Goodreads Reviews for the Dr Po

The Darkening Sky (4.44 Stars)

'Absolutely enjoyed this first novel.'

'I have read many a crime book, but this book was different. I never for one moment guessed how the story would unfold'

'Loved the way the two main characters (Superintendent Lynch and Dr Power) interacted with one another. '

'Illustrations were brilliantly drawn and brought the characters to life'

'Thoroughly enjoyed this debut novel from Hugh Greene'

'Brilliant. Very much enjoyed - a new detective series based in England.'

The Fire of Love (4.62 Stars)

'good plot and enjoyable read - away to locate more books in the series'

'This is a gripping story, I was hooked from the first page and found it difficult to put down. The description of the house and its history and the man who built it was very true to the time and the author really brings it to life.'

'I love the illustration by Paul Imrie on the cover, it is very striking and beautifully drawn as are the black and white illustrations

'A well written book with a well-thought out s Series..Dr. Power, l definitely want to read the next one.'

'There are lots of twists and turns and comple Shelved at....

from you and difficult to guess' Local Interest...✓ local author

'After the first chapter I could not put it down

'The illustrations were brilliant evocations of Notes....

'I love the little links between the books in the illustrations. Dr Power as drawn is quite dishy. I think I'm falling in love with Dr Power!'

'What I enjoy about Hugh Greene novels are not only the illustrations, but the twists.'

The Darkening Sky

Hugh Greene

Illustrated by Paul Imrie

THE DARKENING SKY

The sky is darkening like a stain;
Something is going to fall like rain,
And it won't be flowers.

W H Auden

ISBN 1500832537

First Edition Published Worldwide in 2014.
Revised Edition March 2015.
Proofreading by Judith Eddles.

ONE

And was it all a dream ?
Something conjured between
Night and Day,
Something Born of the Dark,
Something Stirring and Sliding
In the Slime of the Unconscious,
Was it all a dream ?

The moving ?
The taking ?
The images flicker in the mind
Memory or Imagining?
Wish or Dread Fear ?

Was it all just a dream ?

In the darkness of the city the Royal Liverpool Hospital was a floodlit, grey monolith that jutted into the sky. Its concrete bulk had squatted on the side of a hill. The ground it now occupied so heavily had once played host to street upon street of small redbrick terraced houses. Narrow cobbled streets and their gangs of working class Liverpool children had been swept away by the bulldozers of the seventies. The houses which had survived the predation of Hitler's Luftwaffe could not escape progress. The houses were replaced, as they themselves had replaced the fields and farms that had once fringed the fishing village that had once been Liverpool. Where the Royal Liverpool Hospital stood in 1992, buried under metres of concrete and steel had been a healing spring, a place of pilgrimage in medieval times. It was a measure of how modern man despised his roots perhaps, that his hospitals, palaces of disease and technology, should so totally bury the old ways.

This night was different. Although the city lived and breathed as normal and its buses and taxis ploughed the streets, something infinitely older had pushed its way up from the past, as if buried roots could not be denied any further and were striving to send out new shoots. This night something was born in the fertile mind of a man.

The man could have been observed running, barefoot, from Lime Street Station, a large Victorian city station that catered for the Inter-City trains. The rain drummed upon the road and glossed the pavement his feet slapped upon. Passers-by scowled and shouted abuse after him when he ran into them, uncaring and wild-eyed. They wondered who he might be, but their concern lasted only moments, for the attractions of the bright city centre on a Saturday night held greater sway. This stranger followed the string of orange sodium lights that stretched up the hill, away from the city centre, away from the River Mersey and towards the Hospital. A police car was gliding silently past the Medical Institute building nearby, but its occupants did not even register the wild man. Perhaps if they had registered him and stopped him they would have aborted something that was going to occupy a great many of their colleagues over many months to come.

The unseen runner kept to the shadows of the car park, avoiding the taxi rank. His bare feet walked across the consultants' car park and passed the row of waiting ambulances, their doors wide open, having disgorged their occupants into the casualty. The man blinked against the bright light from the main door of the accident and emergency department. He felt the wet clothes sticking to his skin and heard his breath as he gulped oxygen after his run. This was his goal, and the beginning of his quest. He heard the voices from the shortwave radios that crackled away in the ambulances nearby. A warm draught issued forth from the open doorway, smelling of that clean, alcohol smell that all hospitals wore. Tentatively he stepped into the world of light and approached the reception desk.

One of the casualty sisters showed the doctor into the patient's cubicle. Dr Allen was unfamiliar with casualty, and especially that of the busy Royal Liverpool Hospital. He was beginning to regret the easy way he had agreed to do a locum covering a Saturday night. The agitated bustle, the noises and bleeps of technology, the flurry of white coats and clean uniforms did not sit well with his relaxed manner. His world was that of the suburban G.P. Used to his leather-patched corduroy jacket and now thrust into this crisp white coat he felt out of place and unsure of himself.

He closed the cubicle door. This act did little to buffer them, doctor and patient, against the noise of casualty, but it afforded a little more privacy. He introduced himself to the man opposite, "I'm Dr Allen, one of the casualty doctors. I'd like to talk to you..." He'd been warned about the patient by the sister. He was treading carefully, and his voice sounded uncertain. "Is that all right ?" There was no reply. Allen recalled that the casualty sister had not just been uncertain about this patient; she had been frightened of this man. And now that he was in the patient's presence Allen himself began to feel uneasy.

The patient was a tall and willowy man, with a narrow, sallow face. His long hair was plastered onto his forehead which was beaded with droplets of perspiration. The pupils of his eyes were wide and unmoving, stared unnervingly at a point past Dr Allen's right shoulder. He sat almost rigid in his seat. Though he was dressed in shirt sleeves, Dr Allen noted that the shirt was an old-fashioned shirt, like the ones that his grandfather had worn. His hair needed a cut and his face a shave. His feet were bare and streaked brown with dried blood.

Allen tried to engage the man enough to shake hands with him, but all the man would do was stare straight ahead in silence. Allen coughed nervously. He settled himself into a chair and looked at the floor, whilst still keeping the patient in the periphery of his vision. Allen waited a few moments, before trying again. "I suppose things... are...difficult for you." There was no response to suggest that the man had heard. "Would you like to talk about things?" Nothing. "Can you tell me your name?"

They sat together in silence for some minutes. "Are you frightened of something, sir?" It seemed ages since the patient had even blinked. His breathing was shallow, almost imperceptible, but rapid and as if he dared not breathe in his terror. "Sir. I am going to touch your arm." Allen wanted to test the patient's muscle tone, but perhaps also wanted to check that the man in front of him wasn't a statue. He reached across the gulf between them and gripped the soft hand of the man opposite. He tried to move the hand at the wrist and the arm at the elbow, but he met with firm resistance. No matter how hard Allen tried he could not coax him to move his arm.

Sometimes immobility can give way to violent activity, and after a few attempts Dr Allen cautiously sat back again and sighed. "The sister who saw you before, told me that you wouldn't talk to her either, and that you wouldn't eat or drink anything she offered. You wouldn't tell her your name either. If you told us...we might have some records that could help us..."

The man looked into the doctor's eyes. Allen shifted backwards in his chair, conscious of the angry arousal his words had caused. The sterile grey walls of the cubicle were chipped and smeared with years of use. Perhaps the concrete walls had not been re-painted since they were built. They seemed to press in on Allen. His chest tightened.

The man in front of him spoke his first words since he'd asked to see a doctor at the reception desk. "I want Dr Power. I want to see Dr Power."

"Who's he?"

"The psychiatrist, Dr Power."

"Oh..." A visual memory of a tall, rounded man. The medical students had laughed at his jokes and admired his lectures. " I remember him. He was here when I was training. Used to teach me. But he doesn't work here now."

The man frowned, narrowed his eyes. "Don't believe you."

"He left a year or so back."

"I know he moved house. Know the address. But... I want to see him at work. I wanted to tell him something."

"Tell him what?"

The stranger drew a deep breath as if he were about to launch into a lengthy, but garbled explanation. When he spoke he said only three words. "That it's beginning."

"You want to tell him that it's beginning? What is?" The man looked away again and became as motionless as ever.

Allen felt afraid. The man's eyes seemed so keenly alert. He might jump up or lash out at the doctor.

Allen got up to go: there could be no meaningful contact with this man. He yearned to leave the unearthly man who stared into nothing and spoke of nothing. Allen turned to open the cubicle door. For a moment he stood on the threshold. The noise of the busy casualty beckoned him, drawing him away from the patient and back into life.

The patient mumbled something, but Allen could not catch his words and perhaps he had not been meant to fully understand anyway. "I'll ask the duty psychiatrist to come and see you."

"Get Dr Power. It's beginning."

Allen was surprised at this further communication, a clear command uttered into space. The patient's head never moved, his eyes never met the casualty doctor's. Silence. No acknowledgement. The command, once given, would not be re-iterated. "I think Dr Power has left. I'll check for you." Dr Allen left, closing the door behind him, and made his way to the internal telephone. The switchboard were unhelpfully brusque with him when he asked how to contact the duty psychiatrist. They told him with the bare minimum of courtesy and cut him off as he thanked them. Allen vowed not to repeat this locum job another night. He punched out the key sequence he had been told would activate the Registrar's bleep, listened for the tones that signalled the system's acceptance and replaced the receiver. He knew that somewhere in the night the psychiatrist's bleep would be chirruping insistently away.

It took a few moments for Dr Ashton to wake and, her heart racing in alarmed protest, switch on the bedside light and dial the number her bleep insisted she ring.

Dr Allen picked up the phone at the other end, hopeful of some assistance with this most odd of patients.

"Hello, is that the duty psychiatrist?" Allen waited for some reply. There was a pause, then her groggy voice.

"Alice Ashton, Registrar in Psychiatry. Can I help?"

"I hope so. This is Graham Allen in A & E here..."

She sighed. "Oh please...not another patient. I've got another forty hours to go...it's." There was a pause. "My watch says it's two a.m. This isn't another drunk, is it? You know, you should be screening them out before you refer them to me."

"I'm sorry, but this patient is no drunk. He's a genuine, one hundred per cent psychiatric patient." His words were chosen carefully in deference to her weariness, but Dr Allen would still defend his judgement."

"There are no beds in Liverpool tonight. We can't offer him a bed. We've accepted a twenty-five per cent cut in our bed quota."

At the other end of the phone Dr Allen felt she was almost accusing him of cutting the hospital's resources. He counted to five and swallowed his impulse to tell her just how junior she was compared to him. "I have an unknown man who looks about thirty, of no known address who has just presented himself to casualty. For most of the last three hours he's been waiting to be seen he's been mute and absolutely motionless. I guess you'd call him catatonic. You know, at times he almost seems terrified. He has spoken though. About twice. Once was when he came into reception asking to see a doctor, the second time was three hours later when he demanded to see Dr Power. I think Power's left, hasn't he?"

"He got a consultant post in Cheshire. I wonder how this man knows Power's name...perhaps Power was his doctor, perhaps Power wrote notes on him when he was working here. Have you checked records?"

"There isn't a name to check records with."

"That's a pity. You know he must have been a patient of Power's. I'd be interested to see him. Power used to teach here. Wrote a book on the murkier aspects of the unconscious. I've got a copy. You know him?"

"Yes, taught me when he was a Registrar and he was on the news last year, wasn't he? The hostage business."

"Yes, that was Power wasn't it? They roped him into helping. That was one of Power's patients."

"Yes, but not the same one as we've got here. The patient who took the hostage died if you remember. Now...much as I'd like to discuss the famous Dr Power..." said Dr Allen, mindful of an elderly patient who was being wheeled in by two paramedics. "Are you going to come down here and see this man?" Allen's patience had disappeared like water in the sand. Work was beginning to pile up while he was on the phone. He only half-listened to her words of assent. The rest of his attention was focussed on the words of the incoming ambulance crew. He heard words about the old lady's chest pain and her breathlessness. As long as the psychiatric registrar was coming – that was all that mattered. He was about to put the phone down, but Dr Ashton was still speaking.

"And make sure that a nurse stands by while I interview him," she said. "And prepare some intramuscular chlorpromazine. The last catatonic patient I saw became very violent, very suddenly."

Dr Allen heard her putting the phone down. "It must be your charm Dr Ashton," he said. Allen replaced the receiver. From down the corridor came a thin wail of pain from the eighty year old lady in the resuscitation bay. A thoughtful sister was opening the controlled drugs cupboard to get out the diamorphine that she knew Dr Allen would request to control the pain from the old lady's myocardial infarction.

* * *

Dr Ashton washed. She had felt hot and sticky from her sleep. As she stood at the basin in her on-call room she now felt the chill of the night air and shivered. She hurried to put on her clothes. Pausing by the door she picked up her Filofax. It had the phone numbers of the consultants, senior registrars and social services she would need to phone if she needed to admit the patient on a section of the Mental Health Act. She closed the door and double-locked it behind her. The Doctors' residence was quiet except for some insomniac two floors above who was strumming plaintively on a classical guitar.

Fifty yards of darkness lay between the residence and the hospital rear entrance. The hospital stood on top of a hill that fell away towards the city centre and beyond that the Pier Head and the River Mersey. The wail of a police siren from the city announced another clubland fight. Further on still a lone police car moved slowly down the dock road past Pier Head, checking on the sleeping bodies in the bus shelters. Occasionally they could prevent another suicide from throwing himself into the lapping, chemical-ridden tidal waters.

Dr Ashton promised herself that her next post would not be one anywhere near a city centre. She passed the doctors' cars. Her feet crunched on the cubes of sparkling glass from someone's broken car window. The light above the car park flickered and died and she was in darkness. An adolescent warcry rang out in the night air. She jumped. How close? A few yards? A half-mile? Sound travels at night. If she screamed, who would come to help her? The fifty yards seemed interminable. She fumbled in her pocket as she walked. Where was the electronic door key? She'd left her bag at home. It wasn't safe any-where in the hospital and carrying it outside in the city night it would be the perfect bait. She looked about. The shadows around her seemed to be empty. She couldn't be sure. You could never see what was mov-ing just behind you. Holding her breath she pushed the key card into the slot on the door lock. Nothing happened. Footfalls behind her. She pulled the card out and turned it round.

"Are you opening the door?" A man's voice behind her. Don't look round, she told herself. She pushed the card in again. The door buzzed and she pulled it open. The footsteps behind her quickened into a run. "Hold on, Doctor!" She leapt into the light of the entrance hall and reaching behind her, slammed her palms against the door and with her full body weight behind them rammed the door shut against its frame. Head down, eyes shut she tried to catch her panicked breath. Her hands still rested firmly against the door as if to ensure it was still safely shut. At last she looked up. Through the finger-smeared plate glass an angry face stared at her, mouthing swear words. Dr Ashton looked at the man's clothes; a white coat, here and there spattered with flecks of blood, but also adorned by a stethoscope and a security name badge. "Dr L. Durrell, House Officer in Geriatrics."

She opened the door shamefacedly. "Sorry. You frightened me."

"Excuse me," he said, brushing past her. "I'm late.I've got someone in heart failure in casualty." She watched him hurrying away up the stairs and down the labyrinth of corridors to casualty. In the distance he looked like a scurrying white rabbit.

* * *

Dr Allen was nursing a cup of black tea in the staff room. It was three a.m. The other casualty officer had allowed Allen to slope off for a break. The casualty was quietening down as Sunday morning took over from Saturday night. Allen was just relaxing when Dr Ashton appeared like an avenging angel in front of him.

"So you're here with your feet up, are you? You've woken me up, dragged me across the car park in the dark and the cold and the rain; putting myself at risk and when I get here the casualty is deserted; no nurses, no you and no patient."

"No patient?"

"He's gone."

Dr Allen took his feet off the coffee table and sat up, spilling a small quantity of painfully hot tea onto his leg. He swore under his breath as Dr Ashton continued her tirade. "He should have been watched. Closely watched. Where did he go? Do you have an address?"

Allen shrugged, "No, he wouldn't talk, remember. I think he was manipulating to see Power really. When we couldn't deliver, he just upped and left."

"And he's probably psychotic. Very ill indeed. And we don't know where he is."

"Hold on now. You seem to be inferring I'm to blame."

"I'm implying you're to blame, not inferring."

"I don't care. I referred that patient to you. I asked the nursing staff to look after him. I did all that I could. If he deliberately left I can't help it. The fact that I'm taking my break has nothing to do with it. I've been working non-stop for seven hours on my feet, and I'm not going to take this kind of shit from a junior. I want an apology."

"You won't get one. This man is a real suicide risk. I'm angry because I'm bloody worried. Let me show you why. Why I'm so worried about his being left alone, and about my nearly having to see him on his own. Mr Nobody left something for me. Besides his shoes, which for some mad reason of his own he left behind on the seat, he left this little beauty." From behind her back, Dr Ashton brought out her right hand. Snugly fitting into the palm of her hand was a leather-bound handle. From the handle ran a glittering seven inches of steel with a tip so sharp that it was painful even to look upon. "A present from a grateful patient?" she said sarcastically.

Allen was taken aback. "Oh...I didn't know. I...er..." He looked at the home-made knife. "It looks like it's been made from a crossbow bolt."

"Hardly relevant. Did he say anything else. Anything that might give us a clue as to where he came from. I could send someone out for him if we knew. We could stop something."

"He just wanted to see Power. To tell him something."

"What?"

"I did ask. It was pretty vague. Something like...er... 'Tell Power it's beginning,'" said Allen.

"That what's beginning?"

"Don't know. He wouldn't say. I did ask. Should we pass his message on?"

"To whom?" she asked.

"Dr Power," said Allen.

"There's nothing to pass on is there? 'It's beginning.' What's that meant to mean?" She sagged down into the battered chair opposite Allen, wilting visibly. She bowed her head for a second, then looked up into Allen's eyes. "I'm sorry," she said, her voice losing its adrenaline edge. "I can't stop biting people's heads off these days."

"Would you like a tea or a coffee?"

"No. The caffeine will stop me sleeping." She looked down at the weapon she held in her hand. "This will stop me sleeping more though."

"I'll make you that drink." Dr Allen felt able to help. The end of his shift was now clearly in sight and he had promised himself never to do a locum on casualty again. He told her so. He told her that he was no city centre doctor. He looked forward to returning to the safe predictability of a weekday suburban surgery. He could afford to be generous. "Would you like a chocolate biscuit, too?" he asked.

"Yes, please." She put the sharpened crossbow bolt down on the table. "If this is your last night here, I'll leave this for you. A souvenir of the Royal Liverpool."

TWO

Dr Carl Power sped along the tree-lined Wilmslow road and curved round the long bend into the outskirts of the village. He passed Alderley Edge Station and the newly-contrived 'Merlin' public house and glided over the bridge and into the High Street. The green-leaved street of the Cheshire village was lined with the shops that stock the trappings of professional commuter life: boutiques rather than clothes shops, delicatessens rather than supermarkets, and wine merchants rather than off-licences. The names of these middle-class emporia traded on the quaint history and geography of the area; references to the Edge, King Arthur, Merlin and wizards abounded. This was elect suburbia anxious to project its character.

Carl Power put his foot on the brakes and slowed to a halt outside the nearest bakery. He ignored the yellow lines, mainly because it had been a trying day. The stress of starting a new job had torn at his nerves. He was anxious to get back to his equally new home and relax. Power got out of the car and hurried into the bakery oblivious of the approaching traffic warden.

He cut an unfashionable, but smart figure standing in the bread queue. His dark brown hair was turning to grey at the temples and his lively face wore a heartening smile. He had disarming brown eyes, that like a chameleon could adapt their expression second-by-second to their owner's requirements. If Power wished to charm they would twinkle good-humouredly, but if he wished to challenge or discomfort it was his eyes, not his voice, which held his opponent's attention. The shop assistants viewed him with interest. This man had presence, but it was not immediately apparent to them what held their attention. He was handsome, but not overly so and in his mid-thirties though not in any way plump, it was clear he was a man who liked his food and drink.

While he stood in the queue trying to decide what he wanted

from the cakes and pies that were left at the end of this Spring day the slim warden was standing by his Saab estate and alternating her glare from the lime green car to the back of Power's neck. Feeling uncomfortable, for some unknown reason, he bought a large crusty white loaf and some fruit pies with brown butter pastry and headed out of the shop.

He was not to be hindered by the warden however, her attention had been suddenly diverted by another crisis. Completely unaware of his luck, Power stowed his purchases in the car, debated whether to hunt for other food in the rarified air of The Wizard's Pantry, but his temper was so frayed that he decided to make do with his meagre purchases. There would be something in the fridge and the freezer. It would be a challenge to create a dinner for two out of whatever he found. Power relished a challenge of any nature.

Sighing, he rested back in the driver's seat. His day as a consultant psychiatrist had been as busy and fraught as any before. For so many years now the title of consultant had been his goal. Like all goals, once attained, this one was rapidly losing its tempting glow. A ward round, an argument with a psychologist, difficulties with his secretary and a Registrar on maternity leave, a suicidal patient trying to hang herself; all this had been his domain since his appointment almost a year before.

He checked his mirror and moved out into the street. He comforted himself with the thought that tomorrow was Saturday. Cheered, he began to accelerate. Ahead of him though a black BMW was static. Power slowed to a halt.

The driver of the BMW was hanging out of his window waving his fist, with the heel of his left hand he occasionally beat at the horn. Ahead of him there was a short queue of traffic. It was towards the cause of this jam that the traffic warden had so hurriedly run. Power could see none of this however. He watched the agitated driver in front with detached fascination. The red-faced BMW driver emerged from the black carapace of his car and strode moodily up the village high street. He looked at Power, assuming him to be a comrade in distress, and walked over to him. "Traffic's absolutely jam-packed. Bloody hippies, that's what it is."

"Hippies?"

"They've taken us over, invaded the village like last year. Sleeping on the streets, holding their bloody festivals in the fields. Found they'd parked one of their wrecks on my lawn the other morning. Ruined it. They didn't give a fart, just buggered off, taking my lawn mower with them and my morning milk. The police wouldn't do anything, of course." Power looked at the irate face above him. Tight curled black hair well-groomed, sharp black eyebrows, angry blue eyes and the whiff of an expensive after shave mingled with the perspiration born of irritation and a long drive.

"What's going on up ahead then?" Power asked.

"God knows. Looks like one of their wrecks is blocking the entire street." He looked at the dilapidated appearance of Power's Saab and wondered whether he had been tactless. Power's Saab looked as if it would leave a nasty patch of oil on your drive if you invited him to stay. Power had nursed the Saab through student days and house jobs. He was fond of it, though the police, who obviously suspected that the green hulk would soon disintegrate, were forever stopping him. The frequent contact had sensitised Power further towards his dislike of authority. Colleagues at his last hospital had nicknamed the car the 'Batmobile'. Standing beside the Saab the BMW driver surveyed the variegated coat of green paint, that had long since lost its polish, and red rust. He looked at Power. Power was wearing a smart suit. He couldn't be a hippy too, could he? He decide not and returned to his theme of outrage. "They need a sorting-out...a ruddy good belting. They wouldn't know what'd hit 'em. They won't pay the poll tax you can bet...if we all lived like that there'd be anarchy. Bloody anarchy. Scrounging bastards. Let's go and sort them out. Are you coming?"

"Er...I think I'll wait. It'll sort itself out."

"I know your sort too." He sneered and turned his back on Power. Power leant out of the window and watched. He could just see the coach deliberately parked across the road. In front of it a milling crowd of protestors with long hair, banners and placards. They swarmed about the post-office and chanted, "Give us the dole", "Give us our rights", "This is England, give us our rights". Power could just see a traffic warden waving her hands about, clutching her notebook and gesticulating at the coach. Someone had taken the precaution of barricading the post office door shut. An anxious bespectacled member of the counter staff stared out from behind the glass window. The BMW man had reached the New Age people and casting about chose a suitable male specimen without a placard. Power didn't see the actual blow, but he did see the youth clutching his face as he fell on to the tarmac. The fist went up again and another hippy closest to hand, this time a female, was punched to the ground. The crowd seemed to close round the violence, containing it in a sea of placards.

On Power's right-hand side two police cars, sirens blaring, roared towards the confusion. After some minutes peace was restored, a social services official promised help in streamlining social security benefits, the bus was removed from the highway and the BMW driver was escorted to the police station, muttering, "Typical, bloody typical."

Power had finished the apple pies and listened to the five o'clock P.M. programme whilst waiting. Somewhat refreshed he was glad to rev up the ancient Saab and to continue his journey. He drove through the village and then turned sharply left, climbing the hill past a signpost which simply said "To the Edge".

He sped past a ragged group of hippies, dressed in khaki and red, and climbed the steep wooded slope in third gear. A mile further on with dense woodland on either side, Power arrived at two towering sandstone gateposts. Carved into one pillar was "Alderley" and on the opposite pillar, "House." Gratefully, Dr Power indicated and then turned into the driveway of his home.

The walls of Power's house basked in the sun and yellow sandstone became burnished gold. Across the golden sandstone grew the lizard-green leaves of a Virginia creeper that fluttered gently in a warm and balmy breeze. The House sat high up on the edge of a massive escarpment called The Edge, and here the air was usually crystal clear except today it carried traces of woodsmoke from a distant fire. As the breeze shifted about it played with distant sounds of children laughing, or maybe even the sound of music wafted from the fields below.

Power parked at the edge of the wide, gravelled forecourt and climbed out of his car. Standing outside on the firmly crunching gravel Power closed his eyes and let the warmth of the day envelop him. Here, surely, was the peace he had always been seeking. He drank in lungfuls of the crisp air and slowly let them out in sighs of relaxation and contentment. His hair bore traces of grey that belied his youth, but testified to the hard work that had taken him to the early height of his career. Carl Power was thirty-one years old. He had striven for so long to control his life that the prospect of settling down in a new job and a new house offered a chance to relax his efforts. The prospect was alluring and also a little frightening. For now the moment of sunlit contentment was most welcome.

Smiling Power turned to the house. Every time he saw the house there was a feeling of 'rightness' in his stomach. Even when he had first seen the house in a photograph, it had been like coming home. After a succession of student digs, hospital flats and terraced houses near Victorian hospitals, here was his first home, a place in the country to settle down in, but near enough to the city for the hospital and his first consultant post.

The house was a unique Victorian gem, by an architect more used to designing cathedrals, universities and town halls. Power's father had been an architect and he had relished showing him Waterhouse's 'ideal Victorian Lodge'. He had eagerly shown his father the entry in the *'British Guide to Architecture'* that mentioned the listed building. Was the emotion he felt in doing this a form of triumph? Power looked up at the arches of the porch and the windows that rose up in front of him. Power's father jokingly referred to himself in self-derision as 'The Great Architect of the Universe, if not Salisbury', where he worked. Was it so important to triumph over the ageing father?

The house stood in two acres of land formed into a square bounded by a sixfoot dry-stone wall. There was a winding driveway leading from the wide expanse of the forecourt down a thickly wooded hill to the road below. A second entranceway in the wall, perhaps leading to a larger house which was never built, was inexpertly filled in.

The house itself was at the precise centre of the square-walled garden. An entrance framed by the most Gothic of arches was let into the South side. Power gazed lovingly up at the stone walls. Here and there were small, intricate carvings; in one place a vertically sited sundial, in another the engraved plan of the whole house signed for eternity in stone by the nineteenth century architect. Above the pointed roof of the porch stood a stone mastiff, but his head had long ago broken off. Inside the entrance hall a pair of entwined hunting dogs stood at the top of the steps to welcome entrants to the house. Despite these flourishes the rest of the house was as conventional as could be.

Beyond the high wall that ran around the property the branches of the trees moved easily in the evening breeze. The evening light was waning, but perhaps there was an hour or two left. Just over the other side of the thick stone wall were acres of National Trust forest that covered the Edge – a sandstone escarpment overlooking the Cheshire plain. The woodland beckoned him. Power yearned to set himself free in the cool green darkness that the woodland offered. Maybe he had a little time before he had to start preparing the meal. After the fractiousness of the day's work a walk in the wild wood would give him the space to think. There were things he wanted to say to Eve. A walk would let him get his thoughts straightened out.

Power walked through the forest humming gently to himself, revelling in the smells of the earth and the dark green undergrowth. This was the place visited by Cheshire commuters on a Sunday afternoon wanting a brief contact with Mother Earth before submerging themselves in the fumes of the city. This was a place to run with children and the family dog. But Power began to feel proprietorial – this forest was his back garden. When he stood on a high cliff top overlooking the plain and saw the hippy camps lodged in the lush fields of pasture below he felt vaguely irritated. He looked at their ramshackle lorries and buses and wondered who would clear up the mess from their fires and latrines when they left? He listened to the beat of their drums and the wail of guitars and wondered why they had chosen this peaceful spot to invade. A rare rebel voice inside questioned his values. Why shouldn't they behave this way and be what they wanted to be? Power knew himself to be a man driven by the need to conform and to be needed. They had different values to him. He had different values to them. What did that matter?

Power moved on through the wood. In the distance he saw a tall, thin man dressed shabbily in strips of red and golden cloth. The man was talking animatedly with two young women who sat on a fallen log at his feet. He leant over and kissed one of the young girls deeply. The other girl laughed, a high ringing bell-voice. Both girls were dressed boyishly in camouflage and khaki, both were skin-head-ed and wore black jack-boots. One was fair, the other dark. They might have been boys, but for their laughing doe-eyes. They were latter-day wood-nymphs to a post-industrial Puck. In the thin man's hand was some kind of long cane. It glinted in the orange sun and only served to exaggerate the man's eccentricity. He was the image of a gangling, threadbare medieval jester. An angry explosion of ginger hair and beard fringed a sharp, pink face. As Power approached the group the jester turned and two slightly exophthalmic eyes fixed Power. The jester smiled and licked his lips. Keeping Power all the while in his gaze, he lifted a flute to his mouth.

Dr Power listened to the lonely flute filling the forest with a clear voice so sincere that any anxiety Power might have had about the man was deftly smoothed away. The bliss of the music seemed to evoke the very heart of the ancient wood. Under the burden of this talent the Piper's shoulders were hunched, but his eyes danced as he played. His long beard draped itself over an ancient silk cravat. As he played he danced with shuffling feet in leather moccasins with narrow points to the toes.

All at once Power's hunger and tiredness intruded upon the music. He wanted to move away; to journey back to his new home, but the glittering eyes of the musician had caught and held him. The phrase of music died away. And as Power was about to move away from this stranger, the bearded man spoke. "That's elegant, Doctor. Have you not a farthing for the Piper? So that I might pay my way?" Dr Power stopped as if poleaxed. He turned slowly and walked nearer to the Piper. He looked guilty. The Piper grinned at him shaking his straggly haired head.

Power looked puzzled, "I don't know you, do I?"

"We haven't met this side of the Dark Ages, but we might meet again, I suppose."

"Do you know me or something? I don't really understand..."
Was the Piper's thought disordered by drugs or was he deliberately
using hypnotic confusion techniques?

The Piper moved closer with a serpentine grace. "For a long
time we have known each other, before we came out of the sea, before
they were sent forth from the Garden even. My name is The Piper.
Did you like my playing?" He stared at Power, weighing him up. "The
Moslems say that the flute is the call of the soul wanting to return to
heaven."

If he had been on safe ground Power might have stayed to find
out more about the Piper; to dissect his mind as only Power could.
Power felt distinctly uneasy in the darkening wood. Something was
waiting for him here. Some old anxiety, long-buried, had re-surfaced to
haunt him. Troubled by encountering the trio of hippies and an unconscious memory they evoked Power turned away, "I must go."

"Have you not a farthing to buy a little fish and bread?"

Power rummaged in a pocket and chancing upon a five pound
note put this into the Piper's outstretched hand. Agitated by the
encounter he then practically ran up the forest path towards the road
that led home. The Piper and his girls laughed and watched Power
running away. At the roadside by the sign that pointed 'To the Edge',
Power slowed to a shambling walk. He tried to gather his breath. His
chest felt tight and his heart beat rapidly. He could not quite place the
stranger in the forest, but something unfathomable seemed all too
familiar.

The evening sky was beginning to darken in the west producing a plush red sunset. Tall Scots pines stood sentinel-like as silhou-
ettes against the night. Power was glad to be heading home. He presumed now that the unusual Piper had been with the New Age convoy.
Strange that he should appear just as he was meditating upon them.
Gratefully, Power turned the corner and climbed the gravel drive to
the House. The windows of his rooms were like dark and empty eye
sockets . He would get someone to install an infra-red lighting system.
A burglar alarm too. The place was too isolated for no security at all.

The last soft, yellow blur of sunlight bathed Dr Power as he opened the front door. He looked back at the gathering night sky. The Mayday moon was beginning to rise.

* * *

He stepped gladly into the mouth of the porch and unlocked the stout oak door. He pushed against the dark solid wood as it glided open in a smooth welcoming arc. Once behind him the same door shut with a muffled report like a distant cannon that echoed in the hallway. A chessboard floor of black-and-white tiles clattered under his heels. Power sometimes wondered whether perhaps past owners had held Christmas parties here. He conjured up a tall Christmas tree in the corner, and for an instant or so he could smell the sweet pine needles and see the presents arranged around the tree's base. He imagined Victorian Christmas Card children in flouncy dresses and bold silk bows. They laughed; they danced. He looked at the hall now and shivered. Only shadows danced here now.

Power's home enfolded him in a soft and comforting embrace. He sighed happily as he moved through the calm and certain order of his world. Although the rooms were comfortably decorated they were neither pristine nor obsessionally tidy. This was a safe and warm world full of books and autumn colours.

He had stayed in the wood longer than he had meant to. The challenge of producing a meal from the surprise contents of his kitchen had been doubled by the pressure of time. He would have to hurry. Power crossed the wood-panelled hall and went into his kitchen. He needed to check the contents of his fridge and the freezer in the old pantry.

Power had chosen the house for its warm, large kitchen with its scrubbed deal table standing foursquare upon a quarry tile floor. Power was not a fussy man, but he revelled in good food and wine, and he enjoyed cooking, which he always did with gusto, tasting sauces and supping wine as he did so. Power's kitchen was a robust and functional place, crammed with heavy blue and white crockery and copper pans. He took great pleasure in growing some of his own fruit and vegetables in the large garden behind his house. Bunches of dried herbs festooned racks hung from the ceiling. A Welsh dresser nearby was crammed with an equally large array of bottles of herbs, and preserves of all kinds: damsons, plums, pears, raspberries, loganberries, redcurrants and sloes. Glorious dark bottles of red and white-green wine lay arranged in racks that lined one wall. And in Power's kitchen there were always good smells of garlic and spice.

Power had retrieved tubs of frozen soup and stock from the freezer. His fridge had yielded lamb, kidneys, cream and broccoli. Plenty here. Power set to work with energy, deliberately pushing the memory of the Piper away and replacing it with the sights and smells of good food. He poured himself a full glass of Merlot and began browning some chopped onion and garlic. He closed his eyes and savoured the smell with a smile.

Half-an-hour later Power had tidied the living-room, (throwing copies of *Psychological Medicine* and the *British Medical Journal* under the seat cushion of his chair), showered and changed. He was pulling on a loose white cotton shirt when the doorbell rang.

He opened the door to see a slim female figure silhouetted by the evening sunlight. Power had the welcome impression of her long hair and the sinuous curve of her hip as she casually leant against the door jamb.

She stepped inside and kissed him tenderly on the cheek. A slim young woman in her late twenties with long golden hair. Eve regarded him with green eyes and a self-contained smile. She wore an unbleached cotton dress with cornflowers embroidered front and back.

"Hello," she breathed softly. He kissed her on the mouth. She tasted sweet and warm. He wanted her already, for each time he saw her again was like meeting her for the first time.

"Come in." He closed the door behind her.

She wandered into his living-room and stood pretending to study the spines of the books that lined the walls. Her eyes strayed over their titles without registering them. Likewise she glanced unseeing at a watercolour over the fireplace that she had painted for Power some years ago. She was conscious of Power's eyes on her and was trying to avoid them for now. When they met it was always as if he was hungry for her. Eve grimaced. She found his childishness vaguely irritating. Yet she usually found that after they had been together for a few hours her hunger matched his. He could seem a playful adolescent, even acquiescent. But with Power looks were sometimes deceptive. She forced herself to look hard at him...there seemed to be a ruthlessness in his eyes, something altogether harder than his slightly rounded face.

"Something smells good," she said with the old awkwardness.

"Would you like a drink?" She usually had a fino. He had opened a jar of olives for her.

She nodded and Power went to fetch the alcohol he had already poured for both of them. This was a relatively safe part of the script they always followed. She heard him returning to the room and spoke as he came through the door. "Had a good day?"

"Difficult. Saw a patient's wife today." He shook his head as he ran over what the wife had told him.

Eve smiled. She liked his stories. Power seemed to have an endless stream of anecdotes about people and their lives. Some of them seemed utterly incredible, but she knew him; they were all true. "What was it?" She drifted into one of his comfortable wing-back chairs and began to relax in his presence. Power admired the elegant way she sat down; the way she held her glass.

"He was an alcoholic. Forties. Businessman. Made good. You know, rags to riches job. Well, someone might say he married above himself. Oxford graduate and debutante."

"Sounds like this was a private patient?"

"Well they did have enough money to go privately, I say they did, because he's lost the lot. Gambled some of it away and lost his job through...an indiscretion when he was drunk. Actually he crashed his company Mercedes through a car showroom window. It was made worse by the fact that it was a Rolls-Royce showroom. So he's unemployed and the word is about that he's just about as unreliable as you can get." He sucked some of the fino into his mouth and swallowed it with pleasure. "Started drinking to calm his nerves during business deals. Moved on to a bottle of scotch a day. The thing is...he became impotent."

"Don't ever do that to me."

Power laughed somewhat nervously. "He got a bit sensitive about this. Blamed his wife. Alcoholics always blame somebody else... for everything. He began to suspect she was having an affair."

"Was she? I mean if he was impotent and he'd been bad to her..."

"No, she wasn't having an affair. But he didn't believe her when she denied it. He confronted her every day with 'the evidence' that she was having an affair."

"Like what?" asked Eve.

"That she flirted with the milkman when she paid the bill. That she was tempting him...when she said 'Good morning' to the postman she really meant 'Come inside and take me'. If she went to the shops and was half-an-hour late he said she'd been having sex instead of going to the supermarket. If she showed him the goods she'd bought he'd say she had bought them the day before as a ruse to cover her tracks. If she showed him the timed and dated receipt he'd say she had sex with a man in the park on the way home. There was no rest from his accusations. He searched her bed, (they were sleeping separately by this time), for traces of any men. He inspected her underwear for their semen." Eve made a face. " No, he did, honestly. That's what he did."

"How did she stand him?"

"I don't know," said Power as he drained the glass. "I really don't. He listened in on her phone calls, opened her letters. It took her and his GP months to get him to come to see me about his alcohol addiction and the jealousy. We call it the 'Othello' syndrome. Morbid jealousy. By the time I saw him he was convinced she was a slut, a whore. I couldn't shake his ideas. I tried a course of pimozide. Sometimes it helps with paranoid ideas. I warned her not to bow to his pressure, never to try and appease him by just admitting to having an affair."

"Why not?"

"Because it would confirm his worst fears, confirm his delusions. And jealousy is a dangerous thing. I told her she may have to leave him altogether."

"Hey, hold on!" Eve sat forward in her chair. "Telling her to go...I thought you weren't meant to play God. Telling her to pack her bags. That's doling out some pretty heavy advice." She looked flushed and angry.

Power was taken aback. "Well...of course, you're right. Generally I don't try to interfere. I let people make their own decisions. I don't want to give the wrong advice and be blamed for something dreadful happening...but this was different..."

"How?"

"After they saw me that day he took her home and thrashed her. Beat her up. Broke her arm. He said that while she'd been in my office, while she'd been giving me her version of things, she'd had sex with me. It was ridiculous."

"I should hope so."

"Well of course it's ridiculous," said Power irritably. "Anyway to cut a long story short...things got even worse. he stopped taking the pimozide, refused to come and see me. I saw the wife today. He was meant to come for an appointment, but he couldn't; he was on remand for her attempted murder. What happened was that a week ago she had finally broken under his pressure. All his accusations were true, she said. He was right. Would he just leave her alone? Yes, she'd had sex with the milkman, the supermarket manager, the baker, the postman, me...everybody...now, would he just leave her alone. She did the thing I'd told her never to do."

"Like those fairy tales where the little girl is warned by the good fairy never to open up a certain door or a certain box. They always do."

"Yes, well, this was a real Pandora's box. He stabbed her with the kitchen knife. Luckily she moved as he lunged at her. She still got a chest wound and a pneumothorax. Somehow she managed to get out of the house with this wound still bleeding and get help. He's been arrested and is on remand. No bail granted. He was still champing at the bit to kill her. And he made threats to do the same to me."

"Nice people you work with."

"Hmmm...yes, it's the nature of the work I'm afraid. I'm pretty sure he'd try too. I'm rather glad he's behind bars. When people get such strong emotions they often transfer them onto their psychiatrist. Listen, I don't want to think about this man...it's been on my mind all day. Tell me what kind of a day you had."

Across the room the windows were long slabs of darkness. Somehow they made him uneasy, as if they were an act in the theatre and there was an audience in the darkness beyond. He crossed the room and began drawing the curtains. As he waited for Eve to speak Power could just see the outline of the sentinel trees against the stars.

* * *

On the periphery of the clearing, under the canopy of trees, they moved into the darkness. The sounds of laughter and music around the New Age Encampment seemed dulled by the trees as they moved into the night. Through gaps in the undergrowth Sian could still see the orange coloured glow from the roaring fire. Long shadows rose and fell, floating amongst the trees as the New Age people danced to the music of the flute and drum. Sian looked back, now slightly anxious at having left the group to follow the stranger. He seemed not to have noticed her pause. As she left the dance Sian looked at the Piper. Did his eyes meet hers, could he see what she thought as she edged into the night?

The stranger pressed insistently on through the trees, staring ahead into the gloom and striding out confidently, crunching through the bracken on the forest floor. For a moment she thought of going back to the group she had joined only a few weeks before. The night's festivities had only just begun after all. Why should she follow this tall, straggled-haired man with his sack slung over his shoulder? There was something in that bag, something he had promised her, something she craved, and something, curiously, that he had divined that she would desire.

A resounding crack shot through the forest as one of the huge logs on the bonfire behind them split. Laughter from the group, drawing her back into the light. The stranger was marching quickly out in front of her, receding into the shadows. If she delayed any more he would be gone and the stuff in his sack would be gone with him. Gathering her courage she started after him, breaking into a run when she realised she was losing him. When she breathlessly caught up with him, the clearing was a quarter of a mile away. To their right, equally far away, sat a tall Victorian house, surrounded by a stone wall, on the rise of the Edge. In the distance the house provided a bare glimmer of light, and this pinpoint of light was the only sign of any other humanity. All she could hear was his breathing and the sound of their feet on the forest floor.

"It's so dark. I can hardly see. I'm afraid I'll trip on a root or something."

"Hold on. Just wait." He stopped and set his sack down upon the ground. "My bag of magic tricks has many marvels." He extracted something from the dark mouth of the bag." Just stand in front of me will you? I need shelter from the wind. A scrape of glass on metal. The scratch of a match against the sandpaper side of a matchbox. A bright flame, almost dazzling to eyes now accustomed to the night. Then he stood up with the gas lamp. Its light and persistent hiss seemed welcome company in addition to the stranger. "Better?" She nodded, his gaunt features lit from below, looked slightly wolf-like. He noticed that she shivered. "Not long now."

She had promised herself that she would not do this again. Temptation had led her from her terraced home in South Wales to the capital and the dubious comforts of a squat in Acton. She remembered the others there now, she remembered their smell and their cynical camaraderie – the fellowship that dissolved when someone collected enough money to score. Looking for work in the city became another existence within the hours of darkness. Her body could transform itself by miraculous spells and the enchantment of others into money and thence transmute into euphoriant substances. Life itself transformed into a treadmill of sexual activity, brief ecstasy and, with daylight, an uncomfortable sleep. Through her own temptation and the use of her sex to tempt others she could possess what she desired, but in doing so became the possession of that which she desired.

Caring parents eventually found their fourteen-year-old daughter, were duly shocked and guilty, and restored her to their small terrace, bought from the council. The temptation though followed and could be satisfied just as easily in a small Welsh town as in a busy city. The old man at the corner was very grateful. His trips to the doctor for temazepam prescriptions became more and more frequent. Sian felt superior to the local thugs on glue and drink. Her choice was altogether more dangerous. For satisfying more unusual tastes than the old man's one could achieve, the rewards of cocaine or heroin, which she smoked, fearful of needles. Though in time this fear would no doubt eventually be conquered too. If all else failed, if the town became as dry as a Welsh Sunday, there were psilocybin mushrooms from the park, or a trip into Swansea with money filched from parental pockets.

Eventually a family conference, the general practitioner, the police and then the forensic psychiatrist. When social services intervened , Sian decided to abscond again, promising herself to stay clean, but never return. The New Age people offered something. It seemed to feed an emptiness inside her. Then after a few weeks with them came this man, who sought out her hunger and offered to feed it again.

"We've come a long way," she said. "We're climbing the Edge." She half-stumbled, put out a hand onto the rough bark of an Scots pine tree to steady herself. "Where are we going?"

"We don't want to be disturbed, do we?"

"I thought you might have a tent or a caravan or something for us to do it in. I'm not going to do it here on the hillside."

"You want the stuff don't you?" he sneered at her. "People have been living here for thousands of years. Look up there, at the rocks that form the Edge."

"Rock. Sandstone. More trees. I don't see anything at all."

"Come on," for the first time he touched her, and his grip seemed warm and reassuring. He led her towards the sharply rising sandstone slope that formed one face of the escarpment. Amidst the jumble of rock and clay were fissures that ran from the top to the bottom of the Edge. As they moved round an outcrop she saw it, a black maw that seemed to open up in front of them.

"A cave..." she breathed. As they climbed, the circle of light touched the walls of the cave mouth, ten feet high. There was a slightly fetid animal smell that rose from the interior. A smell of stale urine, and the charred smell from a dead log-fire. He lured her inside. Once she was in the cold darkness he pushed her more roughly, deeper into the mouth.

Only five hundred metres separated Power's house from the caves. Two couples spaced apart by privilege, one in a world of light and good food, the other in fumbling darkness. Both couples had seduction in mind as a game, but all four individuals had very different agendas to reconcile. One male would make no compromises, for his was an uncompromising and unfamiliar world that ruled him ruthlessly.

"My day?" Eve thought about her life, so different from Power's life of hospitals and patients. "You want to know about the world of art?" Power nodded. She set the empty crystal glass down on a nearby table. "I've got my exhibition coming up at the gallery in Manchester. I've been getting the canvasses sorted for that. Some pictures to be framed. Writing entries for catalogues. Not so easy to describe your own work. Especially when...well, you know I do portraits and how..." She struggled for the word.

"Unconventional?"

"Something like that. You know I put in symbols to describe people."

"Yes, I know." Power had watched Eve's career developing over the past two years from an unsuccessful art graduate to a sought-after portrait artist. Business and society queued up for her rich and un-orthodox portraits.

"Well, you know, how I use symbols like a code...they mean at least two things."

"Like travellers' scratch marks on the walls outside houses; 'generous woman', 'mad dog here'...that sort of thing."

She frowned. "A bit like that...but I'm not a tramp, and these are no scratch marks. It takes me a few months to get these things done. Carl, I'm tired of them, the portraits I mean. People just want the same thing again and again. Like so-and-so had before them."

"They think each portrait's different, because of the symbols and they pay well don't they?"

"I keep on putting up the prices to deter them. Only they keep on coming. I hate being committed. I hate being labelled. Tied down." Power felt the last words meant something more, but said nothing. Eve went on, " When you have someone sitting for a portrait you talk to them, get some idea of them. I use the things they tell me. I put their secrets into the painting. They don't know it, of course. I did this business-man last week. I put a plump red rose in his buttonhole...that was for hs mistress, close to his heart. In a vase on a shelf was another faded bloom, that was his wife. On the floor, by his feet was a discard-ed dead flower, petals scattered...his mother."

"When are you going to come clean about these things you've woven into their pictures?"

"I don't know. It's difficult, when they're so proud. I mean they appear in magazine articles with these damn pictures. You know, I can't tell anyone but you what I've done. If I did tell people what their portraits really said..."

"But if you don't like these people, doing their portraits...surely coming clean would stop them bothering you...faster than putting up your prices."

"I know...I just can't bring myself to break away from it all. It's uncomfortable to stick with it and the alternative is worse. The money's nice though..." she giggled and Power felt vaguely irritated. Not that he minded her artistic duplicity, it was something else about her talk that unsettled him. He looked at her smile, her eyes and her breasts and knew that he desired her. If only he could square every-thing, resolve everything between them.

"Come on, let's eat," he said. They got up and drifted into the dining-room. He seated her down and then he brought in a tureen of steaming soup. Eve sniffed the air appreciatively. Her stomach rum-bled. Power hoped her hunger was two-fold.

Power sat down and flapped a crisp white napkin onto his lap. He picked up a soup spoon and began to eat. Between mouthfuls he told Eve of his encounter with the Piper in the wood. "Made me feel uneasy. Seemed to know me in some way, but I couldn't place him. He sounded either as though he was trying to impress me with pseu-do-philosophy or he was ill...you know, thought-disordered."

"He'll be from the hippy convoy," said Eve. "I hear the locals are up in arms. Someone overturned one of their vans last week and set it on fire."

"Really? Well, perhaps the village deserves the New Age people. For years they've made out that the Edge is where Merlin put Arthur's knights to rest....you know I don't know how many sites in the coun-try are linked with poor old Merlin. He must have spent most of his life travelling. All the places must have made a mint out of old Merlin. Now, these New Age people have taken the legend seriously. They've had a festival here for the last two years around May Day. And it grows year-by-year. Most of April and May the roads are filled with battered coaches. For the last couple of weeks I've heard the Convoy Camp, you know, in the distance. Sometimes it's chanting prayers to Mother Earth or whatever, then Celtic harps and things, sometimes it's heavy metal."

"Well, they're trying to resurrect the past, all that crap about earth mothers and earth magic. They should jettison the past. I've chucked mine out. Threw all the photos of darling mummy and daddy out years ago." She tore a piece of bread in half.

"There speaks an angry woman."

"Don't mock me Carl Power."

He ached to follow her lead, but to do so and expose her feelings might close her forever to him. She would bury him as she had the past. Instead he said, "Our roots lie in our past. Have you ever seen a living tree without roots?"

She was brittle, "But then I'm not a tree." And then she seemed amused, as if her threadbare awkwardness had been designed to provoke him. She seemed gratified by her success and softly now moved back into caring for him, "You must think me odd or rude or both. You touch a nerve inside me, I suppose. I've finished my soup. What's next?" She smiled at him and Power was again disconcerted and excited by her ambiguity.

When he brought her main course of lamb and kidneys in a cream and brandy sauce, she caught hold of his arm as he was about to return to his side of the table. She drew him down and planted a lingering kiss on his lips. Their tongues touched and Power knew that Eve would be asking to stay the night.

Sitting opposite her again and settling his napkin discreetly over his arousal, Power thought to chance his hand with her again, (as he had done several times before).

"Listen, I've been thinking," said Power. She nodded as she sliced the tender lamb and he continued as she took a mouthful of his blissful food. "We've talked about it many times before."

She swallowed. "And it sounds like we're going to talk about it again. And why not? Go on."

"You could move in here...for good."

"You know I like my freedom. I like to be with you, sure. I like this knowing we're together. But I like being apart too sometimes... so I can work...sometimes I like to drive all night – I'll drive into the North Wales countryside; stop by a lake or a river and watch the sun rise. Feel the earth waking up. Couldn't do all that if we were together. Sometimes I like to dance close to people, sometimes I like to dance on my own – away from everyone."

Power thought. She didn't like the success of her paintings either. Didn't want to be defined, maybe? "I could give you that freedom?"

"It's mine already. Not yours to bestow." Her voice was steady and calm and she was smiling. The first time they had had this conversation she had been anything but calm. Power remembered her standing over him; screaming, red-faced. The first time she'd walked out on him. They had fallen back together again. They always did. She had grown to rely on him, trust him too much. She seemed to resent that sometimes. He was too dependable. He looked at her finishing her meal. Perhaps if he shook her view of dependable Dr Power. If he became as mercurial as she, would that change her?

"I want to settle down. I've put it off for so long, put all my energies into research and clinical work. I'm a consultant now. I've got more money than I can sensibly spend. I want children."

"That'll get rid of your money problems...if having too much can ever be a problem."

The meal was nearly over. He wondered how long he could afford her this way? The urge to settle down had become insistent after so many years of casual love and casual sex. "I love you, Eve, but..."

"But?"

But maybe if nothing's going to happen we'd better call it a day? What had he been going to say? Power shook his head. He couldn't think clearly. He spent his day sorting out a hundred problems that people brought him; problems with their lives, their children, their marriages. When problems were this close, when they were his own, he couldn't see any solution. He was right there in the midst of, part of, the problem.

"What were you going to say?" He thought he could detect anxiety in her voice. She pushed her empty plate away decisively. "Is there a pudding?"

"Nothing special." He looked down at his hands.

"Good, I don't want any. Carl, can we..." He looked into her green eyes. "Can we go upstairs?"

"I suppose apricot sorbet can wait, can't it?"

"I suppose so." She stood up with all the grace embodied in her slim twenty-six year old figure. Power snuffed out the table candles, and followed her silhouette out into the hallway by the stairs.

* * *

"Come inside." He pulled at her arm, felt her resistance.

"What's inside?" Sian pulled back against the stranger's grip. "There could be an animal in the cave."

He sounded exasperated. "There's nothing in there. People come to the entrance, but they don't go deeper. They don't come prepared with lights and things. I've been in here earlier tonight. I know it's safe." A slight relaxation of the tension in her arm. He cajoled her, "It's shelter and we can do what we've got to do, get what we both want." He patted the bag to try and entice her. " Come on, I'm not going to leave you alone. It's all right. This was a home, a thousand years ago. Neolithic man...and woman lived here. Did what we're going to do. The cave's no virgin." The cave floor tilted abruptly downwards beneath her feet. Not expecting this she almost fell against him. "Are you?"

"Sorry," she said, looking about her at the walls. The air in the cave was quite fresh. "What did you say?"

"Are you a virgin?"

"No."

"Didn't think so. You done this before for stuff?"

"Once or twice," said Sian quietly. "Listen, I want to know about the stuff you've got first. I want to see it."

"You need it quickly? You in withdrawal or something?"

"I'm tired of this, why are we going deeper into this place, it's scaring me," she said. "Let's stop here. There's no one about, so let's do it. Show me the stuff first though, I've got to see it."

"No. A little further." He led her round a small outcrop of rock. "The cave gets very low here. Crouch down." The cave height suddenly fell to one metre or so and twisted back upon itself for a few more metres in length before narrowing to an orifice shaped like a mouth set up from the floor and measuring some sixty centimetres in diameter. "Crawl through here."

The short-haired girl protested, her eyes wide with apprehension. "It's too dark. I can't see in there. There might be a drop or anything."

"I've been here before, I told you, it's all right."

"Give me the gas lamp then."

"Just get in!" He pushed her angrily from behind. She felt the stone lower lip of the mouth bite into the front of her thighs. Sian gasped. She fell forward into the darkness. She held her hands instinctively out in front of her as she toppled into the mouth. They made contact with the floor of this inner cave. There was the rustle of soft, dry straw beneath her fingers. He pushed her again. He seemed agitated now he was so close to his goal.

He pushed her into a cloying world of darkness, so extremely black that he could hear her breathing had become panicked. She could not see the extent of the walls, but from the echo of her panting breath she guessed the hollow space was small. She reached her hand up. Not more than a foot above her was the dry-stone roof. It would have been impossible to stand up. She could only crouch. Gingerly, trying to avoid knocking her head against the stone she turned around. The mouth of the cave was a circle of light. Outside he was bending down, rummaging again in his sack. When he stood up he was holding two packages.

"This is what you wanted...the smack." He showed her a plastic bag partially filled with a white powder, but when she reached out for it he withdrew his hand. "Not yet. And this," he waved a box in front of her. "This is a free gift, if you're good enough."

"What is it?" Sian asked.

"Benzo's. Benzodiazepines, you know, tranquillisers. Do you like them?" She nodded, eyes glued on the two packages, but the stranger was cautious. "But you've got to do exactly as I say. You agree?" She nodded once. "You agree to whatever I want?"

"It depends."

"If you don't agree I'll go now." He was putting the bags back in the sack, tying up the neck. Sian cursed herself. She had misjudged him, and prejudiced her deal. She couldn't bear the idea of his going. The price for what he offered her seemed low enough to her, probably he was new to the game. Perhaps she could take advantage of his newness.

"Don't go. I know what you want. Okay, I'll agree to do anything you want me to do. It shall be my command."

There was a pause that seemed infinitely long to Sian. Would she get what she wanted? He had hoisted the sack onto his shoulder and was bending down to pick up the light. She wondered if he was just going to walk away from her, leaving in the enfolding darkness.

Suddenly, the light was thrust through the orifice and the sanctum was lit up for the first time. "Take it," he said. "Put it down somewhere safe. Don't set the straw alight though." She took the light gratefully and looked around the sanctum for somewhere to put the hissing lamp. The floor of the mini-cave tilted towards a gully that ran along the length of one of the walls. At the end it ran into a small reservoir that was now filled with straw. Neolithic men had carved it to store water for the night. A level portion of rock that jutted out from the wall opposite seemed the logical place. She set the lamp down and looked back at the mouth and outside.

"What now?" she asked. With the movement of the blue-white gaslight into the sanctum, it was the larger cave that had grown dark. She could no longer see him, and only his breathing gave him away. There was a pause, then his voice came back, slightly slurred all of a sudden. Slurred with lust?

"Take your clothes off and pass them out here."

She wanted to protest, but bit back her words at her own inner promise of the heroin and the benzo's. It had been so long since she'd had either. In the absence her unconscious desire for the drugs had grown the longer she had denied it. Wordlessly she began pulling off her camouflage jacket and pulled her tee shirt over her head. She passed them outside to him. She didn't see him stuffing her clothes into his sack. "Where's the straw come from?" she asked.

"I brought it." He took her boots from her hands. They disappeared into the darkness and the stranger's bag.

"You really planned this didn't you? The straw and everything." Silence. She imagined his eyes gloating over her body as she unzipped her crotch and slowly, teasingly, peeled the tight khaki trousers from her thighs. She felt a perverse frisson of delight at the idea of giving herself to this unseen audience. "This wormhole of yours is getting quite warm. Neolithic man wasn't so stupid living here. Do you think he used this place for this too?"

A voice from the depths, "I know he did."

She pulled away the bra that she still wore, despite the teasing of the other New Age women. She half-imagined, half-hoped he admired her firm young breasts. She had left the best till last, for him. But when he took the panties from her hand they disappeared into the cave beyond with no comment. She sat back on her haunches and felt the warm blades of straw pressing into her bottom. His hand lifted the sack into the sanctum first and then he clambered in. Outside in the darkness he had undressed without ceremony. He looked at her nakedness with dispassion. His eyes were cold. Sian looked down. He was erect, but she got the strangest sensation that the erection wasn't for her, but about something else. She giggled nervously, partly to try and lighten the proceedings. He prescribed her a half-smile to pacify her.

"I want you to lie down for me," he said. "With your head towards the back of this place."

"With my feet at the exit, you mean?"

"Do it." Nastiness in his voice. He had nearly won. As she lay back, he moved round her, rustling the straw until he knelt by her right side, at the level of her waist. The rock beneath her sloped to her left, down to the runnel. She looked up at him as he leant over her, inspecting her groin. She opened her legs slightly, inviting him to stop this distant and silent examination. He seemed oblivious.

"Have you got some protection?" she asked.

He looked blank. "Oh...I would use that, of course I would. I don't want AIDS. I think you're being very good." He smiled the semblance of a smile. It almost calmed her. He leaned over her. His face was in shadow. "You deserve a present now."

"Could I...could I have it later...to take away?" She would rather enjoy the fruits of her labour later, away from him. She could try to forget how she had earned the smack if she had it later. Something to look forward to.

"You can take it away, of course you can." She felt that her control was re-established and she relaxed a bit. "I just want to give you an extra present. Some benzos...you look a little tense. Some diazepam will relax you, help you enjoy things. It's a small price to pay for heaven, after all."

"What do you want me to do?"

"I want you to turn over onto your front." She rolled over obligingly. The straw seemed harsh against her excited nipples. He began brushing off the straw that clung to the soft skin of her shoulders and the back of her thighs. She felt him reach over her, lifting her pelvis up; she moved with him as he drew her across his knees. She felt the hairs of his legs against her belly and the hardness of his penis pressing into the plumpness of her left buttock.

Sian chuckled dirtily. "So, I have to be spanked to get my smack. Go on then."

He didn't understand her joke. "I want you to be quiet now. No more talking. You're going to get your reward now." She lay exposed as he opened the sack and retrieved a box that lay inside. He opened it and drew something, she couldn't see what, out of it. "Stay still and be quiet. Open your legs a bit. I'm going to give you some diazepam." She opened her mouth to ask something. "Be quiet. You'll get the point." Suddenly she felt his hands moving over her bottom, pulling the buttocks apart.

"Hey! What are you...?" Something hard and cold, like a thin tube pressed against her and then entered her. She gasped at the suddenness of it. His fingers squeezed the tube and some fluid flew out of the nozzle, spurting into her. Then, just as suddenly the tube was gone from her.

He was explaining. He sounded pleased with himself. "The rectal mucosa absorbs the diazepam almost like...like an injection. Are you getting it?"

He was right, the drug he'd squirted into her behind had already started to act. "Oh yes...yes...you know, I didn't know what you were doing then. It's good, so mellow. Oh...." She sighed softly and whispered, "...oh I wouldn't mind whatever you did to me now."

"Good. That's ideal. The effect should take you deeper still. While you can I want you to get onto your side facing the wall, away from me. Can you do that?" She was almost asleep as the ten milligrams of diazepam took hold of her central nervous system. Mumbling to herself she shifted her pelvis off his knees and rolled onto her side facing downwards towards the runnel. "I think you're nearly ready." She grunted assent, but sleepily drew her knees up, curling herself into slumber. Irritably, he unfolded her so that her now unconscious body lay perfectly straight. In this position she tended to roll either onto her back or her front. He propped her up with his knees. "Such a small price to pay for heaven," he said.

Softly, she entered the long night.

THREE

The New Age Encampment was wreathed in early morning mist. Dew covered the trampled grass of the fields, but could not quite extinguish the smouldering, blackened wood fire at the centre. The ring of makeshift shelters and wigwams might have been that of the first settlers to move through the virgin forest that had covered the land thousands of years before. Only the detritus of modern-day packaging and the rusting green behemoths of ex-service buses that flanked the camp betrayed its latter-day origins.

A lone woman, shivering in the morning air, moved about the fire, tending it with bits of dry brushwood until it spattered back into flame. She placed a blackened kettle of water over the fire and waited, patiently, for it to boil.

* * *

Eve shut the front door of Alderley House as softly as she could. She was leaving early. If she stayed the temptation to stay forever would be too great. She must cut herself off from him again, at least for a little while. As she unlocked her car she happened to look up at the curtained windows of Power's bedroom. She had left him warm and blissfully asleep. Part of her yearned to be with him and sharing his warmth. The same part of her bitterly regretted teasing him so ambivalently the night before. Did he, could he ever understand her?

She saw her relationships and particularly last night as a dance, sometimes too close and sometimes too distant, but never finding the comfortable mean. She started the car and angry with herself revved the engine half-aware of her vengeful fantasy to disturb his sleep. Her car moved off, wheels crunching through the brown wet gravel, headlights casting over the wall in the morning darkness. The road down the hill away from the Edge was deserted. She stopped in the village at the 'T' junction, she paused for a second and since there was no car behind her, took her time to adjust the seat and switch on the radio. As she turned right Eve glanced up at the mirror, she noticed a distant figure walking down the hill behind her. It was only a brief glimpse which she did not even register as she accelerated away.

At the bottom of the long hill, by the old coaching inn, parked early the night before was a white van, spattered with mud and grime. The van's rear windows had been whitewashed. So early in the morning there was no-one else to see the tall shadowy figure walking jauntily down the winding hill road and into the village of Alderley Edge. The man whistled, as if some burden had been lifted miraculously from his shoulders. He passed the blinking orange glow of a Belisha beacon and its light showed him to be smiling happily. He swung the heavy weight of his bag as if it were lightness itself. The bag described a rhythmic arc through the air as he swung it like a pendulum from his right hand. When he reached the van and locked himself inside, its engine roared into life the first time he tried the key. Slowly, the van pulled away from the kerbside and, unobserved, headed south.

* * *

Carl Power sensed the cool dampness of the air in his bedroom and burrowed his way deeper into the warmth of his duvet. The peace of his home was a balm to his soul and the satisfaction of Eve's body had given him the most blissful of sleep. His mind swam gradually up from five fathoms of sleep to the surface of consciousness. Somewhere, he could not place it, there was an urgent noise. An insistent tapping from somewhere below. Mice? Power rolled over and stared at the ceiling trying to re-orient himself. Where was the noise? From downstairs? A thin voice, pitched high with panic. "Help! It's important, please help!"

The thin, sharp, shrill voice pierced Power's peace. He growled unhappily, he wondered about waiting until whoever it was went away. But the voice was insistent, and sounded genuine enough. Was it Eve? No, it was a stranger's voice. Power roused himself finally and pushed away the edge of the duvet. Dizzily he scrambled to his feet and dragged on his blue towelling dressing-gown. He gingerly crept down the still unfamiliar staircase to the hall. Whoever it was had now resorted to banging on the door with both fists. Power could hear hysterical sobbing. "All right, all right, I'm coming," he called out to try and pacify her. His words had no effect; she went on pounding at the door until it was opened, and pulled away from her flailing fists.

"What is it?" There was a hard edge to his voice. The woman's agitation was infectious.

She stood in front of him, eyes wide open, staring at him while her mouth hung open; speechless, but gasping for air as she hyperventilated. She was a young woman with cropped hair, taller than average and elegant in a white trench coat. In one hand, clenched in her fist, was a yellow silk scarf and in the other a knotted leather dog leash. Of the dog there was no sign.

"What is it?"

She stared at him, visibly trying to marshal some coherent sentence to describe what she had seen. Eventually she fought down the panic that forced her breathing, "I've got to phone for a doctor. I need your phone...can I?" Then she felt ridiculous asking his permission. Didn't the circumstances warrant something more decisive than weak polite requests? She pushed past him into the hall and cast about, looking for the telephone. Power could not believe this. Was he still dreaming; perhaps this strange woman would disappear if he awoke? "I'm a doctor," he said. "Are you all right? Can I help you?"

She snapped, "Not me. Not me," at him without taking her eyes away from her search for an instant. Then she spied a phone on the hall table. She pounced upon it.

Power tried again to help. "Has there been an accident? A car on the road?"

She paused at last, uncertain in her dialling. "You're a doctor?"

"Yes, I am. Now, I know something bad has happened, but take your time and tell me what it is."

"Come on, we've got to go there. She needs you." She grabbed his arm and pulled him towards the door.

He wrenched his arm away from her grip. "I'm not even dressed. I'm not going anywhere until you tell me what the matter is...." He looked at her horrified face. "...because I might need something when I get there – if you tell me I can get some things together." Power's sudden refusal to be hurried put a brake on the momentum of her panic. She sank all the way down back onto the floor and rested her head back against the wall. She covered her eyes and sighed.

"I don't know what I'm doing; don't know what to do."

"You're running around like a headless chicken," commented Power. She gave him an alarmed look. "Can I get you a drink of water or anything?"

"What did you say?"

"I said you were running about like a mad thing."

"I thought you said something else. I'm sorry. It must seem very bad of me. I've had a dreadful shock, you see." She looked up at him. "I wanted a doctor, but there's no point. I can see that now. I'm not very good in an emergency."

"Tell me whats wrong.."

She yawned suddenly, "I'm sorry...I do that when...I don't know why. I was walking the dog..." She grimaced as she launched herself into her story at last. "Like I do every morning. I park my car at the sign, 'To the Edge' and I walk him, before breakfast you know. Oh God....I couldn't get him to come away." She began to cry.

"You're safe here." Power knelt down by her. "Go on now."

"I was near the foot of the ridge, amongst the rocks, where the caves are, when I noticed that B.J....that's the dog...had disappeared. Then I saw him around a rock, standing there, looking puzzled...if a dog can look puzzled, you know at the entrance to this cave. I moved around a bit, saw past the boulder this time and I could see, could just see, a bare foot, lying on the ground outside the cave. Then as I moved round further there was a leg, hips, a stomach, arms...but no...er...no..." She swallowed; trying not to be sick again.

"A body then?" She nodded.

"I couldn't get B.J. away. He went berserk, oh, I can't take any more. I can't." She began to shiver uncontrollably. Power fetched a blanket and wrapped it around her. Then he phoned the emergency services.

* * *

By noon the Edge had sprouted another encampment. It was as if the towering sandstone ridge was a fortress besieged. The forest that encompassed the Edge had been closed to the public. The curious were turned away politely and, if persistent, not so politely by the Cheshire Constabulary. The trees of the forest were be-ribboned by orange fluorescent tape that divided the forest floor into sections. Painstakingly, the police had started to search each section; scouring the bare rock, clay and broken bracken. They searched for clothing and weapons, any clue no matter how small. "We are archaeologists: brushing away the dirt from fragments of the past," said Superintendent Lynch in his lectures. "We have a different time scale, that's all."

At the cave mouth the most intensive search of all was taking place. The body had been photographed from every conceivable angle and then removed by the forensic pathologist for examination in his echoing, enamelled morgue, on a bed of cold unyielding steel. In his wake, other experts explored the cave.

At Alderley House, two police trailers, mobile offices in effect, were being set in the forecourt. This was the most convenient point to tap into the electricity and telecommunications networks. Power watched the police taking over his home with dismay. Part of him grimly acknowledged that the large forecourt accommodated the police so well that it might have been waiting for them. He retreated into his house and closed the door. Power wondered if the Edge had been waiting for this event, like an empty stage waited for its actors, perhaps the Edge now welcomed the start of its own play, the beginning of a new myth. Power shivered. He had seen the ghoulish visitors watching outside, summoned by the news of the murder on the radio. When they had heard they must have dropped everything, got into their cars and raced to the village. What did these voyeurs expect to see? They were spectators at an event and Power felt he was in the arena. He imagined how in the months and years to come people passing by in their cars would give themselves a vicarious thrill of horror by recounting the murder, and would intensify their feelings by walking to the spot where the murder had occurred. Power had been invaded and he knew things could never be the same. At the back of his mind Power had a nagging fear, which he could not even acknowledge to himself, that the unknown body on the rock was Eve.

The command trailer was Superintendent Lynch's office, the other trailer his special operations room, where he and the rest of the Special Crime Squad would work. The logistics of siting the operations room were complex and it was a near-miracle that the base had been established, all the telephones and computers linked, within a few hours of Lynch's demand. But people didn't like to cross Lynch. He was said to have God on his side.

Lynch had spent the morning at the cave. Now, as he climbed the hill back to his office, he noticed his clothes were muddied by the clay he had crawled upon in his quest for knowledge. He had a passion for fact that would have gladdened even the heart of Dickens's Mr. Gradgrind. Lynch knew that in these early days every effort must be made to find and collate every possible fact. Even the most insignificant detail would sometimes lead to a conviction. He brushed some of the dry clay off his trousers. He growled inwardly as he saw the thicket of reporters and camera crews that had grown about the gates of Alderley House. As they saw Lynch approaching them some reporters ran forward asking questions. Microphones were aimed towards him. Long-suffering constables held the reporters back, creating a path for Lynch. Lynch listened to their questions as he passed silently, his eyes fixed on his destination.

"Isn't it premature for you to be involved, sir?", "Do you know anything we don't?", "Was she a hippy, sir?", "Superintendent, do you have a comment?"

He moved silently on. I must phone the Chief Constable, he thought as he climbed the drive. He was pleased to see the operations room installed and ready for his command. The noise of questions had died down behind him. Then a voice was raised amongst the others – a shouted question that stopped Lynch in his tracks. "Have you found the head yet?"

Lynch turned and glowered at the reporters. The look itself was murderous. Cameras clicked and flashed and whined. He had given the daily papers one photograph at least. It would appear in the tabloids tomorrow to once again glower vengefully out of the page at the reader, captioned, "Head of the Lynch Mob".

He crunched across the gravel drive and ducked inside the portal of his temporary office. He was greeted by his Detective Sergeant and the welcome smell of freshly-brewed coffee. "You've got everything sorted out haven't you, Philip? Like a home from home." Detective Sergeant Beresford shrugged. He had worked long enough for Lynch to know the way he always wanted things done.

"The press seem pretty rabid today, sir."

"It's impossible to keep something like this quiet. This murder is too unusual to be ignored. On top of all the publicity about the hippy convoy this last week. The eagerness of the media seems almost reasonable."

"Has the body gone, sir?" asked Beresford.

"Yes. I didn't want it here any longer than absolutely necessary."

"We stopped a camera crew climbing the rocks, trying to get pictures of her body."

"Well, it's gone...she's gone. Isn't it striking how our language tries to deny the fact that not so long ago the body was a person. She was a person yesterday. Today she is only a body. You saw her...the whiteness of her...did you see how white she was? Perhaps the pathologist can say why." Beresford poured two mugs of coffee. Lynch went on, "She was like a statue of that white stone...what is it called?"

"Alabaster...marble?"

Lynch nodded. "The body...the legs and arms were splayed out... posed...displayed on the bare rock. No attempt to hide her at all. Not the usual, not by any means. I've seen bodies dismembered and separated for disposal, an arm here, a torso there; but not for display. Remember that prostitute cut up and put into plastic bags...thrown into a lake? The bags were a mistake. They slowed up the decomposition.

"Phillip, we'll have to prepare a statement for the hounds of the press. We need to think about what details we have that can be released. I don't want to trigger a copycat. Philip, think about that, try and jot some ideas down and then can you get the press relations officer sorted out? Can you do that?" Beresford nodded. "I'll phone to the pathologist for his initial ideas. While I'm on the subject of doctors I'd like to talk to that Doctor...Power, the one who lives here."

"The psychiatrist bloke?"

"I'm sure he must have noticed something yesterday. The cave is less than a kilometre from here."

"Do you want me to take a statement?" Beresford offered.

But Lynch wanted to talk to Power himself.

After three phone calls, to the pathologist, the Chief Superintendent and the Chief Constable, Lynch sent Beresford for Power. Wherever possible Lynch never interviewed people on their own territory. Despite the fact that his mobile office sat in the forecourt of Alderley House, Lynch knew that being interviewed in here rather than in his own home would throw any individual off-balance. Lynch saw this as an advantage, 'a confusion tactic' he called it.

None too happy at being summoned, Power accompanied the Sergeant from his kitchen, where he had been consoling himself with food and Tsingtao beer, across the driveway to Lynch's office. The sun was falling in the sky, becoming burnished as it settled into a bed of evening clouds. Power looked about uncomfortably at the uniformed police milling about. They seemed to be picking their way through the garden of the house. Power was irritated by this, but with difficulty controlled his impulse to protest. He wondered if he should ask the Sergeant what they were looking for. He looked at the policeman who walked at his side; noted his slightly pock-marked face and determinedly averted gaze. Power remained silent as he was shown into the ante-room outside Lynch's office.

"Wait here, please, Dr Power. I'll just see if the Superintendent is ready to see you. Please have a seat."

"I'll stand." Power watched as the Sergeant knocked at Lynch's door and entered. A moment later Beresford re-appeared and opening the door wide gestured to Power that he should go in. Without a flicker of emotion Beresford introduced him as he passed by. "Superintendent...Dr Power. Superintendent Lynch is just about to say Evening Prayer." Power half-turned to the Sergeant, not sure if he had heard him correctly. Lynch grimly noticed the hesitation in Power's step.

A quiet, calm voice called from inside the room and drew Power in. "Dr Power, please come in and sit down here." Lynch was standing behind his desk, a neat, tall man with a pinstripe suit and an elegant silk handkerchief arranged in his top pocket. His welcome was crisply formal. He proffered a dry, firm handshake to Power and guided him by the right arm to a seat. This done Lynch sank into silence as he sat behind his desk. He did not look at Power as he bowed his head in contemplative prayer. On the clear expanse of his desk was a small, well-thumbed copy of Cranmer's *Book of Common Prayer.*

If this performance was designed to confuse Power, it worked. Power watched the dark-suited Superintendent as at last he began to say the words of Evening Prayer, which he had long since memorised, "Enter not into judgement with they servant, O Lord; for in thy sight shall no man living be justified. The Scripture moveth us to acknowledge and confess our manifold sins and wickedness; and that we should not dissemble nor cloke them before the face of Almighty God..."

Throughout the other's prayers Power remained silent, watching the man opposite. Lynch seemed genuine and serious in his devotions. Finally, after the Grace, Lynch looked up. He smiled sincerely at Power. "Morning and Evening Prayer are a source of reassurance for me. Something changeless in a bitter and unstable world."

Power nodded. "I am not a religious person, Superintendent... er..."

"The name's Lynch. Do you think my faith is unusual, Dr Power? I find that we English make allowances for other people's faiths. But we...we don't make a fuss of these things. It isn't English to be anything more than quietly cynical."

"It is unusual for someone like yourself to be so open."

"I think you are wondering, as a professional, I think? Let me explain. My faith gives me the strength to go on. Crime, even though it is other people's crime, lingers in the heart. Like this murder...even if the investigation is successful and a murderer is convicted...some things have no earthly solution. And I know that your work can be harrowing too. What reserves of strength can you draw upon? A God? A wife? Children?"

"None of those things." Unfortunately, thought Power, but he kept his private desires silent.

"You will...you must need some reserves. Anyway, we all have our own agenda Dr Power. I have mine. First of all I must thank you very much for letting us use your land." Power hadn't been able to refuse. " We need a base close to the caves, and this is the only site. Your house is the nearest to the caves, I think?"

"I used to like walking there. Only now I'm not so sure. I feel as though someone's spoilt it...in some way. Does that make sense?"

"You're a doctor. Trained in Medicine, Surgery, Obstetrics..."

"What do you mean?" Power felt uncomfortable. Lynch saw him shifting slightly in his seat, crossing his legs and arms in defence.

"I mean you're trained in all sorts of things that the layman could not begin to understand. Trained to observe, for instance. What did your trained eyes observe yesterday, I wonder? The woman who discovered the body made her way here first because it was the nearest house. A house from which you could easily observe things. What were you doing yesterday? Did you see anything unusual?"

Power thought about saying he hadn't seen anything at all, but experience with the police told him to check this impulse. "I went to work; I got back at about six, I think. There was a hold-up in the village though. The hippy convoy people stopped the traffic. Some row about benefits."

"I know that. I was briefed on that. What did you do then?"

"I came back. I met my girlfriend Eve Pearson. We had dinner together."

"Your girlfriend? Have you known Miss...er...Pearson long?"

"A couple of years. We're thinking of settling down together." Power didn't say 'living together'; he thought Lynch might not approve.

Lynch coughed a dry cough. "Were you with her all night?"

Power frowned; was Lynch really asking him if he'd slept with Eve? "No," he said. "Before the evening meal I went for a walk in the wood." Power glumly noticed how Lynch pounced on his words.

"What time was your walk?"

"About seven."

"Not later than that?"

"Maybe. I was out for an hour walking along the Edge."

"And what time did you get back?"

Power resented the detail of Lynch's questions. It was as if the detective was trying to catch him out. And although Power knew the answers, the truthful answers, Lynch's pressure made his thoughts stumble in his brain. "I got back about eight. We had dinner then. We...er...we slept together." Power glanced at Lynch's face to see if he disapproved.

Lynch was amused. "There's a lot of it about, Doctor. Miss Pearson, is she a good cook?"

"Yes, but I cooked last night. Not her."

"What was on the menu?" asked Lynch. Power told him. He omitted to tell him about the apricot sorbet, which had remained untouched when the couple had gone to bed. Suddenly Lynch had pulled a pad of paper out of a drawer and was writing furiously. There was a brief silence as he wrote.

"What time did you both go to bed? The timing is important, as you will appreciate."

"But I'm not a suspect!" protested Power.

Lynch regarded him closely as he spoke, "I explained why I was interested in what you had to say earlier."

"We went bed about ten-thirty or so. We stayed together all night."

"But she wasn't there when you were woken this morning. When the police arrived first thing she wasn't there."

"No, no...well she likes to drive in the dark sometimes...watch the sunrise."

"A sun worshipper?" Lynch laughed. "Like the New Age people...pagan?"

"Of course not! She's an artist."

"And that explains it? Where is Miss Pearson now?"

"I don't know. She'll turn up."

"I don't doubt it. The woman who found the body said there was only the one car...that Saab...in the drive this morning. And she discovered the body very early this morning. How old is Miss Pearson?"

"Twenty-six or so." Almost ten years younger than Power. "Superintendent Lynch...this body..."

"Yes, Doctor?" Lynch smiled and Power felt even more disconcerted by this.

"How old was the woman you found?"

"You're wondering if the victim was Miss Pearson?" Reluctantly, Power nodded. "I'm waiting for the pathology report...but, in my poor judgement the victim was a young teenager. It's difficult to say, of course..." Power felt that Lynch was scrutinising his reactions. "You look uncomfortable, Dr Power?"

"Something like this, happening so close by...it..."

"Yes it is, isn't it? Well, I dare say Miss Pearson is safe and can corroborate what you say. Did you see anyone when you were in the woods yesterday evening?"

Power tried to picture the scene in his mind. "Two girls, yes. I was walking and all of a sudden I ran into this group of New Age people. Two young girls and a man. A thin, bedraggled man with long hair and clothes...a bit like a jester, you know a court fool. He was playing a flute...quite beautifully."

"You're sure it was a flute?" Lynch paused before he committed it to paper.

"No, a pipe maybe...some kind of pipe."

"Pan pipes? That would be apt for the woods."

"No, like a snake-charmer's pipe, you know."

Lynch raised his eyebrows. "I see. If you don't mind me saying, your recollection seems a little hazy, Dr Power."

"I came across them suddenly. I was...actually I was frightened, I thought he was rather sinister. He probably wasn't...it was the surprise. He asked me for money. He spoke as if he was two hundred years old or something – quite archaic language. And the girls laughed. I must be honest, I thought they were all mad or on drugs. I gave him some money and ran."

"How much money?" Lynch wanted to see how much detail Power could supply.

"Five pounds...I didn't have less. I wanted to get away. I felt embarrassed...threatened...the girls laughing at me."

"What did they look like?"

"Young, one with very short hair, like a skin-head cut. The other girl, I don't know, fair I think. They looked unclean."

Lynch grimaced. "Unclean? That's an odd word, as if you imagined them to be lepers or sinners...to be blamed for something."

"No, no...I just meant dirty, that's all. I've got no grudge against these hippies. They'll be gone soon enough."

Lynch smiled. "So will we, once we have done all we can."

"Can I go now?" Lynch thought that Power was like a timid little schoolboy in front of his head teacher. He looked guilty for no reason. Lynch found people's different reactions to authority intriguing.

"Of course you can, Doctor. Thank you for coming." He let Power move to the door. "Oh, Dr Power, just one thing. I will want you to make a formal statement about what you've told me. The Sergeant will arrange that with you. As for me, I'll say good afternoon, Dr Power."

* * *

Power hurried back to his kitchen in the house and brewed himself a pot of coffee, to stabilise his nerves. The imperative thing was to get inside and shut the door behind him. His encounter with Lynch had been profoundly disquieting. Power stood by the kitchen windows at the rear of the house and stared out at the Edge, numbed by his memories and submerged in reverie. He must have been standing this way for several minutes when he broke out of his trance. He'd dealt with the police on numerous occasions. He must have written hundreds of court reports, stood as an expert witness for defence and prosecution in dozens of cases. That was different, they were dealing with someone else's future. All this, the murder and the questioning this afternoon, it was all too close to home. His stomach rumbled for attention. He looked at his watch. It was later than he had thought.

Feeling hungry he went to the fridge. Somehow his trance of reflection had enabled him to put his worries back away at the furthest reaches of his mind. Now his senses seemed heightened; he was flooded with joy at the very redness of the tomatoes and the brown smoothness of an egg's shell. With gusto tempered by hunger he poured yellow sunflower oil into the old frying pan he had dragged out of a packing case. He lit the gas and clanged the pan down on top of the cooker. He parted three rashers of bacon and threw them in the pan. The bacon sizzled agreeably as he selected then cracked two eggs on the side of the pan. He poured the eggs' glutinous contents into the fat. The rich aroma of bacon and eggs filled the kitchen and took Power back to his childhood – a holiday with his grandma. He could see the old white-tiled kitchen now, filled with sunlight and the smells of just such a meal waiting to be downed with strong sweet tea. His grandfather would be sitting at the table in the morning-room, carefully cutting thin white slices of bread into small, precise triangles, like the Communion host. Grandfather would dip the triangles, with evident pleasure, into the saffron yolk of his fried egg.

Power sliced two tomatoes, doused them with white pepper, and consigned these too to the sizzling oil. In an attempt to re-create the nostalgic breakfast, Power brewed a pot of strong tea. Pouring himself a mug he added three large spoonfuls of sugar. This whole repast was a decadence beyond imagination, a no-holds barred defiance of dietary advice. This distracting rebellion felt so very good that Power seemed buoyed up with elation.

Half-an-hour later, as he was finishing the last mouthful of food, Power heard the doorbell ringing. Power got up and strode to the door. It was Eve carrying a wrapped-up canvas under her arm. She rested the painting down against the wall and looked up at him.

"Carl?"

"Yes?"

"I heard the news this afternoon. I came back...the police..." She gestured to the police trailers in his drive. "You've been invaded by them."

"Did they tell you they wanted to talk to you?"

"Yes...they've taken a short statement. They wanted to know about last night. The Superintendent even wanted to know what we ate."

"He was checking my story out...he was checking what I'd said to him before." He was so very glad to see her. He drew her in out of the sight of the policemen outside. "You're my alibi you know. Did you know that?"

"Oh," she looked upset. She hadn't mentioned the murder specifically yet. Her gaze suddenly became averted. "Can I have a wash, please...freshen up a bit...then a drink. I need a drink. The news...I feel so strange about it as if suddenly real is unreal." He moved towards her. "While we were eating last night...out there... so close by us... maybe while we were in bed." She struggled with her feelings, trying to acknowledge them and translate them into words. In a quiet small voice he heard her say, "Carl, I'm frightened."

* * *

"Gentlemen, here is the statement which you have waited for so patiently." Lynch had waited until eight-thirty to make his press statement. He was aware that throughout the day regional and national news coverage had been picking up on the story. His choice of time would launch the statement into the nine o' clock and ten o' clock national news. Lynch had eschewed advice from the police public relations adviser. The conventional thing was to hold a conference where Lynch would be seated at a desk, flanked by his subordinates and the press adviser. Lynch spoke alone, a lone figure in the open, floodlit against the dark maw of the cave entrance. He knew how to achieve the greatest theatrical effect (and his superiors and contemporaries disliked him for it). The goriness of the story together with the dramatic and elegant figure he assumed against the night would guarantee national television coverage. Lynch did not necessarily crave publicity, part of him hoped that the immediate publicity might induce people with fresh recollections of the murder victim or murderer to come forward. It was a gamble. Lynch would face criticism if a copycat murder took place.

The rock of the cave, floodlit bright orange against the blue of the night sky, made a supernatural stage set. The mouth could be clearly distinguished from the New Age Encampment down on the plain. Some reporters had decided to film additional clips from down there. The distant lighted escarpment made an eerie backdrop.

Lynch spoke from his near perfect memory, as the cameras hummed and clicked, "At 7 a.m. this morning, the naked body of a young teenager was discovered by a lady out walking her dog on Alderley Edge. The body is that of a fair-haired adolescent girl. Her clothes were missing and still have not been found. There is no initial evidence of a sexual attack. Her identity is unknown.

"Identification has been made almost impossible by two things, firstly there are no personal effects whatsoever, and secondly the victim has been decapitated...there is no head...we have therefore no idea of her facial image or resource to dental records.

"This girl was murdered on the evening of May 1st here at the cave on the Edge. We are appealing for anyone who has noticed such a fair-haired girl's absence or who may have seen anything unusual happening in the last few days in the Alderley Edge area to come forward urgently. There is a special incident number on 061-321-6666. We need your help. We must find this dangerous murderer, and find him quickly." He paused to enable television editing of his piece, then he spoke again. "That is my statement for your use. I will take a few off-the-record questions now please. Can I have that light off please? Just that one. It's in my eyes. Thank you."

"You said she was beheaded. Have you found the head?"

"No, the murderer has retained this." A shocked silence followed his words. A cold wind began to blow amongst the trees and chilled them all. "We have searched the area for the head, the weapon, her clothes...the murderer has planned carefully and removed them all."

"Where was the body exactly?"

"Where you are now standing, sir. Next question."

"Was there a sexual motive? A sexual attack?"

"We cannot rule that out, but the initial pathology report does not suggest it."

"Were there any other bizarre features to this crime?"

"If there were any," said Lynch. "It would not be politic to reveal them."

"Was this girl one of the hippies?"

"Maybe. We are continuing our investigation amongst the people in the temporary encampment and hippy convoy nearby. It would be unwise to exclude anything this early in the inquiry." Lynch was ever-cautious.

"How old was she?"

A mental image of the body flashed in front of Lynch's eyes.

"Only about fourteen or fifteen, ladies and gentlemen. It is difficult to conceive of any understandable motive for this vicious crime. If you can help us...any information at all..." Suddenly Power broke off, ~~LYNCH~~ speechless; for what more did he have to say? He nodded a curso-ry thank you to the assembled reporters and turned away, hurrying for his car. The press statement had drained him, and as he walked away he realised how tired he was, how keyed-up he must have been through the day. He must snatch some hours of sleep, but for him there would be no real rest until like an archaeologist he had stripped away the blinding earth and uncovered the truth.

FOUR

The hospital boasted a splendid Victorian red-brick facade. A great archway led into a lofty hall, with a bright glass dome, and azure tiled walls. A mosaic frieze ran around the walls and climbed the wide marble stairway up to the wards. Grafted onto the excessive Victorian splendour was the most modern of buildings opened only the year before by the Prince of Wales. In keeping with the Prince's conservative tastes the architect had specified russet brickwork and a Welsh slate roof. The facade of the building had been purchased from an architectural salvage firm and had once graced the Royal Southern Bank in Manchester. The architectural journals had feasted upon *"The Prince's psychiatric hospital"* and depending upon their allegiances had variously described the edifice as 'a sympathetic and harmonious blend of styles' or 'a bastardisation of modern architecture of which the Prince should be thoroughly ashamed'.

Power found the interior of the building most pleasant. It was cool and clean without the horrendous buzz that accompanies the air-conditioning of most such buildings. The rooms were grand, spacious and with windows large enough to admit sufficient light to preclude fluorescent lighting during the day time. And what pleased Dr Power most of all was that his own office was very much his own domain. It was decorated the way he wanted, and the comfortable things that he liked best were all in that room. It was a room he could relax and think in, and it was a room he was happy to show his patients. The room said enough about him to make a personal impression, but not so much as to be threatening or to reveal too much of his inner self.

His office still had that new smell bestowed upon it by newly laid blue carpets and recently varnished woodwork. And he had crammed a set of shelves full of his books on psychiatry, psychology and symbols. The walls ached under the weight of his paintings. The desk though was still relatively clear of clutter, it looked eager to be covered by Power's customary mess of papers and case notes. A set of comfortable armchairs had been purchased at his insistence. In psychotherapy the patient must be comfortable to disclose.

Today Power felt the office was a little too warm. He opened the windows and stared out at the early summer day. A gentle breeze riffled through the branches of the trees that fringed the car park. Down below on the tarmac Power could see his Saab waiting patiently for him. As he moved away from the window a sudden gust of wind passed him, and out of the corner of his eye he saw a note of paper flutter from the desk through the air and onto the carpet.

He picked it up. It was written by his secretary, Laura, and it read, 'Monday, 8.45 a.m. Dr Power, please contact ward 4. They want to discuss a patient, Susan Parkes, when you get in.'

Power felt somewhat panicked by this. Was there time to go to the ward in person or would he have to make do with a phone call? He had a meeting with the Clinical Director at 10.00 and decided to phone. Perhaps he could ask one of the juniors to sort out Susan Parkes, whoever she was.

He found the ward's phone number in the directory and punched it out on the telephone. "Hello, Dr Power here. Is the nurse in charge there?"

"Speaking. It's Stephen Morris, Steve, Charge Nurse."

"Hi Steve, you wanted to talk about Susan Parkes. I don't know her. Is she one of my patients?"

"Yes, your team was on take this weekend gone. Susan was admitted on Sunday...a transfer from the medical wards by the Registrar. Er...I wonder if you could come down and see her please?"

"I've got a meeting at ten. Is there a Registrar there perhaps?"

"Well one's on study leave today and of course your registrar is on maternity leave. I wouldn't press it normally, but...I'd better explain. She's seventeen. She was on the medical wards after an overdose of tricyclic antidepressants. She actually had to go on coronary care for a while. An arrhythmia caused by the tablets. The psychiatric problem is that, she's anorexic and very depressed. We can't get her to eat anything and she wants to discharge herself. I don't think she should go."

Power groaned. "The depression may be secondary to the anorexia. How much does she weigh?"

"Four and a half stone."

Power whistled through his teeth. "When you're that undernourished the brain starts functioning differently – moods and reasoning abilities become distorted and slowed down. Steve, I don't really want to section her – we need her co-operation in the long term."

"I've tried everything to coax her to stay and eat. She said if we force-feed her she'll vomit it back until her oesophagus gives way. She says she can vomit at will. If we put a drip into her she says she'll rip it out of her vein."

Something in Steve's manner irritated Power, but he didn't let it sound in his voice. "I'm coming down there now, Steve." He told his secretary to let the Director have his apologies if he were late and hurried out of his office and down the corridor, past the Professor's office, to the wards.

* * *

She was sitting in bed staring at the wall in front of her. The room was warm, but the bedclothes were tightly wrapped around her. She didn't move, didn't even register Power as he came into the side ward. He sat down beside her white island of a bed. She stared at the blank wall opposite and tried to think, but her thoughts felt sticky and unwieldy. If they came in with the food what would she do? The question reverberated in her brain, but had no logical answer. She would ask herself once, forget the question then repeat it over and over again. What about their food, their drips? How they must hate her to abuse her so. This place smelt of food...it had become a stench, a foul stink of earthly corruption. How could she face the food when a glass of skimmed milk seemed like liquid fat to her.

Power looked closely at her. He found it difficult to assess how old she was from her appearance. She was small, childlike, but paradoxically she seemed preternaturally old. Her hands lay still upon the counterpane. His trained eye saw the blueness of the nails and fingers. He knew that if he touched her hands they would be icy cold. Her body, desperate for food, was shutting down. In her frantic pursuit of thinness she had starved herself for many months. Her heart would be beating slowly, perhaps only once a second. On the back of her hands were calluses. This was Russell's sign. The calluses were produced by the friction of her teeth against her knuckles every time she stuck her fingers down her throat. His eyes moved up her sticklike arm. If he gripped it hard he imagined the arm might snap like hollow dried bamboo.

At her shoulders the bulk of her deltoid muscle had gone, used up by her body to preserve life. The bones of her shoulder showed through the skin like a living anatomy specimen. The ridge of her spine stuck out of her back and pressed through her nightie. Round eyes stared out of hollow eye sockets at nothingness; the only windows on a gaunt and skeletal world. If he asked her how she looked Power knew she would say, 'fat, horribly fat'. She had tried to kill herself with tablets at the weekend, but Power knew that she had been killing herself through starvation for months.

"You're frightened we're going to force-feed you," he said. Slowly, painfully she turned her death's head towards him. A gradual, almost imperceptible nod. "My name is Dr Power. I'm here to help you. I know how frightened you are of losing control." She looked into his eyes. He understood her. How could he do that?

"Are you the psychiatrist then?"

"Yes," he paused then spoke softly, but firmly. "I am a psychiatrist, but the doctor in me looks at you and sees how very ill you are. Your body is so starved that you will die in a few days without food. I know how you feel about food, but your body is dying, believe me."

One of her frail hands scrabbled under the sheets. Trembling with the effort, but determinedly she held out a sheet of paper for him.

" Read it," she said.

Power picked it up and looked at the blue scrawl, he read aloud, "Depression is an inky blue lake. It smells like fried sausages swimming in brown gravy. Fear is a cream cake covered in chocolate." He looked up at her, waiting for a response, but her thinking was very slow. She was still thinking of the sincerity in his voice.

"The other man...the nurse read that. He laughed at it. He was laughing at me." She looked away, and waited for Power to fail the test too.

"I guess that food doesn't frighten him, but it frightens you. How do you feel?"

"Confused. I can't concentrate anymore. Things used to be so clear...so good."

His voice changed. It had been soothing and understanding and she had felt accepted and understood. Now his voice had acquired a rhythm, a hypnotic rhythm. "Early on, the starvation produces a high, but it wears off and decisions get difficult...difficult to focus...and the high, it becomes a depression. As you eat, that feeling of well-being will return. You feel the hunger, but you can rest with the idea that you can save your life if you can make the decision to eat something. You feel the hunger now?" She nodded slowly, eyes half-closed. "But you used to feel you shouldn't eat. Now, perhaps, I wonder if you can make the decision?" She looked at him. He seemed so refreshing and she felt so calmed by him. "I wonder if you would like something?"

"Yes...something to eat. A little something."

"A little something...yes...to help you live. I know how you can make strong decisions. We can talk later about a programme to help you back to health." Susan smiled; a thin watery smile, but a smile nevertheless.

* * *

Dr Jones, the Clinical Director, was a short man with a balding red head. His twinkling brown eyes set in this rubicund face made him look younger than his fifty-plus years. As Power, twenty years his junior, entered, Jones looked round stiffly. It was as if his powerful neck and shoulders found it difficult to move. Indeed if he wished to look at anyone he had to move his whole body rather than turn his head.

"Power? How good to see you." He extended a firm handshake. Power felt Jones' thumb pressing on the back of his hand. "Here, sit down." Jones drew him over to the easy chairs. Power was always amused that the office was twice the size of his own. "Have you had a coffee?"

"That would be an excellent idea."

Jones rang for two coffees and then sat down opposite. "Well, how are things?"

"Yes, well... My registrar's away so I've just been seeing an anorexic girl on ward 4. Left her eating some yoghurt and fruit...a minor triumph."

"Don't like anorexics. Look weak and thin, but are really very powerful people. Have to be strong minded to starve themselves so. Don't like 'em at all.
"Look...we need to talk about various things; the Department budget is a little overspent...we can't get you a locum for your registrar I'm afraid." Power doubted he was at all troubled. "We need to sort out student allocations, audit that sort of thing..." Power wondered if Jones really preferred managing budgets to working with patients. Power started thinking about Susan Parkes. He needed to talk to her family. In a way he was a detective too, rooting out the cause of illness; that was the criminal Power sought. Jones talked on as Power nodded absently.

Half an hour later Jones sat back in his chair, pleased with himself. Power had raised no objections to his plans. "Good, well that's sorted." Power wondered what it was that Jones really wanted to talk about. "Heard from your predecessor this morning. She wanted a reference." Jones snorted. "Nice woman though she was, was hardly ever here – always off having babies. Did you ever meet her?"

"An excellent clinician I believe," said Power diplomatically.

"Spiky purple hair one week, shorn redhead the next. Used to leave her baby and dogs with the secretaries. Her patients could never depend on her."

Power heard the loathing in Jones' voice and couldn't resist opposing him. "She wrote some interesting stuff on M.E. in the eighties."

" I didn't renew her contract though. Got you instead. Professor liked your book on the unconscious. Well, you know that, don't you? Does it sell well?" It was well known that Jones abhorred psychotherapy and everything to do with the unconscious. A book like Power's would be anathema to him.

"It sells tolerably well. Keeps me in pocket money for a week or two when the royalty cheque comes in."

Jones laughed. "I appreciate your sticking up for your predecessor, but you never had to work with her. Intolerable." Jones was skirting around something. Why had he mentioned Power's predecessor? Was he trying to make Power uneasy. To confound Jones, Power relaxed. Jones launched into another topic.

"I hear you've got a house up at the Edge. Beautiful countryside. Nice pubs. Wasn't that where the murder was?" Power groaned inwardly and nodded. "Thought so. Dreadful. Young girl, no head I believe."

"That's right."

"Did you see the body?" Jones was sitting forward in the chair again, his lobster face all anticipation.

"No." He wanted to add, 'why should I have done?'

"Well...." Across the desk Jones noticed how tense Power had become. "You seem upset by something, have I..."

"No...I don't mean to...it's just I could have done without this murder happening on my doorstep. My house was the nearest one, you see."

"I'm sorry," said Jones. Now he looked more closely he could see the stress in Power's eyes. "These things have a way of sucking you in...even if you're not really involved."

"It feels like that, yes. I've got the police crawling over my land. They actually set up their trailers in my driveway."

"I know a couple of Chief Superintendents if that's any help? If I can put the right word in the right ear?"

Power looked at Jones in a new light. He regarded the news of Jones' contacts with some suspicion, but he welcomed the offer of help for what it was. "Thank you, Dr Jones, but I don't know if that will be necessary. I have been told they'll be moving out soon. There's only so much they can do at the site."

"Well, I'm sorry you've been put upon, Carl. Once it's all cleared up, perhaps you should take a holiday. As you know, I'm going abroad for a week or so soon. Does you the world of good. That's what I wanted to talk to you about." Power knew he didn't have to like Jones, or approve of his attitude to other doctors or patients, but he did need to be able to work with him. The practicalities had not escaped Jones either. If he could get Power to see him as a kindly benefactor, Jones could put more trust in him. "You know Carl, now you're in one of the most prosperous areas of the country...you should start a private practice...there might be a session free at my private rooms...I share them with the Professor and Dr Thirlgood. Your predecessor never took up the option. Socialist, you see. As a taster I wondered if you could look after things while I'm away. If there are any emergencies from my private list of patients. There shouldn't be, but I would be very grateful if you could help me out. It would be a foot in the door for you, as a younger consultant. Are you interested by any chance?"

Private work was something he had always eschewed. "David, like my predecessor I don't altogether approve of making money out of the ill. But I can see that you're going to need someone while you're away. I'll do that for you, as a friend, but I don't think I'll be taking up that offer of sessions at your rooms."

Jones smiled. He had what he wanted. If Power was too principled to make a bit of money he, Jones, wasn't bothered. Jones didn't bother to point out the flaw in Power's argument. He already benefited from his patients' illness. What else was the forty thousand pound salary Power drew? Jones grinned at him, the proverbial Cheshire fat cat.

* * *

Eve had risen late. Sleep had dulled her, but as consciousness overtook her she leapt from Power's bed as if electrified. It was not any anxiety about time that provoked her flurried rising, but a worry that perhaps some window or door had been unlocked. She hurried around the house, dressed in one of Power's blue-striped shirts, checking window frames and outside doors. When she was sure that the house was secure she stood in the hall and let out a deep sigh of relief.

The front doorbell rang. Eve opened it gingerly, peering around the edge of the oak door to where Superintendent Lynch stood. Beyond the tall and immaculate figure Eve could see the police trailers. The full memories from the day before came back to her. The police had been working since early morning, whilst Eve had been wallowing in the smooth bed upstairs.

Lynch smiled a reassuring smile. "Miss Pearson? I've been going over the witness statement taken by my sergeant. There are one or two things that I'd like to flesh out with regard to the investigation. May I come in?"

She opened the door wide and he stepped past her. He smelt clean. Eve was conscious of her own unwashed, undressed state. She smelt of Power and beneath the thin covering of Power's shirt-tails she was nude. Lynch showed no sign of having noticed. He stared straight ahead as she made her excuses. "I must go and change, Inspector."

"I'm a Superintendent actually." He corrected her without pride or hubris. He just liked things to be right.

"Well," Eve said, hiding behind the newel post of the bannisters. "Perhaps you could make yourself at home. Make yourself a coffee or something. I'll only be five minutes, I promise."

"That's kind of you. I'll make you a coffee too, shall I?" said Lynch and he wandered off down the hallway, his hands folded behind his back.

Eve ran upstairs and showered, uncaring of the needle hot spray that peppered her skin. She brushed her teeth as she dragged on a blouse and skirt and slipped her feet into her shoes. She came down the stairs as she fixed her hair. A model of female efficiency she began to search the house for Lynch.

She tracked him down seated by the bookcases in Power's study. On Power's desk was a tray of coffee, two mugs and a plate of home-made biscuits. Lynch was munching these contentedly as he surveyed the spines of Power's books.

"Said he wasn't a religious man. Look at all these books - *The Koran, The Bardo Thodal*, the *Bhagavad Gita*. All the world's most holy books."

"And a good many others," Eve sounded defensive on Power's behalf.

"I hope there's depth as well as width to his reading. A man can only follow one religion...not some mish-mash...like those people from the hippy camp. I've been interviewing some of them this morning. I didn't find the one I want...but I think they are a sorry people. They are searching for a god, but our godless society betrayed them, never gave them the one God. So they wander about inventing their own. Sad, don't you think?"

Eve was only half-listening. She was wondering how she might paint the Superintendent. She suddenly realised that he had asked her a specific question. "I'm sorry, I didn't quite catch that?"

"I asked you what Power was like...as a person?"

"You know...it's difficult to describe someone as a person. He's kind enough...sometimes too kind..makes me feel guilty, I suppose."

"He's never been cruel then, asked you to do things you haven't wanted to?" asked Lynch.

Eve flushed, "No, no. Surely you don't think he could have anything to do with...with the murder?"

Lynch sighed. He picked up his coffee. "See, Miss Pearson, it's like this...when there's been an offence all kinds of people are affected. All kinds of people are linked in to the central offence...most of them by coincidence...most of them innocent, but to an outsider, like me, it's not so easy to disentangle people who've become linked in. Dr Power is an unlikely suspect, and his alibi is good. Although he was alone for some of the morning, my guess is that you were with him...sleeping with him...when the murder was committed. Are you a heavy sleeper?"

"No, I'm a light sleeper usually."

"There you are. It's just me. I call it the halo effect. When something happens like this...an offence against nature...everybody is coloured by the halo that spreads outwards. Before I can eliminate anybody I have to feel very sure about them. You know, one thing that puzzled me about the doctor...yesterday when I was interviewing him... he was nervous. More nervous than he should have been. Can you shed any light on that?"

"I don't know," said Eve carefully.

"I was wondering whether he'd had any contact with us before...that made him so nervous."

"Perhaps you'd have to ask him yourself...he works with the courts sometimes...reports on patients...that sort of thing. And recently there was a jealous alcoholic who's been charged with attempted murder."

"There you are then," said Lynch. "He's had more than the average person's dealing with us, but you'd have thought that would have... desensitised him to us."

"About a year or so ago...in Liverpool he was asked to help the police." Lynch's eyebrows rose. "A man had taken a hostage. The first person he'd met...a young girl...and taken her up to the top of the Liver building. do you know it?" Lynch nodded. "He was ill, acting on a delusion. He wanted the Home Secretary to come and substitute himself for the girl. I don't know why. Presumably it all made sense to the madman. Carl happened to be this man's psychiatrist. He was woken out of his bed by the police and taken through the night to the building. Hoisted up to the top in one of those fire engine things. Dramatic stuff. He hates heights anyway. Carl tried to talk the madman down. It was no good. The voices were telling the madman to jump.

"So he jumped, and he pulled the girl with him. Carl managed to get hold of her ankle as she was falling forward. He almost got dragged down with both of them. He couldn't hold onto her...let go...he had to, or else he'd have gone with them. The madman died. I think they saved the girl. She was lucky. Carl...well, can you imagine how he felt?"

Lynch nodded. "He sounds like a brave man." There should be records on that, thought Lynch. He'd ask Beresford to check them, but Lynch had already made his mind up about Power. Just a few more questions. "As a psychiatrist, how good is he?"

"Psychiatric patients do kill themselves." She was defending her lover again. "It doesn't reflect on..."

Lynch interrupted. "Oh, I know that, I wasn't implying anything else. To a certain extent we have a similar clientele to Dr Power. I'm more interested in his expertise."

"Well, he's published papers and a book. He's a world expert on delusional ideas."

"He doesn't sing his own praises though...or he didn't when I saw him."

"Carl's too modest. He's a bit too reserved at times...part of him is always thinking away...removed, you know? He would fly higher if he appeared more sure of himself."

"But he's a world expert, you say?" Lynch looked at the Apple computer on Power's desk, the racks of 3" discs, the piles of correspondence and closely annotated papers for Power's new book.

"He was in line for a University Chair. He could have got it easily. It was as if...as if he just decided to let the other person walk away with the Professorship. You know, sometimes I can't understand him."

"I see," said Lynch. It sounded as if Power would need a certain amount of pressure if Lynch was to get him to agree to what he had in mind. He'd asked Eve all he wanted to. Time to close the interview down. "This...all this happening so close to you. You must feel unsettled by it?"

"Last night I caught him, Carl, looking out of the bedroom window into the dark woods. Just staring. He said he was thinking about his new book, about the collective unconscious, or something.. something to do with the New Age people. I didn't think he was...was thinking about that."

"What did he say?" Lynch had picked up a copy of Power's first book on the unconscious. He was admiring its cover, then he looked for the index.

"He was just staring into the night. Talked about how this house is surrounded by the past. All the people that were here before, as if they were still here."

"What people did he mean?"

"The cave people, the Celts, the Romans...all of them as if they'd never really gone."

"Well...I would agree they've left their mark physically. Their huts...round here the Neolithic people hollowed out the caves, the

Celts had their hill forts and the Romans their mines and farms, but..."

"Other things...things they left behind."

"What do you mean? Ghosts?"

" I don't know. Not ghosts...no, that's too simplistic. Maybe he meant that places become...well, like if they're lived in for a long time... by generations and generations...like this place, like this house even... well then the place itself absorbs something of them."

Lynch frowned "It's an idea, I suppose." He didn't think that physical things like stones, trees and bricks could do any of the things she suggested. He doubted Power thought that either. "Do you think something like a murder could change physical things, change the world?"

"No, well, maybe in one way..." Lynch had confused her. She wondered if Lynch thought a psychiatrist was an appropriate boy-friend for somebody so apparently deranged. She blushed.

"I think things are more straightforward. The murder hap-pened, sure. But that was two days ago. There's not a trace of it out there. There are only traces left, but those are in our memories. Out there, on the rock, there's nothing left. All cleared away."

"Yeah, yeah that's right." Eve wasn't going to try and explain her feelings any further. Lynch made them sound stupid.

Lynch had found something in the index of Power's book, *The Unconscious.* "Here we are...the collective unconscious...let's see what Dr Power has to say...see if I can understand." He read from Power's text. "The collective unconscious was part of Jung's idea that we all share a common past. We evolved from the same ancestors. We have similar genetic material. Our brains have remained structurally the same for millions of years. Our ways of thinking haven't changed. We still have our magic and our gods. Different names maybe, but we hav-en't changed.

"He had a dream, about a house. He went down into the cellars, found more and more rooms, each below the last. Every flight of stairs he went down there was a different room. Each room had different furniture. The first was Victorian, the second Medieval, then Roman and so on. Eventually he came into a cave...with cave paintings and a raging fire at the entrance. A human skull on the floor. He felt this room was incredibly old...older than we could conceive of. And yet he felt there were layers below this, layers he couldn't explore. Our sense perhaps of there being something else, something more than everyday life and thought.

"That gave him the idea that our unconscious is multilayered and each of us has things in common...forms in our brain, patterns of memory and behaviour. In my own opinion the things that all of us do have ramifications for all mankind, our thoughts live on in the physical world – in the unconscious of us all and in the form of our conscious ideas, whether written in books or music or on film."

Lynch looked at Eve. "I'll have to think about that," he said. "Have you read the book?"

"Once. It's a fascinating book...I found that reading it was like finding part of yourself...part you didn't know existed..."

"May I borrow it? Do you think Dr Power would mind?"

"No, he's got several copies. I think he'd be flattered to think you wanted to read it."

"I'm going to ask a favour of him, so maybe that's no bad thing. I'll leave you be now, Miss Pearson. Thank you for the chat and the coffee. Listen, we'll be moving out this afternoon. There's only so much we can achieve at the scene of the crime, and we've done that. If there's anything that comes to mind...please let me know." She showed him to the front door. "Well good-day. God bless." He said, and was gone.

* * *

When Power returned to Alderley House he saw, with relief, that the police murder squad had gone. He might have imagined it all had he not seen the evidence of the deep grooves left in the gravel by the trailer's wheels. As he parked the Saab he recalled a few minutes earlier passing the village churchyard, clogged with a collection of the dead. He had seen a few battered buses from the hippy convoy juddering along the road in the opposite direction. The New Age people were decamping too; partly because the intrusion of the police asking questions about a dead girl had unsettled them and partly because it was almost time to move on anyway. Power had seen the faces of those in the departing buses. A pall had obviously been cast over their enjoyment, not least by the press who had dubbed the murder, "The Headless Hippy case".

Alderley Edge was returning to normal again; with time the village's pain would fade away and the murder merely add to the myth of the Edge.

* * *

At the same time that Power was falling into Eve's welcoming arms, the Superintendent was phoning his wife to let her know he would be late home. Lynch was gathering his murder squad at the Chester police headquarters. When he had got through his excuses, Lynch was ten minutes late. They were waiting patiently for him; thirty assorted officers. They were keen young detective constables for the routine door-to-door enquiries. Lynch had ensured that only the most methodical constables had been selected. Above them he had selected a team of experienced Sergeants and Inspectors, none of whom were so ambitious as to threaten him, but all of the first rank. They were drinking coffee and chatting excitedly when Lynch swept through the doors.

"Good evening," he treated them all to a smile and made eye contact with as many of them as he could. "Welcome to the Edge investigation. Thank you for staying late. I'll try to be brief. I want us to start early tomorrow. I want us to pull together from the start, that's why I wanted to see you all together, and later this evening as task teams, so that we all start at the same point tomorrow morning.

"Either fate or the murderer has been unkind to us. Our scene of crime investigations have unearthed no clues that point directly to the identity of the victim or the murderer. He, and I'm going to presume it was a 'he', (please notice the assumption there), left no personal effects of his or the girl's. No clothes. Nothing. Not a trace. As if our murderer was a ghost or something..."

Lynch switched on an overhead projector and picked up a felt-pen to write on it. He fingered the pen for a few moments speculatively. There was little enough to write down. "I've got the report from the Home Office Pathologist. Let me tell you how I think it was done.

"First of all though, what did we find? We found a body. You've seen the pictures?" He looked around at the assembly. They nodded soberly. "A fourteen or fifteen year old girl, blonde haired. Naked. Splayed on the convex surface of the sandstone escarpment. In full view...on her back, with limbs flung open wide, and minus her head. A neat, bloodless cut between the cervical vertebrae.

"There's no evidence of sexual molestation. No vulval bruising. No semen. A few old puncture marks on the arms. This girl abused drugs at some time in the last few months. And in her groin...a single large puncture site. Fresh. She'd been dead between eight and twelve hours of the corpse's discovery.

"Around her the rock is unstained, equally bloodless. But the body lies twelve metres from the mouth of one of the largest caves that are carved into the Edge. Inside the cave, in what Neolithic man once used as a bedchamber was a pile of straw, partly bloodstained with her blood. This was where she was killed. In a gully and a kind of rock basin that used to be a water cistern is almost a gallon of clotted blood." They were listening closely, most of them apparently unmoved by what he said. Lynch wondered how brutalising a police career could be. Let's see how they take the rest, he thought.

"How was it done? The murderer seems to have been very careful about the blood. Either he didn't want blood on him or his clothes or he was worried about her blood..remember she was an i.v. drug abuser. Maybe he was worried she was HIV positive. Maybe he wore gloves, I don't know. Somehow he got her, alive into that cave, somehow he lured her there. How? We don't know. He's planned it. There's straw there, fresh straw. He gives her something. The serum from what was left of her body blood had high concentrations of diazepam. He must have given her repeated doses of the drug, and while she was unconscious he inserts a wide-bore cannula, a needle, into the femoral artery. He uses the cannula to direct her blood into the back of the cave, into the water cistern. Already drugged under the diazepam and losing all that blood, she drifts into a cold nothingness until she simply expires. When her heart stops pumping out its life blood, he removes her head. Without getting drenched in blood.

"This is the coldest, most calculated, most clinical murder I've ever heard of. And after, when he's done he places her, displays her under the night sky, under the moon, then he gathers up her clothes... and her head, and he simply walks away."

One of the female officers began to cry. The others were unnaturally silent. "Why have I asked for such a large full-time team? Why have I asked that you all be prepared to work for the next few months on this case alone? I believe that this man has denied us his victim's identity as well as his own. I believe that he's as clever an individual as you're likely to meet in your whole careers. Keep this to yourselves. Don't tell this to anyone, not your colleagues, not your loved ones, no-one outside this room. Because I suspect that we won't catch him quickly. And we may not get enough clues to catch him until he kills again. And he will kill again. It's just a matter of time."

Somewhere in the distance a phone was ringing.

FIVE

Power finished the last morsel of scrambled egg and bacon with relish. He checked his watch. A busy day lay ahead of him. With his consultant colleagues on holiday he faced a heavier workload still. Urgent telephone calls from family doctors would plead with him to visit their patients at home that day. He knew that Laura, his secretary, had arranged for him to go to the Risley Prison. A prisoner was voicing suicidal thoughts; would Dr Power please see him and assess his mental state? Part of Power relished the excitement of such a day, another part of him groaned under the stress of it all.

He drained the last of his black coffee and switched off the music he had been playing – a recording of the Chicago Symphony Orchestra playing Stravinsky's Rite of Spring. The music had been tense, wild and discordant. "Not music to eat to," said Power aloud to no-one in particular. "God, I'm talking to myself now." With a chuckle he put on his jacket and made for the door. A nagging thought stopped him however. Had he switched off the gas cooker? He went back to check. "Obsessional." He grunted self-critically.

Driving in to work Power listened to the *Today* programme on the car radio. Brian Redhead was closing the programme down by running through the news headlines one last time. Power was looking forward to the reading of a book extract that he knew followed *Today*. He let the words drift over him without squeezing out the juice of their meaning. An announcer came on and said that the book extract had been postponed 'for technical reasons'. Disconsolately Power switched to Radio Three which was churning out a piano concerto by Mozart. "Wish they'd play something new," said Power as he continued his drive into South Manchester.

* * *

"Balance, that's what's needed," Said Power, glad that his morning clinic was drawing to a close. "A balance of vegetables and fruit, carbohydrates, fat and protein. Not too much of anything."

"Once upon a time all I ate was oranges," said Susan Parkes. "My skin started to go orange. And now I'm eating everything. I'm being force-fed, stuffed, fattened up." She sat opposite Power, her knees hunched up in front of her so that only her face could be seen above them. Power saw, with some pleasure, that her once stick-like arms, clasped about her shins, now sported a thin layer of flesh. The sharp edge of her jawbone was covered with a softer layer of skin. She looked thin, but recognisably human at last. "I'll explode like Mr. Creosote in that Monty Python film." She smiled and the feeling between them was warm.

Power laughed, then grew serious. "You're joking, but under the humour...there's some tension. You are worried we will ram the calories down your throat...like force-feeding a goose to make *pate de foie gras* out of its bloated liver."

"I won't eat that. It's cruel...tastes horrible anyway."

"But Susan, you're worried about being made huge."

"Obese and ugly."

"We won't let that happen. You won't be overfaced."

"Sometimes the meals that come up from the kitchens have different things to what I ordered...chips for instance." She shuddered at the thought.

Power was feeling hungry. He found that anorexics had an insatiable appetite for talking about food. An image of chips doused in vinegar floated into his mind. Power had once known a restaurateur in the *Good Food Guide* who had had anorexia. The man's whole life had been providing the most exquisite of food for others, but not a bite would he eat himself. Power's stomach rumbled. Today he had seen so many patients that he had been forced to miss lunch. He suddenly remembered a fast food restaurant on the way to the prison at Risley.

"Susan if you can eat what we've agreed from the contract we drew up, if you're prepared to do your bit, then we should do ours too. I'll have a word in the right ear...make sure that each meal time you get what you're expecting."   A hot chicken sandwich, medium French fries, a medium Cola. Power ran through the order he would make in his mind. Uninspiring food, eaten in a noisy children-ridden atmosphere, cholesterol rich, ecologically unsound, but somehow satisfying. He tried to rid his mind of hunger. He thought, her body must make her feel like this all the time. Her body is crying out for food.

"It makes me anxious if I don't know what to expect...what I have to deal with...I'm angry if there's a change."

Power knew this inflexibility could be addressed later. For now he was content that her weight was coming back to normal, and as it did so he could see her personality and enthusiasm returning too. It was nearly time for the family work to begin. "Susan...I need to see your family...all of you, together. In our sessions together you've given me a hint of your difficulties...how very distant your father is..."

"He goes out bowling, drinks. Mum doesn't see him at all...except at mealtimes."

"Which are difficult for you. And also these difficulties with your Mum that you have..."

"Last night she admitted...told me about how when she was sixteen she stopped eating for a week."

"So there is a food problem...food is a problem for someone else in the family – even more reason to invite everyone in. Yes?" Susan nodded enthusiastically. Power was lifting a burden of responsibility from her shoulders.

"I feel as if you understand me...what's been going on between Mum and Dad, and me being stuck in the middle."

"In the middle of what though...a war?"

"A cold war." She looked at Power. His eyes seemed to accept all she said. For the first time ever she felt understood. He could make anything possible. This new feeling of hers might bubble into laughter at any moment. She looked at her watch; 1.30 p.m., 22nd June. The hour-long session was up. Time to go back to the ward. Susan stood up.

"I'll have a word about the food, Susan, and I'll talk to your Mum and Dad about a time to see this family of yours."

She moved to the door, gripped the handle, thought about saying it, but could not muster the courage. She wanted to say, "You're the best doctor I've ever met." She wouldn't say it, couldn't say that. She didn't know why. She just couldn't, but she left his room smiling anyway.

* * *

At four Carl had finished his consultation at the prison and done two home visits. Now he was racing across the city (or racing as much as the pre-rush hour traffic would let him) to get to the private clinic that Jones and the other consultants used. One of Jones' private patients was ill – his relatives were asking for urgent help and the patient himself had agreed to attend at four-thirty.

The clinic was set in the lush and well-tended grounds of a hospital run by the Amed Corporation. Once upon a time this had been a country house for the Earls of Derby, now a brand new surgical wing spanned the drive, while behind it the original eighteenth century house by Kent played host to various consultants and their clinics.

The guard on the gate let Power's green Saab through with a disapproving sniff. No consultant he had ever seen had driven such a tin can as this.

A breathless Dr Power launched himself through the reception doors just on 4.30 p.m.. Beryl, the receptionist, looked up alarmed as he stood panting in front of her. "Dreadful traffic," Power explained in staccato phrases as he caught his breath. "Don't think I'm late. Patient here?"

"Yes, he is indeed. This gentleman is one of Dr Jones' and has been for many years – so I did try and put the family off until Dr Jones came back next week." There was something about her tone which rankled Power. "But they insisted he be seen. He's been on a spending spree with his credit cards – over two thousand pounds worth of stuff yesterday. He can't afford it. He was a top executive in chemicals until last year. Lost his job. Too erratic, I suppose." There was a smashing sound and a loud shout from behind the waiting room door. Power could see that the receptionist's alarm had preceded his arrival.

"Is he irritable?"

"He seemed very joyous...he was singing. Kissed me and Dorothy. You've met her, she's one of the secretaries here." Dorothy peered out timidly from behind a doorway. She gave Power an anxious smile. The receptionist continued, "I asked Dorothy to stay with me just in case."

"Very wise," said Power. There came another smash from the waiting room. "I'd better see him. What's his name again?"

"Mr. Hammadi, a foreign gentleman," Beryl said primly. "Rubici Hammadi. Here are his notes." Power accepted the thick file and picked up the case he'd brought from the boot of the car. "I'll take room number one. If you hear me shout, call security. Will you do that?"

"Yes, Dr Power, I have them standing by anyway."

The waiting room was in chaos. Paper bags and plastic beaded wrapping lay scattered all about. In the midst of this shambles stood one of the largest men that Power had ever seen. Six foot six inches tall, and with a barrel chest of fifty inches, black-bearded Rubici Hammadi rolled his eyes and glared downwards at Carl Power. In his hands he held a large blue Wedgwood vase.

"You like this?" Hammadi demanded spitting inadvertently at Power through his beard.

"Yes, I do."

"I don't like the colour! The colour is duller." He hurled the vase at the floor where it exploded into fragments only to join the shattered remnants of the other two he had bought that afternoon.

"They must have been very expensive."

"Who cares about money? I have a plan for the Channel Tunnel that will make me a million pounds a day."

"My name is Dr Power. Please come and talk to me. Come through to my office." Hammadi was staring at the broken pieces of pottery at his feet, fascinated. "That can be cleared up, you know," said Power.

"No! No! It must stay where it is. It is a masterpiece. The way each piece has fallen...a miracle of art...I must phone the Tate...hate to miss a work of genius." His mind was racing so fast Power sometimes could not follow his pressured speech.

"Come with me, please," said Power. Hammadi's mood was swinging like a pendulum. Now he was a meek lamb following its mother. Power shepherded him into his consulting room under the watchful eyes of Beryl and Dorothy. They sat down. "Have you brought anyone with you?" enquired the doctor, anxious to gain some history, because he was sure that Hammadi would be an unreliable witness. Hammadi shook his leonine head.

Once inside the consulting room Rubici sat down for only five seconds before he launched his bulk into pacing about the room. Power opened the notes at Jones' last entry:

"Current regime:
    Haloperidol 1.5 mg tds
    Lithium carbonate 600 mg bd."

Power looked up at the big man who strode relentlessly about the room humming an aria by Puccini. He asked, "Have you stopped this medication?"

"I am the fittest man in the world, who has no need of medication, the fittest man, Dr Power, yes, yes, YES! In this world and the next!"

"So you stopped your maintenance medication...the medicine that kept your mood stable." It was a statement of fact.

"Mental illness is a doctor's pillness...no such thing." Rubici looked down at his sandalled feet. "See these shoes, Dr Power? third world shoes...road to Damascus shoes...convertational shoes." He sat down heavily on a chair. "So tiring being God," he said. "Responsible for everyone and everything."

"You sound as if they were your responsibilities?" Hammadi nodded sadly now. "Sleeping?" Hammadi shook his head. "Suddenly feel down?" Hammadi nodded.

Power noted down in the next page of Hammadi's case sheets, '22nd June. Emergency consultation.' He scribbled down Hammadi's appearance, his behaviour, speech characteristics, thought form and content and then the inevitable diagnosis: 'Acute mania. Plan: Admit to hospital for stabilisation.'

He spoke to Rubici about coming into hospital. Excitedly the big man reached over the desk and slapped Power's face gently, squeezing his cheeks together with the palms of his slab-like hands. "Dr Power!" he grinned into Power's distorted face. "I love you very much but I am not ill. Now I must be going." He released Power.

"No, Mr Hammadi. You can't go home. I am worried about you, because as your doctor I think you are ill. Tell me...how much money have you spent in the last couple of days?"

"I am the richest man in the world."

"How much?"

"Two...three...four thousand?"

"And how much do you earn?" Power knew Hammadi was unemployed. "Not two thousand pounds a day, I know that. You're over-active, spending too much money, not sleeping at all. You know, in your heart of hearts, that you need hospital help."

"You will admit me here?"

"I am being honest with you when I say that you cannot, must not try to, afford this private hospital..."

"I must have the best...the very best..."

"And that best treatment is in another hospital, near here, under my care."

"But Dr Jones always..."

"Today I am your doctor."

Hammadi threw his hands up into the air as if surrendering to the enemy. "Okay." The turnaround was unexpected. Power had imagined a protracted debate, maybe even having to resort to a section of the Mental Health Act to compel Hammadi into hospital.

"I'll arrange admission then." He rang through to reception to call an ambulance. "While we wait together, we can start the treatment. Would you prefer some chlorpromazine syrup or an injection?"

"An injection my good friend. I don't like the taste of the syrup."

It was a quieter, more rueful Rubici Hammadi who was driven away in the ambulance, watched by Power. When Power walked back into the clinic to collect his things, the clinic receptionist was angrily staring at the clock. "This session ends at five o'clock, Dr Power. We're half an hour over."

"Nature of the work. I'm sorry if you've been inconvenienced. Mr Hammadi was in great distress really. Under that joviality he is a very sad man."

"Dr Jones won't be pleased," said Beryl tartly. "Not at all

pleased. Mr Hammadi was always admitted to his private beds. I don't know what he'll say when he comes back."

"Neither do I, and to be quite frank with you, I don't care. Mr Hammadi cannot afford private fees. I will see Mr Hammadi for free. Patients come before profit." Power turned on his heel and walked briskly out to his car. His battered Saab roared agreeably into life and he sped off.

"Well!" exclaimed Beryl. "And he seemed such a mild man."

"No," said Dorothy as she put on her coat. "He's the type that looks easygoing, but underneath he's tough as old boots. Well, I'm off, see you tomorrow." She hid her pleasure at Power's putdown of Beryl and her interpretation of Jones' wishes. She always had had a soft spot for Hammadi and now Power would enjoy her tacit allegiance too.

* * *

Relaxing at the end of the day, Power sank back into the recesses of his wingback chair. His hands clasped a mug of hot coffee to his chest. He was warm, contented and comfortably tired. After the meal he had cooked of carrot and coriander soup and cashew paella he even felt sleepy.

In the companionable silence between them, Eve watched the doctor closing his eyes. Could she trust him? He looked so calm and strong stretched out before her. Could she tell him? He had told her of his day and his proven ability to relax with her seemed endearing. He had tried so hard to create a vegetarian meal for her from his dog-eared cookbooks. Inside her there was a physical yearning, an emptiness that only he could fill.

She crossed the room to him and took the mug of coffee from his hands. She set it on the tray nearby. He opened his eyes, "Eve?"

"I think it's about time for bed don't you?" She took him by the hand and urged him to his feet. "It's up to you to take me there though." He smiled and led her to his bed.

Like the careful unwrapping of a Christmas present they peeled off the layers of clothes that ensheathed them. She revelled in the warmth of his firm hands as he smoothed off the tissue layers of her white underwear. She pulled back the coverlet of his bed and burrowed into the cold smoothness of his sheets. Luxuriating, stretching in the heart of his bed, she arched her back as she tensed and quivered under the touch of his lips. The very tip of his tongue explored her belly and teased at the hardened nipples of her pert breasts. Eve's thighs opened in response to the sure quest of his hands. His fingers slipped easily into her ready moistness. A golden shaft of evening sunlight penetrated the bedroom and ennobled the couple as they moved together – he between her legs, she thrusting her pelvis upwards to sacrifice her crimson joy.

This is like the first time, the first time, the first time, he kept silently repeating to himself.

Afterwards as they lay entwined, still murmuring endearments, they were interrupted by the insistent staccato of Power's bleep from its resting place in his trouser pocket on the floor. They laughed, all tension between them dissipated. He pulled himself gently away from inside her and retrieved the pager. "I've got to phone the paging service. Don't go away." 'I won't let you this time', he thought to himself.

She watched him slipping into a dressing-gown and making for the phone next door. Eve heard his voice muffled and distant. At the same time she tried to reconcile the feelings of contentment and guilt she always felt afterwards. She put on a smile when he came back. "Problems?"

"Superintendent Lynch. You remember him? Doesn't sound as if he ever stops work."

"What did he want?"

"Wants to talk to me about the investigation. I don't know what he wants...really, I...the police give me the creeps...I..."

"I like him. He seemed to care about things. He even cared enough to ask if he could borrow one of your books. Did I tell you?"

"No...no you didn't. I wonder what he wants."

"You'll have to wait until you meet him. When are you seeing him?"

Power allowed himself to laugh. It was a nervous laugh, but it broke the tension he had been feeling since the phone call. "Lynch wants to meet me on Friday morning in Chester...at Morning Prayer in the Cathedral. Can you believe it?"

* * *

Power could see Lynch now, crouched low in the bank of wooden stalls that lined the choir. Though Morning Prayer had clearly ended and most of the clergy and congregation had filed out, Lynch stayed quite still, deep in prayer. Power's attention was momentarily taken by the richness of the carving of the stalls around Lynch: Sir Gawain, unicorns, foxes, monsters and angels jostled in a profusion of symbols. Power could see Lynch's deeply lined face was etched further by concentration. His shoulders were hunched as if he carried upon them all the weight of the stonework above. As he concluded his prayer there was a transformation; the lines on his face smoothed and his shoulders relaxed as he uncurled from his kneeling posture. He stood, bowed his head reverently to the altar and turned. As he turned a shaft of multicoloured sunlight burst through the stained glass and illuminated his face. He walked forward, out of the light, and came face-to-face with Power.

There was a flicker of surprise then Lynch had collected himself. He held out his hand, "Dr Power, it's good to see you again."

"They said you were in the choir. I wasn't quite sure where... they seem to know you here."

"Thank you for coming, Dr Power. It's good of you. I wasn't sure whether you would join me for the service or not."

"No...I...er..." Power was embarrassed. He couldn't make up an easy excuse.

"No matter. Each to his own. On Friday's I always try to finish my working week here in prayer. But we are all...governed by time. Sometimes our lives are too random. Presumably yours can be dictated by the health of your patients, mine by the crimes of others. Neither are predictable things." Lynch consulted his watch. "There's some time for something to eat. Will you let me buy you lunch? Do you have the time to join me?"

"Well, I haven't eaten. I've come straight from the hospital."

"Come on then," Lynch led Power down the stone-flagged nave, through an oak door, blackened by the centuries, out of Chester Cathedral and into the leafy St. Werburgh's Row. Off a street of half-timbered shops, down a small cobbled alley was a small Italian restaurant. This early, at noon, there were few customers and they had the luxury of choosing their table. Lynch opted for a table outside in the warm early summer sun.

"I like June," said Power. "Not too hot, not too cold and the feeling that things are green and growing."

Lynch didn't look up, he was busy flattening the voluminous linen napkin across his knees. A waiter arrived and left two leather-covered menus and a wine list. Lynch began to flick through his menu and talked as he scanned the food on offer. "I've asked you here to talk about the Edge murder. I want to pick your brains, if you don't mind." He looked up and saw Power's face. "Oh, relax, Dr Power. It's not the third degree. I'm hardly interrogating you in some sweaty, grey police interview room am I?"

Power had to concede that as he hadn't been arrested and was in fact in a most pleasant restaurant there was little reason for him to be so uneasy. "So, er...how can I help you?"

Lynch smiled. "There are factors about the crime which puzzle me, Dr Power. I intend to ask all the people I can for all the help I can get too. Can we keep what I'm about to say confidential?"

"If that's what you'd like." Power was irritated by the arrival of the waiter. Lynch clammed up. They ordered. Power chose a seafood fettuccine as a starter and a pork escalope for a main course. Lynch ordered soup then a Pizza Napoli. He asked for spring water, but allowed Power to order a Peroni beer.

As the waiter departed Lynch tore open his bread and spoke again softly. "Murder is an extreme thing. You'll agree with me there. But some murders are...how shall I put it?...understandable in some way. That's not to excuse them, but..."

"Sure, I understand. Like a crime of passion."

Lynch agreed. "A man stabs his wife's lover, or a woman stabs the husband who is beating her. Done in the heat of the moment. Or revenge...you remember the father of one of the boys killed by Brady and Hindley in the Moors murders? He hid a knife on himself to kill Brady at the trial."

"These are people moved by an overwhelming emotion," said Power. "Some part of them screams out in pain at the betrayal of the wife or the hideous loss of the child. Violence seems the only answer because of the blinding fear and hate. Although...do you remember the vicar whose daughter was raped in front of him. He forgave the rapists. Do you remember that?"

"I remember the publicity, yes," said Lynch. "And such a reaction can appear more bizarre than retaliating; wanting revenge."

"I'm glad you can see that," said Power who had wondered what such a religious man as Lynch might think. The waiter arrived and laid out their water and beer.

Lynch was in full flow though and his words were not curtailed by the waiter's temporary presence. "Oh, I do see it. If my children were threatened in any way I have no idea what I would do. The anger would take me over, so I don't know. God forbid." Lynch assayed a spoonful of the vegetable soup that had arrived. "But in this case there is no story, no explanation that makes things understandable." Lynch went on, once the waiter had left the table, to describe the post-mortem findings and his analysis of how the murder had been committed.

His theories had changed little since his original briefing to the murder squad a week or so before. Power listened carefully. He ate his steaming seaweed-green fettuccine deliberately as if refusing to show his appetite was affected, which it was. When Lynch attempted to show him the scene of crime photographs though, Power waved them away until they were out of sight.

"I'm sorry," said Lynch, looking at Power's abandoned plate. Power had hated the forensic pathology lectures at medical school. He had found psychiatry something of a refuge from the bloodier side of medicine. "Well, anyway...," said Lynch as Power resumed his meal, (for his love of food had overcome his squeamishness),"...you can see from what I've told you that the murderer was planning his murder and the display of the body...like a scene – like a tableaux even – this is not spur-of-the-moment revenge. And I can't provide myself with the story that fits it, that lies behind what he's done. It's too much for me to take in. I thought that finding the identity of the girl would help...would tie things together."

Power spoke, "And did you find out who she was?"

"Yes...yesterday...a whole week after the murder... the headless hippy as the Press called her. Crass of them."

"Yes...I mean to say there was a great flurry of activity after the discovery and then nothing." Power realised what he had said. "Nothing in the news I mean. Not to say you were doing nothing, of course."

Lynch smiled at Power's attempt to cover his gaffe. "To be honest, we are doing precisely that; nothing. And if that sounds shocking, let me explain.

"We contacted your flute player, one of the hippies. Well, with some difficulty we found him. It was quite an achievement to winkle him out from that herd of drop-outs. They closed ranks against us, against our inquiry. Even though the victim was one of their own, we're fairly sure of that now. This bearded flautist of yours had, or was given, a very good alibi by his friends. He was probably playing at a night-long concert. Apparently, he was in full view of everyone when the girl was murdered. But he did tell us the name of a friend who had gone missing. In fact, you probably saw that girl...one of the unholy trio you met in the wood that night. At least he said that you were the only stranger he or they had met that night."

Power felt suddenly cold in the June sun. "I didn't even speak to her."

Lynch paused, savoured his soup and mulled over what Power had just said. "Yes," said Lynch. "He said you didn't talk to them. He gave her name as being Sian from Wales. Where else with a name like that? He didn't know any more about her. Nobody knew or would tell us any more. Just Sian from Wales. We searched through the missing persons' files for several Welsh police forces. As you can imagine we only had the vaguest of clues...a first name and an estimate of her age... fourteen or fifteen.

"We found five names. One after the other we discounted them. Two Sians had been young runaways who'd eventually gone back home after a taste of the city streets. They were safe and well. We visited them to make sure. Another Sian happened to be in a psychiatric ward at St. George's in Tooting. One was sleeping rough under a flyover in London, we found her by DHSS records...pure luck really that we could account for all the Sians except one. The one Sian left over. From the missing persons file we got the address of her parents. I visited them myself last week. That was my duty, I think." He sighed and Power could imagine how difficult a visit it must have been. "They'd had a card from her, posted recently from Wilmslow...the town near Alderley Edge. I was asking about her...distinguishing marks...for identification. The parents told me about a broken leg...a fracture of her left tibia after falling from a horse. The Home Office pathologist had taken X-rays of her body anyway. And the X-ray of her leg confirmed her identity. We even matched her post-mortem X-ray to her old orthopaedic X-rays taken in hospital after her riding accident."

"Getting her identity...that's something," said Power. "It sounds as if you were incredibly lucky to manage it."

"Some of my officers put in very long hours Dr Power, but yes... some of the links in the chain were pure luck. Missing persons records are notoriously unreliable. Not centrally collated. A mess frankly...we put in all that time though...in the belief that the identity of the poor girl...Sian...that that would solve everything. The story would fit into place. Perhaps a jealous boyfriend. Or a father trying to keep something secret." Lynch paused while the waiter removed their empty plates and returned with their main courses. Lynch asked for another round of drinks.

"So," Lynch continued. "We have an identity...but there we are. Stuck. Unable to find a coherent link between Sian and her killer. There isn't any we can find. We asked her friends, her relatives, interrogated her father, talked to her social workers, doctors even. Nothing. Even the most suspicious characters had cast-iron alibis. So I am unable to understand a motive for this sacrifice of a young life. Forgive the cliché, but the trail seems to have gone icy cold. And all of this, the scene of the crime, the precautions, the display of the body...makes me think the murderer cannot be understood...that he is, must be, mad."

"Hence the psychiatrist," said Power thoughtfully. "But the things that people do, even if they're mentally ill, still have some reason. It may be fleeting, it may be wrong or bizarre, but to the person themselves the reasons seem logical enough." Power tried to think of an example.

"I once saw a mother who'd killed her children. Four year old twins. How could a mother kill her own children? It seems the depth of perversity. It stands the Universe on its head...that a mother's love should be so reversed. But it was precisely because she loved them that she'd killed them."

"I don't follow," said Lynch.

"Mother was suffering with a depressive psychosis...a very severe depression...so severe that she was deluded. The world had grown so bleak, so black, that as far as she was concerned there was literally no future. She believed...completely believed...that the world was corrupted by evil, full of maggots and that she had AIDS, syphilis and every kind of disease under the sun. She felt completely, utterly worthless. It was all wrong of course. She had been a model mother up until her illness. But because of the depression she was convinced she had all these diseases and had passed them onto her children.

Killing them seemed logical to her. She was sparing them pain by gently smothering them in their sleep...then she tried to kill herself. Failed. That's when I started to see her."

Lynch sighed and found he could eat no more. He was afraid to ask his next question, afraid in case the healer had not been up to the test, afraid in case the healer was not as good as he had imagined. He had to ask, because he had to know about the mother who had made herself bereft. "And now...what's happened to her?"

"The legal system was compassionate...only mauled her a little bit. It's five years on now. She is as well as she can be. She no longer lives with her husband. He couldn't resolve things with her. She's had individual therapy...is on lithium tablets. She's well, and she lets me think that every day she forgives herself a bit more, but I know she has the heaviest cross to bear." Lynch said nothing. Power could tell he had gone inwards, was mulling over some private emotion. Power had the sense not to probe.

"But you see what I mean?" asked Power. "Killing the children made no sense objectively...but inside her head...inside a momentarily dark world we can only imagine...it seemed just. She believed that world so intensely and was moved by such strong emotion that she committed the act."

Coffee arrived, Lynch sipped it pensively. He was looking away from Power avoiding eye contact with him. "These ideas are very strong stuff, Carl. Difficult to swallow at one go. What you're really saying is that inside the murderer's head the murder makes sense?"

"To him, yes."

"I...the investigation...needs your help, Dr Power."

"I guessed you were leading up to that," said Power. "You know there are psychologists that specialise in profiling..."

"I read your book. I think we can work together."

"I...er...when I consider this kind of material, I find it difficult, unsettling...when you try and understand these thoughts, understand psychotic minds..." But this was precisely what Lynch wanted. This was how he proposed to catch his murderer. Know his mind, find the murderer. Power struggled for words. "I would rather not if you don't mind. Forensic work is something I do occasionally, but an investigation like this will take a long time."

Lynch jumped on his words. "A long time? Why do you say that?"

"This man has arranged all this...carefully. He won't let you catch him. He's no disorganised schizophrenic. He..." Lynch was listening avidly. This was exactly what he needed. Power saw the policeman's rapt attention and dried up. "I..er..I would help, but I'd rather not...selfish of me, but..."

Lynch stuck to his guns. "Why will the investigation take a long time?"

Power shifted uncomfortably in his chair. "This isn't a one-off. This man has already planned his next murder."

"How do you know, Doctor?"

"If he acted on a delusion, it's been a long-standing one. He planned according to the delusion...the deliberate display of the corpse...the delusion won't have gone away. It will be stronger now. Whatever inhibitions he may have had about murder...the inhibitions we all share...they'll have gone, have been blown away like sand...and he'll find the next murder even easier to commit. It may be less elaborate. His mental state may even have deteriorated as a result of his... success."

"I want you to help me stop him."

"I can't." Power pushed his chair back from the table. He knew the longer he stayed with this earnest polite man, the more likely he was to cave in and agree; letting himself in for all the worry and the fear of failure. Power stood up. "I just can't." He threw his napkin down. "Thank you for lunch. 'Bye." Power hurried from the restaurant like an asthmatic craving the fresh air outside.

      Lynch sat in silence, uncaring that the other diners were staring at him. Lynch had become even more convinced that Power was essential to his investigation. Somehow he would have to get Power to work with him.

SIX

Philip lived on the edge of the Delamere Forest; a few hundred sprawling acres of open land covered by green trees, as if by a blanket. There were only a few houses nearby, a lucky few that had preceded planning regulations. In one of these Victorian houses Philip lived with his parents, a baby sister and his dog, a red setter called 'Floppity'. Philip, just turned twelve, was becoming sufficiently self conscious to wonder if a dog called Floppity was altogether a good thing. Floppity had been Floppity since Philip's memories began. Floppity had always been there. Hadn't he had another name before Philip had christened him Floppity? Philip couldn't very well go round shouting out "Floppity!" now he was twelve. He cringed at the thought of his schoolfriends mimicking him. Perhaps after the Summer holidays, he thought, Floppity would have to be re-named. What had Floppity been called before he was Philip's dog?

For now though and throughout the long, hot days of the summer he could race through the forest with Floppity as he was – free of the fear of his friends' teasing. And this summer was so hot – the best that Philip could remember. When he ran with the dog at his side Philip felt he was flying and could race forever beneath the trees. He tried to imagine the forest as it had been. Maybe it was like this in the olden days. His father had said that once a huge forest of oak and ash and beech had covered the whole of Britain. Sometimes, in his mind, Philip became an explorer from those times. The first man to cut through the undergrowth and enter the dense forest. The first ever to conquer the land. And in the clearings he, Philip, created Philip's kingdom. He imagined his primitive world; a stockade filled with huts, livestock, his women, his children. An army of men to protect them all. He imagined them to be like Vikings. He had seen pictures of them with helmets and flowing fair hair and beards.

Perhaps he would take Floppity today to a clearing in the real wood. He could take some food and drink too by way of a feast. Then he remembered the man he had met out on the road, a few days ago. He'd talked about the old fort at Eddisbury Hill. He had given Floppity a biscuit and offered to take Philip onto the hill the next day. Philip had been on Eddisbury Hill many times before, but he'd never known it had been a fort. The man had mentioned ruins. Philip had told his father, but his father didn't seem interested; he seemed more concerned with the man and had told Philip not to talk with strangers again. But wasn't everyone a stranger until they had become a friend? He had seen the stranger several times since then. He'd been walking in the forest with a map and a compass. Seemed lost or looking for something. He'd looked harmless enough. Philip had seen him another day crossing the fields across the road from their home. He was just a walker. There were thousands of those all year round in the forest. He didn't tell his father he'd seen the man again. After all Philip didn't think the man had seen him watching him from behind the hedge. There was no point in telling Dad. Dad would only shout at him.

The day stretched out in front of Philip the way they do when you are young and on a seemingly endless holiday. He went down to the kitchen and threw together some sandwiches – beef spread in one and apple and sultana in another. A bar of chocolate. People always took bars of chocolate on expeditions as emergency rations. With his trusty hound Philip set off down the road, past the old red pillar-box that glinted in the sun. Floppity surged on ahead of Philip down the lane, ears streaming out behind him like red, furry banners. They passed the disused school house. Ahead of the explorer and his savage beast was a ridge of high ground. As they got nearer Philip could see the farm gate that led up on to Eddisbury Hill. On front of the land were two well-kept houses. Philip could see the washing on a clothesline flapping in the breeze. The white sheets were dazzling in the sunlight.

Philip stopped at the gate. A white van was standing at the side of the road. He'd seen the van before. That walker...the one who'd told him about the Celts who'd built the fort...he'd driven that. When he'd followed the stranger to the Forest car park Philip had seen him getting into the van. It was a Ford Transit van, A registration, battered and spattered with mud. Philip went up to it and peered inside the driver's cabin. Empty. The windows in the rear doors were whitewashed over. The van was pointing east. If the walker had set off that way he would have reached the South side of the forest. Philip thought about what his father had said as he was walking back to the gate where Floppity was waiting patiently, his tongue lolling out of his mouth. Perhaps, thought Philip, he should take down the van's number. He fumbled in his shirt pocket and took out a small black diary. Using the small pencil inside he wrote down the registration number on the page with the day's date. He calculated how old the van was. Not only was the van a wreck, it was an old wreck.

Eddisbury Hill is carefully shaped. It stands at the strategic corner of the upland. For the most part it is a conical hill. Philip went through the gate at the bottom and began to climb the deep-cut and narrow lane that wound round and up the side of the hill. He thought about how clever these people had been in building this. You could see it was a fort now. They'd moulded the hill so that from above they could see everyone who tried to climb it; and anyone who wanted to get to the upland had to climb it. Perhaps if their enemies tried the fort people would hurl rocks or spears or rain arrows down on their heads. Philip wondered if they would pour boiling oil down the hillside like they did in castles.

Philip half-walked, half-ran up the spiralling road. Floppity was waiting above at the edge of the upland. When Philip got there Floppity shot off again into the bushes on the right. In front of Philip were fields. He could see the shoots of wheat beginning to grow. He turned his attention to the unchecked vegetation on his right. Here an overgrown coppice of small trees and bushes had formed over the years. Philip stepped forward to follow Floppity and stumbled over a ridge of stones that just poked through the earth. This must have been a wall, he thought, may be the guard-house. The man had said there were ruins here. They must be here, because something would have to stop the farmer from ploughing here. There must be more stones buried here, submerged in the thicket.

He called out "Floppity!" self-consciously. He thought that he heard a scrabbling noise. Perhaps the dog had found something...an old Celtic bone may be. A hoard of golden treasure? Philip wanted to be famous one day. Appear on television. He pushed his way through the branches of trees, and stepped, as well as he could, over the brambles. The shadows of the trees were cool and had prevented the morning dew from evaporating. Philip's shoes were soon soaked with water from the long grass. Sticky seeds from the grasses and weeds clung to his trousers. Yes, here was a wall; part of a house? Here a tunnel...going deep underground...where to? Should he go down there? Was that were Floppity had gone? Then he saw the dog away over to his left.

Floppity was lying down on his side, about ten feet away. Philip stared at him. You couldn't see him properly because of the grass and the overhanging branches. There was something by the dog's mouth. Red meat. Had Floppity killed something? Philip hurried over. The meat looked raw, but there was no fur. Floppity hadn't killed this. Floppity lay so still. Was he breathing? He knelt to touch the dog's ribcage.

Then, suddenly, a noise behind him. Simultaneously something tight round his throat. Sharp, pressing in, something like fingers at the back of his neck. He couldn't tell. All so fast. No time. He thrashed wildly. Agony round his neck. Cutting into his skin. He tried to move, but it hurt. He tried to scream, but no air reached his vocal cords. Fear. Things growing dark. Struggle some more then gradual numbness, a blanket of comforting night.

He slowly unwound the ligature from round the boy's throat and looked at the boy's pale, blue face. He felt a little uneasy. You could never tell. He was always a bit worried they'd come back to life. No, he was safe. No time to waste though. He hurried to pull off the boy's shoes and socks, his trousers, his shirt. Put them all in a canvas bag. As he was putting the shirt in something fell out of its pocket. It fell into the grass. He noticed its fall into the damp grass. Slightly panicked he searched for it. The place was so overgrown, where had it gone? He must find it. When he did he saw it was a pocket-book. It fell open at the page where the boy had written the registration number of the van. A good thing he'd found this, and lucky the boy had come today, and not someone else with their dog. Obviously fate had chosen this boy. It seemed so right somehow. He put the pocket-book carefully in the bag. Now he looked down at the naked boy and then at his watch. Not much time. Must get back. Mustn't leave any clues. Get to work. Quick!

Half-an-hour later he walked slowly down the spiral hill path. 'Go slowly now,' he thought. 'Pause. If someone sees you, look natural. Pause...take our time. Look at the Ordnance Survey map. If you look normal they won't suspect. Take our time about it, eh? Just carry the bag down to the van. Pretend it's only got your sandwiches inside. You've got sandwiches in there anyway. The boy had some with him. Carry the bag as if it's lighter than it really is. Nearly at the van now. It's all right.'

No-one noticed the white van. No-one saw it leave.

* * *

Power swung the battered Saab into the Consultant parking space in the hospital car park. He switched the engine off and listened to the last of the *Today* programme. Brian Redhead was winding things down. "...well, those were the news headlines on June 22nd...and in *Thought for the Day* earlier, we heard the Archbishop of Canterbury condemning the violence that centred on Stonehenge in Wiltshire last night, when 10,000 New Agers broke through police ranks to touch the stones on their holiest night of the year, as police helicopters lit up the sky and police donned riot gear. The Archbishop urged us all to keep the faith. And in Cheshire, my home county actually, police and volunteers begin their countryside search of the Delamere forest for missing twelve year old, Philip Wray; missing now since early yesterday. Good luck to them and good day from the *Today* programme." Power put the news of the hippy riots behind him. Wiltshire was a long way off. He switched off the radio and got out of the car into the morning sunlight.

Power strode happily down the hospital corridor, unaware of the role that events were to forge for him. He heard voices coming out of his secretary's office and his step faltered. He slowed almost to a standstill.

"...I've never seen him like it. We've been up on Eddisbury Hill since five this morning.... Never seen him react like this. Adults you can take, perhaps, but children, no. It's something else...hits you inside and you feel so...bloody angry. As for him, his face went white...he just stood there shaking. Asked me to drive his car here. Once or twice I looked across at him there sitting in the passenger seat. He was just staring ahead, not seeing anything. When we got here he said 'I can't see the parents. You'll have to get someone else to break the news, I can't.' And that's something he always does himself. Wanted to come straight here instead."

Power heard his secretary Laura. "Sounds like he needs a psychiatrist...you know to talk to..."

The other voice, male, was defensive, "We've all got our weaknesses. I think his reaction is understandable, normal."

"He seemed to want to be alone," said Laura.

"He prays...that's how he copes. His way."

Hearing this, Power wondered what Laura's reaction would be. Her world was purely a secular one. "Me, I'd want a cup of tea. Something warm and soothing," she said. "Like mother's milk I suppose."

Beresford's tone became inquisitive now. "The Superintendent really rates this Power bloke. He's your boss, what do you think of him?"

Power hurried into the office interrupting them both. He couldn't bear to hear Laura's opinion of him whether or not it was good or bad. He had an aversion to receiving any personalised criticism. He had dreaded school reports, interviews with University Tutors and video feedback sessions as a junior doctor. When he came into the room the conversation stopped like a car running into a brick wall. Power looked at his secretary, Laura. Her blue eyes smiled back at him. Half-sitting on her desk was Detective Sergeant Beresford. They had been talking animatedly and their body language spoke of some physical attraction between them. In reaction to his entry they shifted slightly away from each other. Beresford eventually stood up to meet the challenge of Power's presence. With some amusement at himself Power noted that he felt jealous of the Sergeant. Laura, pretty, intelligent Laura was his.

"Laura, can I have a word please?" asked Power.

"Of course, Carl."

"Shall we go next door then?"

"Superintendent Lynch is in your office." Another liberty taken.

"Across the corridor then!" Power said testily. He led her through the door opposite. He shut it behind them and in the cramped confines of the photocopying room they stood close together.

Laura felt guilty. She couldn't think why. Power made her feel guilty. She had to apologise, "I'm sorry, but..."

"It's all right. You've done nothing wrong. I just wanted to know what's going on. I wasn't expecting all this."

"Well," said Laura, looking up at her boss. "A body has been found...a young boy...on Eddisbury Hill. I think it's the boy they've been searching for. You know, it was on the news last night." Power shook his head. Sometimes the news just didn't register with him. "This Superintendent has come from Eddisbury Hill. He seemed so shocked... wanted to be left alone...so I put him in your office. I thought you wouldn't mind."

"I don't. I have met him before, but I didn't think I'd see him again. I hoped I wouldn't have to anyway. What does he want? Do you know?"

"They want your help."

"Helping with enquiries? That's what they say when they're about to arrest someone."

She could see him frowning; could see the fear in his eyes. Laura laughed at his concern. "You're too much of a worrier, Carl. I think they genuinely want your help. This Superintendent seems to have a little faith in you, even if you don't."

"He's all right I suppose, quite human really." Power was slightly flattered, but tried to suppress any smugness. It would only distort any decision he made. "But I don't particularly like the police. Never have. I've always tried to steer well clear. Don't you think people will get the wrong idea if I go off with them."

"You can be sure I won't let them 'get the wrong idea', Carl." For an instant she laid a reassuring hand on his arm. She pulled it away. They both seemed embarrassed at this impulsive gesture and ignored it, pretending the contact had not occurred. Power opened the door and they hurried out. The Sergeant was watching them with a wry grin. "Carl, shall I get you a coffee?"

"Please, and could you postpone my appointments for this morning. I have a feeling this could take some time." He watched Laura disappearing down the corridor towards the kitchen. All of a sudden he was seeing her in a new light. Could he have been missing something right under his nose?

The elegant figure of Superintendent Lynch was leaning against Power's bookcase, a book by Sigmund Freud open in his hands. He greeted Power in a civil and urbane manner as the latter entered his own office. "Just reading a little Freud, Carl." Yes, thought Power, Lynch did look tense and drawn, different to their last unsatisfactory meeting in Chester. The investigation was taking its toll on him.

"What book is that? *The Psychopathology of Everyday Life?*"

"Yes. Except that life isn't quite so everyday recently. I was dragged out of my bed and spirited across the county at four o'clock this morning." He paused, the images of the morning running through his tired brain, he looked at the pages of Freud's book, but the words made no sense.

Power tried some humour. "You know, I have a word processor. It has a programme that checks words to see if they're spelt right. If they're not it substitutes the correct version. It can't handle proper names though. When I write about Freud it always substitutes Fraud."

Lynch laughed, but seemed lost in an inner world of tension. He collapsed into one of the chairs that Power put his patients in. "You psychiatrists can joke about Freud, but you respect him in your heart of hearts. I like this too." He pointed to a page of illuminated manuscript that Power had had framed. Lynch read out the inscription. "Visita inferiora terrae rectificando invenies occultem lapidem."

Power translated automatically, although Lynch had already worked it out. " 'Seek out the lower realms of the earth, perfect them, and thou wilt find the hidden stone.' It's about the philosophers' stone."

"You used it in your book of the unconscious."

"Yes, but once you start digging in the earth of the unconscious you never know what you're going to find."

"No..." Lynch looked downwards at the floor. "I feel cold inside, Dr Power." He spoke softly without emphasis. "I'm trusting you when I say that this morning has left me cold with anger inside. This morning I stood on top of a hill, under the arc lights. The scene of crime people hurried round me, but it felt as if the world had come to a grinding halt. I was a statue and I looked down at the body of a boy. I don't know how long I stared. I wanted to move away, but I couldn't. I couldn't uproot my feet. Whoever killed him had taken off his head. All I can remember is his bare skin against the cold, wet grass. No head."

Each word hung in the space between them. Despite the hospital warmth Power felt a coldness growing inside him too. Lynch's feelings seemed to transmit themselves to Power. He could feel the other's horrified sadness. Neither of them seemed inclined to speak.

"Like the girl on the Edge." It was Power who broke the ice.

"Yes, I've got no doubt now. You were right, Carl. I'm looking for a serial killer." Power noted how Lynch used 'I' not 'we'. Lynch had personalised the hunt for the killer. It was Lynch's quest, his duel with the killer. "Serial killers are very rare. My nightmare come true; I didn't think one would come my way and it makes me feel old suddenly. I feel like er...er...this is my final test and, you know, I don't feel up to it... it says in James that the Lord won't test you more than you can bear... but, today I don't feel up to it...not after what I've seen today. I trust...I pray that the boy...that he has crossed over from death to life."

Power ignored the biblical quotation. "And so, how do I fit in?" he asked, but he knew exactly what Lynch had come here to ask of him.

"I want some help." Lynch's words had a demanding tone.

"There are criminal psychologists who specialise in profiling..."

"I know that you would be better. I've read your book. I know you can add something, some insight, that I don't have. I wouldn't ask unless I thought it was necessary."

Lynch continued, "The motive isn't sexual. As far as I can gather, the bodies haven't been touched sexually, although their clothes have been removed. Why? And the heads? You see when the girl was murdered at the Edge in May I thought the murderer had removed the head to prevent us identifying her. I thought that once we'd hunted her...identified her, we'd have a link...some understandable...detectable link to the murderer. But when we did identify her, by chance good fortune found out her name, her parents, her home...we still couldn't find any link. Nothing to explain why her in particular. It wasn't a jealous boyfriend or a guilty father or anything so mundane. She seemed to be a random choice. And now a second victim – naked under the sky. Head severed neatly between the second and third cervical vertebrae, probably two days ago now – in dense undergrowth. No other disfigurement. No evidence of sexual molestation of boy or girl. (Sex is an understandable motive, although unforgiveable.)

"So why remove the head? You would initially assume it was to prevent identification, but the murderer would know that, in choosing a twelve year old, identification of the body would be swift...immediate in fact."

"I suppose if they had been sexually interfered with in some way. If there were any semen stains these could be used for DNA fingerprinting?" Lynch nodded, but his face showed his distaste. Power continued thoughtfully. "So if the motive isn't sexual...and I'm not totally sure we've ruled that out, by the way...something about the head then?"

"Something that I cannot comprehend."

"You want help with this?"

"I want all the help you can give me. I can negotiate all the fees you need. I want you to think your way inside this murderer's mind."

"You want a profile of the likely man?"

"More than that. Something more. I can't see any point to what he does. There's something though, some explanation. This killing behaviour seems almost random – random victims, random circumstances...why?"

"No, not random. If we could just find some way into his way of thinking. Into his head. Something about the heads." A memory surfaced in Power's conscious mind. "When I was a medical student...in my first week...we went up to the Anatomy Department. I remember there was a smell about the corridors that surrounded the dissecting room. The preserving fluid they used to keep the bodies fresh. The smell got on your clothes – in your hair. You'd be having lunch and suddenly you'd catch a whiff of the dissecting room on your jacket. Horrid.

"I'd been dreading actually going into the dissecting room for the first time. They let us in in groups of ten. Someone in the group before me actually fainted. He didn't stay the week. He switched to psychology. When I got through the doors I saw why he'd fainted. I felt sick. The first thing you saw when you got in there – in a sort of transparent plastic box, on a marble slab – was a head. The head of a fat old man. Shaved head – a few grey hairs, like pig bristles. Sliced cleanly across the neck – by a machine. A cross section through the neck – oesophagus, trachea, carotid arteries, vertebrae, spinal column. The worst thing was his face – they'd sliced away the greasy grey skin in flaps to show the course of the facial nerve – its branches spreading over the jaw and cheeks. I won't forget it. That image. I couldn't eat meat for weeks."

Lynch's mind had been free-associating: "They used to impale the heads of traitors on pikes and display them at Traitor's Gate in London. I feel as if I could do that to the murderer. And that makes me annoyed with myself – that I can't detach myself from this case. Can't find any forgiveness. Not a shred. Just a hatred I can't set aside; that damages me too in the end. I'm praying that in the end I will be able to let go of all this, but I...can't see how at the moment...Lynch sounded weary, desperate. "Can you help with the investigation, please, Dr Power? I would get a temporary Home Office Appointment. The pay would be quite good. You would be allowed all the resources you needed...Can you help, please? Carl?"

Power knew this was a decision he could no longer postpone. Instead he felt impelled to answer, "If I can be spared from my work...I'll help you all I can. I'll discuss it with the Clinical Director."

"You'll get your time, whatever he says. I'll see to that. And speaking of time, I've got an appointment with the Chief Constable this morning. I'd better get going. I'm trying to keep this case mine. If I can make an arrest soon there'll be roses all around. If I don't....well, the stakes are high aren't they? And it's not just me who'll pay them." Lynch stood up, leaving the patient's chair. He already seemed to be recovering his usual urbanity and composure. "Look, I'll get my secretary to copy the files we've already built up...for you to study, okay ?"

"And I'm going to see if I can get to the library this evening."

"The library?" Lynch could not see the relevance.

"They have a CD-ROM computer. Allows you to scan the world scientific literature for the last ten years or so. It'll give me access to forensic psychiatric case reports worldwide."

"Oh," said Lynch. He was impressed.

* * *

After Lynch had departed, Power sat back in his office, hands behind his head, eyes closed, thinking. He was relieved not to be interrogated as he had paranoically imagined he would be. Yet he was puzzled as to why Lynch seemed to focus upon him. Lynch must know that even if murders are outside normal behaviour, they are by no means the sole province of madmen. Most murderers, even multiple murderers, tend to be more sane than insane. So why involve a doctor of the mind in the investigation?

And Lynch. His religiousness seemed a curiosity in these days. Yet his faith seemed one of the mainstays of Lynch's character. Without it, Power thought, Lynch would not function. Something in Power envied Lynch. Lynch believed it all without reservation, without any of Power's cynical questioning. Despite having read most of the world's holy books, Power saw them as phenomena of man's need for religion, not as evidence of God. He envied Lynch his simple faith, and his certainty. And Power also wondered what function religion held for Lynch. Cynically he assumed that Lynch used his belief as a prop against something else. Against what?

Power heard Laura moving round in the room next door to his office. He was struck by how much he had minded when he had seen Sergeant Beresford chatting her up. Underneath this jealousy was what? What feelings had he harboured for his twenty-two year old secretary these last two years? He was amazed that it had taken him until now to realise that he genuinely cared for her, more so than for a colleague and more so than a friend. He had been so wrapped up in Eve that he had never even allowed himself a glimpse into these feelings before and he was surprised by himself. A thing which did not often happen. Power always thought he knew himself inside out. When he found he was wrong, that his unconscious mind had kept things from him, Power was full of wonder. He would have to explore the feelings more, especially if Eve really didn't want to. He pushed the thoughts away. There was too much running through his head for him to give the matter adequate consideration. All the same, his mind's eye kept returning to an image of the bright bubbly girl outside his office. Power laughed at himself and tried to focus on the reason for Lynch's visit.

Something to do with heads. The seat of four of the senses – eyes, ears, nose and tongue. Inside the cranial vault, cushioned by cerebrospinal fluid was the brain. The site of the mind itself. Mind and body. Hadn't Descartes analysed the split between body and thought? Was thought a product of the billions of nerve cells in the brain, or more than that? What was the interface between thought and body? Didn't the heart race when an exam candidate thought of his embarrassing lack of knowledge? Didn't the function, or lack of it, of the cirrhotic liver produce confusion?

It was a bad doctor who forgot the role of the mind and emotions in the course of an illness. But doctors were more than able to separate the mind and body. They separated themselves into doctors of the mind and doctors of the body.

Cartesian dualism aside, thought Power, it was the murderer who had executed the crudest mind/body split of all.

* * *

A vast expanse of emerald green heathland stretched limitlessly in front of him. No tree, no bush, no shrub broke the flat line of the green horizon. The horizon was a world-circle that surrounded him and was touched by the lip of the grey sky-rim. Below him the wet grass, above him the battleship-grey clouds tumbled and rumbled incessantly.

Light managed to penetrate to the surface of this world only with great difficulty. When it had struggled through a darkening sky the light seemed somehow exhausted, drained of life.

Power turned. Behind him, out of nowhere, something was running, bounding, at great speed in an arrow-straight line towards him. As it drew nearer Power could see that it was a large black dog. Something like an unholy cross between a Rottweiler and a Great Dane. An unnaturally dark shadow followed the dog. Strands of thick saliva trailed from the hound's gaping mouth. Power, impressed by the size of the canine teeth, began to run. He had never liked dogs and this specimen seemed particularly hostile. He ran, but he didn't know where he was running to. The bare green earth offered no shelter. The sky flickered with lightning, one or two streaks of lightning radiated out from the centre of the sky like some brilliant, but jagged, spokes of a wheel.

Behind him the silent dog seemed to be gaining ground. Ahead there was a forbidding horizon.

Power woke abruptly. He was breathless. Sweat drenched him. He felt it running down his face like the wine had done. Feeling panic inside he flung the covers of his bed back and sat up. 'What did the dream mean?' he asked himself. His mind had assumed an extreme importance to the dream. He knew it was of critical importance to him, but he couldn't work out what the symbols in the dream represented. The dream had had a particularly vivid quality and the affect of fear that pervaded it had been strong enough to wake him from deep sleep. What was Power's unconscious trying to tell him? What did the dream mean?

* * *

The council had provided a portakabin toilet by the picnic site. He washed his hands in there. A coach load of walkers had just left the car park to have lunch at the nearby Ruthin Castle Hotel. Weary after their exertions they looked forward to the rewards of a chicken in the basket meal. When he came down the steps out of the public conveniences he was more than gratified to see that the white van stood alone in the car park.

For most of the past two days he had waited and watched in the shadow of Foel fenlii. He looked up at the side of the mountain. In his mind's eye he traced where he would be climbing shortly. To his right the slopes of the mountain were devoid of much vegetation bar grass and bushy heather. The high ridge of the mountain was equally bare against the skyline. Further to the right the edge of the mountain fell away from the eye. If you followed the single-track road that way you rounded the hillside and were greeted by a vista that dropped precipitously away from you over the lush expanse of the Vale of Clwyd. Looking South-west you could see first the market town of Ruthin, then the purple of the high Welsh mountains beyond, where the ancient spirit still lived on.

There wasn't much time. He began to climb. The canvas bag in his right hand was heavy, it unbalanced him. It would be heavier when he came down straight afterwards. Depart before anyone suspected, they said to him. Hope that no-one saw. It had to be done. Must be done. It was always a gamble, part of the excitement – if it all worked it was further proof, (if any more was needed) that he was right and should continue.

He almost ran up the mountainside at first. He couldn't last though and coughing and spluttering slowed his wheezing pace to a slow, plodding climb. The wind caught at his green jacket and he filled his lungs gladly with the crisp oxygen.

Over to his left was the pine forest. The trees covered the eastern slopes of the mountain as a tufted blanket might cover a sleeping giant. Best to climb up through the trees. Less chance of being seen. He opened the gates that prevented the sheep from entering and began to push his way up through the trees. Thin, leafless branches whipped at his face and body. (Better than being in the open and being stopped before he could finish it). Last summer's dry twigs snapped under his feet. (No-one to hear though).

The foresters had left at eleven thirty to go to lunch at the nearest pub, The Druid's Inn, on the A 494. The last two days they had come back to work at twelve forty-five or thereabouts. He had been especially careful they didn't see him. He'd watched them congregate in the car park before they left – the three men each coming from a different part of the forest. One man had been planting trees around the picnic area. Another had been thinning the established growth. The last had been repairing fences near the top of the ridge. (Gloriously near to where it needed to be done. Another sign). He had found the fence where the forester had left off. His tools lay scattered about. The forester had been convinced there was no-one about to steal them.

Now it was just a matter of waiting. The bag could be unpacked. The foresters looked powerful so this time he had brought his crossbow along. He unpacked it and the shining steel bolts, all with a tip so sharp it was painful to look at. Just a matter of waiting. (The police had no idea, weren't even close).

SEVEN

It was eight o'clock in the morning. Unable to sleep Lynch had come into work and, in the absence of his secretary was opening his morning post. A variety of items: a polite request for a newspaper interview from Lynn Barber of *'The Independent'* (not all the media were so polite, with the killing of the boy the press had become noticeably more aggressive to Lynch); a copy of the divisional budget and *'Management Implications'* a newsletter which Lynch filed in the bin; a letter from someone who had been eliminated from the enquiry, but who persistently sent in confessions, each one different from the last. Perhaps he was a case for Power, thought Lynch. Then he came to a thick envelope from the forensic pathology laboratory. He opened it with a sense of foreboding.

First, Lynch read the post-mortem report on Philip Wray. It was difficult for him to separate the emotions he felt from the facts he needed to know as a police officer. Yet he knew he must read this. He was desperate for some mistake, some quirk overlooked by the murderer that would give him away. He tried, as best he could, to focus on the boy's post-mortem. There was some evidence that he had been dead before decapitation, ('high levels of deoxyhaemoglobin and methaemoglobin in blood samples', 'damage to distal portion of tracheal cartilage', 'ligature marks in cervical skin') Lynch told himself this meant the boy had been strangled first with a piece of wire or something. There was no evidence of any sexual attack.

Essentially the pattern was the same as with the girl – a swift death followed by expert decapitation. Lynch read the pathologists's description with distaste, 'a clean and knowledgeable dissection with few blade marks suggesting swiftness and precision'. It sounded almost as if the pathologist was full of admiration.

Lynch was surprised and perturbed though by the second report he had requested. Detective Sergeant Beresford, who had come into the office, watched his superior. Insomnia had made a companion of him, like it had done Lynch.

The piece of paper trembled in Lynch's hand as he read it. When he put it down he noticed he felt different in himself, as if ice water was trickling and running over his head. D.S. Beresford saw Lynch's reaction and picked up the report statement and read:

"Preliminary Report on the third organic specimen (Lab. No. 2140) from the Alderley Edge/Eddisbury Hill investigation. Results of a microscopic examination and further tests :

"MACRO: A piece of severed red muscle tissue or meat (10x15x5 cm)
Dermis and adipose tissue attached to one edge.
Origin – "Undergrowth on Eddisbury Hill. Last meal of
Dog (See Separate Autopsy Report).

"MICRO: Skeletal muscle tissue, adipose and dermal layers. Human origin.

"DNA PROFILE: Not compatible with other human tissue from crime sites. Separate origin.

"CHEMICAL PROFILE: Traces of potassium cyanide within lacunae in meat, injected by hypodermic syringe into muscle layers. (See Cause of Death/Dog)"

Beresford looked up, "I can't quite get this, sir. Is what he's saying that..."

"What he's saying is...that the meat that the murderer deliberately fed to the dog was laced with cyanide. The dog wouldn't have lasted more than a few seconds after eating only a small bit of it."

Beresford protested. "But the other bit says.."

"The meat...the tissue that the murderer threw down for the

dog was human muscle. The DNA profile gives us an idea of who it was from." Lynch paused to let the uncomfortable truth settle in Beresford's mind. "All the lab can say is that, because it didn't match the bodies we have; that it wasn't the boy or the girl. I'm saying that this was part of a third body and a third murder."

"But where's the missing body then?"

"Where are the missing two heads?"

Lynch sat back in his chair and pondered the unwelcome news. "I'll need to let Power know. Can you ask him here for me?" Lynch watched Beresford leave, he felt so perplexed he could hardly think any more. Minutes later Sergeant Beresford was back on the phone to Lynch. "I phoned Dr Power, he's on his way over."

"Good, now can you get me the Chief Constable?"

"He won't be in till nine, sir."

Lynch scowled, "Then get me a coffee while I wait, two sugars please." He considered settling down to his customary time alone at Morning Prayer, but now he felt he should delay this at least until he felt a little less angry, a little less harassed.

* * *

From the summit of Foel fenlii the world is a rolling patchwork of fields and hills stretching seemingly forever into the distance of England and Wales. An ancient cairn of heavy granite stones, shaped into a conical mound, sits at the summit like a vacant throne, commanding a 360 degree view of the world.

Five well-worn paths radiate out from the 500 metre summit and trail down the mountainside like tentacles, or the points of a starfish.

Around the long hill were the continuous oval ditches and banks that once had formed the defences of a Celtic hill fort. It was no wonder that the mountain had once been strategically important given its lofty and supreme view.

On 24th June at 10.35 a.m. a party of sixth formers, led by their school history master disembarked from their white Ford minibus. Rucksacks were unloaded from the back, opened and anoraks and cagoules extracted. Despite being June, the morning was cool and grey clouds covered the mountains of Wales. There was a keen wind blowing, and though this was cold, it promised to shift the cloud and unmask the sun.

Mr Bell, a graduate of far-away Cambridge, a history man, envisaged a gentle climb to the summit of Foel fenlii. By the time they reached there he estimated that the sun would be pouring down on their backs, the view would be appreciated and picnics eaten. Then he could begin his lecture on the nature and purpose of the hill fort. He smiled at the prospect.

The gaggle of eight students clustered randomly about Mr Bell, shivering after the humid warmth of the minibus. Unlike their leader they looked up at the summit with some dread at the amount of energy that would have to be expended before lunch.

Mr Bell was a clean-living enthusiast for hill walking. The class viewed the evidence for this; his ruddy, weatherbeaten complexion and sandy hair, his well-worn frame rucksack, his practical walking boots, trousers tucked into thick khaki socks, compass, plastic map and Gore-tex jacket. By way of contrast they wore ill-fitting designer trainers, jeans and anoraks. Some had canvas haversacks, others clutched plastic bags limply holding sandwiches and cans of drink. Some pupils had sneaked along cans of Carlsberg and Guinness for surreptitious consumption.

Mr Bell locked the white van carefully and hoisted his back pack into place. It was heavy. He was training for a July walking holiday in the Pyrenees and he had deliberately increased the weight he would carry by including extra full water bottles.

The party left the Forestry Commission car park at 10.50 a.m. and climbed the stile one-by-one. Mr Bell walked ahead, striding up the slope. The initial gradient was easy enough and the party of teen-agers kept close by Bell. As the gradient steepened the party became more strung out. Poor shoes and general unfitness held some back. They struggled on the loose stones. The path between the knee-high heather and bracken was well-worn. In places it had been replaced by steps, and in others protected by lengths of hessian to prevent erosion. The hessian had become torn over the months under the boots of hikers. Some of the girls tripped and fell.

By the time Bell was half-way up his group was trailing some two hundred yards behind him. He took a bottle out of his pack and drank the ice-cold water whilst he waited for them all to catch up. When the last one had staggered to his side Bell waited a further ten minutes to give this wheezing fat boy a rest.

"Dreadful," he muttered darkly. "I'm twice your age. You're all knackered...You're horribly unfit. Don't any of you start smoking or you'll be having a coronary by the time you're forty."

"Sir, can I pay a visit?" One of the boys pointed to the woods.

Bell thought about making a sarcastic comment, but he restrained himself. It was a day out. He nodded and first one boy, then another, headed into the trees to relieve themselves against pine trunks. They ran into the dark forest through a gap in the fencing where some repair work was taking place. The old fence and pieces of new wood were lying nearby.

* * *

Power entered Lynch's office at eleven o' clock just as Lynch was on the phone. Lynch smiled a welcome and waved Power to one of the deep leather armchairs that he had salvaged from the clear-out of the old police headquarters. The chairs were deep and comfortable. Power marvelled at being engulfed by one of them. He listened to Lynch's voice; it sounded just a trifle more cultured than normal and also as if Lynch was making an effort to contain his temper. "No sir, I haven't requested that be done....Well, I can, but it will soak up the manpower that I've already got....I am aware that with this third...

event...that the political pressure will grow on us all to get a result, but there is no evidence of sexual assault and to question all the...No, it's just the time...I would welcome that...No, I really hope that I can keep the investigation...a more senior figure?...But I've just got a team organised...Dr Power yes...no, not that unusual. A hunch...yes, so do I. I will keep you informed, sir, good-bye and thank you." He put the phone down and sighed with relief.

He looked up at Power. "Keeping the wolves at bay, Carl. That was the Chief Constable. In a case like this the political pressure mounts with every victim, as it were. He's given me more manpower, but in return I've got to demonstrate that we're leaving no stone unturned. He wants us to pull in every ex-con we know who has ever committed anything against a child. In return for getting the Chief off my back I've got to assume the role of Witchfinder General. Do you think this murderer is a paedophile, that this is to do with children in particular?"

"No," said Power. "This isn't to do with children. I guess he just wants victims. As if they were sacrifices or something."

"It's about someone who is so damaged that nothing is sacred." Lynch told Power about the pathology findings.

"There's someone here whose put a lot of thought into staging everything. Whoever it was had to prepare the meat by injecting it, had to get the poison, had to know how to handle the poison. And there again the pathologist refers to the expert removal of the head."

"Almost praises his technique!"

"The murderer knows his job, like a surgeon perhaps. Surgeons always have seemed odd to me. They have to be able to dissociate themselves from what they do. They dissociate to cope. If they thought about what they were doing...cutting open someone...maybe they couldn't do it. They have to dissociate themselves from the operation and dissociate the body in front of them from the personal being it is."

"I see," Lynch looked down at his hands. "You think maybe this is a doctor at work."

"Could be. It runs against the whole tradition, but this man whoever he is, has some proficiency. And doctors can be quite cold... quite inured or desensitised to suffering."

"But it could also be a vet. A vet knows anatomy and operates. Nurses know anatomy. Dentists do dissections don't they? Butchers know how to dismember animal carcasses. You don't particularly need to stick to professionals. It's unlikely to be a medic, because they don't have the time. These murders can look quite random, but they're not, as you say, they're carefully planned. The murderer must have known who the boy was, and that he had a dog before he brought the...er, flesh. And in the Alderley Edge case there was fresh straw in the cave."

"And the blood was there too...all of it...as if he'd drained her."

"Well, he had, " said Lynch, remembering her almost transparent pallor. "...but why, why do that?"

"When a surgeon operates he likes a bloodless field. Surgeons cauterise the microvessels that bleed when they operate. The blood obscures your vision of what you're trying to do to help the patient. In the murderer's case he wanted to control where the blood goes."

"Doesn't want it all over him, you mean."

"That's right. He probably has to walk away from the crime... doesn't want to be caught covered in blood walking down the road. And if he severed one of the carotid arteries when the heart was still beating there would be a cascade, a literal fountain of blood." When Power imagined the fountain of blood it made him feel sick. He had hated anatomy classes and had had bad dreams about dissection. Post mortems in pathology had been even worse. No wonder Power had settled on psychiatry. He continued, "So the murderer has to kill the victims...to stop their hearts pumping the blood around before he..."

"Yes," said Lynch. "I can see where your logic is going. It seems to me that the murderer is taking immense trouble over all of this."

"To drain the blood..."

"Yes," Lynch interrupted again. "I can see that. All this trouble - to get the heads."

Power closed his eyes and raised his hand. "I understand. Excuse me." He stood up and left the room, leaving Lynch somewhat bemused.

When Power returned, his face was grey. He smiled wanly at Lynch.

Lynch frowned, deep in thought. He had scarcely noticed Power's discomfort surrounding the bloody details of the murders. "I must get to grips with what you're saying. Have you thought any more about what links the crimes?"

"I've been through everything you sent me. The house-to-house statements, the statements of the parents, neighbours, teachers, doctors, hippies. Nothing strikes a chord."

"You're baffled?" Lynch raised an inquisitive eyebrow.

"Yes."

"I am glad there are two of us, at least."

Power's stomach rumbled. He had been awoken by Sergeant Beresford's phone call at eight-thirty. He had overslept after the exertions of the night, and consequently missed breakfast. He looked at his watch and reasoned that he must let Laura know of his whereabouts and ask her to take messages until he could get back to the hospital. His stomach rumbled again. "I need to phone the hospital, let them know where I am," he said. Lynch gestured to the phone as if to say 'feel free'. When Power had finished he was aware that his hunger had re-doubled. He wondered if his stomach needed some ballast, to steady him.

Lynch laughed as Power's belly gurgled again. "Shall we get some breakfast then, Doctor?" Lynch knew of a French patisserie cafe in the Medieval Rows in Chester. "I know a place only five minutes' walk away. Fantastic pastries and coffee. What do you think?"

Power grinned broadly at the prospect of food.

* * *

"Where the bloody hell are they?" Mr Bell was asking no-one in particular. Having excused themselves to go into the forest to urinate, the two lads were taking a long time. "I'm going to get them," said Bell, suspecting they were having a cigarette.

"Going to have a look at them more like," whispered one of the girls to another. Bell didn't hear. He went closer to the broken fence. He could see the forester's implements lying about: a hammer, nails, saw and axe. He noticed they each had droplets of water on from the early morning rain. Bell thought it strange that the tools should have been left so carelessly out to rust. It offended his obsessional sense of rightness.

Bell peered into the dark depths of the forest. He couldn't see anything moving, couldn't hear anything. No voices, nothing. Tentatively he walked into the trees. Suppose one of the boys was injured? Lying with a broken ankle or something? He moved into the silent gloom.

"BOO!"

From the undergrowth, both boys sprang up at him. "Oh God!" shouted Bell, genuinely alarmed. "Don't be so bloody stupid! Get back to the group. Now! We've been waiting for you." He was beginning to get his composure back, but he was still slightly ruffled. "Silly buggers," he muttered to himself as he followed them out of the trees into the light. Through the clouds the sunlight was growing stronger as the day progressed.

Bell started the climb again, purposefully moving up the mountainside. This time Bell resisted the temptation to make any allowances or breaks for the group. Not far to go now, only fifty metres or so to the summit. He pressed onwards leaving the students straggling behind. He made the summit just as the sun broke through the clouds and burst onto his face. He let out a shout of triumph and elated ran to the stone cairn. None of the others had even mounted the lip of the hillfort below. He turned round on the spot and, looking at the view, surveyed the magnificence of the world laid out below him. He hummed to himself, "I'm the King of the Castle. I'm the King of the Castle. Get down! You Dirty Rascals. Get down..."

It was a small mountain as mountains go, but the feeling of conquest of any summit was always joy to Mr Bell. In fact he was looking forward to his sandwiches when he realised he wasn't alone at all, and to make things worse, his companion was a most unpleasant one.

Bell had moved around the cairn to view the Welsh mountains across the Clwydian plain. Out of the corner of his eye he glimpsed that someone was sitting on one side of the ancient cairn.

Bell was about to speak when he looked properly at the man. No words came out of Bell's mouth, although it had fallen open. The man half-sat, half-sprawled in a seat, hollowed out of the cairn stones. His hands seemingly gripped the stones like they were the arms of a chair, or a throne. Bell was taken by the bare knees of the figure. They jutted forward and for some reason they fascinated him, mainly because he could not bear to look at the man's shoulders. The man was naked and pale, although the underside of his arms and legs looked mottled and purple.

The figure seemed to occupy the cairn almost regally, despite his nudity. Bell was put in mind of the *Emperor's New Clothes*. He was surprised by his own reaction; that he could find any humour in the situation. Nervous laughter seemed about to possess him. In fact, this reaction of his frightened him most of all, for this king, sitting on his stone throne and surveying his domain, had no eyes to survey with. No eyes, no nose, no mouth, no head.

Bell caught sight of one of his teenagers in the distance, just about to ascend the summit. He was on the other side of the cairn. From there, like Bell before him, he wasn't able to see the dead man. Bell thought he had to spare them this sight. He brought his voice back into play, from silence to a sudden cracking, but demanding roar. "Stay there! Don't move another step. Nobody, nobody move!"

Ashen-faced, Mr Bell left the occupant of the cairn and escorted his party down the hill again. He snapped at any questions they asked and continued the rest of their journey in silence. One girl cried. Mr Bell had never been like this before. He drove them slowly, deliberately, into the nearest civilization, the nearest town, Mold. He stopped the van outside the police station. The perplexed sixth formers watched him as Bell left the van and went through the blue doors of the station entrance. The more observant of them saw that Mr Bell's hands were shaking.

* * *

The *Cosi fan tutte* cafe was all dark wood and sparkling glass and silverware. Here in the most English of towns, the walled city of Chester. The medieval styled rows lay at the heart of the old city. At first-floor level, a covered wooden walkway surrounded most of the Rows' shops. Sitting in the French cafe Lynch and Power could watch and admire the beautiful women who passed the glass windows. Their spirits rose through the meal of chocolate croissants and bowls of dark strong coffee. They relaxed and joked in the warm, convivial atmosphere of the cafe. Then Power noticed some other figures standing around outside. They seemed to be looking at the Superintendent and he. He watched their lips and could swear they were speaking their names, Lynch and Power.

"I don't think there is a back way out," said Lynch ruefully. He had been watching the reporters outside for several minutes longer than Power. One had even had the temerity to worm his way inside, where he stood nonchalantly reading a paper and trying to eavesdrop. "When we go out there I want you to say nothing. There's some reason they've come looking for us. You can be sure it's not to praise Caesar, but to bury him. Oh, and don't appear surprised by anything they say. They'll be looking for reaction. You can imagine them starting a piece with the sentence, 'Superintendent Lynch sat laughing and drinking coffee while....' Come on, let's go." They paid and made their way to the door.

At first Power had thought Lynch's reaction to the media a little paranoid, but as he saw the reporters jostling for position when they neared the glass doors, he was beginning to change his mind. They looked like a pack of hungry dogs to him.

Power made his face serious and tried to avoid their eyes. He heard their barked questions, couldn't fail to. "Who's this you've got with you Superintendent? Is this Doctor Power? The mind expert? What's his theory on the hippy killer? Have you heard about the third murder?" Power nodded before he could stop himself. "What did you think Dr Power?"

"Are you going to Foel fenlii to see the body?" shouted out a particularly strident woman. Power tried hard not to frown. 'What are you talking about? What body?' he wanted to ask. But taking Lynch's example he said nothing at all. He merely followed the Superintendent who parted the reporters as a galleon in full sail parts the waves.

By the time they had returned to Lynch's office in the Chester police headquarters, even Power had realised that the third murder the reporters were referring to was in fact a fourth.

* * *

Lynch eschewed the offer of a ride in Power's decrepit Saab. Instead he led the doctor to his own Volvo 740 Estate. "Safest cars on the road," said Lynch, pointing to the Volvo, and implying that the faithful Saab was a death-trap. Power sank into the opulence of the leather upholstery without a word. The smell of the leather reminded him of his father's Rover. He noted with distaste that Lynch had the car stereo tuned to Radio 2. Thankfully Lynch switched it off as he started the car. Lynch drove the mighty car out through the back entrance to the HQ car park, thereby avoiding the flock of reporters that had gathered by the main entrance. Unhindered they took a side road that flanked the high city walls and led to the roundabout opposite Chester Castle. Lynch waited impatiently for the traffic flow to ease before shooting off and round the roundabout to the right and the A483 road towards North Wales, before turning off on to the A55, then on the A549 to

Mold. The roads became congested around the market town of Mold. A bypass and several roundabouts made Lynch mutter to himself under his breath. It was several minutes before he could accelerate onto the A541 and raise his speed to sixty-five miles an hour.

Power noticed that Lynch was exceeding the speed limit, but kept his own counsel. He watched the small globe compass that Lynch had fixed to the rear view mirror. It swung round crazily and uselessly, its magnetic white sphere inside whirling round in its cushion of water. The brain floated in a sea of cerebrospinal fluid. In a car accident, at the moment of impact, the brain would do the same. He shuddered as Lynch angrily overtook a slow-moving Lada. "What time is it, please?" grunted Lynch, too engrossed in his quest to look down at the clock.

"Two o'clock."

"The Chief Constable's secretary said he would be available now if I wanted to phone. Can you open the dashboard, please?" Power was slightly mystified by this latter request until he opened the glove compartment and saw the car phone nestling inside. "Press the 'transmit' button, then the 'scramble' button and then the 'loud' button in that order." Power complied and then Lynch gave him the direct line number. As Power punched it into the machine, Lynch asked him to keep quiet. The ringing tone sounded on the four in-car speakers. "We'll soon have the chief in stereo." Lynch's voice had changed from its angry imperative to a tone of mild apprehension.

"Good afternoon." The Chief Constable's voice sounded disagreeably loud. Lynch's steering deteriorated slightly and ever-cautious Power fiddled with the volume control.

"Good afternoon, sir. It's Chief Superintendent Lynch again, sir."

"Yes, this is getting to be a habit, twice in one day."

"Have you heard?" asked Lynch. It was a vain question.

"Course I've heard! It's all over the news on radio, on T.V. If we're not careful they'll solve the murders before you do." Lynch winced at the jibe.

"We're on our way to view the body at Denbigh General Hospital." Lynch said.

"They've moved it?"

"Yes, God knows what else they've done wrong. That's why I'm phoning, sir, I need a mandate to..."

The Chief Constable interrupted him. "Have they invited you there to see the body? This is another police force you know. Have they asked you over?"

"Well, not exactly." Lynch had had his secretary ask a reporter where the body was being kept.

"Have you talked to them at all?"

"Er...no, that's what I'm..."

"And you criticise their procedure! Lynch, Clwyd's a different county. It's their ground, their investigation."

"Sir, I'm ringing to ask you whether I can take over...create the supra-regional task force that's going to be needed. I need to be able to co-ordinate this myself. If the investigation gets split up..." He left the dire consequences to the Chief's imagination. "It's only logical."

In the silence you could sense the Chief Constable's disapproval. Eventually, he spoke. "It should be a higher ranking officer in charge."

"But I'm here," protested Lynch. "I'm in the thick of it all. To bring someone else in now...could lose valuable time."

"Lynch, are you anywhere near a solution?"

"We're finally getting places, sir, with the extra manpower you drafted in." Lynch was being extremely economical with the truth.

The Chief Constable paused again. It was difficult to assess the validity of what Lynch was saying. He liked to see people's faces; to see if they believed what they were saying. "All right, Lynch. Now I'm sticking my neck out for you. God knows why. I'll see what I can do. Let me thrash it out at my level, okay? Just don't ruffle any feathers."

"I remain in charge, sir?"

"For now, Lynch." The phone went dead with a 'clunk' that resounded in the car.

Power looked at Lynch, was intrigued by Lynch's deviousness. He hadn't seen the political animal in the devout policeman before. It was something of a shock. "We're getting places? Where exactly have we got with the investigation?"

Lynch suddenly swung the car round to the left. "Where have we got? Denbigh General Hospital, that's where."

* * *

They took their jackets from them and bade them don white plastic aprons that covered them from chest to ankle. They gave them blue plastic overshoes to snap on over their shoes. "In case of splashes," said the mortuary assistant. Power wrinkled up his nose in distaste at the slightly sweet odour of the department. The duty pathologist met them at the entrance to the mortuary room. Power could just see the wall of cabinet drawers beyond. Behind each one... He hated this. When he had been a house surgeon attending post mortems had been the bane of his life.

"The Inspector has already been to see the body," said the pathologist. Lynch sized up this young man, Dr Campbell, with his short blond hair and golden rimless spectacles. His arms were crossed and his stance was defiant. This was his territory and his world. To Power it was an underworld, and the pathologist was welcome to it.

"Dr Campbell, my name is Chief Superintendent Lynch of the Cheshire Constabulary. I am heading the supra-regional inquiry. The officer you met before is local and under my command...."

"Oh yes, I remember you...I saw you in Eric's copy of *The Sun*, this is the fourth isn't it. Not going too well is it?" Presumably Eric was the mortuary attendant, thought Lynch, or perhaps the doctor was trying to distance himself from *The Sun* newspaper.

"...and this is Dr Carl Power."

"It's not often we see a psychiatrist here, or are you a medium as well, Dr Power?" Power ignored the comment, but nodded politely. He was beginning to feel increasingly moist beneath the layers of plastic that protected his clothes. "Well, we're very busy, shall we get on?" asked Dr Campbell, leading them into the bare confines of the morgue. "We're so busy that I don't think I'll be able to get you a written report until next week."

"That's all right," said Lynch. "I'll be asking the Home Office pathologist to do the post-mortem. Get some of our scene of crime boys here too. The body shouldn't have been moved to this place at all. We might have lost evidence in the move." If the remark was designed to discomfort Campbell he showed only the merest ruffling of feathers. He had a thick skin.

"The local coroner has asked me to perform the post mortem. That is the procedure here. If you want your own expert to do a second P.M. you'll have to talk to him." said Campbell, approaching a trolley. A white plastic cover was spread over it. He whipped the cover back with a flourish.

'You insensitive bastard,' thought Power, as he caught sight of what the pathologist had so dramatically unveiled. He could sense the pathologist was smiling at his horrified reaction.

Campbell indicated the severed neck. "Good way of curing schizophrenia, eh, Dr Power?"

Power looked into Campbell's eyes. "Thank God you don't practice on anyone who's living."

"Have you seen all you need?" asked Campbell, impervious to all criticism.

"No," said Lynch. "Can you leave us alone, please? If it's not too much trouble." He watched as Campbell retired unshaken into a nearby office, then turned to Power. "What do you think, Carl?"

"I'm no pathologist...I..." Power looked at Lynch's expectant face.

"I'd rather ask your opinion than Dr Charming here."

Power nodded. Steeling himself, he made an external inspection of the body. After a few minutes he looked up at Lynch. "No obvious damage to any part of the thorax, abdomen or limbs. Even the neck is clear of ligature marks. The head...er...would probably show the site of the pathology."

"What do you mean?"

"The injury that killed this man was to the head. A bullet or something."

"Something, more like," said Campbell re-emerging from his hole, unable to resist commenting.

"But I am right about the head?"

"I haven't looked at the internal organs yet. But, for what it's worth, in my opinion, you're right Dr Power." He looked down at the dead forester. "This is a strong, well-muscled man. The murderer probably wanted a swift and sure way of killing him. Nobody would fight this man voluntarily. No, I know it's speculation, but a bullet might cause blood to spatter over the torso...from the explosive impact. I think it would be something like a crossbow, silent and swift."

Power nodded, here at least was a point he could agree on with Campbell.

"Thank you for your time," said Lynch, tearing the sweat-encouraging plastic apron from him. "I'll send the Home Office team over to collect the body."

"Of course," said Campbell watching the retreating figures. He covered up the body and went for lunch.

* * *

Dr Jones yawned, scratched his belly and sank into his favourite armchair by the fire. The cloudless night had grown chilly and against Jones' judgement his wife had set and lit some of the dry logs from the old oak tree that had been felled the year before. Now he felt the benefit of the crackling warmth the fire brought. He almost said, 'It is cold for June isn't it?', but thought his wife might derive some satisfaction from having been right about lighting the fire. He stayed resolutely silent. Mrs Jones regarded him out of the corner of her eye and went back to the tapestry of a peacock she had been stitching for the last eight months. Her husband reached out for his coffee and the copy of the *Manchester Evening News* the paper boy had delivered earlier. She noticed that he had moved his chair closer to her fire and derived some comfort from this.

Pausing to sip the coffee and then set it down again, Jones eventually put his reading glasses on his nose and unfolded the tabloid. The headline declared, "Four dead!", and Jones tut-tutted to himself. "North Wales body and other links to Alderley Edge Murder," said a subtitle. There wasn't much room on the page for anything other than the headlines.

There were a few lines of text about the murder enquiry that neither excited nor intrigued Jones. It all seemed quite a remote world to him. But something else on the page....

Mrs Jones watched her husband convulsively jerk to his feet, his fingers clutching at the paper until the knuckles were white. Should she call an ambulance, was her first thought. She worried about his health more and more these days. He appeared to be going even redder in the face, but he wasn't clutching at his heart, so she presumed it wasn't the heart attack she had dreamt about. She worried about him. Of course the insurance was all in order, but you could never be sure. It was a great worry.

Dr Jones appeared to be making his way to the telephone, angrily chunnering to himself. The emergency was over as far as Mrs Jones was concerned. She confined her attention to the tail of the peacock which she was finding so difficult, while he dialled a number he had found in his diary.

He listened to the ringing tone and when a male voice answered spoke, "Mr Preece? The Regional General Manager?" With the answer being affirmative Jones launched himself into his speech with pride in his voice. "This is Dr Jones, Consultant and Clinical Director of Adult Mental Health. I'm sorry to phone you at home, but I really must discuss this with you tonight. It will require urgent action in the morning. It's about one of our newly appointed consultants – have you seen the paper?"

"No, I have not." The Regional General Manager had only just got home after a stormy business meeting at one of the Hospital Trusts that was lurching into the red. He was upset at being disturbed at home and he thought he could tell by Jones' pompous and officious manner that probably there was no good reason for the interruption.

"There's a photograph of Dr Power splashed all across the front page."

"Oh?" A vague stirring of interest. "Is that the psychiatrist whose working with the police on the Alderley Edge thing?"

"Yes..." The Manager obviously had prior knowledge, but not from the news. Jones felt the wind being stolen from out of his sails. "We can't have this – a new junior consultant waltzing off and leaving his work to tour the countryside with the police. The caption says 'Superintendent Lynch discussing the Alderley murders with psychiatrist Dr Power' – they're having coffee in some cafe in Chester. He just swanned off and I find that this is where he got to. We can't keep him, I'm afraid. He's unreliable, an idiot, getting us a bad name."

"I thought the General Medical Council prevented you from discussing colleagues in such derogatory terms? It's hardly professional of you is it?"

"I...I...I've never been spoken to like that before...who are you to..."

"I'm the Regional Manager. You asked to speak to me. Dr Jones, I can understand your..." He stopped himself from saying 'jealousy'. "...feelings about Dr Power being co-opted to do this police work, but actually I have been asked, just this evening, to release him from his clinical duties on paid leave - whenever he deems it necessary – to assist Superintendent Lynch."

"But who agreed to that? I'm the Clinical Director, how can I maintain services when..."

"The directive came from the highest place. If you like I can give you the phone number of the Minister at the Home Office I was speaking to. The Secretary of State has requested that we release Dr Power for this inquiry. But maybe I should give you the Home Office number when we speak again in the morning. Now, goodnight."

Mrs Jones didn't notice her husband shamble off disconsolately to find the whisky bottle. She was too engrossed in her needlework.

* * *

Had Dr Jones been watching television later that night he might indeed have had a heart attack had he been watching the *Newsnight* programme. The editor, grey-haired journalist, Adam Raphael, had persuaded Lynch to agree to his interviewing Dr Power. Persuading Power to be interviewed was another matter. He had the feeling that he was being sucked deeper and deeper into the investigation. He was frightened of becoming something he wasn't. To catch the murderer he already knew that he would have to chart the depths of the murderer's unconscious. To make any kind of chart, would mean an exploration, a journey into the murderer's way of thinking. Power felt he had to keep his identity intact to find his way out again. Knowing who he was, where he lived, who his friends were...these were all touchstones that would help him navigate his way back.

It was a reluctant Power that allowed himself to be made up

by a woman who clucked over his complexion ('not as clear as it could be, is it?'), sat in a studio and wired up to a microphone, opposite a television screen. The interview would be conducted at a distance. The presenter Jeremy Paxman would be in the London studios, Power would be slumming it in Manchester's Oxford Road studios.

When they had positioned him and lit him to their satisfaction, they left him alone. He sat in the studio, which, apart from the three brilliant lights that were trained on him, was distantly dark. Hardly visible in the blackness was the single eye of the camera, just above the television screen. Power watched as Paxman effortlessly and delicately tore a politician to shreds and went on to introduce a report on Afghanistan. Power wondered what he could say about the murders that wouldn't make him sound too stupid. Lynch had thought the interview might stimulate some more help from the public. Power was feeling alienated by the remote-controlled studio.

From somewhere a disembodied voice sounded. Power looked around, but could see no-one. It was a director from some distant control room. 'Was this what it was like to hallucinate?' thought Power.

"We'll be coming to you next, Dr Power. You're the next item on Jeremy's menu."

'Am I to be eaten?' wondered Power. 'Thrown to the lions?' He thought of all the millions of pairs of eyes that would be on him in any moment. He thought he was about to panic, but suddenly, from somewhere he found a reserve of calm. He thought about how assured Lynch had looked when he had spoken in public. If he could do it...

The footage on Afghanistan was over. Paxman was back on screen. "In this country there has been increasing alarm voiced about a dramatic series of murders in Cheshire. Today police revealed that a further two murders have to be added into the total. The latest was of a forestry worker in Clwyd, North Wales. All of the corpses so far discovered have been beheaded. Despite the problems this posed for identification, three of the four known victims have been named. Forensic science, much trumpeted in recent years, has been hard-pressed to give some clue to the identity of the killer. So far, there has been no joy. Police have turned to a psychiatrist, Dr Carl Power, for help...." Paxman turned to Power, staring at him through the glass screen. "Dr Power, are the police turning to you in desperation?"

"No...no, I wouldn't say in desperation."

"But what does a psychiatrist have to offer in such a case as this, beyond pronouncing the murderer mad?"

"What he does...the murders...may seem mad, but he may be quite sane, or he may be a psychopath, or he may, as you suggest, be psychotic. I'm trying to get some idea of what the murders mean for him...they're pointless to you and I...to him...no doubt they have a private meaning."

"You said him? How do you know it's a him?"

"Well statistically serial killers, (and this is a serial killer), are male. He would probably be in his twenties or thirties, probably a bit of a loner...but he may have a job...might live alone or with parents... serial killers often have problems with their parents. There have been a few with fathers who have been senior police officers or public prosecutors. Almost as if the murders are a rebellion against a father who personifies authority. A strike against authority might seem to the murderer's unconscious as the same as a strike against their father."

"You're an expert on the unconscious aren't you?"

"I wouldn't say that," said Power modestly.

"But you have published on the subject...I'm intrigued by what you say though...all these facts about known killers like the Ripper and others...in following these 'profiles' might you not make an unwarranted assumption...like the murderer is male when they're female, or acting singly when they are a group?"

"That is possible, but as time goes on we add to our knowledge of the killer."

"You mean with each murder?"

"If you want to say that, yes...we get closer to him. And it is a him, because we doubt that a female would have the strength necessary." Power was conscious of the sweat beading his forehead under the hot lights. He went on to explain further. "The last victim was killed on the edge of a forest and carried some two hundred yards or so up a hillside to the summit of Foel fenlii, a Welsh mountain. Not an easy task. But yes, you could say that we're playing a game of blind man's buff with this man...and all the time we play he's calling us... taunting us. He comes close then he moves away again...calling names at us through the darkness."

"What's his motive?"

"We don't fully understand it yet. It's not directly sexual. He hasn't sexually interfered with the victims. He murders in isolated places, outside places...and it seems to me as if his victims are displayed...under the open sky. This has a meaning for him...and I don't know if it has echoes with anybody else, but it seems like a ritual...er, that he repeats."

"What do you mean by a ritual?"

"Mankind loves rituals. We all have rituals. We thrive on them. They make us feel safe. Little children have rituals...they don't step on lines in pavements or they have to have a special piece of blanket at bedtime, a certain story repeated again and again. Adults have rituals too...the way they go to work every day or church services are a perfect kind of ritual...warding off evil, propitiating God. It's magical thinking. Say a charm and nothing will harm you. We all have some kind of ritual that reduces our anxieties."

"So how is this linked in with what the murderer does?"

"Well, the function of his ritual is no different...he feels compelled to follow it through...if he doesn't he might feel calamity will befall him, or perhaps he feels the ritual will give him great power."

EIGHT

"What music are you putting on?"

"Suor Angelica."

"Puccini. Good. It's a bit sad though," said Eve. "About a lost child." Power nodded as he slipped the CD into the player. "Can you open the wine I brought?" she asked as she handed him the bottle and the corkscrew. The music began to swell and fill the room. Eve sat back down on the couch where they had been lying together. "There's a bit in the music which is so...moving...it raises the hairs on the back of your neck. Haunting."

"You gave me this CD," said Power. It was Eve who was a fan of opera, not Power. But this opera stirred him like no other. He handed her her glass and sat down beside her. She nestled into his shoulder and wondered if she had the courage tonight. It was difficult to form the words. He sipped the wine and pursed his lips, musing over its different taste. She wanted to tell him about something in her past. Something so personal that it ached inside her, so that she kept it hidden. Hidden for so many years. He must know if he were to finally understand her, understand why she sometimes danced close, sometimes far apart. If they were ever to settle down, surely he would have to know? If she was to be certain he loved her, he must know. And she knew it wasn't her fault, but it might change what he thought of her. He might not love her then, might not even like her. But it wasn't her fault! She had been too young to know. To tell or not to tell? To know or not to know? Eve looked at this silent man, listening to his music and sipping her wine.

"It's the same colour as communion wine...that deep, deep red," he said. She shuddered. "Are you cold?" he asked, putting his arm about her.

"No, I..." The mention of communion wine made her feel some- how guilty. "I hope it doesn't taste as bad as communion wine."

"No," he said drawing her close. "It's quite marvellous."

And he was marvellous too, she thought. She knew she wanted him inside her, and suddenly tonight was the wrong time to tell him. And the longer she knew him, the less she wanted to spoil it all by tell- ing him about that man she had known when she was a girl. And, sure enough, Power was never to know. Some things cannot be said, even to the ones we love most.

"I saw you on the box. On Thursday night...you didn't phone to tell me you'd be on." she rebuked him teasingly.

"I...er..."

"You're too modest, Carl. I thought you were great."

"I'd rather be known for something less ghoulish. You know what? My publisher rang me today...told me that the book chainstores had cleaned him out of my book. He's reprinting. They think people who read the newspapers and saw *Newsnight* will want to buy."

"Isn't that good?" Power was frowning.

"It's...don't you think it's a bit distasteful?" He'd written the book as a piece of academia, not as a bestseller.

"It's just the way of the world, Carl." She reached over and smoothed his hair. "You came across well on television. But did you mean it when you started talking about rituals and sacrifices. Sounded a bit wild, you know."

He looked at her and weighed her words. "Blood sacrifice isn't an everyday thing in our society. I'll agree with you there, but then our society is pretty new and we're the same old human beings we've ever been. The same brains as the Incas. They used to waste a thousand lives at a go. In the Bible, Abraham seriously considers offering the life of his firstborn to God... Human sacrifice was a worldwide thing. The Celts used to sacrifice slaves and unwanted children. How did the children's skeletons get put under the stones of Stonehenge?"

"I didn't know that."

"They talk about the fear of God...they must have been terrified of theirs. To sacrifice your children...that reeks of a great fear. Don't you think?"

"I don't like to think about it."

"We've forgotten about it. But I'll tell you there...it's all stored up here. " He pointed to her temple then his own. "In our race memory or our collective unconscious, whatever you want to call it."

"That's frightening...you're frightening me, Carl."

"It frightens me too. I tried not to take this on. I told Lynch I wouldn't, but he managed to change my mind. It's like this, if I'm going to catch this man I've got to have a good idea of how his mind works. That involves sacrifice."

"Let's talk about something else, shall we?" Power smiled and nodded. He welcomed the opportunity to put the images behind him. "How's work on your next book going?"

"Oh, the publisher was asking me about that. Wanted me to hurry up! I told him I wasn't going to compromise. You know I wonder if he...the murderer...whether he's bought a copy of my book?"

Eve decided that topic wasn't nearly far enough removed from the investigation. "What's for supper?" she asked, trying to get Power into the realms of food, where he was at his happiest.

* * *

Lynch chose a pew near the back of the small parish church. He took off his great coat, neatly folded it and placed it beside him on the dark pine of the seat. His eyes took in the crisp whiteness of the walls and above it the steep dark wood that rose into the high roof space. He had been pleased to see that, as a mark of respect, the media had largely stayed away from Phillip Wray's funeral. Lynch had felt it his duty to be here. He must face his own failure and guilt at failing to stop the killer, but there was more than that that Lynch had to face inside himself. He put down the service sheet he had been given by the funeral directors and picked up the pew Bible as if it were a talisman. He read quietly, reverently as the boy's family and friends arrived in twos and threes and seated themselves. Lynch smelt the flowers and, out of the corners of his eyes, saw the crow-like pall bearers carrying in the coffin. He could not bear to look directly at this. He tried to erase the memories of the arc-lit scene on Eddisbury Hill from his consciousness; tried not to think they were only burying a part-body.

The minister was saying, "I am the resurrection and the life..." Lynch clung on to his Bible and read, blotting out the church around him.

The white-haired vicar had taken his place at the side of the coffin. He looked at the flowers on top of it and his etched face reflected their light. His tired voice equally reflected the hurt felt by the black-suited men and white-faced women. "The death of a child seems a cruel thing, and when a life has been robbed in this way..." His voice faltered and the vicar sought firmer ground, resorting to the old Book of Common Prayer he was holding. "Lord, thou hast been our refuge..."

Lynch's mind wandered over his life, considered his own losses and as the words well-known to him washed over him Lynch sought some comfort from them.

"There are celestial bodies and bodies terrestrial; but the glory of the celestial is one, and the glory of the terrestrial is another. There is one glory of the sun, and another glory of the moon, and another glory of the stars; for one star differeth from another star in glory. So also is the resurrection of the dead: It is sown in corruption; it is raised in incorruption: It is sown in dishonour; it is raised in glory: It is sown in weakness; it is raised in power: It is sown a natural body; it is raised a spiritual body."

Lynch was aware that the mother of the boy had turned round, had recognised him, was staring at him. He could not meet her eye. Feeling a coward, he bent his head and addressed his Bible again, conscious that she was turning away from him now. He read, 'There are those who rebel against the light, who do not know its ways or stay in its paths. When daylight is gone, the murderer rises up and kills the poor and needy; in the night he steals forth like a thief. For all of them deep darkness is their morning; they make friends with the terrors of darkness. For a little while they are exalted and then they are gone; they are brought low and gathered up like all others; they are cut off like ears of corn.'

The congregation filed out slowly to the sombre organ music. Lynch hung back, wanting to stand, as he did, on the edge of the crowd around the graveside. He watched the small coffin being lowered through the gaps in the black-suited figures. He watched it remorsefully, and he wondered how the sun dare shine so brightly on a day such as this. The July sunshine burst upon the mourners in searing hot streams. So brilliantly did it fall that the contrast between the mourning black and the rest of the colourful world was transmuted into simple black-and-white on Lynch's retina.

At last the thing was done and Lynch turned, glad to be able to cast aside the pall of gloom that the service had created within him. But he was not to be allowed to slip away unnoticed. He was not to be allowed the part of a silent walk-on player. As the mourners turned away from the graveside a burly, black figure in dress and veil bore down upon him through the crowd. The grief of this woman was central to the moment and the unwilling Lynch was now to find it focussed upon him alone.

"Are you the police Superintendent who interviewed us?" She lifted her black veil. Lynch looked at the face of the woman who was staring up at him. The red rims of her eyes were raw with crying. Her face seemed pudgy and pale. She wrung her hands in agitation; large beefy hands that Lynch imagined kneading and pummeling dough in the kitchen at home. This small, rounded country mother seemed to dominate the crowd, who followed her with their eyes.

"Superintendent Lynch, Mrs Wray. I wanted to pay my respects. I hope that it doesn't seem an intrusion...I'm sorry if..."

"What are you doing about getting that animal?" She was paper-pale and there was a dangerous light in her eyes. Lynch wondered if she was about to strike him. He remembered how Power had talked about people in the thrall of strong emotion doing things they might not otherwise do. If she swung out at him he would not mind so much, what he did mind was the audience that had now gathered round them.

"Our team is working round the clock. I know we haven't got any results so far, but..."

He had answered her question as fully as she wanted. She interrupted. "When you get him...will you bring my boy back to me?"

At first Lynch could not understand what she meant. He wondered whether she was fully orientated. He knew grief could play tricks on the mind. Then he gathered she was talking about something more down-to-earth. She wanted her son whole again, in death as he had been in life. He could almost feel the mother's driving imperative to have his body in one resting place.

He nodded. Tried to find the right words. "We'll bring him back for you, Mrs Wray."

"Good. Thank you for coming today." She smiled, and her anguished face seemed almost to compose itself in calm. She turned away from him and was about to walk to the waiting black limousines when she looked back at Lynch. "I've remembered something," she said.

"Yes?" Lynch came a little closer to her.

"The day Phillip...died. There was a...." A sudden flash startled both of them. The brilliance, superimposed on the sunlight, was over in the blink of an eye. Away to his right, running through the gravestones, was a press photographer escaping with a perfect image of the tall and elegant policeman comforting the grieving mother.

Lynch was tempted to run after the man, so incensed was he by the callous intrusion, but to do so might only compound the indignity the media had wrought upon the mother's grief. "Go on Mrs Wray, what were you about to say?" he asked softly.

"I remembered when I looked onto the road just now. On the day Phillip died I went to post a letter at the post-box. I can see the red post -box now in my mind's eye. And there was a van parked just a little off the road...where one of the farmers sometimes parks a trailer. That's all you ever see there normally. And I knew the van wasn't his." Lynch wondered why she hadn't told him this before? Sometimes people did this though. Some detail would escape their memory for days and then be triggered by what? An emotion, a smell, a taste of something, some trigger would spark a whole field of detail.

"Can you tell me about the van?"

"It was white, all over...like a butcher's van." She began to cry.

"Thank you, Mrs Wray. That may be important, it may be nothing...but we'll check that. If you remember anything more..."

She nodded as her husband came forward, grey-faced and tight-lipped, to put an arm round her and gather her into the car. Lynch hurried to his own Volvo and drove back to Chester, stopping at 'The Miller's' public house for a Kaliber lager and a bowl of oxtail soup, which he only ate after a few seconds' silent prayer.

* * *

"Another busy afternoon clinic ahead," thought Power as he crunched across the gravel towards his car. He had been working on his book all morning and had dined on lentil soup. Now there was just time to race to the hospital for his outpatient clinic. With the extra time he was giving to Lynch's investigation it seemed there was always a backlog of clinical work to catch up on.

The summer had moved into a glowing July. His working relationship with Jones had cooled down to a simmering mutual discontent. In the corridors and on the wards the two were civil, but nothing more. In his personal relationships, Eve had taken to spending more and more time with Power, but still resisted his idea that she could settle there. The couple seemed easier together, because Eve had finally decided how much she could trust him.

Eve had taken to moving easily about the house, coming and going as she pleased. When they wanted to be together or apart they were. Their individual homes had changed over the weeks, modified to suit the other's tastes. Eve's flat was noticeably less tidy. Occasionally Power's old newspapers, copies of the *British Medical Journal* and discarded socks could be found littering the floor of her bedroom. Power's living-room was noticeably tidier and often filled with bowls of fresh-cut flowers.

This gentle July morning Eve had crept into his bed as dawn broke. They had made love and luxuriated in each other's warmth. Satisfying one hunger was one thing, but when a sublime thought of fried bacon, tomatoes, and fresh white bread danced into Power's head, the image was so succulent he could almost taste and smell it. He hurried into the warm bathroom, showered, then ran downstairs to the kitchen where he made breakfast for two. Eve left as Power was settling to his work on the word processor.

Now it was after lunch, getting late and his clinic was booked up. Power looked at his watch as he approached his car. "Oh God," he murmured to himself – partly because of the time, but mainly because of his car. The Saab's nearside tyre was completely flat. The car listed to starboard. Power gloomily and automatically wondered if the spare tyre was adequate, indeed, whether there was a spare tyre. He would need the tools. Now, hadn't he taken them inside for some odd job in June? The inconvenience of it all provoked him to cry "Damn!" out loud, which made him feel marginally better so he repeated the experiment, "Damn!".

Then he looked down at the tyre itself. Seeing something amiss, he inspected it more closely still. This was no slow, overnight puncture. The tyre had been slashed. A neat cut, about three inches long had been made just above the wheel rim. Sometime last night someone must have stolen up the drive and deliberately knifed the Saab's tyre. He looked over at Eve's car. Each tyre was intact. Instinctively he looked about him, but he knew he would see nobody watching him. Whoever it had been would have long since gone.

Feeling hunted, Power stormed back into the house and set about searching for his tools. Having found these he realised he would have to cancel his appointments. From the hall phone he rang up his secretary, Laura and explained the situation. She was sincerely sympathetic, "Can you try and cancel my clinic, Laura?"

"You've got an appointment with Dr Jones at four-thirty. Would you like me to cancel that as well?"

"Oh...I was trying to remember what I had on...I couldn't remember that."

"I shouldn't think you'll be too upset about missing it," said Laura.

A noise from outside intruded.

A sort of understated deep bass thud. It was nearby though and close enough for the impact to be felt in the pit of Power's stomach. The smile disappeared off Power's face and he dropped the phone. Laura found she was talking into silence.

Power ran to the front door, opened it, and was faced with a thick acrid cloud of black smoke. He coughed. His eyes ran. He felt heat on his face. The billowing jet black cloud drifted with the breeze and beyond it Power could see orange flame cascading upwards into the sky, like a fiery waterfall in reverse. In the midst of the fireball the green Saab blackened and twisted and melted. Power could feel the hot, dry air sliding down his throat like a knife and down into his lungs. He shut the heavy front door hurriedly. After the fire-ball the house seemed dark and cold.

He picked up the phone. Laura had rung off. He punched in the number for the fire services. "My car...it's exploded!" He shouted as the voice answered. The calm voice at the other end seemed unaffected by

his agitation. Was this such an everyday occurrence that the telephon-
ist was simply immune to Power's panic?

After he had answered all the questions Power sat down on the
nearest chair. He had begun to shake. His initial disordered thoughts
were not how lucky he was not to have been trapped in the blazing car,
but rather that he had lost something like an old friend. The Saab had
been engulfed, destroyed in seconds. He had seen its metal skeleton
wracked by the heat. He remembered the students who had shared
journeys with him in the old Saab; to the University, to parties, and
home. He recalled the girlfriends he had kissed in the car. There was
the time he'd slept in the Saab when a tent had blown away on an
ill-fated continental holiday.

Only later did his angry tears give way to a more rational fear.
The slashed tyre and the explosion had both been manufactured by
someone.

* * *

The Emergency Services operator had taken the precaution of
requesting all three services, fire, police and ambulance to attend the
explosion at Alderley Edge. By the time the fire appliance had arrived,
the Saab was a blackened skeleton surrounding a few flickering flames
as the last of the upholstery and carpet turned into ash. The yellow
sandstone front of Alderley House was blackened with soot from the
explosion of the petrol tank. The police were already searching the
area for hidden explosives and clues as to how the bomb had been detonated. The local force had alerted the bomb disposal team, which was
on standby in Liverpool minutes away at the other end of the M62.

The ambulance man looked down at Power. Power lay on the
hall floor, breathing noisily, his reddened, shiny face smudged with
carbon and devoid of eyebrows. "You got caught in the flash." It was a
statement of fact.

"I'm all right," said Power, not moving. He was vaguely aware of
the uniformed men that milled about him.

The ambulance man was experienced. His grey hair spoke of

many years dealing with the victims of accidents, crimes and sudden illness. His voice was calm as he tried to assess how badly Power was burned. It looked superficial...a few flash burns...the victim must have only been exposed to the blast for a few seconds. "What's your name, mate?"

"Dr Power." He looked up, saw the wrinkles at the corner of the ambulance man's eyes. He thought about saying something and changed his mind. His thoughts seemed to be far away and he no longer seemed to care. He felt unreal, as if time had slowed to a meaningless crawl.

"If you're a medical doctor you'll know you're not all right, even if you say so."

"I'm all right. I'm waiting for Superintendent Lynch. He'll sort all this out."

"You're not waiting for any policeman. You need to be seen in hospital."

"I'm all right, I've told you." He thought about standing up and walking away to prove the point, but suddenly realised he couldn't make the effort.

"I worked at the Manchester air disaster, remember that? It was years ago, but I don't forget. I saw what smoke inhalation can do. Listen to yourself...wheezing away."

Power listened as he drew an experimental breath. The air made a strangled whistling noise in his throat and chest. When he breathed out it was as if his chest was an old squeeze box squeaking a final sigh. "Maybe you're right," he conceded.

"It's the smoke and the heat...you breathed it all in."

"When I opened the door...yes."

"Come on then, Doc," the ambulance man said kindly. They brought him a stretcher for he was too weak to stand and his chest had begun to ache. The ambulance men exchanged glances, but said nothing. "You asthmatic, Doc?"

"Cats...only with cats." Suddenly Power was finding he didn't have enough air to talk. They settled him in the ambulance and strapped an oxygen mask to his face. They were talking but Power could no longer hear them properly. Somebody had stuffed his ears with cotton wool. He was feeling very tired.

"Just 24% oxygen. I'll radio in." The driver looked at Power. "Better be quick. He's losing consciousness."

* * *

The bed felt rather hard and there weren't enough sheets. He shivered. Something tugged at his arm as he tried to roll over in bed. There was a clatter and the noise of cheery shouting in the distance. Power stretched his feet out and encountered the hard uncompromising metal if the footboard. Groggily he came to. He was propped semi-upright on pillows as comfortable as hard sacks of grain. On opening his eyes he gradually realised that he was not in his bedroom at home. The surroundings seemed familiar though, because this was undoubtedly a hospital side-ward. He stared over at the other three beds. The occupants seemed to be either in the process of getting up or unconscious. A young boy opposite lay dead to the world, a drip posted by his side on a dripstand.

Power looked at his right arm. Here too a yellow venflon had been used to give him a drip. He followed the clear, curling tube that ran from his veins up to the nearly-empty bag of saline that hung on Power's own dripstand. That was what had been pulling at his arm. If he craned his neck he could read the intravenous additive label the house officer had stuck on the saline bag. "Hydrocortisone 200mg. Aminophylline 250mg." Shouldn't be given together, he thought critically, but shrugged it off. He was alive that was what mattered. He ran his attention over the various parts of his body. His legs felt okay, his trunk too. His chest seemed a bit tight, but not as bad as...when? How long had he been here? He remembered the ambulance man. Nothing else. His left wrist was hurting. He looked down at it. It was bruised and several small brown puncture marks peppered the skin overlying his radial artery. 'They must have been taking my arterial blood gasses,' he thought. 'Christ, I must have been really ill.' His burnt face smarted too from where the explosion had scorched his skin. He recalled telling the ambulance man he was alright. 'I'm a bloody fool,' he thought.

A staff nurse came by. "Oh, you're awake now."

He uttered the classic line and smiled at himself. "Where am I?"

"M.2." she said, looking at the drip. Power was none the wiser. "This bag is nearly finished. I wonder if there's another one made up in the fridge."

"When did I come in?"

"Yesterday," she said, moving away.

The nurse was already halfway down the ward. "What time is it?" he called out after her.

"Breakfast time," a student nurse was standing by his bed. "You're a little bit late, but I don't think sister will mind if you have a bite to eat then get washed."

"Have I been in here for a whole twenty-four hours?"

"Oh no," she said cheerily as she put a roll and butter in front of him. "You were on intensive care until last night. Do you want tea or coffee?"

"Coffee. Black, please."

She fetched him a cup. It tasted marvellous, but he winced as he drank. His throat felt sore. He wanted to ask if he'd been intubated on intensive care. Had he been that ill? She was more excited to tell him something else. "There's police outside. Been one here ever since you came in. You done anything wrong, then?"

"Is he a Superintendent?"

"No..." she laughed. "It's a WPC. Keeping guard. What you done then?"

"Nothing." He was tired of her. He wished she would go and leave him to the stale bread roll that passed for breakfast. There wasn't even any jam.

They put up another bag of hydrocortisone solution. "Just to be sure." And after a hour or two of trying to piece together what had happened to him, the house officer came by. Her hair was untidy, her eyes were red and her white coat and skirt looked as though she had slept in them. In fact she had. She looked pale and tired. Too tired to be burdened by his questions. She listened perfunctorily to Power's chest and pronounced it free of wheeze. He felt a bit of a fraud. "Have you been on call all night?" She nodded wearily. "Much sleep?" She shook her head and staggered off. Maybe somebody else would tell him what had happened, Power hoped.

At eleven o'clock a tall, dark-suited Detective Sergeant, who had just arrived on the ward, managed to persuade the sister to let him ask Power 'a few questions'. Power watched Sergeant Beresford as he found a chair and sat by Power's bedside. He introduced himself. Power knew that Lynch relied heavily on this man, but up till now he had been largely unaware of him. Unaware except for the time he chatted up Power's secretary, Laura. They regarded one another warily. Beresford found the idea of talking to a psychiatrist unsettling. They always said they couldn't read your mind then seemed to proceed to do just that. He decided to hide behind questions. "Glad to see you're better, Doctor. Can I ask you a few questions?"

"If I can ask you a few questions too," said Power who was feeling thoroughly bemused by his last few days, if not weeks.

"No, I meant, if you were well enough to talk."

"Quite willing. Fire away."

"It's about the fire bomb..."

Power seized on the information and interrupted. "It was a bomb then?"

Beresford nodded. He could appreciate why Lynch liked working with this man. Both of them were direct, certain of themselves. If Lynch was a maverick police officer then Power seemed to complement him. Power had these most penetrating eyes and he seemed to hang on every word. Beresford felt a bit more uncomfortable, as if he was under the microscope. "It was a bomb, yes. We found a radio-controlled device just under the petrol tank."

"Because just before it went off I noticed the tyre was flat."

"Ah..." Beresford reached into his pocket and took out a small voice-activated tape recorder to catch what Power was saying. "Beats a notebook." He explained.

"Well," said Power. "When I came out to the car I saw the tyre had been slashed. So I had to go indoors to get my tools and phone the hospital...to tell them I'd be delayed, you know, while I fixed the tyre."

"See anyone about?" Power shook his head. "And you're sure the tyre had been tampered with?"

"Of course I'm sure. There was a four or five inch rip in it. I thought it was a malicious trick, a prank of some sort...you know I meet some strange people...have to do court reports on some nasty types...I thought perhaps...that...but, I never thought that someone would try and kill me. You know bomb the car."

"No, we don't think they were trying to kill you. Superintendent Lynch doesn't think so anyway."

"But they exploded my car!" Power looked as if he might explode too.

"But it was a radio-controlled bomb. Whoever it was waited until you were safely in the house before they detonated the device. They wanted to explode the car, not you."

Power thought about it. "But that would mean they had to be watching me...to know whether I was by the car or in the house. Someone had to be watching."

"That's right." A dumpy lady volunteer with a tea trolley clattered her way up to the bed and offered some tea. They both asked for some. She turned to the police officer.

"You can't have tea, love. It's only for the patients."

"Oh, I'm like part of the staff," he said charmingly.

"They don't get none either," she declared and gave Power his tea before stumping off. "There you are, doctor. Hope you're better soon, love."

"Only the best..." muttered the Sergeant in her wake. "Right, well...back to more mundane matters. We know that whoever set off the device was close by. In fact, he was just over the other side of that stone wall of yours. We found that the earth there and the grasses had been trampled down. He must have been waiting for a few hours, wanting you to see the tyre, go back inside, then trigger the device.

"He used one of those things like for a car alarm...you know you can turn it on and off with a thing that goes on your key ring. You can switch it on and off from about thirty feet away. Not far...but he would have stayed behind that solid wall during the blast. I believe you opened the door of the house...got caught by the heat?"

"That's right."

"You ever had connections with Irish terrorists?" Power shook his head. "Or Animal Liberation people? Ever done any research on animals?"

"I dissected a few rats as a sixth-form student along with thousands of others," said Power. "Nothing more sensational."

"Ever been the target of this kind of thing before?"

"Not bombs! I've had letters...from different people over the years. Abusive phone calls from ex-patients. Threats from people when I wouldn't admit them or give them some psychiatric let-out when they went to court. So many really."

Beresford's face fell, "Over the years?" How many grudges were there against this doctor?

"Yes...an assortment. When people are unwell they often get a kind of fixation...we call it transference...to their doctor. They feel all sorts of things for him or her...love, sympathy, anger, hate."

"Any recent letter we could think about?"

"I can pass the letters from the last few months on. One stood out though. Addressed to my home address. Patients don't usually do that. Takes some researching to get your home address."

"What did it say?"

" It said I was at the end of the road or something like that. No, it said 'You're at the end of the line, Power.' I think it's all connected you know."

"What is?" Detective Beresford was lost.

"The murders and this bomb. It's all connected."

"How? I know you're helping Lynch, but this bomb...well, we have to rule out what you're saying. That's why I'm involved, but to tell you the truth, Doctor, it's more likely to be a personal attack. How do these murders fit in with it? Why can't the two events be completely separate? You got hate mail before the murders started after all."

"I have a feeling..." Power went on. Beresford tried to keep a straight face. "...have you ever heard of synchronicity?"

"You what?"

"It's an acausal connecting principle that Jung..."

"The two events aren't connected though. Except in that you're the subject of one attack and advising the police about something else." Beresford tried to reassure Power. If you thought about these things too long you would mis-trust your own shadow. "What was it you said...'synchronism'?"

"Synchronicity."

"Wasn't that a song by someone?"

"Yes, it was an album by 'The Police'"

"Oh yes..." Beresford grinned. "You were having a little joke with me weren't you, doctor?"

"No, I was being serious."

Beresford laughed. "Well, well..." he said. "I must be going. Your local force is keeping a police guard on you for now. For your safety. Tail it off after a few days. Don't worry. I don't think they meant you any real harm. Just wanted to frighten you."

"They succeeded," said Power. Beresford laughed dutifully again. He never knew when Power was joking. "Before you go, Sergeant. Where's Lynch? I was expecting to see..."

"He's a bit busy. Gone up to Durham to a see a remand prisoner. Apparently this man's confessing to all four murders, the girl, the boy, the forester and the owner of that poisoned flesh we found on Eddisbury Hill."

"I'd like to have gone with him."

"I'm sure. But you're still not right are you, sir? And anyway, this is the umpteenth confession we've had so far. All of them fakers. Oh, and he's got us looking for a white van now." By 'he' Beresford meant Lynch. "He doesn't know the make or year yet though. Does he know how many white vans there are?" He shook Power's hand and left. As he passed the nursing station he noticed the blue-garbed sister.

"That Dr Power...the psychiatrist, you know?"

"Yes." She looked at Beresford warily.

"Does he always talk like that? He didn't have a bump on the head or anything?

"Don't think so. What's wrong?" She got on with filling in a segment of a patient's nursing notes.

"He didn't make much sense to me. Rambled on, making connections where there aren't any. Very odd."

She looked up again and gave the police officer a 'professional', all-knowing smile. "I'll ask the house officer to check him over, Sergeant."

"Perhaps it just rubs off on them...working with the mad, I mean." She ignored his semi-joke and went on with her work. Her bleep began to go off. Beresford shrugged his shoulders and left the ward, more puzzled than when he had arrived. Could Power be right in assuming that all the events were related? Back in his hospital bed though, Power was even more discomforted by events. He wondered if there was a phone he could use.

The ward was getting hot in the late morning sun. Power got up from his bed while the nurses weren't looking and pottered around the bed, pulling the dripstand behind him like a dog on a lead. He opened the ward window nearest to him as wide as it would go, then drew the blinds. They rattled slightly in the breeze. He drew in a deep lungful of air and coughed. His chest still wasn't one hundred per cent. Wrapping his dressing-gown around him he sat down in a chair by the coolth that the window provided. Someone must have brought the dressing-gown in; he wondered who.

"A penny for your thoughts?" Power looked up and smiled at the face above his chair. She bent down and kissed him. Her lips were cool and gentle upon his scorched cheeks. It was Eve. "The sister let me through even though it wasn't visiting. She seems a nice soul. She was a bit concerned about you. Thought the explosion might have given you a knock on the head."

"Well, my thoughts haven't been making overmuch sense I agree. How are things?"

She sat down on his bed and unloaded an armful of cards and fruit. "Fine...they took away your car...you wouldn't really know that there had been anything wrong. I've had the windows that were damaged replaced." Power nodded, he hadn't registered any breaking glass in the confusion of the blast. "Just the scorch marks on the walls left and I suppose the creeper looks a bit charred at the edges. A bit like you."

"You all right?"

"Me?...I'm fine." She didn't sound particularly fine, but Power didn't probe. "I'm getting used to the police searching through everything and asking all kinds of questions." Power nodded distantly. There was a pause, and unlike other pauses between them, this one felt uncomfortable. It was as if a blue sky was beginning to cloud over. Power felt uneasy. She tried saying, "I miss you." But it didn't sound right, as if part of her was glad he wasn't there.

Power looked away, out of the window. There was something about her he'd never realised before. About the way she acted...always a little guarded as if there was something unsaid between them. He felt it now more than ever. The enforced separation seemed to have highlighted it in some way. How much can anyone know another person? How much are we individual islands in a sea of society? What should he do to make things right? His fault was that he couldn't stop trying to heal people, to turn them into patients. He felt confused and unable to cope. Coming to terms with everything that had happened in the last few months was taking its toll on his reserves.

In the end he said, "I miss you too." But it sounded empty and they both knew it. He tried again to get to something more hopeful "Perhaps...when I get out...I think there are things we need to talk about, if you want to...maybe a short break away somewhere nice?"

"I've got an exhibition...a retrospective to arrange for August.

I'm too busy." Dancing far apart.

"I see."

"Yes, I see too." She sounded brittle and he wanted her to leave him now. "Anyway, you've got to do your Sherlock Holmes bit. Lynch was asking about you."

"Is he coming here?"

"Don't know." And she didn't care.

After a few more conciliatory exchanges, they reached a compromise. Somewhere to work from next time, but Power was dreading it. Abruptly he had realised how much they had to work through together and it had come as rather a shock. Was he up to it? She'd done everything to help him, to care for him. He looked at the clean clothes, cards and fruit she'd brought him. And yet things needed working on. He watched her leaving the ward and felt guilty because he was relieved to be on his own again.

* * *

After a meal of leathery ham and cold boiled potato Power was getting restless. The senior house officer had listened to his chest and disconnected the drip. A trip down to X-ray had provided Power with a normal chest film and he was anxious to be off. Being on the receiving end of medicine and its rituals was not to Power's liking.

It was with relief then that he greeted the pin-striped consultant who had bounded onto the ward specially to see him. The other patients looked on enviously. They only saw the consultant once a week. To tell the truth they were all a bit put out by the attention the sick doctor attracted. He didn't mix much either, and he read *The Independent.*

"Well, Dr Power," Dr Parkes sat down by his patient's bed. "You're lucky to be alive. Nasty case of Adult Respiratory Distress Syndrome. Rather unusual. Mind you, Doctors can't have anything too mundane. My SHO says you're back to normal now though. Good powers of recovery, if you'll pardon the expression." Power smiled thinly. "When do you want to be going?"

"Now. Is that possible?" To Power's joy, the consultant agreed.

"I want to see you in my rooms in a few weeks. Do some respiratory function tests. That okay?" Power nodded. He felt that if he didn't agree the consultant wouldn't discharged him. He had no intention of keeping the appointment though. Power was a good doctor, but a very bad patient.

Power expected the consultant to go now he had made his magical appearance and muttered his benediction and dismissal. The physician seemed disposed to stay however. He seemed to be trying, unsuccessfully to formulate some sentence. Eventually he overcame his embarrassment.

"I have to thank you Dr Power. We all have to thank you."

"Thank me?" Power was incredulous. It was not as if he was Royalty gracing a hospital after breaking a limb at some polo match.

"Yes," said Dr Parkes. "You treated my niece. She'd stopped eating. You know, Susan, you discharged her a week ago."

The names and the memories connected. "Oh yes...you mean Susan Parkes. She's your niece?" Power was struck by the connection between two different parts of his life. There seemed so many coincidences in life, more in real life than you'd believe in any novel. He had felt the connections between the bomb and the murders. To him they were as real as this coincidence of consultant niece. And yet Power hadn't been able to convince Beresford of any links between the arson attack and the murders. Power wanted to see Lynch.

Dr Parkes was talking about his anorexic niece. "She's a different girl now, thanks to you. Got some flesh on her bones. You know, there was a time when I thought she was going to die. For a time I thought she had some wasting disease." He lowered his voice in case anyone else should hear. "Never thought psychiatrically, of course. Don't think to, you see. Not in your own family."

"You're close to Susan then?" Power probed.

"Yes, we live quite close by my brother. Susan and I were very close before...before she started to slim." He started to say something else, but stopped himself. He frowned, then carried on as if no doubts had troubled him. "I was very pleased at the work you'd done."

"It isn't started yet. There's more work to be done."

"What do you mean?" The consultant physician looked perplexed as if Susan's weight was the be all and end all. "What do you need to work on?"

"That's between Susan and I, if you don't mind me saying."

"No, of course not. I was just..."

"And thank you," said Power. "Thank you for everything. I've no doubt you saved my life...well..." Power felt awkward. "I'll be going then, and I'll take my police escort with me." They shook hands. Power watched Parkes as he walked away. He looked unsettled. Power wondered why he, Power, had to go and unsettle everybody?

* * *

A police car, not an ambulance, sped him back to his house in Alderley Edge. Pleased to be there he took a tour of the rooms, revelling in the appearance of home.

He was pleasantly surprised to see that all was as he had left it. The police constable who had escorted him home had talked about the anti-terrorist squad having been asked to search Alderley House. This search had been minutely conducted. They were anxious to find any traces of explosive, suspecting that the house as well as the car may have been booby-trapped. Power imagined the sniffer dogs moving from room-to-room, nosing through cupboards and sniffing at the chairs. Yet even the knowledge of this invasion and the current presence of the police constable waiting and watching at the gate did not detract greatly from the pleasure of being alive and home.

He sank onto the settee and his mind roamed free. His body might rest, but his mind was embarked upon a quest and it would not cease its travels until it had found the solution that linked it all together...the murders...the bomb attack...the coincidences of the past few months. It seemed a mammoth task that dwarfed him. His attention focussed on the dog dream he had had. In the past few nights the dream had recurred several times, each time frightening him with its theme of pursuit. He could see the dog's jaws snapping at him. His mind flowed to think about the coincidence of meeting Susan's uncle, Dr Parkes. In all these ideas what was the important seed and what was the redundant husk?

Power felt satisfied that he had achieved the cure of the anorexic girl. 'Why should this thought be so satisfying? What was it about doctors that they should want to heal people? We need our patients,' thought Power. 'Why do I need to heal?'

And the murder enquiry, and the bombing...somebody wanting to frighten him...terrify him, but not actually kill him...why did he want to link them up and solve the crime? Perhaps because all the acts reeked of sickness...like some festering infection that challenged the doctor in Power. In trying to find the solution Power was trying to heal again. He would heal himself and others by solving the mystery, by destroying the focus of the fiery infection.

Struck by this insight Power suddenly felt hungry and eager to begin his quest once more. He went to raid the fridge. Finding it bereft of anything vaguely tempting Power slammed the fridge door. He wondered if the policeman would accompany him if he went to the take away.

To add to the coincidences of Power's day the doorbell rang. When he opened the front door it was Lynch who filled the porch. In one hand he held a brown paper carrier bag, in the other a plastic bag from the off-licence.

"Can we talk? I hope you're not too tired after the hospital. "

Power shook his head and smiled. "What have you got there?"

He nodded at the bags. "If it's what I think it is," said Power sniffing the air, "you must be telepathic."

"No I'm not telepathic, I'm just getting to know you Carl." He lifted up first one bag then the other. "Chinese food...junk food and... beer. I'm sure you're rather fond of both."

Power was warmed by his friend's humour. Laughing, Power invited him in. And whilst Power ate and drank, the abstemious Superintendent drank mineral water, (knowing that his wife would have some supper waiting for him at home). They talked about the investigation, about the false confession that Lynch had just heard in Durham. As friends now they were beginning to work well together. They would have to if they were to stand any chance of scenting their quarry.

NINE

Superintendent Lynch wiped the last smear of the Lancashire Hot Pot off the plate with a hunk of brown bread. If anything the Hot Pot had only been improved by its lengthy sojourn in the oven. The potato slices on top had crisped to a glorious brown, and the lamb, carrots and onions had reduced to a marvellous sauce beneath. Mrs Lynch was well aware that food cooked for her husband had to be designed to endure long waiting. Unlike the food, she could not endure waiting for her husband whilst he was caught up on an investigation. Prudently she had retired to bed, leaving the Hot Pot in the oven on a very low light. It was a wise decision, for when Lynch returned from Headquarters she had already been asleep for two hours.

Lynch sat alone at the dining-room table. Downstairs all was quiet. Darkness, except from the glow of the kitchen, had greeted him when he entered. It had been twelve hours since he had last eaten. He mused about Dr Power. Power didn't seem to be able to go without food for five minutes. Lynch wondered how Power stayed so slim given his appetite. Perhaps Power was an anxious type and worried all the calories away. Lynch wondered whether he could manage a pudding, then wondered what there might be in the kitchen. He stood up from the table and carried his empty plates out of the dining-room.

He passed through the dark hallway. He heard the muffled music coming from his teenage daughter's room. For the last few months she had been touring India. She'd taken a year off between finishing school and a going up to Cambridge to read Law. For twelve glorious months she had done as she wished. Lynch had had reservations, particularly about her plans to tour India by train alone. He'd thought about putting his foot down. He'd imagined having to go out to India to search for her or bail her out or something of that ilk. He was surprised and gloriously happy to see her return in one piece, looking thinner, happier and wiser. She was even beginning to study again to get herself 'back into the swim'. Wonders would never cease, he thought.

He found a tin of peach halves and emptied it into a bowl. This he took into the lounge with a cup of decaffeinated coffee. It was getting late. He wondered about phoning Carl Power, but hesitated. They had only just talked, but the conversation was buzzing around Lynch's mind. Lynch didn't want to burden him and at this hour he might well be asleep. Then he thought of a way round the problem. He phoned the Alderley Edge police station and asked them to radio the constable they had placed at Power's gate. The Desk Sergeant answered Lynch's enquiry efficiently, "Our officer says that Dr Power's lights are still burning. Seen him moving about a few minutes ago." Lynch looked at his watch. It was midnight. He knew that whatever his enthusiasms he should let Power rest. And he would have to force himself to rest. The Desk Sergeant went on, "I'll be pulling the constable out from Dr Power's tonight. Won't be continuing the vigil from tonight. Can't keep twenty-four hour watch. Budget won't allow it."

"That's the way," commiserated Lynch who was himself, facing some questions about the budget of the murder enquiry. "Everything these days seems to involve some risk. I myself think that it was... someone who wanted to scare the good doctor rather than kill him. Still, that's only our judgement. It's Dr Power who has to live without police protection. It's him who's being made to take the risk, not us." Lynch wished the Sergeant good night and rang off.

He sat down on the sofa with his coffee and kicked his shoes off. He might read a little before bed. He would read downstairs rather than disturb his wife. As he picked up his copy of Power's book the murder still dominated his mind. During a murder enquiry Lynch found it difficult to settle to anything else. He loved cricket, and yet this year he was unable to focus on the Test match. He thought about what Mrs Wray had said at the funeral. It was one of the only new leads he had. Using her information about a white van Lynch had featured the Foel fenlii murder on the *Crimewatch* programme. He was looking for witnesses; not necessarily to the murder, but to anything that went on in the car park. The mountain was quite deserted really. The only road that went nearby was a single lane track that ran through the car park and down the other side of the mountain. Lynch knew that the murderer must have used the car park. Accordingly the car park was featured on the *Crimewatch* programme. There were about a hundred telephone reports from people who been in the car park in the week of the murder. Several came from a coach of tourists that had been passing through on June 23rd.

Two people on the coach remembered seeing a white van. And a retired colonel and a lady in a separate car who had been there the day before saw it too. Of the other reports, none really matched. And after Sergeant Beresford asked the forestry workers they remembered the white van too. The problem was that nearly all the people gave a different make of van. It was either a Vauxhall or a Renault or a Ford. Its number plate was a Y or a B or an A.

To confuse matters further the discoverer of the forester's body, Mr Ball, had driven a white van. Lynch had interviewed the indignant man himself. He was upset at being treated like a murder suspect, and more so at having to provide alibis for all the known dates of the murders. On the whole, having checked these alibis out, Lynch felt that Ball was not a prime candidate for their suspicions.

Lynch felt that he was shadow-boxing with the murderer. All that he could see was the man's shadow...what was left after he had passed by. Lynch could only ever hope to find him by considering the man's acts...or his ritual as Power put it. 'By their fruits ye shall know them'.

And now, Lynch held the glossily-backed fruits of Power's labours in his hands. *The Unconscious Mind* by Dr Carl Power. A Heart of Darkness or a Heart of Light? Lynch opened the book and found his place.

'I have shown how the mind can cope with the most unpleasant thoughts and described Freud's work on psychological defence mechanisms. The Unconscious Mind may reduce the psychological hurt that acknowledging murderous impulses or motives may cause the conscious mind. The purpose of this mechanism is to prevent the overwhelming nature of anger and aggression that threatened to possess the individual.

'The most extreme act of aggression is murder. How do the minds of people cope with the nature of this heinous crime? How do people come to terms with what they have done?

'The act of murder usually results in a corpse and a murder investigation in the here and now. But the 'act' has a life of its own – a past and a future – before the crime in the aggressive impulses and fantasies of the murderer and after in the distress of relatives and for the murderer, the way he or she acknowledges, or fails to acknowledge, his or her act or the motives for it.

'To illustrate let me take the cases of three individuals who committed murder: a psychotic patient, a mentally handicapped woman, and a person of normal intelligence with no psychiatric illness.

'CASE A: A 46 year old man; a quiet, controlled person who was a rigid perfectionist in his work as a town planning clerk, and a perfectionist in his hobby of model plane making, became suddenly aware of his wife's infidelity. This fact disordered his regular existence and destroyed his lifelong composure. In an uncharacteristic blazing fury he argued with his wife, becoming so heated that his neighbours two doors away overheard him. In an escalating temper he lashed out at his wife with a poker, fracturing her skull and damaging various intracerebral arteries. He was picked up by the police in a town two hundred miles away, wandering aimlessly with a vacant expression on his face. He claimed not to remember his own name, address, job or any other personal detail. This appeared to be a hysterical fugue state. His unconscious mind would not let him be overwhelmed by the painful memories of his crime. Over the next few days his unconscious mind leaked more and more details into his consciousness. After three days in hospital he made a full confession to the police who were able then to link him with the murder two hundred miles away.

'CASE B: A mentally handicapped woman of eighteen with an I.Q. of 70 had been physically and sexually abused over a number of years by a care worker in a local authority home. In the early hours of the morning she stole out of her bed and went to the separate wing of the home where she knew this member of staff was sleeping. She lit a fire downstairs in the sitting room below his bedroom. It was a small fire, made of a mound of shredded newspaper and cardboard, set near the sofa. She waited until the paper had caught fire and then went back to bed. The fire spread to the foam in the sofa and very soon the staff block was destroyed.

'When interviewed the woman resident said that she had set the fire, but that she hadn't killed the worker. She attributed a 'life of its own' to the fire. It was the fire 'who' had jumped from the papers to the sofa. It was the fire's fault, not hers. In this we can see errors in logical thinking, perhaps secondary to learning difficulty, but also a clear attempt to "rationalise" away her guilt.

'CASE C: A psychotic woman of 36 was seen in a prison cell by a forensic psychiatrist. She was on remand for allegedly stabbing her brother to death. When she was questioned she admitted stabbing him and laughed. "You see, " she said, "he was not my brother. He was the devil himself. He looked like my brother...exactly like my brother in every way...same clothes...same face...same hair. But he was a replica of my brother. Just looked like him. That's all. I knew he was the devil impersonating my brother. So I stabbed him."

'In case C the woman, who had paranoid schizophrenia, had the well-documented Capgras symptom (or l'illusion des sosies) where a close individual is misperceived as being an impostor or double. Dostoevsky's *The Possessed* contains an example - "You're like him, very like him, perhaps you're a relation - only mine is a bright falcon and you're an owl and a shopman".

'In case C the psychotic unconscious sanctions an aggressive act towards the brother on the basis that he is not the real brother. There may have been a real grudge towards her brother that she was not permitted to express in any other way. [See delusions; dangerousness and acting out].

'In this way we see how the state of mind before the act of aggression is part of a continuum that runs to the act itself and the state of mind after the act. All too often we focus on one of the aspects to the exclusion of the others.'

Lynch closed the book, having marked his place. It was twelve-thirty. He closed his eyes for a moment's prayer. He prayed that his wife and children would forgive his single-minded determination to hunt his quarry, that Power would be given the insight that would help them catch him, and that the relatives of the victims would be given some comfort. This done he switched off the lights downstairs and climbed the stairs to bed. His wife stirred slightly as he climbed into her warm bed. She reached over to him and they cuddled in the darkness.

* * *

Power had had a bath, on his way downstairs Power looked out of the landing window and down the drive. The lone policeman had gone off duty and, as Power had been expecting, had not been replaced. Tomorrow he planned to go back to work. Staying around home any more would frustrate him. He needed his work and his patients, because he had this compulsion to heal. It wasn't altruistic, it was a deep-down drive, and he couldn't survive without his patients.

Power had furnished the living room sparely. Two green wing-back chairs flanked the fireplace. The grate was empty except for dried flowers. It was late summer now and Power was thinking of having the chimney swept. He fantasised about having a roaring fire in the grate on winter evenings. Tonight though the weather had been hot and now only in the early hours of the morning was it getting cool again. Next to the fireplace were bookshelves groaning under Power's collection of novels. In front of the fire, between the sentinel chairs a Nepalese rug in red and green covered the woodblock floor.

Over by the window, crouched on an Ottoman and surrounded by cushions sat Power. A barleysugar standard lamp illuminated him with a cone of light. Despite the aching heat of the day Power had, by now, wrapped a duvet around his shoulders for the cloudless night was cold. He looked at his watch, 2 a.m. Like the fire he hoped to build in the grate his mind had been leaping like a flame, licking at first one idea and then another. Power had been concentrating on the mind of a murderer. The only way to catch him was to understand the murderer's thoughts, Lynch had made that plain. Exactly what motivated the murderer though was almost impossible for anyone to conceive. Power was nearer than he imagined, but after a busy day back at work and with the lateness of the hour, Power's flames of thought had reduced to glowing embers.

The key was in the murderer's mind. What compulsion drives him to commit these things? How could Power penetrate an unseen, unknown mind? Were these random killings? If so, then no-one and nowhere was safe until he was caught. And yet what Lynch had said... that perhaps the murderer watched his victims before...that spoke of planning and pre-meditation. Hardly random therefore...there must be a rationale. There was the method the murderer used. Hardly random either. Power felt frustrated...if there was a rationale or a link...what was it? The Yorkshire Ripper had tried to focus on prostitutes...there was the link there. But what link was there between a boy, a teenage girl, a forestry worker and another as yet undiscovered victim? They were a random choice...unrelated to each other...or at least no-one could see the relationship between them all. It was like a fire burning out of control.

He tried to think of it another way. He put aside the profiles of the victims, the site of crime reports the forensic psychiatry texts and other documents Lynch had copied for him. Think of it another way. Where did the murderer live? Alderley Edge and Eddisbury Hill were in easy reach of dual carriageways and motorways to Warrington, Manchester and Liverpool. Manchester was half-an-hour away. Liverpool three quarters of an hour. Even Birmingham was only an hour and a half away in a fast car.

Power rootled in a drawer for his set of Ordnance Survey maps. He had a full set covering the North West from the days when he was more keen about walking as a sport. He sat back down on the Ottoman and spread the 1:50 000 map of Stoke-on-Trent on the floor in front of him. Alderley Edge lay at the northernmost margin, south of Manchester, west of Knutsford and east of Macclesfield. He looked at the country villages around: Nether Alderley, Mottram St. Andrew, Adders Moss. Just east of the village of Alderley Edge was the ancient, sharply defined Edge marked on the map in close brown parallel lines. Power could see his own house marked by a tiny square near the 'M' in 'Old Mine'. The other places, where were they? Eddisbury Hill? Foel fenlii?

He found and spread the map for Chester over the other. There was Eddisbury Hill, marked 'Fort' on the map. Nearby was the village of Delamere and north the once-great Delamere forest. Fast roads ran through the forest and led to the motorway network. By the hill lay the remnants of the straight Roman Road that had once run westwards to Chester. Just by the hill was the ominously named Hangingstone Hill. Another ancient site? Where was Foel fenlii? Another map altogether; the Denbigh map. He spread this out too. 'Fort' again marked the summit of the mountain, 511 feet high. Must have a good view, thought Power. You would be able to see down into the valley, down into the medieval market town of Ruthin, more English Tudor than Welsh. He looked at the town. More ancient sites...a Castle, a mound, a stone circle. A half-hour drive from here and you'd be on the M6. Two hours and you could be in London. The murderer could journey North from London, commit his crime, and be back home the same day. Possible, but hardly practical though. An idea was beginning to form in Power's mind.

How far was Foel fenlii from Eddisbury? It was a nuisance them all being on separate sheets of the Ordnance Survey. Perhaps, if he had the room, if he spread them out on the floor, edge to edge, corner to corner as they would be if you laid out all the map squares to form a huge map of the British Isles. He shuffled the maps around, managing in his tiredness to knock a balloon glass of brandy off a nearby table. He cursed as the thin globe of glass broke into pieces on the wooden floor.

Maybe it was no bad thing breaking the glass, he thought, as he headed for the kitchen to get a cloth, carefully carrying the shards of glass. He had drunk nearly a quarter bottle of brandy. It was time to go to bed. He was getting too tired to carry on. The ideas just roamed around in his mind and got nowhere. It was too late to try joining Eve in the flat below. In the kitchen, as he ran the water to dampen the cloth, he could hear the birds outside beginning to sing themselves awake. 'Go back to bloody sleep', he thought.

Intending to clear up in the living-room and then turn in, Power crossed over to the standard lamp to switch it off. He happened to glance down at the maps. Something caught his eye. And then the dying embers of thought that had smouldered into the morning light became a furious flame. He put the kettle on to make some strong coffee, then went searching for a ruler and a pencil. He was going to add

174

fuel to the flames.

* * *

In the morning Power prevailed upon Eve to give him a lift in to the hospital. They had largely patched up their differences on the phone the night before, but as always there was a fragility in the relationship that they were both wary of testing.

At the bottom of the long hill, before they turned right onto the A34 north to Wilmslow, Power asked Eve if she would stop outside the Merlin bookshop. There were some books he needed, to confirm his theory, and this sort of bookshop, (not the type usually frequented by Power), would be a dead certainty for the kind of books he wanted. Back in the car Eve saw the titles he had bought and approved. "There's another book I've got at home. Specifically about Cheshire too, by a vicar of all things. If you're nice to me I might lend it to you. Why are you interested in this all of a sudden. Not really your scene is it?" The question was part genuine and part needling. It highlighted some of the differences between them.

Power took the question at face value and told her all about his discoveries in the early hours, sitting with the maps like some god taking an overview of the world. Eve had to admit, albeit grudgingly, that she was fascinated (and chilled) by Power's idea. "It's like a ritual," she said.

"Exactly," said Power. "His secret ritual." He looked at the tree-lined road ahead and brooded. "I hope the clues are in these books here."

Eve was keen to get back home and find her own books. Perhaps she could solve the riddle before Power. She would like to do that. She was still angry with him, but she didn't know why. It was all locked away from her in her unconscious, and marked, 'Not to be opened'.

"When are you going to get another car?" she asked. "It's as if you haven't accepted that the Saab is dead and gone. Can you grieve for a car? I expect a psychiatrist should know."

"Of course I am in mourning." said Power. "But I'll survive."

She laughed at his maudlin tone. "You really loved that death trap didn't you?"

Power shuddered at her choice of words. A vivid image of the fireball flashed in front of him obliterating the reality of Wilmslow town centre. Eve was going left on the A 538 to Altrincham. In the sky to their right a Boeing 747 was rising into the blue through the shimmering air. But the image of fire persisted in Power's mind. He suddenly felt cold and afraid in the heat of the July day. Neither he nor Lynch had really paid enough attention to the attack on Power's car. If it had been the murderer, (and Power was certain it had been), then it was further evidence as to his state of mind. They were unwise to discount it so lightly. Why then were they doing so? Perhaps because the idea that they, the investigators, were threatened by the uncomfortable notion that they were vulnerable too. Perhaps the murderer felt even more vulnerable himself, that he needed to attack Power after the TV interview? What if the murderer had watched Power theorising about the murders and had felt that Power was so dangerous to him that he had to go? Or was there some other reason for the attack? Like the flames, the idea burned painfully in his mind. Power struggled to keep his composure and shrugged off the vision. "Er...well, I'm going to look at a car this afternoon."

"Oh, what kind are you going to get?"

"I'm going to look round a dealers...called 'Classic Cars'. They sell...well...they sell classic cars really."

"What are they when they're at home?" asked Eve. They were coming up to the hospital gates. Soon Power would be at work, treating his patients.

"Wait and see," he said and, as the car slowed, kissed Eve goodbye.

* * *

Two days later Power was sitting in his office dictating discharge letters on his patients. One copy went to the G.P. and the other was buried in the patient's case files. There were moves to computerise the system, and although Power was an enthusiast for computers he had reservations about the confidentiality of the machines. He had once watched an amateur hack his way into secret Ministry files with no apparent difficulty. Power's patients trusted him absolutely with their stories and confessions. He couldn't bear the idea that someone else might use his notes for their own ends.

Power had booked two tickets to the opera that night for Eve and himself. In addition to his desire to please Eve, he wanted to pay off the guilt he sometimes felt when he treated her less well than she deserved. He had been distant for the last few weeks. He had once felt so very certain that Eve was the only one for him. But in the last few weeks her vague ambivalence had been catching up with him. It was as if she was always holding something back from him. He felt cheated. At times he showed his frustration at being excluded from something hidden inside her. In booking the opera seats Power was deliberately being altruistic. There was something of the hair-shirt about opera as far as Power was concerned. He liked twentieth century classical music, but not opera, never opera. There was only one thing Power hated more than opera and that was ballet. He thought that the outing to please Eve would do his soul good. They planned on meeting that evening in Manchester for a meal before the show. The thought of an Italian meal and his own altruism pleased him.

But there were two other reasons for Power's general good humour. He had succeeded in buying a new car. He went over to the window to check it was still in its space in the car park and marvelled at its sleek black form.

The other reason for his happiness was the way that his theory about the murders seemed to have dovetailed so well with his researches in the various esoteric books from the Merlin bookstore. Eve's book had served to complete the picture. And having refined his theory Power now felt ready to unleash it.

* * *

Superintendent Lynch was less than content. The tabloid newspapers had got hold of a tape recording of someone who purported to be the man Lynch was seeking to arrest. He read the transcript with disbelief. "Superintendent Lynch, I'm so far ahead of you now that you haven't even got a clue. You might even say I've got a head start! I'll just keep on going till you catch me and I know you're so bloody incompetent that you'll never find me or the heads. I can just keep on going, but I'll give you one clue, Superintendent, to make your life easier. My name is Smith and I live in Northumberland. But remember I'm going to keep on killing until you get me."

Lynch had listened to the tape broadcast on the local radio. The male voice had an unmistakable Newcastle accent, but Lynch had worked there for several years when he had been a D.I. He knew there was something wrong with the accent. It was as fake as the Liverpool accents in television situation comedies.

"They can't be serious, can they?" asked Lynch as Detective Sergeant Beresford brought him some mid-afternoon tea.

"What's that, sir?"

"These newspaper people. They can't seriously believe this tape, can they? I can't believe they're willing to lead credence to this rubbish." Beresford made consoling noises as he set the cup of tea in front of Lynch. He knew that Lynch was more perturbed by the very personal attacks being made upon him in the press. The media wanted blood.

"It's the silly season. No news worth printing. If there'd been a proper disaster or something they'd not have printed the story."

"It undermines everything," complained Lynch. "I want someone to go round to the head offices of this newspaper and get this tape. Let's expose this hoaxer for what he is. And if anybody seems particularly difficult at the newspaper, do 'em for obstructing justice."

Beresford sighed, "They've already turned it in, sir. Doing their public duty and all..."

Lynch glowered at the front page of the tabloid. "It's nobody's duty to publish this," he muttered.

Beresford tried to make his voice sound a little lighter as he prepared to give out the little good news he had stored up for the Superintendent. "Sir, Dr Power phoned. Says he's coming here to take you out for a drive...he said in his new car." Lynch looked up incredulously. Had the whole world taken leave of its senses? First the nonsense about the tapes, now Power was proposing a jaunt around the countryside in his new car. Lynch could see his career deflating like a punctured balloon. Beresford continued his news, despite Lynch's pained expression. "Power said he had something new and important to say about the case. Sounds like a new line of enquiry."

TEN

Power's new car purred through the countryside of North Wales. Superintendent Lynch stared through the windows at the rolling green hills that surrounded the fields of ripening grain. He was glad to get out of the office; tired of the demands on his soul, tired of the demands of journalists fascinated by the murder inquiry. At any time the journalists might revolt, turn and attack him, baying for his blood. Lynch opened the side window and let the fresh air flood into his face. The warm sun kissed him with light. "It's so beautiful...you could almost forget...." He sighed at looked at Power who was smiling and humming to himself, seemingly quite oblivious of Lynch.

"I thought," said Lynch, moving almost into Power's line of sight to command his attention. "That you were going to get a new car."

"It's new to me. You know, the insurance company wouldn't give much for the Saab; and besides I couldn't find another Saab...not one exactly the same..."

"I'm not surprised," said Lynch. Power's Saab had been unique for years.

"...so I got a Rover 105S."

Lynch looked around him at the walnut, chrome and cherry-red leather of the interior. "So, how old is it?"

"1958," said Power proudly. "Look at the detailing and the quality of the craftsmanship. Just superb."

Lynch shook his head. "How much was it?"

"Three thousand."

"Not so bad. I mean it looks good, but it'll be breaking down all the time. Large repair bills...if you can find the parts, that is."

"Nonsense," said Power, denying the uncomfortable truth. "Anyway, if it's too much trouble I'll get a new car."

"You mean another old car, don't you?"

"Of course, they've got character."

Sitting in the bulbous black and chrome monster Lynch felt he probably looked like a policeman in a black-and-white Ealing film from the 'fifties. He also suspected that the car greedily drank gallon upon gallon of leaded petrol. Still, it was a most comfortable car and there was that urbane smell of real leather upholstery. (He wondered suspiciously whether the aroma had been added by the dealer with a spray can, anxious to make a sale). However, he was grudgingly forced to admit that the ride was superbly smooth. "Like going back in time." He muttered.

"And that's exactly what we are doing," said Power cryptically. For Power it seemed that with the chain of recent events the past had merged with the present in more ways than one. The Rover, for instance, was an exact double for his father's old Rover. No doubt he would have to analyse his glee at acquiring his father's old car. "Do you know what?" he asked Lynch. "I've thought of a name for this car."

"What is it?"

"Oedipus," said Power triumphantly. Lynch did not understand, but he was not as conversant with Freud's theories as Power.

"You said we were going back in time," said Lynch. "I got the feeling you weren't just talking about the car." He was wondering why the secretive Power had dragged him away from the busy office. "Have you discovered something about the murderer...something to do with the past?" Power nodded. "Go on, tell me...I can't wait any longer."

"Damn!" Power had suddenly noticed that the A494 road had led them past a village which was flashing by the car on the right. This was the village of Llanferres. Power had the impression of a Saxon church and nearby a black-and-white half-timbered pub called, 'The Druid's Inn'. "Missed the turning," he explained as he swung the Rover sharply over to the right. The car behind them blared its horn angrily as it braked. Lynch stared at the juggernaut hurtling towards him on the other side of the road. He endured a moment of panic then they were turning round in the lay-by.

"You didn't indicate," protested Lynch.

"No time," said Power as he set off again to retrace the road back to the turning he had missed. He found it, turned left and then they were on the road between the mountainsides. By the time Power brought the great car to a halt the sun was mellowing into the late afternoon sky. "Come on," he said. "Let's climb the mountain."

Lynch looked up at the daunting slopes of Foel fenlii. "Can't you let me in on the secret here in the car park?"

"No."

"I don't really like going to the scene of a murder more than I have to."

"It's important. You have to be here to understand."

"But understand what?"

"Understand the murderer's mind, of course."

Intrigued, Lynch stepped down from the Rover to accompany Power on the slow ascent. Power was surprised to see that although Lynch was older than the doctor he was considerably fitter. Lynch also had the audacity (and breath) to laugh when Power paused a hundred metres into the climb. "Too much fried rice. Too much beer, doctor."

"What do you do for exercise then?" wheezed Power uncomfortably.

"I play cricket in the summer, go swimming in the winter. What do you do?"

"Mental gymnastics." Power was developing a stitch, but refused to acknowledge this additional physical discomfort in front of Lynch. They set off again, but Lynch kindly slowed his pace.

At the summit the wind blew keenly, buffeting and cooling them down. Power had to raise his voice above it. "It's a fantastic view isn't it – like looking down on a map...down into the green valley and there," he gestured to the South. "There is Snowdonia in the distance – the great Welsh mountain range. The holy mountains."

"Not holy as far as I'm concerned," said Lynch as he stood uncertainly by the summit cairn. 'This was where the body sat', he thought.

Power's earlier light-heartedness had vanished as they climbed. He was serious now as he began to explain what lay behind all of the murders. "The mountains might not be holy for you, but before Christ, thousands of years ago now, the Celts thought they were holy enough. They quarried the Welsh mountain stone for Stonehenge. They carried the stone over water and over land. It was that special, because they were inspired by a great religion. A religion, which had spread all over Celtic Europe."

Was this the past, which Power wanted to talk about? Lynch was more down-to-earth about the inspirations of the builders of Stonehenge. "More likely they were inspired by a slave master with a great big whip. What are you trying to say?"

"The murders are linked in time and space. I'm trying to show you the connections. Look that way." Power pointed northeast, "What's over there?" It was a rhetorical question.

"Cheshire, England."

"Yes, but there was no division in Celtic times. Different tribal regions maybe, but no country boundaries."

"So?" asked Lynch.

"People do things, believe in things we can't always under-stand; because we don't share their thinking. There was a reason why our ancestors built stone monuments – a very good reason for them, as far as they were concerned - but it makes no sense to us now – be-cause three thousand years on we don't share the same mind-set."

"So?"

"We don't understand why our murderer does what he does either. I didn't know what the link was, because the link is hidden...hid-den inside his head. Like the people who built Stonehenge – they've gone; and their ideas have gone with them. All we're left with are the stones. 'By their deeds ye shall know them,' thought Lynch again. "We have to work it backwards – to guess what was in the Celtic minds when they built Stonehenge. And now in the murder investigation, all that we're left with after the murders are the bodies. The thoughts that explain the murders are locked away in the murderer's mind. I think I've found the key."

Lynch looked at the triumph in Power's face and a small bud of hope began to flower in his heart. But he would guard the hope from Power's eyes. He dared not test the hope in case it was vain. "Go on," he said non-committally.

Power answered with a question. "What made the murderer choose his victims?"

"I don't know. I don't see a link between them – a 14 year old girl, a 12 year old boy, a forestry worker: unrelated as to age, sex, fami-ly – everything!"

"There is a link...they were convenient – near to the place the murderer wanted them to be in. He lured the girl into the cave. We know she was a drug addict. How did he get her in the cave nearby? Maybe he offered her drugs? He used the dog to lure the boy into the undergrowth on Eddisbury Hill. He prepared things for both of them... he devised his traps carefully...in the case of the Eddisbury Hill murder he had brought poisoned meat for the dog." Lynch shivered in the wind. Power seemed so certain and the knowledge that he was about to reveal the murderer's soul chilled Lynch. "All the victims were in a place of his choosing, and he probably didn't need to work too hard to get them there. We know the forester was working on the fence, just down there." Power pointed along the ridge of the hill. "He was as near as possible so that when the murderer finished he wouldn't have far to bring the body to the cairn-throne. And each body has been displayed, hasn't it? The display of the headless body has a religious significance for him."

"But maybe the place is immaterial," said Lynch. "He just chooses out-of-the-way beauty spots – spots where people are not on their guard – places with bushes; cover, places to hide. Lonely places like this. Your car down there in the car park – it was the only one, wasn't it?." They looked down the hill at the Rover. It looked like a toy in the distance. "Out here...alone...in the country, he's got solitude, time to do what he wants."

"Yes, he does need time you're right...he'd need at least half-an-hour – more really to do the dissection. And yes, you're right – they're all lonely places – but they're all special places too. And that's what's most important to him."

"Why? Why are they special places?"

"Each one is an ancient Celtic site. Alderley Edge has been inhabited for ten thousand years. There are important caves, mines and fortifications. Eddisbury Hill was a strategic hill fort, a place of Celtic military power, and this, Fool fonlii, another hill fort, a high defensive place. Look, you can still see parts of the defences. This cairn, where he put the forester's body is thousands of years old itself. Okay, nowadays all three sites are just overgrown tourist traps, but years ago the sites were thriving, important places, full of people – soldiers, merchants, farmers."

Lynch looked about the hillside. It was difficult to imagine the ghosts of the past, clawing their way into the present. He needed to be reassured. "Maybe they were special places once upon a time, but you haven't convinced me of a link in the murderer's mind. To me they're just lonely places. Convince me it's not just a coincidence. I can't see the link...yet."

"You will," smiled Power. "I was looking at the maps of the area, then I found a book which confirmed everything for me. How can I best explain?" He reached down to the cairn and selected three stones. Lynch watched the psychiatrist with bemusement. Huffing and puffing, Power shifted three large stones. "Alderley Edge." One rock thumped down onto the summit turf. "Eddisbury Hill." Another thump. "Foel fenlii" Thump. "What do you see?"

Lynch looked down at the three rocks on the ground. "I see a line of stones." He was puzzled by Power's excited response.

"That's right, exactly right...a line. What kind of lines do you know?"

"Hmm..." Lynch thought about it. "Railway lines, power lines... if you're saying these murders follow a line you're wrong, because we looked for that. We looked for railway lines that the murderer might be travelling on; roads, canals, rivers...those sort of links. There weren't any."

"Because you weren't thinking abnormally – like the murderer does. You were being logical...and he isn't logical. He was connecting the murders in his own mind...according to a ley line."

Lynch's eyebrows shot up. "Well, I've heard of them, but...I.."

"I know what you're thinking...but remember, we're interested in what the murderer thinks. When people talk about ley lines they talk about lines of earth forces and ancient magic. They have maps of the ancient sites...these are the people that say that Stonehenge and Avebury and Old Sarum are all built on a ley line. Their idea was that the ancient Celts were more in tune with the earth and the moon and that they said they could tap the earth's energy by their rituals on the ley lines. The ley lines are meant to radiate all over the country...but if it sounds far-fetched to you and I, we have to concede that thousands of people believe these things, and there are more people who do today even than twenty years ago. They believe in all this, as strongly as you believe in your God."

Lynch looked as if he would concede nothing to such people, but he could see the idea that Power was trying to get across. "You're saying that no matter how bizarre this idea seems – if it's the one the murderer has got in his head...the idea he's working to...then... he's creating the murders to fit it." Lynch knew then that Power was right, but the murderer's belief seemed an inversion of everything Lynch stood for. "This ley-line then, how do you know about it?"

Power fished in his pocket and took out two books. "This is a book on the Stonehenge ley lines – how they connect with prehistoric ritual. How the ley line links to the holy Welsh mountains. And this book, " Power flourished a green paper back. Lynch looked at the title, 'The Cheshire Ley by Rev. John Watkins.' "This is all about this ley line. The one we're standing on now."

"I know a Reverend Watkins," said Lynch. "Retired now."

Power wasn't listening. He was caught up in his own exposition. "The ley line we're on is one of the most important and powerful leys in the whole country. This ley has more ancient sites and markers on it than any other. The book shows how the ley line links together hill forts, caves and standing stones. And the ley starts at Alderley Edge. The author even points out how the village's name has got 'ley' in it. We're standing on the ley that links Alderley Edge, Eddisbury Hill and Foel fenlii."

"So, each one of the murders has happened on this line? This is the link?"

"Yes. And each murder is a ritual sacrifice according to the ancient ways. There's plenty of archaeological evidence for Celtic human sacrifices. And how the Celts placed a special value on the human head...as a trophy it carried great power. If you look at some of the ceremonial barrows...some of the chambers below ground are filled with bones. The others are filled with skulls. At Stonehenge some of the post holes were filled with the bones of a child sacrifice." Lynch looked pained by the thought.

The Superintendent stared out over the fields and trees and hedges of the open countryside below them. He had a memory of a childhood spent in a Shropshire village – of English orderliness – the local post-office; the village Green and cricket in the summer; the local market and the Women's Institute stall with jams and bottled fruit; the Church and its lichen-covered, weathered tombstones. He remembered looking through frosty cottage windows at early morning mist rolling over the freshly turned brown earth and diffusing the green of the trees to a cloud-soft whiteness. Every Sunday the bells would ring out over the parish – a regular call to the Christian faithful. This was Lynch's world of law and order. This was how it seemed it had always been. Yet here was Power talking of a time before history, a distant past, filled with brutish ancestors, sacrificing their fellow men to unknown gods. Their days had gone, their bloody rituals replaced by a bloodless Christian Mass. But were the bells tolling now for Lynch's Christian world, just as they had for the pagan gods that governed Celtic harvests and were embodied by the silver, cold moon and the golden Sun? Still, it was difficult for Lynch to comprehend the drives, which could lead men to sacrifice the souls of others, past or present.

"We don't have sacrifices though," declared Lynch, for his own reassurance rather than anything else. "Not now, anyway. This is a Christian land."

"The New Age people wouldn't subscribe to your Christian views...they're probably closer to the ancient Celts with their ideas of Gaia and earth power and what-have-you."

"But it's not the same is it, Carl? They don't practice sacrifices."

How many times must we deny the ideas that we find uncomfortable, wondered Power? Twentieth century man had sacrificed millions to the gods of war and political ideology, just as medieval man had sacrificed millions to the Crusade and Jihad. "The idea that the earth is angry with us...for polluting it. These ideas have the same form as the old ideas...these are the old ideas, over again; that the gods are in every tree and meadow and stream...that they may get angry – and so they need to be placated. These are the old ideas returning."

"So, you're linking the murders to the New Age festival at Alderley Edge?"

"I was just speculating that the murderer is acting out the ideas of a changing society." Power looked up and finally registered Lynch's incomprehension. "I'm sorry...it's just an idea. I'll be more specific. The murderer is probably acting out a delusion – an abnormal belief – centred on his own ideas about this Cheshire ley line." He pointed to the book now in Lynch's hands. "Each murder is a sacrifice at a specific site on the ley line – maybe to propitiate the gods, avert disaster, or gain power or something. He's picking the most important sites too - ancient caves, Celtic hill forts. The heads he removes...perhaps he thinks they are filled with energy...that he is accumulating force as he progresses along the ley line."

Lynch was still assimilating the ley line theory. "And if the murders are on this line...then he'll go on along the line? Then will he always confine himself to this line in the future?"

"Um...yes, probably, I think so."

"He might use the other sites on the line?"

"Yes. He's moving southwards on the line, using the most important sites. But he's moving with time, and that's something else we need to consider."

"Something else? I think you've given me enough to digest..." Lynch's head was spinning with this insight into the murderer's head.

"No, this is important. Keep with me. Keep your thinking head on for a little while longer. You see, the Ley Man, (that's what I've called the murderer), is constrained by place to acting on the ley line, but he's also locked in by time. He has to act at certain times as well as certain places. He feels compelled to...everything is a ritual."

"Yes?" Lynch's mind was filling with all kinds of possibilities. The new idea had elated him; he was suffused with hope. No wonder they hadn't made progress before. Without the key there had been no way of unlocking the door. "Tell me about the times then," he said eagerly. "How do they fit in?"

"Each of the murders has been in a special place on a special date: May 1st, June 21st, and June 23rd."

"They don't seem special to me at all."

"No, but you're used to the Christian calendar aren't you? If it had been Easter and December 25th you'd think otherwise. These are important dates for the Old Religion.

"May the 1st is Beltane. A festival of fire...to strengthen the sun for the Spring...you know, to ensure a good harvest that year. In the old religion they used to bury people alive to guarantee a good harvest. June 21st is the Summer Solstice and June 23rd is Midsummer Eve. All dates for Pagan rites to do with the Spring and Summer. Now do you see?"

"This is the key, isn't it? This is what we've been waiting for isn't it?"

"Yes, I think it is. This is the template he's working to. Now we know what he's got in mind...we can predict what he will do next – where he'll do it and even the day he'll do it."

"When will that be?"

"I looked it up. There are festivals throughout the year, but I'd say the next likely candidate was Lughnasadh."

Lynch didn't catch the name, but his concern was for another detail. "How much time have we got?"

"August the 1st."

"Where?"

Power shifted around to where the headless man had been arranged to face the south-west. He stood where the unseeing corpse had been and facing the sinking sun pointed down the mountainside.

"There." Lynch followed the line of Power's pointing arm, to the slate roofs of the houses and shops, to the church spire of the town of Ruthin, whose image shimmered in the evening heat haze.

Lynch had often used the metaphor of the detective as an archaeologist – sifting through the dirt to find the truth of the past. Now Lynch felt as if the ancient past was reaching up through the centuries, skipping an entire two thousand years of Christianity. The Ley Man was putting the ghosts of the old religion into play once more. Human sacrifice, here, at the end of the second Christian millennium.

He looked at Power and knew that here was an expert in the human psychology, who had given him the key to find the murderer and lock him away.

ELEVEN

Excited after the day spent on Foel fenlii, explaining his ideas to Lynch, Power had retired to bed early. Initially he slept deeply, but anyone watching him in bed later would have seen him turning frequently under the sheets, almost writhing in agitation.

He was dreaming a dream that was starting to haunt him, so often had it recurred. He was once more alone on a flat disc of earth bounded by a white clouded sky. He was running over dripping green grass as fast as his legs would carry him. Behind him, always at a constant distance so that he could never afford to slow his frantic pace was a large black dog, hackles risen and white-toothed jaws gaping wide.

The dream had become embellished with repetition. As he ran Power carried a bundle in his hands. At first he felt it was a precious baby, wrapped in swaddling clothes, but on closer inspection it proved to be a hoard of gold coin, wrapped ineffectually in a fleecy apple-green cotton sheet. With the hound barking at him, the rain falling from the cold, leaden sky, and the uneven earth beneath his feet Power stumbled often, and as he did so the trove of coin in his arm was jostled and jerked, releasing the gold in a minor cascade onto the floor. With the black hound so close Power could not stop to pick the gold up and it fell under his running feet to be ground into the mud.

Ahead a white tower, similar to a lone lighthouse, rose up on the horizon and grew as Power hurried towards it. When he drew within five hundred metres or so he could see a figure atop the highest balcony. He had the impression of a red beard and the sound of pipes, carried strongly at first by the wind. As the wind changed it carried the music elsewhere. If he could only get there, open a door and slam it in the face of the black dog that pursued him as closely as a shadow.

Power chanced a look behind him. The dog had gained upon him, and had similarly grown in size and shape. It now resembled nothing so much as a night-black wolf with shoulders as high as a horse. Now when Power turned round and ran he could feel the hot breath of the creature as it panted on the back of his neck.

At this Power woke up and lay sweating in the pit of his bed. He threw the cotton sheets off himself and let the cool night air bathe his naked body. Still groggy from sleep he tried to analyse the meaning of the dream. It must mean something important...so important that his unconscious would not let him rest until he had acknowledged the correct meaning. Wasn't this why the dream recurred...so that he would, in time, be forced to find an explanation for the dream-symbols chosen by his unconscious? There was something important here, but...but Power was too tired to address the matter. He would sleep on it, if he could, and note the dream down in the morning. What was so important about the dream?

* * *

The next night, after work, Power reached Manchester at seven o'clock. The Victorian city's centre had emptied of the day's traffic and the streets around the banks and city institutions were remarkably free of cars. He found a parking space in St. Anne's square by the Royal Exchange, a gargantuan edifice erected to house the court of King Cotton. For many years the world prices of cotton had fluctuated in concert with the trading of the brokers in the Exchange's vast marble hall. Power walked past the shopping mall it had now become and onto the deliciously shade-filled streets of Deansgate. The evening was warm and Power was in shirt-sleeves. He carried his jacket over his arm. Passers-by noticed his smile. He was feeling buoyed up by the gratifying reception Lynch had given his theory. It seemed as if the Ley Man was within their grasp. It was time to relax and celebrate. All of a sudden Power was feeling very positive towards life in general and Eve in particular.

He looked at his watch: seven fifteen. They were due to meet at half-past. He could afford to walk more slowly past the well-stocked windows of Deansgate. He admired the window displays that dripped with gold or delicacies or vintage wine. Deansgate was a symbol of the very prosperous city that Manchester had become. He passed Kendals, a store which once rivalled Harrods in terms of quality. He was frustrated by the shutters on some shops, and the locked doors frustrated him. Why couldn't opening times be more flexible...like Italy for instance? He longed to browse through the bookstores of Waterstones and Willshaws and stopped thoughtfully on John Dalton Street to look in at the books. But nothing could affect his good spirits, or so he thought. He was certainly anticipating a good meal when he arrived outside the restaurant he had booked. The thought of the entertainment and company ahead only elated him further. He stood outside The Romans and looked at his watch. Bang on time. He peered through the restaurant's plate glass window to the annoyance of an elderly, epicene man who was dining nearby. She wasn't there.

Eve had said she'd get the train into the city and a taxi from the station to the restaurant, in order that they could travel back in the same car. Maybe the train had been slow. He mused about the journey back in the car. Perhaps he might stop the Rover near that wood in Prestbury. It would be romantic to make love in the moonlight. Power waited outside for ten minutes then decided to go in and occupy his table. He ordered a cappuccino and started to peruse the menu hungrily. He was so hungry that when the cappuccino arrived he even ate the amaretto biscuits, (which he usually categorised as inedible).

When Eve hadn't arrived by 7.50 he felt slightly panicked. The performance started at eight-thirty. There was hardly time to order and eat even if she turned up immediately. Power compromised by requesting a large seafood pizza – reasoning that if Eve turned up in the next half-hour he could share this with her. She didn't. Power consumed the pizza anxiously because of the fast-approaching deadline of eight-thirty.

He left it as late as he could before paying and leaving to get to the theatre on time. Perhaps she'd gone there straight away from the station? If so, she would be waiting anxiously outside, because he had the tickets. He hurried through the city streets, which were now filling up with people. He moved quickly between them, dodging and weaving a path towards the theatre. His earlier composure had gone and his tension would only be released by the sight of Eve's smiling face

4

through the crowd.

Bright lights shone out from the Palace Theatre's gold and cream facade. The opera-going crowd, smart in dinner-jackets and evening dresses milled about the disgruntled Dr Power as he stood alone on the pavement of Oxford Road. He felt underdressed and awkward. As the others passed into the theatre behind him the melee about him dwindled until it was just the occasional couple arriving late by taxi. Of Eve there was no sign. He looked down at the tickets in his hand and wondered what to do with them. By now the opera, La Suor Angelica, had started. He could hear the distant strains of the orchestra beginning Puccini's overture.

He tried Eve's phone using a nearby Mercury kiosk. He imagined the phone ringing in the lofty rooms of her flat. He let it ring a long, long time, but there was no response. He hated the phone.

Power decided to go home, because opera was not his favourite entertainment and the prospect of opera alone seemed infinitely worse. He meandered back through the Manchester streets past the couples and gangs of students from the polytechnic and University out on pub crawls. He remembered a comment from his student days, 'A University is a fountain of knowledge where all come to drink'. He smiled a wry smile.

Power drove home through the bright lights of the centre, past Waterhouse's Town Hall and through the campus of the red-brick University into Withington and bed-sit land. He stopped off at a student pub and consoled himself with a pint of Bass bitter. His Rover made an incongruous sight against the battered Fords and Volkswagens in the car park. The Saab would have had no trouble mingling with the students' cars. He drank the bitter thirstily. He thought the name of the drink apt for his present mood. He was only just managing to suppress his anger and hurt at being stood up by Eve. He supposed he had been difficult with her in the past days and weeks. He should have been more...receptive to her and less caught up in himself. But she had agreed to come! It wasn't like her to be so spiteful as to let him arrange everything; go to so much trouble and then destroy it all. Equally unlike her to forget, La Suor Angelica was one of her favourite operas. So she had said anyway.

It was a puzzled Dr Power who drove back through the great city southwards to Prestbury village where Eve lived. As he passed through the suburbs the land gradually became greener and the trees grew more densely, until at last he was driving down the hill into Prestbury. It was ten o'clock and dusk had become night.

As he drove through the country commuter village he saw the lights of the *Admiral Benbow* and *Black Boy* public houses. Besides these the High Street was in darkness. He parked the Rover by Eve's car in one of the small alleys that led off from the shops. She would have walked to the station, he thought, then taken the train into Manchester. If she had started her journey, that was. Had he missed her then somewhere in the city centre? No, surely he'd waited long enough in both places: at the restaurant and the theatre.

When he got out of the car and moved closer to the steps that led up to her first-floor studio flat the passive infra-red detectors he'd had installed picked up his body heat and the stairway was flooded with light. It was as if some unseen hand had switched the light on. It always startled Power when the light switched itself on so suddenly.

Eve lived over the top of an antique shop. She was pleased that it was such and not a grocers or newsagents. The shop was quiet by day and night and the noise of commerce never disturbed her painting. Power climbed the steps at the side of the shop and at the top got out his keys to open the front door. However, the door was already ajar. The flat inside was dark and silent. Eve could not be around. He'd noticed from outside that her curtains were not drawn. She must have gone to Manchester, thought Power, but then if she had, why hadn't they met? And why had she left the front door ajar? Power's apprehension only grew when he switched on the hall lights.

Books were scattered from the bookshelf, which appeared to have been pulled over. Power's fearful anxiety mounted, and was not to diminish over the coming weeks. When he did gather the courage to enter the rest of Eve's flat he was to find more signs of a struggle, but of Eve herself there was no trace.

* * *

Lynch sat in the armchair across the room from Power. He rested his head against the wings of the chair and looked over at Power. He knew that this quiet man was filled with a secret knowledge of people and their minds. He also felt that, because of what had happened, of what they had so far shared, that they were on the threshold of a long journey together. The journey was to an unknown destination, but both their paths were interwoven. Coincidentally this corresponded to the feelings that Power's patients had when they first met their doctor. Power was a healer who would accompany them on their individual journeys – each on an odyssey or quest to find the specific that would render them whole. But with Lynch and Power the healing process might be a more equal process. Power in particular, having lost Eve, felt uneasy and vulnerable.

The morning sun streamed through the window and lit his head from the back. To Power gazing against the strong light it looked as if the crown of Lynch's head was surrounded by a golden halo. Lynch had listened to all of Power's worries about Eve. There was little doubt that, after a struggle, Eve had been taken from her flat. Power looked exhausted. He had spent most of the night awake imagining who had taken Eve from him. Lynch knew that Power had found a phone call from Eve's mother particularly harrowing. Power had been the last person to see Eve, and that had been yesterday now.

"Do you have any recent photos of Eve?" asked Lynch. Power looked up surprised. Lynch explained. "For the 'Missing' posters, and then the press, you know. I was hoping you had one I could use. It would save me harassing the Pearson family again."

"Mrs Pearson is quite...well, she made me feel very guilty."

"Why?"

"We don't have any control over what others say about us... apparently Eve had really built me up in her family's eyes. You...I never really knew what she thought of me...can you understand that? Does that sound outlandish?" Lynch shook his head to reassure Power. " On some levels she was...is very private. Always something held back...in case...Oh I don't know. Her family...I think they were just about to hear wedding bells...you know what I mean. That's what she'd been saying to them. I spent months trying to get her to say...but she never said it to me. Said it to her mother, not to me. And then I go and lose her."

Lynch said nothing. He was trying to deny the thought that he might have prevented something by taking Power's concerns more seriously. He felt that perhaps he should have addressed the car bomb more thoroughly.

"I was wrong to separate that event from the murders. I think they are related...the bomb attack and the disappearance of Eve Pearson and the murders. They must be related, but I can't see exactly how, except..."

"Except?"

"The only constant feature to all the events is yourself. To someone who didn't know you better..."

"What?" There was a more than a tinge of anger in Power's voice now.

"If I was looking at this case from outside I'd look at all the murders, one of which occurs yards from your house...and I'd see you getting your car blown up, and then your girlfriend disappearing. Well, I'd add two and two and make five. You are linked to the Ley murders. You've read the newspapers, haven't you? In fact, to be frank, as far as the murders are concerned you seem to be central to them..." He saw the discomforted horror spread over Power's features. "But I do know you better. I know you as a friend, Carl. I know that you've alibis for some, if not all, of the murders. Know you're innocent, in fact. I'm just asking myself what game it is that the murderer is playing. Is he trying to discredit you? Frame you?"

"I don't know what to say," said Power, disliking the turn of the conversation. "Do you suspect me?"

"I'm aware of how things might look to someone with less grasp of the detail of the case." Lynch was aware of the researches that the newspapers were making into Power. When the news of Eve's disappearance broke, they would have a field day with Power. "I don't suspect you, Carl. But there are others."

"But I've given you the key to the case!" Power protested.

"Yes. And I hope it enables us to catch the murderer, but some people might say that giving us the key might be a very clever ploy by the murderer."

"If this is what you think..." Power was only just managing to keep control. It was almost as if he was watching himself from outside. Watching himself gradually losing control. Understanding, from outside, what a strain Power had been under. Making allowances for the near-hysterical tone of voice. He watched the other Power cover his face with his hands.

"Carl...I'm just showing you how things might look to someone outside." Power looked anything but grateful. "They don't know all the help you've been to us. They can't know...I don't want them to know our theories of the murderer's mind. But doing that put you in a vulnerable position. They don't know your true role."

"I was worried about being identified by the press...I was worried they'd jump to the wrong conclusions."

"I'm sorry. I'm trying to keep them at bay. Don't want them to know everything about the ley line theory. But I can leak that you're not a suspect."

"It won't be long till they get hold of the ideas we've got."

"I've only told a few of the senior detectives."

"It won't be long then till it leaks," said Power.

Lynch frowned. "Perhaps it would be more useful if you were to speculate on the identity of a suspect, perhaps someone near to yourself or Eve Pearson?"

Power had been over and over the question in his mind. He

could only come up with generalities. "A male. Early adulthood, be-tween twenty and forty. Probably unmarried or sex-avoidant. Delud-ed and acting out dangerous thoughts or hallucinations. Lives alone... or...maybe with an elderly parent."

" No-one specific then?" Lynch asked. Power shook his head sadly. He had racked his brains, but the harder he thought the less his mind seemed able to work. " I just keep wondering if...if she's alive still. You know."

Lynch shrugged his shoulders. He knew very well, as did Pow-er, that the Ley Man had not delayed one of his killings. Why would he change his habit of killing? Why would he not kill almost instanta-neously as he had before. What would stop him doing that? If he had meant to sacrifice Eve she would be dead by now. "I don't know," said Lynch, trying to think. Any crumb of comfort he could give to Power. "The only thing is that it's not yet when you said he would move again. You said he would sacrifice again on August 1st. What was it called?"

"Lughsanadh. Lugh's Day. Lugh was king of the Celtic gods. I could have got the dates wrong. He'll know the subject of Celtic rituals better than me."

"I'm planning something for August 1st too, Carl. If your ideas are right he'll feel compelled to act on that date. And if we know where he's going to be and the day he's got to act on.... He'll be want-ing to use Ruthin. It's the next point on the line. Now, we just have to think about it Carl...whereabouts in the town will he act out?"

"There's a castle, or the remains of one and its walls around its land. They built a hotel in the grounds...that's there now, but on the side of a hill there's an old circle of standing stones. That's where he'll want to use." He thought about what the Ley Man would use it for and closed his eyes, but was unsuccessful at blotting out the images in his mind's eye.

"Yes, if you're right, Carl he'll act out in the circle. The place is so important for him...we've seen that...the way he displays..." Lynch stopped himself. "The Ruthin Ring. That's where I want to set a trap. We'll only use a few officers...we need to arrive unseen and stay unseen in the town. Too many men running round the place, and he'll know there's a trap," The need for secrecy was paramount.

Power couldn't bear the thought of waiting to act. "We need to do something now...waiting till then may be too late...we can't wait till then. We need to do something for Eve now."

"Carl, I don't know what else we can do...we're doing everything we can already. I think the only viable theory we have is yours. If it's right we can almost guarantee that the Ley Man will turn up sometime in the 24 hours of August the 1st. And because he won't be able to resist coming, because his madness compels him...we will catch him."

"I suppose..." said Power, "...after all the risks he's run...everything he's invested in the delusion. If he failed to keep the time and the place he'd risk undoing everything he's done. He couldn't bear that...to undo his magic."

"It's only a few days now, Carl. If we can save Eve; this is the best way."

"But..." If the Ley Man had spared Eve's life it might be for this ritual at the Ruthin Ring. If they could catch him beforehand if there was any way Power could expiate his guilt. "I want to come along," said Power decisively. "I want to be there."

Lynch nodded approvingly. Power's earlier self-pity and useless frustration was turning into an angry determination. "Of course, you must come. That's what I wanted you to do. It's the best way of coping. You can come down to Ruthin with me tomorrow. I want to scout out the area...to get to know it...as well as he does." Power nodded. "I'm going to go now, Carl." Lynch stood up and brushed his suit jacket straight. He adjusted his tie and collar. He had spotted some reporters outside the gates of Power's house. Like vultures, they had seized upon the disappearance of Eve. What source of information did the vultures have? A secret trip down to Ruthin would get Power away from their talons anyway, Lynch thought.

"You realise," said Power. " That if things go wrong there'll be another body?'

Lynch laid a hand on Power's shoulder. 'I pray that I will do the right thing, Carl. Prayer is a powerful thing. It will help you too." And with that he left.

***

After someone one dies or is lost those who are left behind sometimes take on characteristics of those who have gone. When Power's shuffling, eccentric uncle had been alive he had chain smoked small panatella cigars and dabbled on the stock-market. After he had died Power had thought himself unaffected by the loss until he realised that he had unconsciously acquired the habits of his uncle. He had begun to crave small cigars and phone calls to his stock broker had become a regular pastime. As soon as he saw the true significance of his actions he was able to stop the cigars and cancel his subscription to the *Financial Times*.

Now Eve had gone he found the same phenomenon occurring. He found that on his way home he had stopped in the village of Alderley Edge. He stood outside the florists under its canopy, painted in crisp green and white stripes. Power stared at a profusion of sweet-smelling flowers, blush pink, yellow, and red. He wondered which to buy. He was used to making decisions, but not about flowers. Flowers were Eve's great joy, she loved painting them and he suddenly realised that he had incorporated this inside himself. He was buying the flowers for her even though she wasn't there. Knowing this, however, he was still determined to buy them. He bought a bunch of glorious-smelling freesias and some big soft yellow roses.

On his way out of the florists he spotted the off-licence and went in to see what beers they had. Power had a penchant for continental beers, but the shop was stolidly English so Power opted for the sweet and heavy Ruddles beer. He put the flowers and dumpy beer bottles on the leather seat beside him. He drove out of the village and up the hill to his home. Tonight, he promised himself, would be the one and only night he would get drunk over Eve. He would drink himself into a forgetful stupor, try for a time to blot out the shadow cast upon him by the world. This was no solution he knew, for in the next few days he must face the shadow himself.

***

Three days later Power drove into North Wales. Here he met Superintendent Lynch at the Ruthin Castle Hotel. Amidst the medieval kitsch and American tourists ordering cream teas Lynch was planning his trap. He had taken over a suite of rooms overlooking the courtyard. From his hotel window Lynch could see the belt of trees that effectively hid the Ruthin Stone Ring from view.

In these rooms Lynch was joined by selected officers from his murder squad, including Sergeant Beresford. They settled themselves into the comfortable plush velvet and rushing fire of the bar and waited for Lynch's commands. Another of the rooms was booked for Power. Lynch himself stayed in his room, surrounded by books on ley lines and ritual magic. A copy of *The Golden Bough* lay open on the small desk that the hotel had provided together with a copy of Power's book and the book by Watkins on *The Cheshire Ley*.

When Power arrived, feeling slightly under the weather because of a hangover, he entreated Lynch to accompany him on a walk 'to clear my head'. They climbed down the sweeping staircase from the police officers' rooms and walked through the great hall. The Americans from various coach parties glanced uninterestedly at them both. Lynch heard the laughter of his men from the bar. He didn't mind as long as they kept their mouths shut about the August 1st operation. He had chosen them carefully though. All three were cautious, tactful young men.

The evening sunlight that greeted Power and Lynch at the entrance seemed all the brighter after the gloom of the Castle Hotel. Well-kept grounds curved down the hill and through the castle walls into the town. The Inspector and the Psychiatrist made a striking sight as they paced the medieval streets deep in conversation. The topic of this conversation was the Ley Man and their plans to trap him. They were so engrossed that they plodded unheedingly through the winding streets, past half-timbered black-and-white Tudor merchants' houses and the old courthouse, past Georgian and Regency buildings.

At last their circuitous route took them back to the Castle itself, where they feasted on roast pork and rich wine. But although the fare was good, Power's appetite had mysteriously disappeared. "Not like you not to eat well," said Lynch as he tucked into a lemon sylla-bub served in a tall and elegant glass. "I think we'll take coffee in the lounge," he said to a passing waitress. Lynch was enjoying this life on expenses, but he knew that after a few nights of this he would be missing his wife's home cooking.

After dinner they settled themselves in two plump armchairs either side of a roaring fire. Despite the heat of the day, the hall of the stone-walled hotel was chilly and the fire a welcome thing. Lynch was summing up the arrangements for his trap. He looked around cautiously from time-to-time to assure himself that no-one was eaves-dropping. "Beresford and two others are eating out tonight. We've tried to keep apart...so that people don't suspect that we're anything more than tourists...well, they're meant to be salesmen from Manches-ter, actually. They're here for tomorrow...you know, help set things up. We really do need a small operation." Power fidgeted uncomfortably. "Don't want anybody to guess, least of all your Ley Man. I'm going to alert the hotel manager. I think I have to unfortunately...because the stone circle is in his grounds. But I'll keep it under my hat until the last minute."

"He's not my Ley Man," said Power, looking at the fire and avoiding Lynch's gaze.

"No...no, I'm sorry. Look, I...er..I don't know what to say, Carl."

"I can't believe...it all seems so distant to me, as if it was hap-pening to someone else...because I was minding my own business one minute, and the next everything is distorted...like I'm watching a film or something. Not the real me...just someone who looks like me. As though it's happened to someone else. I can't really believe Eve's gone...that it happened. I keep on thinking it will stop and it will all go back to normal...and then I realise it can't. And, you know the hardest bit? It's accepting that I'm at the heart of it...that it's directed at me in some way, like I'm being punished...or...tortured by someone I don't know...I can't see."

The fire crackled and Lynch thought over what Power had said.

It seemed to hint at a greater difference between their characters. Power was analytical, and Lynch was borne along by conviction and faith. Through Power's numbness, his loss of appetite, Lynch could sense the other's muted pain. "You don't believe in God, do you?"

"Perhaps there is something. But the Christian notion...Churchianity...that's not for me. I don't think Jesus would have liked the Church."

"I think you have to have courage to pin down your faith in something. Christianity is our faith...the Eastern stuff...that's somebody else's. We water down our faith with theirs and produce something that no side would accept."

"And before Christianity it was just another religion...five thousand years ago our ancestors believed in different gods...celebrated this Lughsanadh all over Europe. It's like politics...religions come and go."

Lynch could have argued the point, but didn't. "I've found my faith a great comfort in times of trouble." Lynch watched the glowing wood as it was consumed by leaping flames. "And without a faith... without some moral code...what's to stop anybody doing exactly what they want without any regard for anybody else?"

"There's the Law for all that. No need for religion."

"No point in any of it without faith either. On their own people want everything...possessions, money, sex, violence...this wanting more and more and taking more and more...it's like a fire burning inside. How do you make sure the fire doesn't spread. Like a fire burning in the hearth – the heart of the home – how do you contain it?"

Power looked up with sudden interest. "You watch it, like we're doing now. Through the hours...through the years. Watch it to stop it getting out of control."

Lynch laughed. "Getting too deep for me, I'm afraid. I think I'll have a brandy or something then turn in. What do you think?" But Power was listening to raised voices outside the hall. Inquisitively both men went to see what was causing the commotion. They arrived at the hotel reception to find it deserted. The two porters had run out into the night. A lone American in plaid trousers looked at them through tinted spectacles. "They've gone to repel the invader," she said cryptically, then went on to explain. "Hippies. Trying to park their buses in the hotel grounds. Something about a music festival in the hills."

"I thought I saw them on the road down here," said Lynch. "They must have been gathering for the past few days."

"I guess the hotel doesn't want any freeloaders in the grounds."

Power waited until the elderly American woman had gone, then looked directly into Lynch's eyes. "Isn't it strange that the New Age people are here just when we think the Ley Man is about to kill again?"

"Perhaps we should take a look."

"Do you remember the Piper?" Though Power had never thought to see the Piper again, the figure's recurrent intrusions into his dreams had sensitised him. "Do you think he'll be there?" The dream of the Piper playing high up on the balcony of a tower...

Lynch had interviewed so many people in connection with the murders that he couldn't recall them all. "The Piper? Ah...hold on... wasn't he the man you saw in the woods at Alderley Edge? The Piper with two girls...Power nodded agreement. "Well, it would be useful to know where he was in June, when the second and third murders were. A traveller like him would be capable of travelling the ley line when he wanted. He wouldn't have the commitments of work and routine. He could come and go as he pleased."

"Yes," said Power. "But if the Piper has Eve where would he keep her? A caravan or a bus would be no good. You could just about lock someone up in a house, but not a caravan. Someone might hear something."

"Whatever...it's late, the New Agers will be stopping nearby tonight...we can talk to them tomorrow perhaps..." said Lynch. "But there's plenty of other things to do...tomorrow night we have to pre-pare our trap. From midnight it'll be August 1st, Lughsanadh ac-cording to the Pagan calendar...that gives him twenty-four hours to complete his next act on the ley line. We'll need to man the site all day, from midnight to midnight at least. I suggest we turn in now. Get in a bit of rest."

When Power reached his bedroom he undressed by the light that filtered through the nets, then he closed the Chintz together and in the warm darkness sank into his bed with gratitude. The thought that the New Age convoy was in Ruthin too had re-awakened the im-ages of his dreams. He hoped it would not plague his sleep again. His sleep had been poor since Eve had gone missing, but tonight he was so tired that he hoped sleep would soon overwhelm him. What if the dream had been a premonition? Power discounted the idea. Perhaps if he analysed the dream more. Dreams were about the day, or about the conflicts of the individual unconscious...Manifestations of the archetypes. Archetypes like the dark side of your own character...the shadow for instance. The black dog would be his own shadow, a con-crete interpretation of the phrase 'dogged by his shadow'...perhaps, it was the kind of sick joke the unconscious enjoyed. But the Piper had occurred in the dream and then the hippies had reappeared, somehow Power was sure that the Piper was here in Ruthin too. There wasn't any logic behind his sudden conviction, but he was somehow sure of it. The dream seemed so real to him. What else did it mean? If he was to continue analysing his own dream...what was the bundle of gold? The gold he had lost? Eve? Had he been losing Eve before? Had he dreamed about the precious baby of gold before or after Eve had been taken? Power felt confused. He felt numbed by loss and by the tiredness of continual anxiety. He felt waves of sleep wash over his conscious mind. It would soon overtake him. Before it did he prayed for Eve. It was his first prayer for some time.

TWELVE

The world was in darkness, an unending void. Though sight was denied her, there was touch, taste, smell and hearing: but the world was a quiet one, (except for the humming of some machine), and there was little to taste and smell besides her own body.

Eve could move across the floor to her right and left. When the chain was as taut as it would go, when it felt as if the manacle would pull her hand off at the wrist, she could just touch the side walls with her fingertips. They were hollowed out of the earth and featureless. When she touched them in the darkness she could feel small rivulets of soil and dust run over her fingers and onto the concrete floor. In places concrete struts climbed the walls to support a steel mesh that held up the earth roof.

Above her head Eve could just touch a low portion of the roof. In a gap between the concrete and steel vault Eve could feel the cool touch of earth again. She would tease and scrabble at the soil above. Thin fibrous tendrils hung down from this part of the roof. Unseeing, she wondered what these might be. Wires, plastic threads? She worked at the soil about them. As she burrowed the soil away the thin fibres became thicker and less pliable. Deeper in, the soil was colder and more moist. She tugged at the cord-like tendrils, then she realised what they were. Roots. She was buried in the earth. She was buried deep; buried below roots that formed a living wooden cage around her. For a while she was too shocked to do anything. Then she began to worry even more at the roots. If she could find a decent sized piece and break it off, then she could fashion some poor sort of weapon.

And into her dark, cold and silent earth he would intrude. The first she heard was the padlock of the outer door. It would slam to behind him, then he would fumble at the door of her tomb, taking off the bolts, undoing the locks. Then if she stayed still she would feel a stirring in the air, hear his breathing, smell him. If he brought food though she could always smell that before he opened the second door. She had become especially good at smelling meat. Like a dog. His meat stew was good, but tasted unfamiliar. She couldn't think why.

Sometimes, like this time, he wanted to talk, but usually at her, not with her. This time he seemed curious about her. In the absolute darkness he spoke, " How are you?"

Since she depended on him for everything, she restrained herself from swearing at him. "It gets cold in here," she said, hoping perhaps he would bring her a blanket. There was silence while he digested this information. The machine outside went on humming.

"Did you like the stew I brought you?"

"Yes. It's very good, " she said carefully. Her life depended on him. He giggled. It sounded a childish voice, slightly false, with a faint but discernible accent. "Perhaps I could have some more? And something to eat it with."

"Don't know about that. Expensive keeping someone alive." It sounded as if he wasn't at all sure of the merits of this policy. "And if you had cutlery you might use it on me. I know women for what they are. Scratchy things. You gave me some good scratches."

"I can't remember." She couldn't.

"That's the diazepam. Knocks out memory formation."

"Did you inject me?"

"In a way." That giggle again.

Eve felt sick, but she had to keep on playing his game. But she hated his game. She hated him. She felt the revulsion rising up in her stomach. Frustration made her want to scream. "Who are you?" she asked, keeping her voice as calm as she could.

"If you can't remember my face I'll be well pleased. And I'm not going to tell you my name. They don't let me take chances."

"What do you mean, 'they' ?"

Silence. She heard him shifting on the earth floor, moving away from her.

"Don't go, "she said and he paused to hear her out. "Tell me when will you let me go?"

"But I'll never let you go. Didn't you guess that?"

She had guessed that. There was no time now to react to his words, she must work quickly to try and get what she wanted, and ultimately prolong things; to devise a way out or wait for someone else to find her. He was leaving. "When you come back, can you bring a blanket? Please?" With an effort she had made her voice sound pleasant. The kind of voice you could agree with.

He considered her request. "No point in your getting settled. Not now." The door slammed behind him and the locks and bolts clicked home.

Overnight, the heart of Ruthin had been captured by the New Age people. St. Peters Square, the quaint market place in front of the fourteenth century church, had been filled with battered buses and camper wagons. Canvas lean-tos propped against the side of these vehicles sheltered those who had slept out through the balmy end-of-July night.

A single police Mini-metro stood parked impotently by the encampment. The local police had found themselves overwhelmed by the sudden invasion. The county forces were weighing up whether to muster enough to evict the hippies from the town centre. Against the proposition was the fact that it would be virtually impossible to dislodge anybody from St. Peter's Square. The streets leading into it were narrow. A defence of the position would be easy for the hippies should they wish to resist. Also, did the police have the manpower? Wouldn't it be easier all round just to let them stay for a few days?

Experience had shown that this convoy always did move on after a few days. Would it be better just to nurse the feelings that the sudden hi-jacking had caused, and allow things to take their natural course?

Lynch muttered to Power about the breakdown in law and order as he picked his way in between the campfires, piles of fuel, squatting figures in loose green and orange clothing, and dogs. A goat brayed at Lynch and scowling lunged at him too. The townspeople, who gathered on the fringes of the square, looked at the camp in the centre of their town with bemusement and disbelief. They were too puzzled to approach the ramshackle band. It looked like something out of pre-history or the pictures on the news of some third-world country. Some of them even wondered if this was a special festival staged by the Arts Council.

Power and Lynch were the only outsiders willing to enter the camp. They did so unhindered by the New-Age people who regarded the crisp-suited figures amiably enough.

Lynch dodged the goat's teeth with alacrity, and glowered at the people around him. Now he was in the midst of them though, and he wondered if he hadn't better modify his expression. He didn't want to antagonize the people. Their presence here was no threat to him personally after all. In fact he wanted their co-operation. He tried to look neutral. Power though wore an expression of uneasy anxiety. He scanned the ramshackle caravans and buses for a sign of Eve.

"She could be here," said Power.

"Be careful not to see evil where there is none," counseled Lynch in a low whisper.

"I'd have thought you'd have more to say about them...being a Christian and everything." Power's anxiety gave his voice an angry edge.

Lynch was unruffled by the jibe. "They're wrong and misguided, but not bad in themselves."

Then they saw him, climbing out of a big, green single-decker bus. The Piper in his bright harlequin rags looked up at the blue sky and stretched his arms and back. He yawned and let out a whoop of joy to greet the day. He looked southwards over the heads of the other travellers seated on the ground eating their breakfast and drinking their tea. Power and Lynch stood in front of him. And Power had the uneasiness that comes with deja vu. Here was the Piper, seen by Power last in reality in the woods at Alderley Edge, and last seen in Power's prescient dream atop the lighthouse tower. It was more than coincidence, it was synchronicity.

The Piper smiled at them and bowed slightly to Lynch and Power. "Gentlemen. Are you pilgrims joining us travellers? Are you seeking enlightenment? Or are you from the council?"

"We have spoken before," said Lynch.

"At the Edge it was," said the Piper. "A police man aren't you?" Lynch introduced himself and the doctor. "Is it about poor Sian? If it is, well, you'd better come in." He turned and climbed the steps into his bus. "Come on, it's quite clean."

And clean it was, though filled with the paraphernalia necessary for living outdoors. These items of hardware were ranged on the old seats and in the luggage racks, but confined to the front half. The rear was curtained off by a crimson rug that hung from ceiling to floor. The air smelled sweet. Power knew the smell from numerous student parties. The Piper stood in front of them holding the curtain aside. Beyond, the bus had been stripped of its seats. The interior had become a soft cave of red and purple and gold fabrics. Soft cushions littered the floor and the low bales of fabric that passed for seats. A thin veil of a curtain divided this inner sanctum, and beyond, Power could see a bed and rudimentary washing facilities. He could see also that the bed, only recently vacated by the Piper, was still occupied by a sylph-like figure. It was not Eve, but a short-haired dark girl. She was sitting up with a white sheet modestly wrapped about her nudity. She stared back at Power and, embarrassed, he averted his eyes.

The Piper had seated himself in the comfort of the cushions and Lynch was struggling to get down as low as the agile Piper. The Piper had chosen a golden flute from the several instruments that rested on a cloth-covered bench. He played a few notes. He played beautifully. Then when his guests were seated, stopped and waited politely for them to speak.

"Bach?" said Power.

The Piper nodded. "I had a Classical training, Doctor." Now he was alerted to it Power could hear the Home County vowels in the quaint speech patterns the Piper affected.

"You were at Alderley Edge," said Lynch, ignoring this exchange. He had his own agenda. "We questioned you about the murder of a girl who you had known. A member of your troupe." The Piper laughed at his choice of words. Lynch resisted the temptation to frown. "Was she close to you?"

"None of us is really close. We are our own."

"Forgive me, that seems rather an evasive answer."

"That was the answer that I thought fitted, Superintendent."

Lynch made his voice calmer. "Then I'll be more specific, shall I? Were you sleeping with her?"

"According to your law, she was under the age of consent."

"I think you are being evasive now," said Lynch quietly.

"I didn't kill poor Sian."

"Who did then?"

"I don't know. Nobody I know did. I make sure the people I travel with have the spirit...are free of anger..."

"You mean some people are excluded from this?..." Power was puzzled that the New Age people could be exclusive in any way.

"All groups have rules, spoken or unspoken. Like families. You know that, Doctor," said the Piper. "We keep ourselves pure by letting the impurities fall away."

Lynch probed further. "Around the time that Sian was with you, was there anyone else about? Some stranger. An 'impurity' who just joined you and later fell away?"

"Sian herself was a stranger. On the Edge of the group. She was falling away herself. Couldn't stay clean. Abusing her body and denying her spirit." All the while the Piper was scrutinising Power. He looked into Power's brown eyes and it was Power's turn to feel judged. Usually it was others who were disarmed by Power's eyes.

"But was there anybody?" Lynch asked again.

"I don't know. You might have noticed...the Edge was a big festival. Difficult to keep track of everybody."

"Are you their leader then?" Lynch had noticed the way the other vans and shelters clustered about the Piper's bus.

The Piper smiled. "I don't have that power. Don't want power. But they travel with me. Ask me things." Power noticed the girl was getting out of the bed. Her movement attracted his involuntary glance. He tried not to let his glance linger on her naked figure. It was difficult.

Power asked a question to focus his own mind away from the bare thighs he knew were so close by him. "You seem to dislike hierarchies?"

"Doesn't everyone except the person at the top of the hierarchy?"

Lynch concentrated the interview again. Ignored the nude figure beyond the veil. "Can you recall anyone in a white van?"

The Piper frowned and closed his eyes. He thought back through the assorted images that crowded his mind. At last he opened his eyes. "There was a white van, driven by a tall, thin man. Long hair.

He sat far away from everyone. Didn't seem to like the group. Sian talked to him once I think. Not more than a few words. He left. Drove off. Maybe she told him to go. I don't know. I never spoke to him. He was...distant. I think he had his own ideas. Not one of us."

Lynch nodded. He felt an inner excitement. The clue about the white van had stirred something in the Piper's mind that had been missing on the previous interview in May. But he wasn't entirely convinced. The coincidence of the Piper's presence at the Edge and in Ruthin was uncomfortable. "And, why are you in Ruthin?"

"We follow the earth magic where it leads us," explained the Piper. Power raised his eyebrow. Lynch, conducting the interview, remained impassive. " Following the magic is like following a tune. You go where you hear the music best."

"How do you know where to go then?"

"I measure the earth magic of a place by dowsing. There is a vortex here now, in this town, near this church. It was here well before Christianity. The energy will be at its height tonight. And at the Edge the power was greatest in May. We followed it there, like the wise men followed the star of Bethlehem.

This was too much for Power. "This is nonsense. How do you measure this earth force? If it can really be measured, how come it's not in any reliable scientific journals?" The Piper smiled annoyingly. "There's no basis for all this. No evidence at all," said Power.

Lynch interrupted again to follow his own agenda. He wanted to know where the Piper was when the Eddisbury Hill murder happened. "And in June, where did the earth magic go then?"

"We followed it south to France. Cernac."

"Whenabouts in June?"

"We stayed there all through June."

"You have witnesses, to back this up...that you were in France all that month."

"All of the people here."

"Besides the people here? I think they owe you a certain loyalty."

"I was playing at the Solstice Festival. Channel 4 made a film of the concert. You could ask them for the video, I suppose." He smiled innocently.

"Have you got any questions?" Lynch turned to Power. He had satisfied himself about the Piper.

"This book." Power fished in his pocket and produced *The Cheshire Ley*. "This book is about the ley line that runs from Alderley Edge right through Ruthin. Did you know about the ley line?"

"I've read it," said the Piper, not deigning to pick up the proffered copy. "It's by an Old Age priest."

"What do you think of ley lines?"

"I feel that you don't believe in anything, do you?" He peered closely at Power, as if divining his spirit by inspecting his face. "But there are ley lines, it's just that over the years they've grown weak... thin...you need worship along them to keep them strong, you understand? They only get strong if there is worship along their length. One day when there are enough New Age people there will be enough energy to open up all the old ley lines again."

"Someone has read about this ley line and misinterpreted things. Someone who is ill, mentally ill," said Power carefully, watching the Piper's face. "We think that there have been sacrifices, murders, along this ley line. Like a kind of ritual."

"You think that's why he took Sian's spirit?"

"We think so."

The Piper considered the matter for a moment then spoke. "I can see how illness might distort someone's soul, might make them do these things, but whoever it is doesn't understand the ley. Not really."

"You can help us if you like," said Lynch. "It's quite simple. Can you keep your people away from the Castle. Just for tonight?"

The Piper didn't ask why, but nodded. "I'll do that small thing for you. We came for a festival of music at Galchog. Near here. We don't need to be at the Castle."

Lynch and Power stood up. The Piper looked up at them. "I would offer you bread and honey, but we have so little gold and I guess you have eaten well already." Lynch took the hint and offered the Piper a ten pound note. He was well-satisfied with the Piper's information. The Piper pocketed the money with shameless gratitude and, as they departed, he began to play a tune he'd composed when he worked with the London Symphony Orchestra, a long time ago.

* * *

At four o'clock Power decided to dine simply in his room. He wasn't feeling very hungry, but he knew that if he was to make it through the long night's vigil he would have to eat something. He ordered two boiled eggs, toast and sweet black tea. He ate this sitting by the long windows that overlooked the terraced grounds. Down by the stone balustrading in the distance it seemed to Power as if there was an elegant woman leaning over to look down into the trees. She wore an elegant blue and green evening dress and her waist was slim and shapely. But when Power looked more closely the woman's dress lifted and twisting upon itself, fanned outwards into a display of peacock feathers. The illusion of an elegant woman had become, (what it had always been in reality), a magnificent peacock. As it strutted around on the stonework the bird let out a piercing shriek and the illusion was truly shattered. Power broke into the second egg, wondering if he shouldn't get an eye test.

Lynch had been fretting about for most of the afternoon, making phone calls to the Chief Constable and surreptitiously visiting the stone ring that stood on the southern-facing slope of the hill in the hotel grounds. Because of its seclusion the ring was secluded and seldom visited. Lynch had taken a compass and tape and measured the stones. Although he did not believe in the ideas behind the books, he was keen to test the accuracy of *The Cheshire Ley*, since it seemed to Lynch that this book might be the template for the Ley Man's delusion. Up to now the Ley Man had followed the book exactingly. Lynch had discovered that the ring of standing stones was set in a way that corresponded to the axis of Stonehenge itself. Correctly aligned the stones would predict the position of the sun at solstice and equinox.

"But this is incidental," said Power when he heard of Lynch's discovery. "A paranoid schizophrenic might fix on anything, any system. He collects murders. He could as easily use any other system for his ritual...the full set of tube stations...or all twelve signs of the zodiac. Remember the killer in New York who worked his way through the zodiac, randomly killing people...except that he chose each victim from different signs of the zodiac. But you need to study the system he's using. You need to become as familiar with it as you can. Then perhaps you can out-think him." Lynch had gone off, pleased with himself and the possibility of snaring the Ley Man in the act. Yet he sensed Power's detached grief at the loss of Eve. And because of his own foreboding Lynch could not talk to Power about her.

He busied himself assessing the ground around the stone ring. Where could they hide so that the ring was observable? Lynch was betting that the Ley Man must appear at the ring itself sometime in the twenty-four hours of 1st August. He wandered about the fields scouting for places to wait. And all the while he tried to be as inconspicuous as he could. For all he knew the Ley Man could be watching him from the hills across the valley. Whatever happened he must not suspect that a trap was being laid.

At last Lynch was sure of his ability to put the ring under surveillance, and allow his officers to come and go unseen as the rota would allow. They would suspend everything now until the few hours of darkness before midnight before settling themselves and their equipment down to wait.

* * *

Eve shifted herself in the darkness. The Ley Man had taken her outer clothes. She sat on the hard cold ground and her limbs tingled because the circulation in them was sometimes cut off. In the darkness time had no meaning. There was nothing to focus upon except the cold and the humming of something outside her door. It sounded like a fridge. The motor would occasionally switch itself into life and thrum to itself, and when the thermostat was appeased the motor cut out. She didn't know how long she had waited, but now she could hear him coming back.

* * *

In the evening Power had declined to join Lynch for a drink at the comfortable hotel bar downstairs. Instead he lay mournfully on his bed upstairs, not sleeping, hardly blinking, but staring out at the evening sky. Imperceptibly it seemed, the clouds were gathering and the sky was darkening. Power lay immobile, his movements as retarded as those of a rabbit frozen in the headlights of a car.

He asked himself over and over again, what had he to do with all these events? Lynch had been right when he said that an outsider would see Power as being inextricably linked in, even central, to the murders and the car bomb, and now the loss of Eve. He tried solution after solution to see if he could explain events. Nothing fitted. He felt confused by a welter of different emotions: loneliness, guilt and the intense fear that someone posed a very real threat to everything in his world. Someone who had murdered at least four times in the last few months, and who would have no compunction about repeating the act. No wonder Power was lying stunned by events. He felt as unreal as if the old world around him had simply ceased to be, and had been replaced by some shifting sand of chaos.

Just a quarter-of-an-hour before midnight Lynch knocked at the door. He waited in the plushly-carpeted corridor outside, and after a while knocked again. Alone in the dark, like a man sentenced to his own execution, Power slid himself round on the bed and sat up. He fumbled in the starlight from the window for his coat. He put it on with all the movements of an automaton.

He opened the door and Lynch outside noted how drained of

colour Power's face had become. "You took your time," he said. "We need to get into position. It's time." He started off down the stairs, and Power followed him wordlessly, vaguely listening to the words that Lynch threw out in his wake. "We'll start out with all five of us being at the stones. Later on we'll reduce down to three. I've said we'll need three there constantly. The two on relief can go and get a drink or whatever before coming back. The others are already there."

There was a hollow some thirty yards away from the stones. It dipped sharply into the earth and was filled with scrubby under-growth, which afforded shadow and screening, but as Lynch had im-pressed on them, they were to avoid unnecessary movements. In the night the sound of a man barging his rustling way through the bushes or cracking twigs underfoot might alert the Ley Man. Conversation was to be non-existent except for any urgent communication, to be conducted at no more than a whisper. If the man with night-sights saw anything before the others he was to wait until the Ley Man came into the clearing before alerting the others. If they were to catch him, they needed to see him, before he tried to escape, as he would.

Beside the hollow was a screen of rhododendron bushes, on one side of which was the hotel's empty auxiliary car park. Here Lynch had parked his car, which he had thoughtfully filled with a supply of coffee flasks and sandwiches. He was reasonably confident that the Ley Man would not approach the stone circle from the hotel side, and so they could retire to the car under the reasonable assumption that this would not be visible to the murderer. Lynch had surveyed the land carefully. The Ley Man might approach from the road that ran nearby, or the public footpath, or through the woods opposite the circle, in a clearing in which the circle stood anyway.

Ensconced in the hollow, and invisible to any who might wan-der into the clearing, Power looked at the deformed shapes of the standing stones. In the moonlight, with the eye of faith and imagina-tion, the heavy stones could easily be turned into broad-shouldered trolls who crouched upon the silvered grass. Power imagined them growling to one another as they struggled to their clumsy feet and be-ginning a ponderous circular rite to celebrate the darkness which lent them life. But the stones did not move, had not moved for countless years, ever since the strong hands of man had placed them there.

He looked about the clearing. The Ley Man might be here now in the shadows opposite, waiting. Or what if he never turned up at all? What if Power's theory was wrong? He checked the time on his luminous watch. One o'clock was not a good time for his self-confidence at the best of times, and he was beginning to realise that not only did the actions of the Ley Man revolve around him, he had become central to their solution.

He was staring intently into the darkness, trying to scan the shadows for any movement at all, when Lynch laid his palm on Power's arm. "Come on, Carl, it's two o'clock," he whispered. "Let's go and get a bite-to-eat."

Lynch let Power into his car which stood alone in the car park. They closed the door behind them, and at first the silence that they had maintained for over two hours now was difficult to break. Wordlessly Lynch had poured two plastic mugs of steaming black coffee. Power accepted the hot drink gratefully, but he didn't need the caffeine to keep him awake, there was that much adrenaline flying about his circulation. Power had been thinking about the policeman beside him. About the conversation they had had in the last few days. They had shared the image of watching a fire to ensure it didn't spread out of control. The image seemed to sum Lynch up. Lynch probably also saw himself as a watch against the fire.

When Lynch silently offered him a pate and tomato sandwich, Power broke the silence. His soft voice sounded momentarily unnatural, until he had grown accustomed to its use once again. "This is like a crusade for you, isn't it?"

Now he was in action Lynch was inhibited by the need to be silent. And yet he knew that their voices would be contained within the car, despite this he replied with one word. "Maybe."

"Do you think we've got it right? I'm worried that perhaps my theory is too way out...that I'm wasting your time and leading you down a blind alley."

"Don't think so," said Lynch stolidly munching away at a sandwich. There was a pause. Power waited. "I understand the theory. That all the murders occur on the ley line. Even if it sounds off the wall...I know it's right. I can feel it's right. It's just the murderer's motives that escape me...what moves him to do these things. Perhaps only someone with your expertise could make sense of Cain's sin."

It seemed to Power that 'normal' people desperately sought to distance themselves from the criminal. In doing so they denied their own darkness. Did Lynch deny his own shadow too? It was 'normal' people who went to war...killed millions. And society too would aver its own dark side. Power tried to find an explanation for the murderer's behaviour. He told Lynch a story.

"When I was a senior registrar I was called to a prison to see a man who'd served two years of a life sentence. They'd noticed he wasn't eating properly and was talking to himself in his cell late at night. To someone he called 'Jimmy'. It seemed reasonable to ask for a psychiatric opinion. His crime had been the murder of his best friend... and although he had confessed to it he would never discuss his motives. Never.

"When I arrived at this ghastly red-brick prison I was shown to his landing. He was lying on his bed. Painfully thin and shivering. But he wore no clothes. He held a towel tightly with both hands over his private parts. And the way he lay...absolutely still like a soldier at attention...catatonic, with his head raised just off the bed, lying on a non-existent psychological pillow.

"I sat by him on the bed and started to talk quietly to him. All at once he shot up. The guards leapt forward in case he attacked me, but he was interested in where I was sitting...he said 'You're sitting in the blood...a pool of blood...it's on your clothes.' And I'm sure that he could see this hallucination of blood. I asked him whose blood it was. 'Jimmy's', he said. 'It's coming from his chest' And he pointed to where he thought Jimmy was, sitting beside me. 'Jimmy's dead.'

"I talked to him for an hour. He had been in the army in Korea. He talked about the army and about recruiting. How he wanted to build a great army. I might have taken it for some grandiose idea, but then he said how he'd been thinking of recruiting various people in the prison. He called the army 'Jimmy's army'. I asked him who Jimmy was. It turned out that Jimmy had been his twin brother." Power looked out into the night. He went on quietly. "This twin had died of meningitis when he was six or seven. Since that time his living brother had re-invented his dead twin. The dead twin accompanied him wherever he went. He'd followed him into prison. They talked to each other...but where as one of the brothers had grown up the other had always remained a silently bleeding child. It seemed to me that this man was a schizophrenic, and I was making plans in my mind to get him some treatment sorted out, when I realised what he had really said to me when he spoke of recruiting. To test the idea out I asked him whether the best friend...whom he had killed...whether he had been recruited into Jimmy's army. He nodded. For to be recruited into Jimmy's army you had to be dead. And bear in mind that he had plans to recruit most of the prisoners on his landing. So...er...you see that motives for murder can be rather unusual, but in the mad there is a kind of...er...poetic reality."

To Power it seemed that Lynch was closed. He gave no sign of having heard Power's story. Lynch merely munched his way through the sandwich and took another. Could Power open up Lynch's thoughts? Would it help? After a lengthy silence, he spoke again. "After the second murder that's when you seemed to change...to me you seemed to change...you seemed to take things much more personally. After the death of a child." Power's voice had now become a deliberately soft probe into Lynch's psyche.

Lynch looked ahead. He suddenly could not bear to look at the man beside him. The words he had spoken held an extra meaning after the silence, as if increased in value by their rarity. Power noticed Lynch was blinking more frequently. Lynch asked himself how Power's words, ostensibly so superficial, had managed to pierce his armour so uncannily. How had Power pinpointed his mood and his reveries? Power imagined that Lynch's eyes were suddenly moist. The elegantly assured man had grown vulnerable.

"A child," murmured Lynch meditatively. "Our second child died. A heart defect. He never really grew properly. No energy to grow, I suppose. He looked about one year old when he died, but he was nearly two. I remember sitting up all night after an operation he had.

Sitting there in the hospital beside his cot. "Lynch looked into the blue velvet darkness beyond the window glass. "You try to forget. You try to come to terms with it. But the death of a child. Never. Never." And Lynch was affected by the memory of being unable to go and see the parents of the boy killed on Eddisbury Hill.

"Was your faith a help?" Power was matter-of-fact. This was no time to explore the grief that had never left the father. It would take longer than this night permitted. Far better to emphasise Lynch's strengths now.

"My faith? After the death I thought it was a sham for years. How could God let that happen to me...to a two-year old who'd not even started to live...done no wrong...it all seemed a hypocrisy and a delusion. Then something changed...something somebody once said to me. And a few years after it gradually became...I don't know...a comfort to me. I was found. That's how it felt. I was found."

A muffled cry from the darkness. Lynch was alert in a second and had the car door open. The shout was repeated from across the stone ring, "Sir!"

"Damn them!" Lynch slammed the car door and launched himself into the night. "I told them to be quiet. He could hear that for miles around. Frighten him off for good."

Again the officer's disembodied voice. "Sir! We've found something!"

Lynch and Power ran around the screening bushes and into the clearing where the three police officers were scattered outside their hiding place. Lynch scowled, then ordered, "Put the lights on!"

'Let there be light!', thought Power sardonically and then felt ill in the pit of his stomach, because this was the moment he had dreaded.

Lynch had reasoned that there was nothing to be lost in switching the floodlights on. Whoever he was would have been alerted anyway by now and the lights could only benefit the police present.

And there was light. The stone circle was flooded with incandescent light and instantly became a theatre-in-the-round. Against the night the major players entered the stage and stood within the ring. "What is it?" Lynch held his hand up in front of his eyes to defend them from the brightness, whilst he tried to identify where the shout had come from.

In the centre of the floodlit ring was a stone platform. The four police officers clustered around the flat slab of rock. A member of the audience for this theatre-in-the-round would have observed that Dr Power stood on the edge of the ring, moving ambivalently first into the light then out into the darkness again. "What is it?" he called out, unable to watch the proceedings any more closely, but anxious to know the worst.

"A bag, a canvas bag!" Sergeant Beresford called back. "One minute it wasn't there and the next it was, propped up by this altar."

"Is that all?" asked Power. "Just a bag?" Power's stomach was beginning to calm down, although he himself was vaguely disappointed that nothing had been resolved. Where was Eve?

"No," said Lynch. "That's not all." He swung the bag up from beside the stone slab where it had lain on the earth. The bag landed on the central stone altar with a soft thud. "The bag is heavy...there's something inside."

Power watched from the ring's edge in frustration, but his fear still would not allow him further. He saw that Lynch was undoing the draw strings that held the neck of the canvas sack together. Somewhere in the distance, a peacock shrieked into the darkness. Lynch lifted up the open-necked bag and tipped it upside-down. Something rolled onto the altar.

"Christ!" said Beresford. "Oh...bloody hell!" He turned away repelled by what he saw.

Power could not see what had happened through the bodies of the policemen who shielded his eyes. "What is it?" he asked softly.

"I think you'd better come and see, Carl," said Lynch into the night. "It's a human head."

"Oh God." Power felt frozen inside. "Is it?"

"It's a woman's head," muttered Beresford, glancing uncomfortably back at what lay on top of the stone altar.

THIRTEEN

"Carl, would you come here, please?"

A woman's head. Power stood transfixed, cold with sudden perspiration in the humid August night. For a while he held himself motionless, then slowly, like an automaton, he stepped into the light. The police waited for him silently like priests at a ritual as he crossed the ring to the centre stone.

It was another Power altogether who forced his eyes to look at the recent contents of the canvas bag. The fearful part of him wanted to run away forever, but he forced himself to look upon the flat-topped, grey stone.

A woman's head. Severed cleanly and, apparently, freshly. Pallid in the police arc lights. Close-shorn hair, moistly tipped with droplets of water.

Power let out a long sigh. It was not Eve. This was the face of a younger girl altogether. Somehow she looked familiar to Power though, who was she? Lynch could see the relief on Power's face, yet it didn't seem right to allude to it. Not here, not now after what they had found. Lynch knew that Power would be relieved that Eve had been spared, but then again, she was not returned safe yet either. And for himself Lynch was already beginning to know defeat again. The sense of failure washed over him like a slow-moving wave.

"Shall we search the woods?" asked one of the others.

"Wait until the daylight," said Lynch wearily. "If you're thinking of catching him, he'll be long gone. He's played his card and he's left the table." All at once he could not face the rigmarole of paperwork and communication that this discovery would entail. Perhaps Beresford could shoulder the burden for him? Lynch wanted to collapse into bed and pull the covers over his head.

"Didn't you see him?" asked Power. "He came into the centre of the ring and you didn't see him?"

Beresford sensed the criticism in the question, and tried not to let his defensive anger sound in his voice. It was there though. "If we'd seen him we'd have caught him. He was so quick."

"And noiseless too, apparently." said Power.

Beresford looked at him with annoyance. "When you're staring at the same scene for hours at a time...you sometimes get mesmerised. You don't take it in. He's good at night manoeuvres...he must have known we were there...planned how he could get across unseen."

"We do know he checks out the scene beforehand," Lynch said quietly. "Perhaps he saw us here preparing things yesterday. I thought we'd taken every care; I hoped we had...."

"There's something else, sir," Beresford felt he might as well confess everything since Lynch seemed to be in a resigned and rather fatalistic frame of mind. "The night sights went missing. That's perhaps why we didn't see him."

"Who had them last?"

"Me, sir." One of the other officers stepped forward, "I was scanning the stones; been scanning them for hours...and I had to go somewhere...to relieve myself. I put them down on the ground and crept deeper into the bushes. When I got back the sights had gone."

Lynch sighed. "Gone where?"

"I thought perhaps they'd slipped into the grass and weeds. I couldn't find the night sights in the dark. I thought I'd just lost them."

Lynch could see the irony of it all, but a smile was beyond him now. His voice was calm, and coldly factual. "And while you were scrambling noisily through the undergrowth to have a piss, the Ley Man took advantage of your absence and noise to pass among you like a ghost in the night. He even took the nights sights off you. He's been watching us instead of us watching him. He's been here all the time. All the bloody time!" He rounded on Beresford. "You clear all this up. Get the pathologist and the scene of crime people down here. Start the paperwork off. I'll meet you back at HQ later in the day. We'll all have some explaining to do."

Lynch walked away into the darkness beyond the circle towards the hotel. After a moment Power followed him, leaving the three police officers alone. Beresford watched the receding figure. He had worked long enough with Lynch to know his moods. This mood of failure was one he had never seen before. Lynch could be caustic in his search for efficiency. He usually conducted his inquiries with a ruthless elegance. He spared nobody's feelings and had shouted Beresford down on numerous occasions. It was actually one of the things that Beresford liked best about Lynch. You always knew where you were with Lynch. Beresford knew that his own mistakes were few and far between, but Lynch never failed to address them directly. But his mood tonight was different. Lynch had not had the courage to bawl anybody out for their mistakes. And it made Beresford feel far worse. In the distance he could see the two figures against the floodlit front of the hotel. The rest of the night would be filled with making all the arrangements for the morning: the pathologists, the site of crime investigation, all would need to be gone through again. Where possible Beresford would try to use the same people as before. He would direct things his way. But he knew that it was very unusual for Lynch not to keep direct control of the investigation. It did not augur well.

* * *

Sometimes she would touch her eyes. Without sight she felt as if sometimes her eyes might have disappeared. She almost expected her eye sockets to have gone, for the smooth skin of her cheek to spread smoothly and uninterrupted up to her forehead. For her eyes to have disappeared. That they had not, and that her eyes, lashes and eyebrows were still there, was a reassurance to her. Her sense of smell and hearing and touch had seemingly magnified to compensate. The boundaries of everything seemed to be melting though. She could smell, taste and feel her own fear. Things were dissolving. The Ley Man was the only contact with reality. He changed the darkness, floating into her consciousness with his distinct smell of dust and soft, high voice. She could even feel the air disturbed by his movements. There were three states of being now, Eve would slip from sleep to waking darkness to the Ley Man's presence.

He was here now, with food and water. He changed the bucket. She had always been repelled by her own excreta, but in this world without stimulation even the smell of her own waste was something she missed. She was so grateful to him when he brought the food. Strange how her ideas had changed about him. Sometimes in the hidden hours and days of darkness it seemed he was everything. The Ley Man was so very important to her now. Everything depended on him. She depended on him. This paradox at first seemed very strange, and then it no longer seemed a paradox. She was becoming quite finely attuned to his emotions, since everything including her life depended upon the whim of the Ley Man.

This was the man Carl had been seeking. They had talked about him. When the Ley Man went away Eve imagined what he had done: murder after murder after murder. Alone in the earth darkness she would tentatively approach a question as if it were a mantrap hidden in her mind. The question was simple; "What did he want her for?" Was he just keeping her to sacrifice her or did he obtain some warped pleasure from binding her into this cell of nothingness? Did he thrill to the idea of power over her every buried breath.

Today he was pleased. She could feel his smile and his excitement seemed to fill the air of the dank earth cell. She could tell this because the air trembled. Sometimes he started mumbling incoherently to himself. The excitement made him do so today. Anything that seemed important, stressful to him would fracture his thoughts. "I saw the powerful car. The power in the car. I saw it." What was he talking about? Horsepower? Engines? It was one of the riddles that formed his mind, but Eve tried to define his emotions, not the content. She felt sure she depended on his emotions. If he was in a good mood she could manipulate him; she thought so anyway. You could never be certain. His thoughts seemed to shift quickly. This mood of distant pleasure might last long enough for her to ask for the blanket. He still hadn't got her one. She got so cold at night that she slowed down. Hypothermia, she supposed.

The Ley Man moved around the cell more confidently today. He was usually hesitant. He wasn't used to the dark like her. Things were different today. He moved easily about the cell as if, in some way, he was able to watch her.

And this man who held her captive...she could not remember his face at all. Amnesia? The drugs he'd given her? Or had he hit her on the head? How had he got her here? From her flat? She couldn't remember him coming in there, couldn't recall the journey here. Was she near her home, or far away? Was Power out there looking for her, or...was he dead?

What would a psychiatrist like Power have called this man...a split personality was it? A multiple personality; maybe that was it. Maybe this man imagined himself to be several people; changing their personas like masks to suit the occasion.

Her curiosity got the better of her caution and while he was moving about her she relaxed her guard on her thoughts and asked, "Why do you do it?"

He sounded distracted as if his thoughts were far away; as if he could spare her only a fraction of his mind. "Do...do what?"

"You killed them, didn't you? You're the killer."

There was a pause and Eve wondered anxiously whether she had dangerously misjudged the moment and overstepped the mark, then he spoke, almost in a monotone. "Killing isn't the word they use. They call it liberation, yes, liberation, that's closer to the truth, I agree, yes. I liberate the souls from the hands of the evil one. I free them so their souls can fly up...up to the sun, where they came from before they were trapped in matter. We are all trapped in matter. Every liberation strengthens all of us...gives us power."

If Eve understood she didn't know what to say. The Ley Man watched the puzzlement on her face. "I thought you would understand," he said. "Your paintings...I thought you'd understand me." There was loss in his voice. "Does what I've said sound unusual to you? Isn't it true?"

She wished she hadn't asked. "I...er...I...it sounds a bit odd."

"Odd?" There was a stunned silence, then she could hear him breathing slowly through clenched teeth. She heard him shifting over the floor. Eve felt a fluttering in her chest. He was moving closer...then stopped. How far away?

"Did you know I could see you Miss Pearson?" She felt his breath on her face. Stale alcohol. "You have a beautiful face in infra-red. You look a little frightened though. I mean I've got special sights...another unfair advantage I'm afraid...but then it's you who's afraid, isn't it?

He thought back over what she'd said. "Do you think I'm a queer?" he asked. "Is that what you mean by odd?"

Her words came out in a rush. "No, no. Of course not.."

His fist caught her hard on the side of her face. She felt the knuckles digging into her soft skin, connecting with the zygoma bone of her cheek. Eve fell sideways to the floor. A stone jabbed into her rib cage, jerking the breath out of her in a short scream.

"That's enough," he said. "You'll be careful how you say things in future. Be more genuine." There was a tremor in his voice. Then suddenly he chuckled. "I wonder if I'll be able to see the bruise in infra-red?" Eve lay on the floor motionless, hardly daring to breathe. Every bit of her yearned to attack him and avenge herself. "Not to answer you though...that would be rude...I'll call you Eve now we've touched...but not the way I touch the others here.... No, no, no." There was a silence. Eve heard him moving away, his feet scraping against the floor. "I've got to go...it's getting busy...the bastard's busy doing the thoughts again." He was talking to someone else now. He'd turned away from her. "Not yet, no, wait. Not yet." He spoke to someone as if they were impatient. But there was no-one there, except for the voices in his mind telling him what to do. Telling him to kill her now.

Eve realised he might be away again for a long time. Each time he went she never knew whether it was hours or days before he returned. She must speak. "Please...before you go. Please could I have some food and water?" He was moving through the doorway. By now he couldn't distinguish her voice sufficiently from the others. She felt the change in air pressure as he closed the door. "Please!" The door closed to and the silence rang over everything again.

* * *

Sitting in his hospital office a day later Power read the newspapers with gloomy despair. The strong sunlight coming through the window was so bright that the whiteness of the page seemed to burn into his eyes, but he felt a still darkness settling upon his mood. The story had assumed front page importance in every paper. *The Sun* ran with the banner, 'Lynch needs Lynching', and a sub-heading 'Barmy cop fails to catch psycho' whereas *The Independent* had a more sober, but cutting article entitled, 'Home Office Row in Ley Man Case'. Power read below, 'Ministerial sources at the Home Office voiced disquiet yesterday about the handling of the so-called Ley Man murder inquiry by senior police officers. Victims of the murderer in the last six months have included a teenage girl, a twelve year old boy and a farmer from North Wales. Some sources suspect that other murders have yet to be detected and attributed to the multiple murderer who has struck, apparently randomly, in Cheshire and Clwyd.

'Chief Inspector Lynch, temporarily heading a supra-regional investigation into the characteristically brutal decapitations, had been following a theory provided by a consultant psychiatrist, Dr Carl Power. This involved the concept of ritual murder at specific pagan dates along a 'ley-line'. Senior ministers have expressed concern about Lynch's methods, pointing to his failure to capture the Ley Man at an operation in rural Ruthin, North Wales, two days ago. Police secretly watched a stone circle for twenty-four hours and failed to capture the murderer. The murderer though left a grisly clue, the head of a murder victim, hidden almost under their eyes.

'Home Office forensic experts have been called in to offer further advice. The political storm has not abated though and a furious row between ministers and shadow ministers seems likely to break out. "The ley line theory seems ludicrous to all right-minded people," said a Tory back-bencher, "This evil person or persons is clearly playing a sick and random game, and the police are listening to some crank psychiatrist, while people are being killed." It seems the theory is likely to be discredited and the course of the inquiry amended in the next few days.'

Later that day, towards the end of his afternoon clinic, Power's telephone rang. He had been listening good naturedly to one of his medical students' tediously overinclusive descriptions of a new patient. Power had had to listen carefully in case he missed something relevant in the welter of information. The shrill noise of the telephone came as a relief, but the voice of his secretary, Laura, seemed panicked. "Carl, I'm under seige. It seems someone has let on about your interest in this killer. The newspapers keep phoning me up. I've had to call security to evict one reporter who was ferreting in your room. They're asking me all kinds of questions about you. Dr Jones is jealous and curious at the same time. He's not very pleased. Keeps muttering about the reputation of the hospital and the welfare of the patients. All the same he keeps hanging about to see if they want a quote from him."

Power groaned. "I think it's time to take a holiday."

"Have you finished your clinic?"

"Just coming to a close," he nodded to the medical student, who grinned back.

"It won't be long before they figure out where you are," said Laura. "You should leave there as soon as you can."

"This is intolerable. How can I work like this?" Laura didn't answer. Dr Jones had just been saying something along the same lines about Power. He had even let it slip that he was considering the option of suspending Power 'for getting us all mixed up in this'. But Laura knew Jones and suspected it for what it was, bluster.

"And I've got a caller on the line. It's all right, it's not a reporter. It's a genuine call, a Superintendent Lynch. Shall I put him through?"

"Yes please." Power swivelled his chair around so that the medical student was out of his line of sight. He could tell that the medical student was hanging on to his every word, and although Power was an open man, the sight of the student goggling at him was off-putting. "Hello?"

"Carl? Have I got through to you at last?"

"I have a troupe of tame and not-so-tame reporters besieging me."

"I know the feeling. Be careful what you say. The press will quote anyone you talk to about anything. Have you seen what they're writing now?" Power grunted assent. "He's winning isn't he, Carl? Not only has he escaped the trap. Not only is he a genius at withholding clues, but he's also got the Home Office on his side."

"What do you mean?"

"They want the Ley Man's head on a plate...if you'll pardon the expression...and I haven't delivered. They don't want me in charge any more."

"There's always a search for someone to blame. If they can't get the murderer they pillory others, usually those they've heaped their own responsibility onto. Like social workers, criticised if they're too vigilant and take a child into care and also criticised if they're too lax and fail to take a child into care. How are you feeling?"

Lynch said nothing for ten seconds or so. Power deliberately kept the silence going. At last Lynch said, "The Chief Constable and I have been summoned down to London. High level talks with the Secretary of State. And I know that none of them are on my side."

"I wonder if you blame me for the idea?"

"How can I? It's the right idea. It's just them, they're so narrow-minded they don't believe anyone would act according to your theory. We're not dealing with anyone though are we, Carl? Well, no-one the politicians would understand. They only know statistics; the number of men on the beat, the annual number of car thefts, the number of victims. Nothing else matters. Mr Public is horrified and wants action, so Sir Politician wants action too. They want my resignation from the case. I'm angry with them not you. And I'm angry with my superiors for deferring to the politicians. But that anger is pointless, destructive...they've already decided. I'm on the way out."

"What will they do about Eve? Don't they understand?"

"They'll try something else. It won't involve either of us."

"Well, I'm not so sure that I can take this pressure any more. I would like to go back to being an obscure doctor again, but...."

"I don't think the Ley Man will allow that do you?" Power tried not to think about it, looked out of his consulting room window at the trees. "Carl, I know that I'm heading for an early bath, but somehow this case has been like nothing else I've ever worked on. It's sucked me inside out. I feel like I'm really fighting something here and I can't let go that easily. If you hear anything, tell whoever's in charge, but tell me as well. Will you do that? Will you keep me in touch?" He waited until Power agreed. "Thank you, Carl. Goodbye. You'll be in my prayers."

Lynch took the five o'clock Pullman in the company of the Chief Constable. At eight o'clock they met the Home Secretary and his advisers. The nine o'clock news carried an interview with the Home Secretary and the announcement that a Senior Police Officer had been suspended. "The intense hunt for this vicious murderer will be re-doubled. We have a new commander for the inquiry and a new strategy," said the Home Secretary, but he refused to be drawn into describing any detail of what this might be. To tell the truth he wasn't sure.

* * *

The journey back to Chester on the Inter-City Pullman was tense. Lynch sat in stony silence across the table from the Chief Constable...who in turn kept his grey eyes down on the paperwork in front of him. From time-to-time he signed letters and read reports switching papers between his executive briefcase and the table. As he swivelled between the case and the table he took care not to glance at Lynch, who stared defiantly at him.

"You will be assigning me to a position in the Ley Man investigation, though." It was Lynch who had broken the silence.

The Chief Constable drew a deep breath. Should he ignore the comment? It was clearly designed to provoke him. Lynch had cost him dear with the Home Office. Now Lynch was just being unbearable. "I don't think that the 'Ley Man Enquiry' is altogether a good title. I would prefer the enquiry to be completely dissociated from 'Ley Men', 'ley-lines' or any of that mumbo-jumbo."

"But that's the way the murderer is thinking. It doesn't matter what you think of ley lines. Your opinion won't change the Ley Man or what he's doing."

"It's not helpful. You're not being helpful. I will ask your section head to re-assign you to some other investigation. That's if you wouldn't like some leave. I gather you've been working very hard on the case. I won't dispute your dedication. Partially of course it's my fault for allowing a...I mean although you're a senior officer, this case has assumed proportions that..."

Lynch didn't like the implication that he wasn't up to the job and was overtired. "I wouldn't wish to be re-assigned, sir; I feel I have built up an expertise in this case and..."

The Chief Constable frowned. Lynch wouldn't back off with any grace. "But the officer I assign to the case will need a free hand. You must see that a fresh mind will see the case differently. I don't want a potential personality clash to detract from.."

"I can take orders. I am a professional who could work under another officer even if it was my case before. It's just that I need to find this man, I need to see the solution through."

The Chief Constable sighed, "No-one would dispute your dedication, Lynch. But dedication, this 'need' of yours, could blind you. Maybe has blinded you. There's no point in endlessly debating this. I will be asking for you to be re-assigned."

"I won't leave the Ley Man case, sir."

"I think you will, Superintendent."

"I will not."

The patience of the elder officer snapped. "If you can't keep out of Barnes' way..."

Lynch's eyebrows shot heavenward at the news of his successor. "You're not letting Barnes get his hands on the case!" Lynch knew Barnes was methodical, indeed obsessional in his attention to detail, but singularly unimaginative.

The Chief Constable ignored Lynch's protest and tried again to say something through without interruption. He leaned over the table and hissed at Lynch. "If you can't keep out of Barnes' way I will suspend you." Lynch gaped at him. He had never come this close to disciplinary action before. It was some measure of how he felt: the importance that this case had assumed in Lynch's heart. The Chief Constable sat back in his chair, gratified by Lynch's temporary speechlessness.

Lynch's next words were as much for himself as the Chief Constable. "I can't leave this case alone, sir."

The Chief looked down at his papers. He was matter of fact, without looking up. "That's simple then. I'm suspending you from tomorrow. We'll review the situation in two weeks. And if you decide to stir things up while you're suspended...if you go interfering in Barnes' investigation we'll have grounds for further disciplinary action."

Lynch closed his eyes. The world had suddenly become unreal and distant. It was time to be quiet. He was far out on a thin and narrow branch, but inside him his conscience was telling him he couldn't leave the case alone. And he knew he couldn't.

* * *

Power awoke red-faced, hot, sweating. He peeled the sheets off him and sat on the edge of his bed trembling. The recurring dream of Hammadi had assailed him once again. Power knocked the bedside light on and crossed the room to throw open the windows.

He stood cooling off in the night breeze. The curtains flapped around him. He couldn't stop himself peering out into the darkness below the window to check there was no-one there. It had been like this for nights now, ever since the Ruthin Ring a week before. After a few hours' sleep he would jump into wakefulness and fight with the temptation to pick up his things and go – to drive his Rover far, far away from this once-happy house and never return. But he stood his ground. He would tour the house, compelling himself to enter each and every room to check it was empty. To check that the Ley Man hadn't stolen into his house in the night. Then when he was quite sure he was alone he would lock his bedroom door tight, bolt it twice and search behind curtains and chairs; underneath the bed; inside wardrobes. When he felt finally safe – when he had laid his own ghosts to rest and taken possession of the whole house again then he could slip back into sleep.

Tonight the dream had come back, but it had been different. The dream returned with insistency every night. What was he missing? What was his unconscious persistently trying to tell him?

Tonight, as before, the shadow-wolf had been hunting him across the flat green earth. He had felt the hot and humid breath on his neck. Turning, he had seen the yellow canine teeth gaping wide, waiting for his flesh. Strands of thick, silver saliva trailed from the black wolf's slavering mouth and danced upon the wind that rushed past them both.

Power could hear the animal growling an unnaturally deep sound that resounded and reverberated deep within him. It was a growl that filled all time, which filled everything.

The tower was nearer now. He could see the open door in the

golden walls. He had managed to keep ahead of the wolf, only just, but he was still fractionally in front. Power put on an extra spurt, although his muscles had ached themselves into a knotted scream. And it seemed that with the effort he almost flew across the dreamland. Through the doorway. He whipped around and gripping the edge of the door swung it, slammed it in the face of the shadow-wolf. He saw the door shudder; heard the dull thud as the wolf's body fell against the stout door. It looked a bit like his own front door.

And he was floating gracefully up the spiral stairway. Up to the very top, through a hatchway and onto the balcony. It was a lighthouse. Now Power was walking around the circular balcony. He looked through the golden railings onto the grass world below. The wolf paced angrily back and forth outside the stout door. And Power was glad that he was safe; that solid stone wall and doors lay between him and the shadow-wolf. From up here he could just see the wolf. It felt safe now. Behind him the vast glass light mechanism was beginning to turn. The glow of the filament was becoming a beacon of light to shine against the darkening sky. And Power realised he was not alone on the balcony. The Piper was here, now grown old. The Piper opened his mouth to talk, and Power knew that what he was about to say would be the most important thing he had ever heard. It was then he woke up, without hearing the Piper's words.

For a while he lay there feeling somewhat cheated. The dream had acquired a most vivid sense of importance. The sense of being hunted, of near death and then defeating the hunter, cheating death. And the dream suddenly made sense to him. In real life he was being persecuted. Lynch had said Power was central to everything: 'inextricably linked.' In one sense the dream merely confirmed his daytime fears. Power was being hunted and all that he held dear was at risk. The wolf was a symbol, but of what? Power's unconscious had selected the dream wolf not just because it thought him the persecutor, the murderer, but because he represented something else.

The wolf was the embodiment of all the dark things in Power's character. It was his shadow, his alter ego. The shadow sheltered Power's negatives: his arrogance, his restless anger, his fears of his own potential illness, the keys that drove him to heal and solve other's illness.

Then Power was suddenly sure of something. The Wolf was ravening madness, the wolf was a mad thing, uncontrollable, something that had to be locked away. Lying in bed Lynch was visited by the certainty that the murderer was a patient.

Sometimes our dreams compel us to look at the truth. That he was being hunted by a patient was something Power had suspected all along. But he had never acknowledged his suspicions completely. To do so would be overwhelming.

True, Power had for years fought the battle to become a consultant, forging his way through medical exams and the ranks of Senior House Officer and Registrar – but it was as if now, from this remove the battle he had fought had been the wrong one. For years he had been drifting with the tide. The real battle, the battle with Power's shadow, had only just begun.

If Power was to control his fear he would also need to take control of the situation, instead of doggedly following the wake of destruction left by the Ley Man. Instead of being buffeted and meekly accepting the havoc wreaked by the murderer he would have to think ahead of the Ley Man. It was not enough to rely on others. After his summary dismissal from the Ley Man investigation, (Barnes had terminated Power's advisory contract without a word of explanation), this would be his own, his sole quest.

Having stirred himself Power went downstairs into the living room. He switched on the heat and scattered the neat pile of papers on the table to find the Ordnance Survey maps. He spread them upon the floor as he had done before and, taking a ruler, drew a long, straight line on the map that linked Eddisbury Hill and Ruthin. This was the ley line, or as Power thought of it now, a front line.

While he was staring at the line and every point that it crossed, the dream wolf image flashed through his mind again, and all at once there was a name, the name, which he hastily wrote down on the key to the map, before he could forget it. After so many hours spent cudgelling his brain and so many years since he had thought of it, the name had simply jumped into his consciousness.

Having delivered itself of the name, his mind could relax, and the tension that had held Power wound like a spring for weeks had diminished. He switched off the lights and made his way back into the softness of his bed.

* * *

She could just hear him talking softly, whether to himself or to her she couldn't tell. "Have you ever had a goal – something you really wanted...that you were prepared to risk everything for? A kind of wanting that was so immense that it hurt inside?

"When I was five I fell ill...meningitis...terrific pain in my legs and my neck and lights looked so bright I could feel my eyes burning in their sockets. I thought I was going to die. They showed me the fluid they took out of my back...I remember seeing it, blurred, against the light...the fluid from the lumbar puncture...it's meant to be clear...mine was white, full of infection. I remember them talking about me. They stuck drips into me, intravenous antibiotics...and I'm coming to the point now. The doctors saved my life. My hearing was never the same, but they saved my life...and in saving my life they gave me one ambition." He made a strange gulping noise as if convulsed by some strong emotion. "From the age of five I wanted to be a doctor."

"You know getting there...to be a doctor...takes application. You don't have to be a genius, just persistent. I wasn't that bright so I had to work harder than most. And the ambition took me over. Still obsesses me. I slogged my way through 'O' levels, limped towards the 'A' levels...but by then I could tell something was wrong. Something battling against me. It was such a struggle, the learning and the exams, I knew I was fighting someone. Then when my father died...just before the 'A' level exam I knew I was fighting a real bastard. I failed the exams. Wouldn't you? They said that if there was a next time...the year after I would have to get even higher grades. The stakes kept on getting raised. I matched them. I shouldn't have done. I know the bastard is so strong, so very strong. And he lets you get so close and then he rips it all away.

"I started to protect myself against him. Wouldn't you? Had to keep myself and my mother safe didn't I? If I did things, certain things in a certain way, he wouldn't bother me, you know, I warded him off. I did all that stuff and next year I passed my exams. I could keep the bastard away from me if I tried hard, if I did the right things.

"I got into medical school. I didn't like it at first...after all that... being away from home...cramming all that anatomy in. It was like learning the A to Z map only in three dimensions. But...I still dreamed of getting my hands on patients...being real, really real. We weren't allowed on the wards till the third year though. Until after the 2nd M.B. exam – the big one – make or break exam. I couldn't wait that long. I started putting on the white coat my father had given me after my 'O' levels and going onto the wards – easy – not like today – they didn't check who I was. I talked to all of them, examined them. Took blood. Put up drips. Once I got the nursing staff convinced I could write in the notes. Once or twice I even signed for prescriptions. I was good at all of that. The patients liked me. I don't think anyone found me out. Different today. I've tried it. You've got to have identification badges and things like that.

"I suppose I neglected my studies...or he made sure I neglected them, I mean. The exams came round sooner than I had supposed and I wasn't ready. I stayed up till 2, 3 ,4 in the morning drinking endless cups of coffee. A friend let me have some of his amphetamines...or ecstasy or something...great...I felt I had superb amounts of energy; I felt on top of the world. I think he was piling it on though, really trying to break me...because before I knew it...he had started to communicate properly with me. I'd known he was there all along – just behind me...a little way behind me...like some kind of shadow. But now he was talking to me. And soon he was talking to other people about me... people I couldn't see.

"One night I was in my room working away...but it wasn't making any sense...hadn't for some time...endless pages of nonsense... just the ambition made me keep going – working at night. Sleeping all day. The memories are distorted...I.... They noticed I wasn't coming out of the room, wasn't coming out for food. I remember being thin. I remember them breaking the door in. I remember lying on the floor, watching, while he talked to me all about it...'They're breaking in now. This is the end. They're going to take you in hand...take you away from all this'.

"I spent months on a psychiatric ward. I was there when Power was an SHO. I watched him being made up to a Registrar. He was a cocky bastard. All the nurses liked him. And as his career took off mine nose-dived into the shit. That was it. Power said I wasn't fit. Couldn't take the strain. Then I knew...suddenly one day I was watching Power laughing with the nurses in the ward office...and I suddenly knew that he was the bastard – the one I had been fighting against all the years. All that time spent fighting him, and here I was in the power of Dr Power. And now he's a consultant...it's my turn to break him." From his voice Eve could imagine that his face was twisted with hate. " You're my bait, and he'll follow you. He'll toe the line, he'll follow the line... and when I kill him...when I kill him...I will have the power."

FOURTEEN

Lynch opened the morning post with less than enthusiasm. The day stretched ahead of him seemingly endlessly. Would this be what retirement would be like in twenty years' time? Mrs Lynch fussed around him, clearing the breakfast things. Lynch took a sip of lukewarm black coffee before the mug disappeared and slit open another bill. He had saved the most interesting looking letter till last.

The long, white envelope was handwritten and posted in Chester. It felt slightly bulky, as if filled with more than one piece of paper.

It was from D.S. Beresford. Lynch smiled broadly as he read the faithful sergeant's words. He spoke of his sorrow that Lynch had been suspended and how everybody thought Lynch had been on the right lines (Lynch wondered whether Beresford's pun had been intentional). It was a dangerous letter to write for someone chosen to be incorporated in the new murder team under Superintendent Barnes. The letter served to demonstrate the trust that Beresford had in his old commander. Beresford wrote that he was sure it would not be too long before Lynch was vindicated. Lynch gave a wry grin; Beresford wasn't as worldly-wise about politicians as he might be. The world of the Home Office and Chief Constables would never allow itself to see Lynch vindicated, whatever happened. To do so they would have to admit their own mistake, and that would never do. Nevertheless, Lynch appreciated Beresford's courage and loyalty in sending the letter.

What Beresford had enclosed with the letter was more disturbing. Beresford had obviously taken it upon himself to leak whatever documents came his way that might interest his former boss. Lynch was torn between reading them and casting them into the bin. His wife had said, of the investigation, 'Put it behind you and start living your own life again.' And she was right, Lynch thought, the investigation would never be his again. The Chief Constable had made it abundantly clear – he would brook no interference from Lynch.

The two photocopies Beresford had sent were still in his hands though and Lynch could not, in the end, resist the temptation they represented. He read them avidly.

The first was an internal memo by Barnes:

'I must thank you all for welcoming me as the new head of the supra-regional murder inquiry into the Alderley Edge killings.

'In the light of recent events in the county of Clwyd we must re-double our efforts to locate the murderer. The key to this will be solid, methodical police work, and though I must pay tribute to those who have co-ordinated the previous inquiry, I must make it clear that we must now progress step-by-step, verifying our sources, cross-checking everything, before making any quantum leaps into speculative New Age theories!

'Our best approach will be to start again and re-evaluate every item of information we possess. This will be an exhaustive task, but I am sure that the vital clue lies hidden, perhaps overlooked, in the statements that we already have.

'I look forward to meeting the entire team on August the 10th at 8.30 a.m. for a special briefing about the future conduct of the investigation.'

Lynch finished the letter and snorted with contempt. "Bloody time-waster," he muttered.

Mrs Lynch looked out from the kitchen. "What's the matter?" she asked, thinking to herself how flushed and angry her husband had become.

"Nothing," he murmured, folding two sheets from the letter away into the chest pocket of his shirt and smiling unconvincingly at her. She ducked back into the kitchen, thereby avoiding any conflict with him.

He opened the second photocopy Beresford had sent him. It was a report by the Home Office Pathologist.

'Initial Report on Specimen 5605 from Ruthin Ring Site, August 1st.

Macro: Female head. Early teenage, (see photo). Shorn fair hair, blue eyes. No evidence of decomposition. Tissue layers intact. No gas separation. No surface abrasion or laceration. No evidence of cranial injury ante- or post-mortem. Features intact.

Intra-cranial contents: Intra-nasal and buccal cavities patent and intact. No evidence of intercourse. No haematoma. Pharynx intact. No haemorrhages. Brain tissue; some evidence of hypoxia (secondary to hypovolaemia, rather than asphyxia). Evidence of ice crystals in hypothalamic region and foramen magnum.

Tissue typing: HLA and ABO Tissue Match exactly with torso and limbs of corpse found at Alderley Edge, May 1st.

Opinion: Head matches body of fourteen year old girl found Alderley Edge three months earlier. Lack of decomposition and presence of ice crystals in brain tissue suggests that head was stored for three months at sub-zero temperatures and had partially thawed at post-mortem examination.'

Lynch sat back in his chair and held the report at arm's length re-reading it. "What kind of a man does this?" he exclaimed. Mrs Lynch popped her head around the door again.

"What did you say?"

"Er...what time is it?"

"Nine o'clock. What are you going to do today? Do you want to come into Chester with me?"

Lynch thought about the prospect. It was not altogether objectionable. "When are you going in?"

"Ten o'clock," she said.

"I will come then," Lynch declared. " I just need to do some phoning...make an appointment with someone."

"Who with?" She suspected he was up to something.

"An old friend...a parish priest I used to know. Thought I'd go and have a chat. It's been a long time."

She smiled. At least it was nothing to do with the murders. "You go ahead then...as long as it's not a lay preacher." Lynch missed the joke, weak though it was. "We'll go in after I've finished in here. Perhaps you could take me out for lunch too."

Lynch nodded, but he was still preoccupied with Beresford's photocopies.

* * *

On Sunday, feeling purified by Communion at the Cathedral Lynch drove easily out of Chester city centre into the countryside and through the meandering lanes to the village of Burton. His passenger lived in an old cottage in the village centre built directly onto the red Wirral sandstone. Against the low, whitewashed walls the Reverend Watkins, (although in his nineties), had hung baskets of fuchsia, lobelia and alyssum. Lynch parked with care at the roadside, hurried out of the car and round to open the passenger door. The elderly Rev. Watkins didn't seem to require this solicitous concern and emerged quite agilely from the car.

"I'd lock the car if I were you," he said, making his way through the wooden gate and up the path to the door. "People aren't what they were."

Lynch followed the old man up the path, admiring the fountains of flowering honeysuckle and climbing roses that festooned the archway of his front door. The scent of the roses permeated even the darkest, dust-laden recesses of Watkins' country cottage. He lavished his remaining life-energy on the garden, but left the simple interior of the cottage to the weekly care of his housekeeper. The old man insisted on making a pot of coffee while Lynch sat somewhat guiltily on the flower-patterned sofa. He listened to the old man rattling saucers and cups in the kitchen outside. The bookcase stood by the side of the sofa and Lynch amused himself by looking for copies of Watkin's own books. To Lynch's knowledge Watkins had written two books, *A Life of Paul* and the infamous *Cheshire Ley* which Power had re-discovered. Lynch could detect only one battered first edition of Watkin's *Life of Paul.* The other book, in all its editions, was conspicuous by its absence.

The old man returned with the tray of coffee and cake. His bearing was straight and he moved with ease. One might have taken him for a well-preserved sixty-year old. He sat down and poured a cup of coffee for Lynch. "Have some cake...it's apple cake. My own recipe. I make it with my own honey. I keep the bees at the back of the cottage. They find plenty of meadow flowers round here. You can taste the wild flowers, or so I like to think." He looked at Lynch through gold-rimmed spectacles. "Well, I am grateful to you for offering to take me to the Cathedral. Since I gave up driving last year I've made do with the local church here in Burton. You miss the choir...they have this real sound of heaven. Well young man, we haven't spoken for many years, since we lived in the same village, in fact. I've listened to you talking about your wife and your children. But you haven't said anything about why you sought me out." Lynch shifted uncomfortably. "Forgive me if I'm a little direct. It is partly my age and partly being of the cloth. We often seem to have to mind-read. Not often people can talk about what really vexes them. I read somewhere, in *The Times* I think, that you'd been having disagreements with the Home Secretary. I've disagreed with every Government since the War...and I mean the 1939 War, but I suspect that you're more troubled by your disagreement than I have ever been."

"It's not been that bad. I think once you've decided to make your stand, once you at least think you're right, then you can stick by the consequences." Watkins raised his eyebrows, but did not comment directly.

"You have no regrets?" Lynch shook his head. "I have regrets. Plenty of them. Some people say that, if they had their time again, they wouldn't change a thing about their lives. I'd change an awful lot of things about my life. You know, I think I know why you've come here today. I wondered when you rang up, I thought about it, and I understand now. It's about the ley line, isn't it?"

"The book? I was looking for it on the shelves."

"Won't keep it in the house. It's only one of the things I regret. I read about what had been going on in *The Times*." Watkins shook his head, and Lynch was fascinated how, in the sunlight from the tiny windows, his paper-thin skin seemed almost transparent. "I asked for forgiveness today."

"Why?"

"You wouldn't be here unless you thought there was a link between my book and those murders. You didn't think you could come here and spare my feelings did you? Just gloss things over and talk of nothings and then casually drop something in the conversation about ley lines? Get me talking like the old fool I am? No. I may be old meat, but I must face the truth about myself. I must face the truth soon any way. You do think there is a link, don't you."

"Yes, it was a friend, an expert in people's minds who suggested the murderer was using the Cheshire ley line, for...well, for sacrifices. But he could have been using any one of a hundred books on ley lines. Not necessarily yours."

"You're trying to spare me again. The truth is that my book was first. Written in the thirties, before any of this was fashionable. I sold it lock, stock and barrel to a publisher for thirty pounds. A young fool I was then, I've just got older that's all."

"Well, it does sell well, if you'd hung on to the royalties...it's been re-printed so many times. Selling even better today, of course."

"You misunderstand. If I'd kept control I'd have let the book die years ago. I would never have allowed the first re-print. But, no, when

I refused to revise the text for further editions they got a ghost-writer to do it. My name still appeared on the cover. I remember when the book first came out though. After the Bishop's comments...I realised what I'd done. It seemed like a party piece at the time...like telling fortunes. The Bishop pointed out I was glorifying the old religions. He spiked my career. But that wasn't the worst of it."

"You mean the book held you back? But it was only a piece of fun."

"Superintendent, you yourself know how seriously people take these things. Don't spare me anything, please. I won't have it.

"Yes, the book delayed my promotion. The little book on Paul helped things, (you can imagine how that sold compared to the Cheshire Ley), I recovered gradually and got my own parish, a nice vicarage, a moderate enough stipend to allow me to marry, but that book has always been a damn thorn in my side. The worst thing about it all was the serious reviews...by the Professors of Archaeology and the like. They didn't just roast the book, they incinerated it!

"Tell me, where was the first sacrifice?"

Lynch replied, "Alderley Edge...outside the caves. A Celtic settlement according to your book."

Watkins nodded. "Yes, the ley line idea is that all these important Celtic sites were built on the ley line, because they pointed to the holy places. They were lines of importance, lines of force, between the ancient sites. So, I wrote the book in a fervour. I'd discovered the ley myself. Fired with enthusiasm after reading books on Avebury and Old Sarum. They were as badly researched as my own."

"How do you mean? I've looked at the maps. The sites line up all right."

"If you plot all the ancient sites in England you can draw so many lines a computer would be kept busy for weeks. It depends what ancient sites you look at. The archaeologists held me over the fire rather like Flashman held Tom Brown in *Tom Brown's Schooldays*. The sites I chose for the ley line were all important, but at different times in history." Watkins hung his head at the thought of this scholarly blunder. "I just didn't see it at the time. Alderley Edge is part neolithic, and part-Roman. I didn't distinguish between the two. Where else was there?"

"Eddisbury Hill."

"Eddisbury Hill. Yes, Eddisbury Hill is a hill fort. But a ninth century fort. The choice of its site can't have been made by the same people who lived at Alderley Edge. They'd been dead for hundreds of years."

"Foel fenlii...the hill-fort there?"

"Iron Age. Another separation of nearly a thousand years."

"The Ruthin Ring then. When was that built? The orientation is the same as Stonehenge."

"Oh..." Watkins blushed. "That's the worst one of all. If I'd talked to anybody in the village. If I hadn't been so arrogant and ignorant as a youth. The ring was built...." He found it difficult to admit this. " The ring was built this century. Er...for a Welsh Eisteddfod."

The two men stared at each other. A bashful smile crept over the old man's face. He chuckled to himself at the dreadfulness of it all. Before either of them could help it they were both laughing. Lynch was laughing at the irony of it all, Watkins was laughing at his own ignorance. "You can see," he said as he tried to regain his composure. "Why I've tried to get rid of the book. Tried to stop its sales. But it sells too well." He suddenly became serious. "That's what the real danger is. What the danger has always been, through all the years, ignorance."

The joke was done and there was a stillness in the room. "It doesn't matter if it is all wrong...even if it's as ridiculous as it is. People believe it. You'd think it'd be difficult after a hundred years of scientific method. No. And your man. It's more than a theory for him, it's his life." Lynch could see the weight of responsibility burdening the old man opposite. His laughter had been replaced by a time-worn dismay.

"There's nothing I can do to put it right, is there?"

Lynch thought about it, but his mind was a blank. "If only there was."

"There isn't. If people want to believe in something or someone they will. What are you going to do?"

Lynch could have replied, 'nothing, it's not my case any more'. He could wash his hands of it all, but that would hardly comfort the old man who faced the barren truth alone. "You've been helpful." Lynch said.

"I don't see how."

Lynch struggled to think of how what Watkins had said could be useful. He couldn't though and it was no use flannelling the old man. He had grown too wise, in spite of, perhaps because of, the cross he bore. And Lynch's visit had only made the cross of the book harder to bear. He couldn't say anything.

At last the old man said something. " Thank you for being honest with me. They aren't always honest with old people. My G.P. makes it always sound as if I'll live another ninety years. People are either unrealistic or patronising." He paused. "What are you going to do about him, the Ley Man? The ley line doesn't stop in Ruthin. What will you do?"

"He works to the ley line, but that fact is the very key to how we'll catch him. He sticks to the line. Has to, I suppose, or the magic won't work. We nearly got him at Ruthin." The problem was, and Lynch refrained from saying it, that Barnes wouldn't touch the ley line theory with a bargepole.

"I see," somewhat relieved by the Superintendent's words. He had always seemed such a competent young man. "But I gather from the press that you're no longer in charge of the investigation." There was no fooling the old man now, despite his protestations of ignorance in his youth. Watkins decided not to torture the young man though. Instead he feigned tiredness. "Thank you for taking me to the communion service. A great comfort, all told. If you will excuse me I usually have a nap before lunch. And after lunch for that matter. Would you mind? You've been so very kind."

The Superintendent said his goodbyes and left. Watkins listened to the car outside revving up and driving off. He had felt so guilty before the Superintendent called. He felt better now. The communion had helped. The ability to confess one's sins. Strange to have sins left to confess at his age, maybe. The forgiveness of sins. Makes you feel better, he thought. Suddenly he did feel sleepy. Maybe if I just close my eyes for twenty minutes or so, he thought, then I can have that cold chicken and potatoes for lunch. Sleep drew him into its soft and welcome oblivion.

* * *

Alone in the cold earthwomb Eve saw no end, no boundary to the darkness. She could feel the damp soil walls that enclosed her, but not see them. Her eyes were simply redundant. Her body might easily enough merge into the darkness and become one with it, for there was no knowing where the darkness began – outside or inside the globes of her eyes. While she slept though her mind's eye was filled with vivid colour. And with every day that passed the waking hours too were being filled with the dream-like imaginings of her mind, projected into the nothingness. The mind abhors a vacuum just as nature does. Eve's sensory deprivation was such a vacuum. Without the stimulation of genuine sight and sound her consciousness was filled with the noise and images from her own mind. The distinction between dreaming night and waking day had blurred, and were dissolving like a wall made of sand.

The threatened dissolution of her being somehow began to seem infinitely more frightening to her than the Ley Man. When he came at least there was a crack of light in her darkness. The images were dispelled by the sound of his voice. Part of her had even begun to welcome the return to reality that his presence gave her. With his voice the noises stopped (except for the machine humming outside) and the images that danced before her collapsed into the ground.

But as he left her earthtomb, the images would crawl back from the edges of her mind. The food and drink he brought would provide some kind of anchor to this world. But once they had been consumed and the taste had dissipated in her mouth, the images would return triumphantly, cavorting through her mind as a kaleidoscope carnival of sight and sound.

Once upon a time the walls that cocooned her became the hexagonal wax sides of a cell in a bee hive. Round about her giant hallucinated bees would dance and hum so that their noise filled the vault of her skull. In the cell beneath hers, a larva stirred. Another time the head of a worker bee, with glistening compound eyes, stared in at her. The images may have only lasted the few brief seconds that the neuropeptides in her brain existed, but for Eve time was no guardian. The brief nightmares might dilate into centuries of experience.

There was food, water, the Ley Man, elimination of her own waste and the carnival of dreams. Nothing else but these things filled her universe.

Once upon a time she was a girl again, and the old man was coming for her, towering above her. "Hell is..." chanted the choir inside the skull. "Hell is Hell is the Condition of those who Cannot. Cannot love." The words echoed in the tomb and the old man reached down to her. Red skin. White hair. Long fingers everywhere. "Do you want this?" Replay. Wanting to scream; but knowing you can't. Mustn't. Daren't. Eve cried peacefully instead. Silent tears fell to fill the void inside.

Now she was Jonah in the belly of the whale, a belly that would metamorphose imperceptibly into the glistening, red womb of Mother Earth. The chain on her wrist a slithering, twisted umbilical cord, an Eden serpent, attached to a concrete placenta. Everything changed, shifting endlessly about her. Her mind felt raw and inside out and she craved oblivion.

* * *

Dr Power parked the car on a convenient verge. He had driven as far as he wanted down a winding, narrow lane he had found on the outskirts of Ruthin. The lane wound between the various boundaries of green pasture fields. The land in front of Power rose up to form a rolling hill, which supported the old castle and also bore the stones of the Ruthin Ring. Power got out of the Rover and locked the door safely. It was eleven o'clock in the morning. He paused to take in the brisk, clean air. He had driven down in a flurry of excitement. Now he wanted to clear his mind and take charge of himself. He opened the glossy, black boot and took out the rucksack he had stowed inside. The rucksack was a large Berghaus one left over from his student days. Power imagined that its drab green colour would merge into the landscape as he hoped his cotton camouflage jacket and trousers would as well. Before he heaved the rucksack out and swung it onto his shoulders, Power took the precaution of unbuckling a pocket and removing the plastic-coated map and his orienteering compass.

He realised he was breathing quickly, still excited by the prospect of his quest. He was alone now, there was no-one to help him. After his suspension Lynch had never rung him. Barnes had no time for him either. Like the Ley Man Power was part of history: yesterday's man. Alone at the centre of everything. At the centre of a campaign that only two people, Power and the Ley Man understood.

He needed to think before he set off. Had he got everything he needed? He ran through a mental checklist of what he had in the rucksack: a one-man tent, (no sleeping bag – the August weather was hot enough), a basic survival kit, some emergency rations, waterproofs, and a small medical kit he had assembled over the last few days, after a trip to the hospital pharmacy.

Hoisting the rucksack onto his shoulders he slammed the boot to and started walking up the hill to the stones.

* * *

"The sun. Gives us everything. Without it, coldness, darkness. No warmth. No light." Eve shivered, but the words washed over her without her comprehending. How long had it been since he brought food? "Without the sun...no food either," he was saying. " No light for the plants to grow. Photosynthesis. Metamorphosis of our world to a barren rock. It's people like me who keep the sun from going down forever. Who save the world from darkness. Who keep the sun coming up every day. If I didn't observe the old rituals. Someone always has observed them. It's down to me to do it now. If I didn't...the sun wouldn't come up. The seasons would stop. That's why I killed her in the spring, drained her blood to fertilise the earth. Grow the crops." Eve moaned softly, lying on the floor of the tomb he had constructed for her. "Without the ritual it all ends. And then I saw a way to stop it, to keep the sun coming up, to keep it on its round. To keep the seasons coming round, to give the earth mother warmth forever." The images and sounds were incessant now, weakened by thirst and hunger Eve no longer cared whether she lived or died. As if they both endured some symbiosis, the Ley Man had become as equally chaotic as Eve.

The last food he had brought had been a chicken, still warm from death, partially plucked and wrapped in aluminium foil for an oven the bird had never seen. It lay untouched in a corner where it had been for two days. Eve was insensible to the smell of the bird or her own body.

"With each sacrifice on the line my power grows, and is finally mine, when I have him here. He's coming. I know him. He'll be coming now. The wait will add more weight to my power. Then we'll be safe, and the mother will be well."

The freezer hummed in the chamber outside.

"He's coming," said the Ley Man, holding his knees and rocking himself back and forth as he squatted on the floor. "Better get ready." He stood up and locked the door on Eve. He opened the lid of the freezer. In the blackness Eve didn't know he'd gone or hear him talking with someone he thought was in the chamber outside. "He's coming, you said he was, yes he is, yes he is."

* * *

Power stood in the centre of the stone ring and took out the map and compass. The map he spread on the warm, dry, lichen-covered altar stone. He flattened it out and laid the compass on top. After several attempts he managed to work out how to orientate the map to the compass. He looked at the horizon, then at the map, and noted the landmarks around him. To the North-East, Moel fenlii itself, where the forester had been murdered. To the East the rest of the Clwydian range of mountains with the beginning of Offa's dyke. But if Power took a bearing on Moel fenlii, and ran it through the Ruthin Ring south west along the ley line, he could see , in the far distance, the high mountain, Craig-Bron-banog. The mountain's broad shoulders were cloaked by the forest of Clocaenog. Watkins' ley line finished in the forest somewhere. Buried there, somewhere, were another set of stones. Since Watkins wrote his book they had planted a vast conifer forest, that had grown thickly over the years, obscuring the stones from view. According to Watkins, the mountainside had been the largest ancient burial ground in Britain. The most sacred of sites, where the Celtic ancestors had lain, overlooking and over-seeing the daily life of their descendants in the valleys below. Now a mantle of evergreens had itself buried the burial ground. This was the end of the line.

Power folded his map into a manageable quadrant and re-placed in its plastic folder, which he hung about his neck. Taking the compass he orientated himself to the bearing of the ley line. He spied a convenient, lone tree in the near distance that was on the same bearing. Now he could begin his lonely walk.

It would have been a beautiful day to relax on a long walk. The sun was rising in a clear blue sky and tall grasses brushed Power's legs like a green sea lapping at the shore. Clouds of grass seed floated on the warm air in his wake. Power could have relaxed on any other day. Perhaps he could have sought the shade of an oak tree and dozed in the summer heat, listening to the soft winds moving through the meadow grasses and fields of wheat. Today he could not relax. His mind rehearsed again and again what he intended to do, and simultaneously he kept his marker on the horizon in view. He must not stray from his bearing, could not leave the ley line. This narrow path would lead him to the Ley Man and, he hoped, Eve.

As he moved cross-country on his bearing he would continually repeat a pattern. He would walk to his next marker on the line, be it a tree or farm building, re-take his bearings and set a new target ahead. Occasionally he stumbled on a hidden clod of earth or fell into a rabbit hole. His progress across the country was slow. He couldn't afford to deviate to an easier path. It was his lot to scramble over the walls and hedges that barred his path. If an obstacle proved insuperable, he had to reluctantly detour and get back to the tree or post he had had in view.

One such target had been the broken trunk of an old elm tree. When he reached it Power sat down on a fallen limb that lay across a field ditch and nestled amongst the weeds. Unshouldering his rucksack he opened the top and took out his water-bottle. He drank greedily from it, then splashed some water into his cupped left hand and washed his face. the back of his shirt and thin cotton jacket were drenched with sweat where the rucksack had pressed against his back. He took the jacket off and spreading it over the top of his rucksack, hung it there to dry in the sun as he walked. He calculated that he had walked only a mile over the gently undulating land. He was making poor time. With the rest it would have taken him almost an hour and he was exhausted in the day's growing heat.

According to the map there was a village over the next rise. Perhaps he could find some lunch there. Of course, he could go back the way he had come, climb into the Rover and drive to the forest. He could have started the walk there. He had a nagging worry though that that way he might miss something important on the ley line. It would perhaps be like the Ley Man to live on the ley line himself. Anywhere between Ruthin and the end of the line might be an important site for the Ley Man.

Power bent down and shouldered his burden once again. The rucksack felt cold and damp against his back now. The sensation would wear off, he told himself. In his mind's eye he had been building up a picture of the Ley Man. The process had been aided by that sudden memory some nights ago, when a name had jumped into his conscious mind.

Power had thought that after a time most of his patients blurred into one another. They were important when he was treating them; when he was seeking to heal them. Once they were better most of them faded in his mind. Some he could not remember no matter how hard he tried. Some his mind suppressed. This name was one of those he had suppressed. Once remembered the name brought back vivid images. Power could see his face as it had been all those years ago. Why had this patient been remembered with such intensity and then buried in Power's unconscious?

Perhaps there was something about the patient that reminded Power of himself? Power had been a medical student, just like the
patient had been. There was something about an absent father too.
Something that had struck a chord at the time Power had been seeing
him. Power had been a very junior doctor then at the Liverpool County
Asylum, Rainhill.

In the years since then the County Asylum had been closed,
torn down, and its patients spilled into the community. Power had
risen inexorably through the grades, as any doctor of promise does,
to be a consultant. But the patient...what had happened to the medical student patient? The notes of the old asylum had been kept in an
archive at a new psychiatric unit in the centre of Liverpool. Power had
phoned them days ago and yesterday the notes that corresponded to
the lost-then-found name had landed on his doorstep with a thump.

Owain Evans had been living in student accommodation when
Power had first seen him, years before, in the County Asylum. His
yellowed case sheet gave a North Wales telephone number for his
mother as next-of-kin, but like thousands of University students Evans
had chosen to live away from home near the University of Liverpool.
And like most students this was his first time away from home. Evans
had thrown himself into his medical studies. His world was his life. He
didn't like people, because they never seemed to like him.

His first preclinical year had been a struggle: anatomy and bio-
chemistry had taxed him with their unfamiliarity. Most students found
the dissecting room unpalatable, but he had taken to the dissection
tables and their work with zeal. He disowned the beery, oversexed life
of the student and focussed obsessionally on his work. To his tutors
though his mind seemed to find difficulty in making sense of his copi-
ous multi-coloured notes. His fellow students in hall found him aloof
and if they approached him he would run away from them as soon as
he could. After he failed his second year exams the pre-clinical dean
had written (in a report filed in his case notes) that Evans 'avoids his
peers and in interviews avoids the matter in hand. He talks about fate
and a struggle with someone who is desperate to thwart his ambition.
Reluctantly I have allowed him to take re-sits in November since his
course work has been more ordered than his exam papers. He seems

to be under considerable strain.'

Soon after Evans had been admitted, (in his third year, after being removed from his hospital accommodation), Power had assumed responsibility for his ward care. Power had re-read his old notes with critical interest. The young Dr Power assumed too much, and didn't investigate everything thoroughly enough. Where, for instance, was an interview with Evans' mother – surely this information was vital. Only a few scribbled comments alluded to her. Mrs Evans was 'elderly, distant and forgetful'. But there were insights from the young Power's keen observation. Power wondered if in some ways he could ever match again the intuitive enthusiasm of his earlier self.

He read that Evans was 'a tall thin youth, with scarecrow hair and features', that he had been 'almost catatonic' on admission to the ward; "'staring wildly into the distance' and responding – yammering away – to unseen voices and moving beneath unseen hands that 'caressed and abused him'. Evans' speech had been incoherent, but occasional fragments could be discerned, and then he would rail against 'the bastard' who was wrecking his life.

When Power could distract Evans' attention back to reality the wild-eyed medical student would admit that the unseen people talked to him and occasionally formed a committee of voices who criticised and 'examined' him, forever finding him wanting.

Tortured by these voices for weeks, Evans' thoughts had become so scrambled that he had stopped studying, stopped washing or changing his clothes and neglected to eat. He was a mad rake of a young man.

Power remembered sectioning Evans under the Mental Health Act when Evans had tried to leave the ward and the frantic battles to give him medication. And later when Evans was responding to treatment Power recalled the uncomfortable interview where Power had revealed that, until he was completely well, the medical school would never accept Evans back. Nobody thought he would be well enough. Even when recovered Evans' delusions about 'the bastard' and his powers over the sun and the moon never receded. At his best Evans was eccentric.

'Without medication,' Power had written. 'Evans will deteriorate again. Unfortunately, Owain Evans cannot see the need for medication and I know he will not comply for long once discharged.'

After Power had told him about his shattered career two incidents were recorded that seemed to justify Power's theory that this student had later become the Ley Man. Evans had attacked Power in the middle of a ward round. Power could recall the consultant pulling the incensed Evans off his registrar. He could remember the flailing arms and legs as the male nurses dragged Evans away.

A week later Evans had escaped from the ward and tried to break into the on-call flat Power stayed in at the hospital. Inside the flat a terrified Power had barricaded himself in the bedroom and phoned switchboard for emergency assistance. The hammer blows on Power's door resounded in his head long after the emergency team had returned Evans to the ward. Not long after both incidents Power had rotated to another post in another hospital. His entries in the notes were replaced by a neater hand in turquoise ink.

There was evidence that Evans had woven Power into his fantasies, because his violence had been directed purely at Power. Power was now convinced that the intervening years had corroded Evans' untreated mind further and turned him into the Ley Man. And yet logically there was no firm link. He couldn't justify his hunch. There had been other patients with paranoid schizophrenia who had assaulted Power and written him threatening letters, but Power's unconscious seemed to scream out 'This one! This is him. You've found him.'

Power may have been sure of his theory, but he was no nearer finding Evans. Evans had left his hospital accommodation long ago. His mother's telephone number had been disconnected for three years. The phone book with page after page of Evans was no help. For that matter Evans might have moved away from Liverpool and Wales. It had been over five years ago now. Logic was no help here. Logic said there was no reason to assume that Evans and the Ley Man were one and the same anyway.

In the notes there was only one clue as to Evans' future. An occupational therapist had written, 'Sad case. Talking about re-training as a builder. Like his father.' Power had looked in the North Wales yellow pages for builders called Evans. Phoning them all proved to be a time-consuming exercise, but unfortunately fruitless too. No builder employed or knew of anyone called Owain Evans.

Power had his eyes on a stone cairn atop the next rise, but to get there he had to cross a field of ripening crops and a small village. He skirted the edge of the field and came to the small collection of slate-roofed cottages that formed the village. A winding track led up the rise and towards the cairn. Out of the corner of his eye though he spotted a small free house on the edge of the village. He looked at his watch. One-thirty. Time for lunch. He pushed his way through the pub's battered wooden door. Inside two or three old men sat round a table talking over their bitter. Power had heard them laughing from outside the door. On seeing Power their conversation stopped immediately and they dropped their eyes disapprovingly. The landlord kept on polishing the bar top and did not look up as Power moved to the bar.

"Is there any food?" The landlord pushed the menu over to him.

"Too late for anything hot, mind," he said. Power chose some ham sandwiches and ordered a pint of bitter. The silence continued all the while Power drank. He bolted this sandwich and left. Once he was outside the door he could hear the conversation starting up where it had left off. He made his way up to the cairn and took his bearings. The sprawling darkness of the forest was closer now. He singled out a field gate on the line he was walking and made for that. The serried ranks of conifers started abruptly on forestry commission land. These were the shadowlands, the territory of the Ley Man. His home ground.

Just outside the forest and still in the hot sunlight, Power shivered. He might easily think that everything in his life had led up to this moment. The thought of some almighty hand directing his fate was a novel one to Power. To be controlled by someone else disturbed him. He shuddered and remembered the note, "You're at the end of the line". He moved past the field gate, re-took his compass heading, clambered over a fence and stood at the edge of the first trees staring into the darkness.

He weighed up what he hoped to achieve. Power sought to find the Ley Man in his own land and reverse the roles of hunter and hunted. He hoped to find Eve alive. He hoped to be able to resolve and heal. Perhaps, he wondered, his hopes were too great. Perhaps his hunches were based on as shaky ground as Evans' delusions. Here on the edge of the vast forest everything seemed meant. Everything that had happened had brought him, lured him, to this point. He must go on.

He abandoned the map to a pocket of his rucksack. He would follow the luminous dial of the compass in the darkness. And it was dark in the forest. The tall pine trees reached upwards for forty feet or so, and their dark branches bristled tightly with green needles that blotted out every piece of blue sky. Doggedly Power pushed his way between the scabrous brown trunks. The thin branches at the base of the trees, dead from lack of light, whipped him across the face and hands as he lurched his way forward into the gloomy silence of the forest. Springy earth, covered in dried needles and twigs, crackled beneath his feet. The sharp scent of pine oils prickled his nose and he sneezed. The sneeze was a lonesome sound that once released faded quickly into the silence. Power could hear his breathing becoming laboured as he forced his way between the densely planted firs. His progress was slow and much of his energy was expended in forging his way between and over dead branches. Afternoon had merged into evening and still Power could only boast half-a-mile's progress into the edge of the great forest.

But for the compass he might have been going around in circles, and since the forest was a changeless and amorphous place this might well have been his fate. Here and there a tree had died and there was a glimpse of the evening sky, but essentially his was an endless progress through identical trees planted equally closely apart.

He paused to drink more water and idly wondered if anyone had pushed their way so far through the trees since they were planted. The only time man visited these trees was to cut them down in swathes for paper pulp. Perhaps he was the only person to have been through these trees for twenty years. The sheer effort of pushing through the sharp-needled branches and the complete absence of any view as a reward would deter anyone but the mad, he thought.

But somewhere round here, on Watkins' ley line, would be the ancient stones he had written about as being at the end of the line. Since Watkins' day however, the stones had been submerged by trees.

He pressed on into the warm, summer evening. All at once he found himself in a clearing. Above him was a round disc of sky, formed by the ring of green tree spires that stretched upwards to the sun. He blinked at the light and peered through half-closed eyes at the clearing.

It was an oval space and quite small, it's largest diameter being some ten metres. In the centre of the clearing was a grass-covered mound that rose up to a metre or so above the ground.

This was one of the burial mounds Watkins had referred to, thought Power, a long barrow. He wondered if the foresters hadn't planted here through their own respect for the dead buried within all those thousands of years before, or perhaps they hadn't planted because of some edict from on high to preserve this archaeological site.

He noticed that no track led to the barrow. It was encircled by trees impenetrable to all but the most determined of people. The circle of trees stood about the barrow like defiant sentinels.

Power took his bearings again and prepared to leave the clearing, but something stopped him. For hours now he had become accustomed to the absence of noise, yet here there was the muffled sound of engines, one close at hand and another over to the left in the trees.

Tentatively he moved into the forest on his left and followed the sound. A hundred yards or so further on he came to a small wooden box that was about waist height. The noise here was unmistakably that of a diesel generator. Up close it clattered away noisily, but it had been muffled and made distant by the trees when Power had stood in the clearing. The generator was locked away behind a vented door. But who needed a generator out here?

Power decided to get back to the clearing, but panicked when he realised that one hundred yards of trees lay between him and the ley line he had been following so patiently. The intervening trees totally obscured his view. He had to find the clearing again, because it was his only way back onto the ley line, his only way of finding the Ley Man and of finding Eve. Which direction should he choose? He chose to go to where the gloom was least and as he crashed his way between the branches he saw that he had been right. The clearing opened up in front of him again.

This time the clearing looked different as if seeing the generator enabled him to discern the hand of modern man more easily. He noticed a stack of old logs on the edge of the clearing – rough logs sawn from mature pine trees. Then Power realised that the only trees these could have been were the trees that had once occupied this clearing. And if the clearing had once been full of trees...

He looked at the barrow. It looked too neat. Too perfect. Too new. It had been built after someone had cut the trees down. The burial mound couldn't be more than a few years old.

The grass-covered barrow looked like the knuckle from a monstrous hand pressing through the earth's skin. Power walked around it. The barrow was set precisely on the ley line's bearing. One end pointed to where the rising sun would be if the trees had not obscured the horizon. At this end of the barrow three massive stones were set into the turf. A horizontal stone, deep within the earth, formed a lintel. Below this two vertical stones lay flat against the wall of the mound. Each vertical was carved with a spiral. He inspected the spiral. This was new work, not thousands of years old.

Ancient barrows of this type were places where the ancestral dead of the Celts were interred to await their descendants who would inevitably join them. The barrows housed the victims of ill-health or death in battle or poor nutrition or sacrifice. That was how it had been thousands of years ago, and how the Ley Man had re-created it. But why go to such lengths? And why choose such a remote and inaccessible site?

Excitedly Power scoured the sloping walls of the mound for something that would explain the Ley Man's action. Either side of the mound he found two circular gratings cut into the earth and camouflaged by the grass that grew in front of them. He waited there a while and periodically he could hear a fan sucking air into the barrow. He wondered why. Inspecting the rest of the outside yielded no further clue. The barrow seemed to cling to its secrets resolutely.

Power went back to the stones that in a genuine barrow would have marked where an entrance once was. The three stones were carefully shaped and expertly cut. The edges fitted tightly except, he noticed, in the middle. There was a narrow groove let into one of the stones. The groove showed up as a pencil-thin black hole against the grey stone. Power dropped down and put his face close to the stone. He tried to glimpse inside. Blackness. He put his ear to the unyielding crack. He fancied he could hear a distant whirring noise, different to that of the fan. Here was the purpose of the generator in the woods. When he lifted his head a few inches away, he could feel a mild draught coming from between the stones. The fans were circulating air through the barrow, which must, Power reasoned, be hollow.

He had an unpleasant feeling, as he crouched down by the stones, that he was being watched. But the clearing was empty and the still trees were silent. Surely the forest was empty, but his discomfort persisted despite his attempts to reassure himself. He felt any movement of his was being observed. He tried to put the thought to one side and concentrate on the stone.

The stones looked massively heavy, but might he move them? He wriggled the fingers of his right hand into the crack between the stones and pulled experimentally. The stone did not move so much as a fraction. Bracing himself, with one foot on the other vertical stone he tried again. This time the stone lifted away from the earth a few inches and then unable to maintain his effort Power let the stone slam down again. It met the earth with a hollow booming sound.

Once more, with all his remaining might, he tugged at the stone. Gradually at first it swung up and out, to stop suddenly and heavily at the full reach of two massive and rusting hinges. He looked at the hinges with a sense of foreboding. A great deal of planning and work had gone into the construction of this burial mound, itself buried within the forest. Power was now certain that no-one came here but the Ley Man. And what was the barrow's purpose here, at the end of

the ley line? He looked around the watching trees nervously and then peered into the earth-dark interior of the barrow. He chided himself for failing to include a torch in his backpack.

He was reluctant to immerse himself in the darkness, and sink into the Ley Man's deathly kingdom. He tried to let more light in by lifting the second vertical stone, but it was shut forever-fast.

Power couldn't see any trap lurking in the gloom below, but that did not exclude the possibility. As he shrugged the rucksack off his shoulders he wondered what produced the humming noise which was now clearly audible within. Now he was separated from the rucksack he pushed it into the narrow opening he had made. He felt the ruck-sack slip down a metre or so into the blackness before it hit the bottom. There was a floor then. It wasn't some fathomless pit. Gingerly he moved the sack to one side and then dropped himself into the mouth of the barrow. The dark cool of the earth swallowed him whole.

His eyes got used to the dim light quickly and he could take in the vault of the concrete roof and walls beneath the turf. Maybe Evans had become a builder after all, he thought.

In front of him was a concrete wall that seemed to support the roof and divide the barrow into two. In the corner of this wall was a stout wooden door. He tried the cast-iron handle, but the door was fixed shut by mortise locks and two great thick bolts held home by padlocks. He could not know what room or rooms were beyond. He could not enter here.

When he held his ear to the wood he thought he could hear something moving inside. He felt the hairs on his back and neck slowly prickling. Was the Ley Man behind the door? He thought he could hear the scraping of a chain clinking against the floor. Maybe there was a devil dog chained up here in the dark? Power called out nervously, but if it was an animal it did not respond. Some living thing was there though, for the Ley Man intended to keep it alive, or why else bother to circulate air in the barrow?

Leaving the door for now he turned his attention to a white metal box, which sat by the inner door. Here was where the motor hummed, and, brilliant in the gloom, was the green 'safety' light of a chest freezer. It hummed impassively.

He opened it.

The lid swung up and he stared in. Grey, formless shapes presented themselves to his eyes. Round shapes, some blacker, some whiter than others, each covered in a frost of ice crystals. He didn't know why he did, but he reached into the cold mist to touch them. His fingers ran over the faces inside. They were like the cold, hard statues of marble that stared at visitors to a museum. But their skin was not smooth. The soft warm pulps of Power's fingers seemed to stick where they touched the frozen skin. He jerked his hand away and closed the freezer lid on their icy stares.

Power was surprised that he was so calm. As if his determination had been hardened by the discovery. His worst expectations about the Ley Man had been confirmed and his emotions temporarily suspended. He crossed to the barrow opening. He reached out and swung the vertical stone back into place, shutting himself inside the tomb.

FIFTEEN

Power crouched down on his haunches, his back against the curved inner wall of the barrow, the closed entrance to his right. After a few minutes he sank onto the floor and rested his feet against the metal cabinet of the freezer.

From his rucksack he took out the medical kit and opened it. He felt for and removed the barrel of a 10 ml plastic syringe, a sheathed wide-bore needle, and two ampoules of crystal clear liquid. In the minimal light that crept between the stones he assembled the syringe with care, making sure the long, white needle was tightly on. He broke the heads off both ampoules and sucked the liquid into the syringe. Four millilitres containing twenty milligrams of droperidol. He hoped it would be enough. He settled down again to wait, but he remained as taut as a bowstring, and all the time his right hand rested on the barrel of the syringe. He listened to the whirring of the air inlet fan and the incessant hum of the freezer. He wondered what lay on the other side of the inner door. He hoped that when he came the Ley Man wouldn't see him hiding here. He hoped he would have the element of surprise and that he would be alert enough when the Ley Man came.

* * *

When darkness fell he parked the white van on one of the few forestry tracks that crossed the forest. He made his way into the trees as he had done countless times before. In all the years he had been here he had never seen another living soul in this part of the forest.

To tell the truth he was getting tired of preparing the food and bringing it here for her. She hadn't eaten the bird he'd brought for her. Maybe he should kill her. He was excited by the possibility. She would be just as much a lure to Power dead or alive, because Power wouldn't know if she was either until he came here. And he knew Power. Knew he would come.

He didn't know why he'd put up with her for so long. A burden, like mother had been.

After half-an-hour or so he found the clearing. He stood there for an instant looking up at the stars in the night sky. They watched him. They approved of the things he did. He sniffed the air and halted. Something different tonight. He crept soundlessly over the grass to the twin stones that guarded the entrance to the barrow-temple.

Power was startled. He hadn't heard anything until the Ley Man wrenched the stone off the tomb's entrance. And he was there, bathed in starlight, standing in the centre of the first chamber, in front of Power. He scrambled to his feet, holding the syringe behind his back so that the other man would not see. He met the Ley Man's dilated eyes.

"Owain?"

"You followed the line." There was undisguised pleasure in Evans' voice. The pleasure at being proved right. "You came." This was what they had wanted. The final sacrifice. Look how meekly the lamb came to the slaughter.

Power spoke, "Are you well? It's a long time since we met."

"I've been watching you."

"Are you well?"

"Never been ill. Illness is invented by doctors like you."

Power had never thought Evans would accept treatment. The idea of him submitting to an injection had never been on the agenda. If the Ley Man had made more noise about his entry to the barrow Power could have stabbed him with the needle as he came through the entrance. The gluteus maximus muscle would have been ideal. Now they stood eye-to-eye and things were awkward. The uncomfortable thought occurred to Power that Evans had simply torn the entrance stone out of its socket without any effort at all.

He could see that Evans had been neglecting himself – long, lank hair, and clothes that were more like rags.

Power was beginning to regret his eternal desire to heal, to make things better. He could scent Evans' dangerous madness. There would be no talking him down. Power wished he a had a gun to blow the nightmare away. Instead he had a thin needle on the end of a plastic syringe. Power felt foolish and very afraid.

"You've got to die," said Evans. "For the sun."

Power lunged at Evans' leg, jabbing the wide-bored steel needle deep into the femoral muscle. Evans squealed in surprise and pain and wrenched the syringe out of his leg and and out of Power's hand. It clattered onto the floor out of Power's reach. Power wondered whether or not he'd had time to press the plunger? Had any of the droperidol gone into Evans' body at all?

Evans fell backwards under the weight of Power's attack, but not before reacting by lashing out at Power's head. The blow carried Power over to the side of the barrow, where his head and shoulders fell against the side of the freezer. The motor chunnered in protest at the sudden shock. Power got to his feet in the darkness. There was a whistling numbness in his left ear where the Ley Man had caught him with his arm.

Without looking at Evans, (who was fumbling in his pockets for something), Power turned and flung himself out of the entrance into the fresh air. He would run; run as he had never done in his life before to try and escape Evans. If he could just get into the forest the Ley Man would never find him.

Power ran only two metres before he was felled by another savage blow from Evans. He fell headlong and the air was crushed out of his ribcage as the Ley Man landed heavily on his back, pinning Power's arms down with his knees. "You bastard. Bastard. Bastard. Bastard." Screamed Evans. "Got you. GOT YOU! GOT YOU!"

The Ley Man reached into his pocket and took out a long piece of strong wire with two wooden handles at either end. Gripping a handle in each hand he pulled the wire until it snapped taut in front of him. Evans grinned in the moonlight.

Power struggled to lift himself off the ground, but the Ley Man was too heavy for him to dislodge. Power fell back against the grass with a grunt and prepared to try again.

With a single, fluid action the Ley Man swung both arms down so that the wire passed beneath Power's head and lay under his neck. Power struggled to speak, to delay the inevitable, but in a split-second the wire was around his neck and being pulled ever tighter by the Ley Man, who rode his back. Power could make no sound at all. The wire bit sharply into the skin of his neck, constricting his trachea. Breathing was difficult at first and then impossible. Power panicked. He tried to open his mouth and suck oxygen in, but nothing happened. His head felt heavy as if it might explode and there was a scraping ache inside his chest.

Power was acutely aware that they were alone; that he was the latest in a line of murders. The Ley Man pulled tighter still and the wire began to cut a bleeding circle around Power's neck. Without oxygen the panic he had felt initially was changing. Pain was becoming a distant thing. Thoughts were closing down. Vision and hearing seemed distant things, experienced by someone else in a remote unfamiliar world. The ocean of calm washed its warm waves over Power's head and all his desires had ceased.

"Owain Evans!" A deep voice rang sternly across the clearing. "I don't like what you're doing. Stop it now, Owain Evans."

The Ley Man looked round in horror. The voice was rather like his father's, but the accent was English. 'Our father?' He thought abstractly.

"Let go!"

He stared around the clearing, but saw no-one. A new voice...

that was a rare thing. He had known most of the voices that afflicted him for years. Occasionally a new one would emerge though to deride him, coax him, advise him or despise him.

The tension on the garrotte slipped a little, but still no air could pass into Power's lungs. He was beginning the long sleep.

"Who is that?" asked the Ley Man. The voice sounded very authoritative. He wondered who it might be. He thought he'd once heard President Kennedy saying 'keep pigs at bay', but he'd never understood that voice. This new voice sounded angry with him. He dropped the wire completely. It fell softly into the grass. "Is that God?"

"You've got it all wrong," said the voice. "What you're doing is all wrong. You've been misled. The ley line you believe in doesn't exist. Stand up and move away from the doctor."

The Ley Man wanted to say 'no', but the voice that challenged him sounded so convincing. It was difficult to tell. Was this the voice he'd been waiting for?

Without the pressure of the wire Power's wind pipe was patent again. A last involuntary movement of the chest succeeded in drawing some oxygen into his lungs. The fading heart caught hold of it and pumped the increasingly oxygen-rich blood to Power's brain. He gasped another breath and his breathing started raggedly again, his ribcage catching jerkily at the night air.

Evans had pushed himself off Power and was standing unsteadily by the barrow a metre or so away. Power lay unmoving and unconscious. A necklace of blood oozed from his neck. Evans waited for the voice of God to sound again. He leant back against the stone lintel of the entrance. He was feeling both tired and calm for the first time in weeks. "You said I was wrong," he said into the night.

"The ley-line was made up."

"Don't believe it." It was difficult relinquishing the idea, because it all seemed so right to him. For the first time Evans began to feel some doubt about the voice being that of God.

"The Ruthin Ring isn't ancient. It was built for an Eisteddfod."

"Lies!" He had been tricked by his own voices. At the moment of final triumph he had listened to lies. The shadow Evans imagined was 'the Bastard' had tried to snatch away his victory again. But Power was still there in front of him, half-alive and half-dead. There was no reason why he shouldn't defy 'the Bastard' and finish Power.

Evans staggered forward towards Power. But the clearing resounded to the noise of a shot fired from the trees, where the voice had appeared to come from. A momentary flash of orange fire from the revolver filled the glade with light and the shadows of the tall trees. Owain Evans dropped to the ground like a lifeless stone.

From where he had been waiting in the trees Lynch took off his nightsights and switched on the strong beam of his torch. Picking his way with care he chose to go to Power first. Lynch set the torch on the ground so that it shone on the doctor's face. He squatted down beside Power, but took care that Evans' body was in his sight and his line of fire. He wasn't altogether sure that his shot had hit Evans and though the Ley Man was undoubtedly mentally ill, his cunning was well-established. A live murderer might well 'play dead' and Lynch was on his own.

He checked Power's vital signs. He was breathing again and his pulse was bounding. His breathing sounded difficult as if he were gagging. Lynch carefully put the doctor into the recovery position, so that should he be sick, his airway was protected.

Evans lay in a disorganised heap at the open mouth of the barrow. He was still breathing and, as Lynch knelt by him with torch and gun in hand, Evans began to snore. It seemed grossly incongruous and Lynch was nervously tempted to laugh. He turned the Ley Man over onto his back and inspected his chest for gunshot wounds. There were none. In fact, there was no evidence to suggest that Lynch's shot in the dark had passed anywhere near the murderer. Lynch was relieved not to have killed him, but puzzled as to Evans' sudden unconsciousness.

Behind him Power was coming to. Shakily, he pushed himself

up into a kneeling position and retched painfully. If it hadn't been for the pain and the fact he was outside on grass Power might have thought he was waking from a nightmare. He looked with difficulty into the glare of Lynch's torch. Lynch turned the light away from his friend and went over to him.

As the spectres of light caused by the brilliant torch diminished, Power stared at Lynch's face. "Oh, it's you. Where did you come from?"

"I followed you over the fields. I was nearby...at a farmhouse nearby."

Power still wasn't in command of the situation, having seemingly woken into an ongoing nightmare. "Holiday? Are you on holiday?"

"No," said Lynch kindly, aware that his friend was far away. "I traced the white van. I've been around the area for a few days. The locals...after a little bribery...told me about a builder who worked from an old farmstead. A wreck of a place. Used to be beautifully cared for by his father. Then he died, and then the mother disappeared too. Name of Evans. After the old lady went, things became very chaotic. Nobody saw much of Evans. Nobody wanted to...the way people on the edge of things are ignored. Anybody who came close though was chased away by his dogs, or a shot fired over their heads...or at them. I overheard them talking about him at a market in Ruthin. When I asked them they told me he had a white van."

Power winced as he got up. His neck hurt him keenly and his head was spinning round. He found that if he spoke hoarsely it minimised the pain. "D'you bring anyone else?"

"Well, you didn't bring anyone else, did you? So why should I? You didn't even tell me you were coming down here!"

"Great minds think alike." Power tried to chuckle but found the experience painful and stopped. He confined himself to a short question. "You been in the barrow?"

Lynch shook his head. "Your friend's in the way."

As he realised how narrowly he had escaped death, Power began to shiver almost uncontrollably. It was with an effort that he managed to tell Lynch about the high dose of droperidol that he had given Evans. It had taken vital minutes for the dose to leach into Evan's bloodstream and seize the murderer's brain. It was Power's medicine rather than Lynch's aberrant shot that had floored the murderer.

"How long will the dose keep him like this?" asked Lynch.

"A few hours."

Lynch put the safety catch back on the revolver and stowed it in his right-hand coat pocket. From his left pocket he withdrew his cell-phone and organised the formal arrest and an ambulance for Power. Lynch imagined the local force blundering through the forest to reach them and amused himself with the notion.

Power frowned at the idea of medical help for himself, but Lynch could see that for Power, facing his fear had cost him dearly. He looked worn and ill. His shirt collar was now ringed with drying blood.

"When I was at the farmhouse I saw you crossing the fields. I could see you were up to no good. Well, the farm was empty, like the Marie Celeste...so I decided to tag along, at a distance of course."

"Have you been in there?" Power pointed to the barrow.

"You asked me that before, you know. Why should I have done?"

Power nodded and winced at the same time. "He built it...built the barrow on his ley line...as a repository. His freezer's in there...and it's full of..."

Lynch stopped him. "If he's got his freezer in there then I know what's in it. The pathology report on the head we got at the Ruthin Ring suggested he was using a freezer."

"It's full."

Lynch couldn't think what to say. He looked at the snoring figure by the barrow's dark maw.

"When he was a student," said Power. "You'd never think...you'd never seen a more normal...more respectable soul. Before his illness, that was." He paused and they waited together. After some time Power spoke again. "You need to go in. There's another door. I couldn't get through. There were noises behind it...like an animal in a cage."

"Something kept in there?"

"Something, yes."

When help arrived it was not brought by uniformed clowns blundering through the darkened forest, it came by police helicopter. As the helicopter roared noisily above the clearing, the air from its blades beating against the trees, Power refused the offer of an immediate transfer to hospital. Floodlit by searing blue-white light, Power shouted "No!" against the row of the engine. He wanted to wait for someone.

He watched as the police helicopter landed men and a stretcher. Later they winched the still body of the Ley Man into the sky. Evans was strapped so tightly to the metal frame of the stretcher that he couldn't have moved his little finger, even if he had been conscious.

As the helicopter chattered away into the night, its tail lights blinked reassuringly, reminding Power of a sane civilisation beyond the clearing. Two police officers armed with axes from the copter's emergency kit hacked away at the barrow's internal door. The wood splintered and eventually gave way under their onslaught. Power crouched cross-legged outside and waited while Lynch and the two others burst into the inner sanctum.

By the time they had sawn through her chains the helicopter was above them again filling the circular glade with its maelstrom of rushing air and light. They carried Eve lightly into the night air.

Power watched as they winched down the stretcher that had so recently carried the Ley Man.

He went over and knelt by her side. She looked thin and frail. Her eyes seemed to have receded into their dark orbits making her face into a taut mask of endurance. He felt her neck for its carotid pulse. A slight bradycardia of 56 beats per minute.

"Do you want to put a drip up or can she go now, doctor?" A globe-helmeted policeman asked Power through his visor.

Unable to marshal words about her he nodded.

"Are you coming with her?"

Power cleared his throat. "Er...no...no...she's stable...I...I..."

"It's all right," Lynch briefly put an arm round Power's shoulder. "It's all right sergeant. If Dr Power feels she's okay you can transfer her to the hospital."

"But...he should really be with us. He needs help himself."

"Take her now," said Lynch.

"But..."

" I think Dr Power will be all right. I'll keep an eye on him."

Power sat back down on the ground and watched the helicopter noisily disappearing from sight. Silence regained its hold over the forest again. He closed his eyes and tried to make some sense of what was happening to him. He needed to assume command of his life again. He looked up at the night sky and spoke to the figure who stood patiently nearby.

"I know I should be good. I know I should go and see a doctor in casualty, but I don't want to. Do you know what I want to do?"

"No," said Lynch.

"I want to walk back myself through the forest. I want to be in charge of myself."

"You can be then. Only wait here until dawn. And then I'll walk with you. All right?"

"All right."

Power and Lynch will return in The Fire of Love

THE DARKENING SKY

11613999R00158

Printed in Great Britain
by Amazon.co.uk, Ltd.,
Marston Gate.